Unexpected
Pleasures

ALSO BY PHYLLIS NAYLOR

Crazy Love: An Autobiographical Account of Marriage and Madness

Revelations

In Small Doses

Unexpected Pleasures

PHYLLIS NAYLOR

G. P. PUTNAM'S SONS   NEW YORK

G. P. Putnam's Sons
Publishers Since 1838
200 Madison Avenue
New York, NY 10016

With special thanks to Ed Legg of the International Association
of Bridge, Structural, and Ornamental Iron Workers.

Library of Congress Cataloging-in-Publication Data

Naylor, Phyllis Reynolds.
Unexpected pleasures.

I. Title.
PS3564.A9U54   1986   813'.54   86-8886
ISBN 0-399-13198-1

Printed in the United States of America
2   3   4   5   6   7   8   9   10

FOR MY HUSBAND REX

ONE

On a barge, two miles out on the Chesapeake Bay, Foster Williams sat listening to all the reasons he should or should not marry a young girl half his age.

He was beginning to feel warm beneath the layers of wool and flannel, his thermal underwear, jeans, and heavy jacket. Up on the gridwork later, he would wish he'd worn more, but now, with the sun on the deck, he could feel a trickle of sweat run down the hollow of his back, to be caught by the waistband of his shorts. Foster shifted, holding his Wonder bread sandwich in one callused hand. He was tired of the way Jack Tulley talked on— Jack, who didn't know beans about it.

"I'll give her six months, and she'll take off after some kid on a motor scooter," Tulley said, winking at one of the crew. He was the oldest, and looked like a turtle, Foster thought, the way his small head protruded from the folds of sweaters about his neck.

Clyde Sheldon—"Bigfoot," the men called him—a large-boned man, bigger than Foster, even, said, "Get her in the family way, that'll keep 'er. Had us three babies the first three years we were married. Sue only walked out on me twice, but after the second one came, she quit doin' like that."

Foster looked from one to the other. The bread stuck to the roof of his mouth and he worried it with his tongue, then swallowed without tasting. He didn't want to think about a sixteen-year-old bride walking out on him; couldn't bear to think of making her that unhappy. The choppy, gray-brown water of the bay slapped at the sides of the barge, whitewashed with gull droppings, and hundreds of birds circled overhead, waiting for handouts. Foster broke off a bit of crust and threw it in the air, as though to dismiss the subject of marriage, but when he returned to his sandwich, his eye caught Juju's. Foster knew by the smile what was coming.

The black man chuckled aloud. "You go 'head and marry that girl," he said. "She be so tight inside her she like to squeeze you to death."

Hoarse laughter rumbled in the chests of the bridge crew, and Juju's high-pitched "heh-hee-hee" seemed to skid across the flat surface of the barge. Foster poured out the last of his coffee and drank it down, his hair blowing in tangles over his face, hiding the frown. He didn't like the men talking that way about April Ruth, giving words to thoughts that Foster scarcely allowed himself. Until a month ago, in fact, marrying her had been the last thing on his mind. He'd offered to give her a home, that's all— raise her, then see what happened. But once he said he'd take her in, the words picked up a momentum of their own. The women took over, and the next thing Foster knew, someone— he wasn't sure who—proposed the idea to April Ruth and she'd said she guessed so. Like it or not, Foster Williams found himself engaged.

"We workin' up top this afternoon, Tulley?" he asked abruptly, closing his lunch pail.

"Up top," Tulley repeated, getting to his feet. He stretched, lit his cigar, and started down the long stretch of deck to the cage.

The 374-foot tower just off the end of the barge was the place Foster wanted to be. The morning spent with the ground crew preassembling the steel yet to be lifted was simply time to be endured; now Foster longed to be on the high beams, far above the water, where he was at his best—where there was more to think about than the skinny-legged girl he'd known since she was three. He slipped on his life jacket and followed the other members of the raising gang, fastening his tool belt around his waist as he went.

The cage was just big enough for three men, but when Foster squeezed in beside Norris Wainwright (Juju) and Jack, he found that the skinny-legged girl had slipped in, too. Outside, the crane operator pulled the lever and the box swung up off the barge. It took two minutes to reach the top, and ordinarily, as the water dropped further and further away, Foster silently counted off the seconds to amuse himself. This time, however, as he watched an ocean-bound freighter below, looking puny as it approached the span, he found himself subtracting the sixteen-year difference between his age and April's when he got to be fifty. Funny how April was half his age now, but when he got to be fifty, she'd be two-thirds of the way there herself. The older they both got, the smaller the proportion, his age to hers, so it seemed like if you stretched it out, there would come a time she'd catch up, but it didn't work that way. Foster shook his head to clear it of numbers. He couldn't see himself fifty any more than he could see himself married, yet it was waiting for him down the road, sure as his dog Vinnie was waiting back at the house.

"They're talkin' '73, now," Juju said.

"Could've told 'em that," said Tulley. "Take one look at this bridge, you can see it won't be done this fall." Jack had built bridges in Portugal and Venezuela and he'd worked on the Verrazano-Narrows in New York. The winds on the bay, he said, were worse than at any of the others because of the open water. It was what Foster liked to hear. Didn't have to go all the way to Portugal; excitement twenty miles from your back door.

From the top of the tower, the sloshing waves on the Chesapeake became mere ripples that gleamed silver in the cold March sun. Foster pulled on his leather gloves. Across the water, the first Bay Bridge stood sturdily aloof, only a few cars on her. Foster knew that by Memorial Day there would be the familiar bottleneck on Route 50—traffic tied up for miles waiting to cross to the ocean beaches.

Tulley must have known what he was thinking. "Come summer," he said, "there's going to be a hundred drivers over there, cussin' us out for not gettin' the second bridge ready on time."

"And not one of 'em willing to trade places with us, neither," Norris put in, and all three faces, Foster's included, broke into smiles as the men stepped out onto the working platform. The cage went back for Bigfoot and the others.

Foster did not think much about the future. He made a point of not thinking about it, and could almost count on his fingers the times he had dwelt on it for any length at all. But something stuck that Tulley had said about the first bridge—the one he had helped build: "When I'm long gone, it will still be here." Foster had noticed the way Tulley always ended his shift by pausing a moment to stare across the water at the older bridge, and knew that someday he would feel the same about this one.

Carrying twenty pounds of tools around his waist, Foster moved toward the edge of the platform behind Jack. Then, as deliberately as he would walk from his own house to the shed, he stepped out onto a beam and started across.

A gust of wind brought with it the fresh, sharp smell of water below. Ahead, Jack spread his arms a little wider for balance but kept going till he reached the corner. Step by step, Foster followed, each foot coming down on a fixed spot on the beam. Out of the corner of his eye, he could see a tanker some distance away, the movement of the men on the barge below, but he focused his eyes on the beam and the place his foot would go next. An eerie quiet enveloped the crew that worked at the top. The clanging and clunks of metal against metal on the deck beneath were muffled here, and the stillness, like the view, seemed to extend outward in all directions.

The wind again. Foster paused, muscles locking, the lapels of his jacket flapping. It seemed to slacken, then returned, suddenly stronger. This time Foster crouched down and waited until it had passed. Behind him, Clyde, who had just come up, crouched too, and swore.

When they reached the corner and took their positions on the gridwork, Tulley nodded toward the barge. "Safety man's around," he warned. Foster impatiently unwound his nylon monkey line and tied off to a bolthole, using a round turn and two half hitches.

Despite the wind, the sun was warm on his back, and Foster felt at home. More up here, in fact, than he did below. Thirty stories down there were truck payments to worry him, Vinnie's leg which had never healed, the leak in the living room ceiling, April. . . .

Foster watched intently as an I beam was lifted skyward. A groundman steadied a tag line to keep the beam from spinning. On the gridwork the men's arms raised in unison, their backs bent, thighs stretched—each man anticipating another's movements.

They spoke more to the beams than they did to each other. While the signalman with his hand-held radio talked to the derrick operator, too far below to see what was happening, Tulley gently coaxed the steel into place like a father—patiently cajoling. Bigfoot swore at the beams and plates, while Juju saw the raising and connecting as something akin to a sexual act. "Slip her in, baby," he pleaded. "Rub up against her, there. . . ." Foster found himself thinking once again of April Ruth Bates and what exactly he was supposed to do with her once she moved in—April with her little pointy chin and her skinny legs and her mule-headed stubbornness now produced in him a speechless terror when he thought of living under the same roof with her.

When the first beam was in place, Foster drove in the driftpins. The wind had risen again, and now the sky toward the northeast was clouding up. Jack Tulley maneuvered past Foster on the gridwork and spoke to the signalman who spoke, in turn, to the ground foreman.

"What you got on the weather, Dave? Lookin' mighty dark up here."

A drop of rain hit Foster on the cheek and he looked at Tulley. Tulley felt one, too. He shook his head at the signalman.

"Put 'er back down," the signalman said over the radio, and as the derrick operator lowered the second beam, Foster and the other men turned themselves around and started back.

"When the first drop of rain falls on you, that's an act of God.

When the second drop falls on you, it's your own damn fault,"
Tulley said as they waited for the cage.

"Hell," Clyde said glumly. "Rained every damn day this week.
Can't seem to get past two o'clock."

Even mist could make the metal dangerous underfoot. The
men did not work when the weather was too wet, too cold, too
windy, too foggy. . . .

They sat huddled together with the other ironworkers in an
old PT boat that sped them back to the mainland, rain pelting
down on their helmets, the horizon a soupy gray mixture of bay
and sky. Norris Wainwright, however, was smiling.

"Foster got hisself a couple extra hours to court that li'l gal,"
he said, nudging Clyde Sheldon. Then, looking directly at Foster,
he added, "You jus' might git more than you figured, ol' man,
if her sister move in with you, too."

"Cool it, Juju," warned Tulley.

Foster said nothing. The wind had blown his dark hair down
over his face again so that his eyes were half-hidden, but his jaw
worked up and down. He could tell that Clyde was warming to
the joke. He and Clyde usually worked as partners, and after
twelve years, they knew what it took to rile each other.

"*Which* sister?" Clyde put in. "Thomasine's bad as Dorothy,
both of 'em goin' to hell in a—"

"Just shut up," said Foster. "Just shut up about April Ruth
and her sisters."

The men exchanged looks of shocked innocence.

"Why, Foster, I'm only sayin' what every last person in the
county knows," Clyde went on, trying to keep his face steady.
Norris Wainwright's shoulders shook with silent laughter.

"Well, you keep what you know to yourself," Foster told him
curtly, and fixed his eyes on the shore as the boat drew up.

There was lighthearted talk in the change shack. Clumps of
men spilled out the door, ready for the hot shower that awaited
them at home. Leaving only his helmet and outer jacket in the
shack, Foster headed for his truck. Clyde clapped one hand on
his shoulder good-naturedly. "C'mon, Foster, let's go get a brew,"
he said.

"Not tonight," Foster told him, and went on. He was several yards down the road when Jack Tulley caught up with him.

"Listen, Foster, I want to say something. The men are just jawin', but you got to think things through. That girl's a minor. Could get you in one hell of a lot of trouble."

"Mrs. Dawson says April Ruth can marry, her father says she can," Foster told him.

"You asked him?"

"Didn't have to. Mrs. Dawson and the other ladies took it up with April, and she says it don't make no difference to her dad."

"Look, Foster," Tulley said earnestly, "you still got time. Right this minute there's no papers on you a'tall. You're a free man and you got no more obligations to the Bates family than I do. All you got to do is tell those women you reconsidered."

Foster's palms began to sweat. A bad choice was still a decision made—over and done with. Tulley had dragged out the option again, however, and it dangled now in front of Foster like a tangled fishing line. To go back on his word meant facing Mrs. Dawson once more. It meant explanations to April Ruth. It meant trying to find Earl Bates in whatever bar he was drinking and telling him he wouldn't be moving April Ruth out of their trailer after all, and that she and Thomasine would have to go on sharing the sofa bed.

"I said I'd raise that girl," he told Tulley, and climbed up into the truck.

"Raise her, not marry her," Tulley pleaded.

"Can't keep her under my roof 'less I do, or they'll have the law on me," Foster explained, and turned the key in the ignition so he wouldn't hear what Tulley said next. Tulley said nothing, however, and the pickup pulled away and headed out to Route 50.

If this wasn't the durndest mess he'd ever been in, Foster was thinking as he roared on by the chicken farm and the cannery and careened onto the highway. It was his habit of not looking to the future that led to this, he was thinking. All those years he'd been taking his wash to the Laundromat between the Amoco station and the diner, the Bateses' trailer parked there in back, he never suspected things would turn out like this. He'd watched those three little girls grow up, and even when Dorothy, the oldest, got to be twelve, he never knew she was headed for trouble. Oh, he saw the way she used to come in the diner, all right, and whirl herself around on one of the stools at the counter, legs flying every which way. Could see clear to China, you weren't careful. The truckers in the booths by the window would smile and grunt and elbow each other, and Dorothy would go right on whirling. But Foster, who never had any sisters of his own, just assumed it was something girls did when they got to be twelve.

Now Dorothy was twenty-one and living with a man named Max, accepting visitors on the side. It was Thomasine, nineteen, who waited tables in the diner where her sister used to show herself, and the way Thomasine would stand at the counter, resting her weight on her hands, squeezing her breasts together in her lowcut uniform, told you pretty much that what you suspected about Thomasine was true. Mrs. Dawson and her self-appointed Decency Committee claimed that Thomasine, when she got off work at the diner, went around from truck to truck parked in the pines, and climbed in the cabs with the drivers. Foster had seen her do it himself, dressed in her tight pants and her halter top that cradled her breasts like a hammock. And because no one could do a thing with Thomasine, least of all the Decency Committee, Mrs. Dawson had turned her attention to the youngest Bates daughter and set her mind on saving April while there was still time.

From Route 50, Foster made the turn on 301, heading south toward Charles County. April was definitely worth saving, though he wasn't sure whether, if it was April up against Mrs. Dawson, it would be April who cried uncle. Seven years ago, when Foster lost his own parents and brother, he had felt more than a little sympathy for the three stringy-haired girls who were being raised, as far as anyone could tell, by the joint efforts of the employees of the diner, the Laundromat, and the Amoco station. April Ruth Bates, however, was not about to be pitied. Since her mother died in childbirth—April's birth—the girl did not miss her at all.

LIVE CRABS, said a sign on a truck by the road. USED PARTS, said another. Past the Arabian horse farm and a church signboard reading, YOU ARE LOVED. Foster turned the radio on, skipped from news to weather to music, then turned it off again and drummed his thick fingers against the steering wheel. He was trying to remember the first time he had seen April. There had always been children back in the Bateses' trailer, it seemed, always toddlers climbing in and out in their dirty pants and bare feet, their legs mosquito-bitten—"Et to death by the 'skeeters," as their father, Earl Bates, described it.

About the time April was nine, however, Foster lost his parents and had begun eating at the diner regularly, parking near the back of the lot in the shade. And on one particular evening—a steamy, August evening, when the big diesels pulling in from the highway seemed to shimmer as they came—Foster had been aware of the skinny-legged girl standing off in the pines as a Mayflower van swung around to park. He had just started for the diner, his back to both the girl and the van, when he heard the most terrifying scream he could remember. To this day he could see, as he'd whirled around, the truck driver's astonished face, hear the grinding squeal of the brakes, remember his heart-stopping sprint around the truck to the other side.

The girl had been sitting on the pavement rubbing her ankle through one dirty white sock, her face screwed up, alternately moaning and cursing under her breath.

Foster and the truck driver knelt on opposite sides of April, the driver's face as gray as the concrete.

"I didn't *see* her!" he said incredulously to Foster. "Like she was dropped from the trees!"

"Where's it hurt, April?" Foster had asked.

She ignored the question and glared instead at the truck driver, her little pointy chin puckering.

"He run right inta me!" she said accusingly. "He run right over my foot!"

"Where'd she *come* from?" the truck driver exclaimed again, sweat pouring off his face. "Didn't see nuthin' ahead but the pines, and then I heard her yell."

A telephone lineman had come out of the diner and was heading for his truck. He stopped when he saw the two men and the girl. Lighting a cigarette, he watched.

"Where's it hurt, April?" Foster repeated. "You better pull down that sock."

April Ruth skidded backward on her bottom. "I'm not takin' off my clothes!" she yelled.

The telephone lineman walked over, and the truck driver looked at him imploringly. "I didn't even *see* her!" he repeated. "Like she dropped from the trees!"

"I want to go inside," April Ruth whimpered.

"She wants to go inside," the driver said quickly to the lineman. He gingerly took her by one arm, Foster the other, and under the watchful eye of the telephone man, they lifted her up and started toward the diner.

"Ankle might be broken or something," Foster chided.

"Ain't broken, it's just hurt," she said.

"Where you come from, anyway?" the driver asked her, still shaken. "I didn't see you when I pulled up."

"Just crossin' the lot like I always do. You couldn't see a elephant if it was comin' down the middle of the road," April replied hotly.

The driver began to sweat again.

"I'm hungry," April said when they got inside.

"Listen, you just sit down and order whatever you want," the driver said. He pointed up to the menu on the wall, above the Pepsi clock.

Foster slid in the booth beside the Mayflower man, across from April Ruth; April's gray eyes scrunched up as she studied the menu.

"I'll have the steak 'n fries with biscuits," she said.

"Steak and fries with biscuits," the driver repeated promptly to the girl behind the counter.

"Still hurts." April reached down under the table and rubbed her leg.

"Ought to have it looked at," Foster said. "Might need an X ray or something."

"You ain't takin' no look," April chided, her voice rising.

The truck driver reached at once for his wallet. He took out two twenties, then a ten.

"Here," he said, handing the money to April. "Just in case you decide to go to a doctor. Okay, now?"

April studied the bills in his hand, then accepted them indifferently. "Couldn't see a elephant if it was comin' down the road," she said again, and stuck the money in her pocket.

It was a week later, when Foster was parking again at the diner, that he saw still another man helping the same little girl across the lot. This man wore a shirt that said SAFEWAY on the back, and the sweat had soaked right through. He was talking earnestly, staring down at the girl, while April shot him reproachful glances, rubbing her ankle.

Foster followed them inside and sat at a neighboring table.

"Steak and fries with biscuits," the driver ordered for April Ruth, and when it came, he paid the waitress, handed April Ruth a twenty, and left.

Foster picked up his own plate and moved over to April's table. She brushed the long dirty hair from her eyes, wiped her mouth, and went on chewing.

"What's the matter?" Foster asked. "Your dad don't feed you?"

"He feeds me," April replied.

"Then what you doing this for?"

A trace of merriment flickered in the girl's eyes. "Thomasine taught me."

"Where is Thomasine?"

April shrugged. "Out playin' somewhere."

"I catch you or Thomasine doing this again, I'm goin' to march you back to your daddy."

"Find 'im," she challenged.

Foster slowly lowered his fork. "He don't take a hand to you, I will."

The gray eyes never left his face. April's pointy chin lifted slightly and she studied Foster curiously. Then, with a smile so slight he could have missed it altogether, April picked up the remaining biscuit on her plate, broke it, and offered half to Foster.

"Grape or apple?" she said, handing him the jelly.

Now, as Foster made the final turn onto a country road, he could still see April's eyes so clearly it was as though her face were reflected there in the windshield. She needed raising, all right; he had seen that even then. But now she was seven years older, seven years smarter, and the very thought made the hair on the back of his neck crawl.

Shops gave way to tobacco fields. TURKEY SHOOT, a sign read, —EVERY SUNDAY ELEVEN TILL FIVE, and further on, JESUS SAVES AND HEALS. The road dipped and rippled like a ribbon. Down the hill Foster went, over Old Woman's Run and up the other side. When he reached his narrow dirt drive, Vinnie rose from the porch and came yelping toward him, ears flopping, dragging her lame leg. The large black dog, second cousin to a Labrador retriever, seemed almost to throw herself in front of the truck in her welcome home. Foster reached out the window and took the mail from two boxes, one with his name on it, the other marked RUSSELL WILLIAMS, then maneuvered the pickup around the potholes in the driveway and came to a stop beside the square frame house. He opened the door and cupped his big hand around Vinnie's head, rubbing one silky ear between thumb and finger.

There was something comforting about Vinnie, the gentle bitch who had seen Foster through the last seven years of his life. Until her bloody fight with a German shepherd, which left scars showing through her short hair and her left rear leg somewhat crippled, she used to go out for days at a time, returning home with dead rats and rabbits that she placed modestly on the back stoop. Even now she would sometimes set out of a morning and head down to the swamp, or spend a day among the sweet gum trees along Port Tobacco Creek, the spiny brown balls of the gum tree catching in her hair. But she always managed to be home when the pickup pulled in, and Foster never let on how much he liked it. As he stepped down out of his truck now, however, he realized that one week hence there would be a pointy-chinned girl sitting there on the porch next to Vinnie, and the sodden feeling in the pit of his stomach seemed to weigh even more heavily than it had before.

The house needed work, for one thing. As Foster laid the mail on the table, he tried to see the kitchen the way April Ruth would see it. Things he had scarcely noticed before jumped and jiggled before his eyes. The rust stain on the kitchen sink. The rip in the screen. The linoleum so worn that the roses hardly showed.

He moved slowly on into the living room, where the door leading outside was never used and the steps beyond had crumbled. His eyes settled on the water-stained wallpaper above the TV. His mother's curtains, gray with age, had hung unwashed at the windows for the past seven years. There was a dark place at one end of the old green couch where Foster laid his head when he napped, and another, for which the dog was responsible, on the carpet. A 1965 calendar still hung on the wall, with birthday cards and newspaper clippings tucked behind it, and a new 1972 calendar hanging in front.

Foster ran his hand over the Formica surface of the magazine stand, and the dust rolled up like lint. When he reached his room at the end of the hall, the bed unmade, the dresser strewn with clothes, Foster went back out and shut the door quickly, his heart thumping painfully against his rib cage. The second bedroom he didn't even bother to open because the squirrels had taken over, and since Foster didn't need it anyway, he let them have it, long as they didn't get in the walls, which occasionally they did. Then he'd go after them with the mop handle, Vinnie barking up a storm.

Foster swallowed. He tried to tell himself that it didn't make any difference—that whatever shape his house was in, the Bateses' trailer was worse. But still, April Ruth, with her mule-headed stubbornness, might take one look at the place and walk out on him the first night, and wouldn't that set folks to talking!

It occurred to him that for a considerable part of his adult life his evenings had been question marks, empty squares on a calendar. Most of the friends he'd had in high school had married young and started families. Up until seven years ago, Foster had gone out sometimes with his brother—to a tractor pull, perhaps, or muskrat trapping in the marsh—but of course Lloyd was gone now. A few of the ironworkers got together occasionally for a bull roast or an evening of poker, but most of them lived in Baltimore or beyond. More often than not, Foster watched TV, and he sometimes went bowling up on 301 with Clyde or to the racetrack with the Harley brothers, if he were really desperate. Now, however, the evenings of the week ahead were filled with something different. He and April Ruth were driving to Denton on the eleventh for the ceremony, and between now and then he had to court her, clean the house, and take care of whatever obligations awaited him as an almost married man.

He went back down the hall, picked up Russell's mail from the table, and strode quickly out the door, the screen slamming within an inch of Vinnie's tail.

A second house, covered with imitation brick, stood at the rear of the lot. It had the same narrow porch along the front, same bare earth yard, same shed at the back. Foster's father had built both houses, one for his own family and one for his brother Russell, who had been widowed. Now Russell's home was shared by a third brother, Shum, and it was even money, Foster thought, which of the two would drive the other crazy.

It was only in the last five years that Foster had stopped calling Shum and Russell "uncle." It seemed to him that once a man reached thirty he should be more or less on an equal footing with his elders, and though Russell's eyes had hardened in their sockets at the new two-syllable salutation, Foster had continued to delete the "uncle" until finally the old man seemed reconciled. It was Russell's name, not Shum's, that was on the second mailbox, however; Russell who paid his own bills; only Russell who could command respect. Shum had always seemed an afterthought.

They were waiting for him now on aluminum chairs.

"Knew you'd be coming," Russell said. Both uncles were dressed in bib-type overalls. On Shum, the taller of the two, they looked like a chicken farmer's, but Russell, his gray hair neatly combed, could have been wearing a three-piece suit the way he sat erect with hands folded in his lap.

Shum giggled, making him sound nearly feeble-minded, which he wasn't. His eyes became mere slits when he smiled, as though the sun were always in them. "Sky darkened up and I says to

Russell, 'Well, they're comin' down off'n the bridge now, any time.' "

"Started to rain," Foster said in answer, handing the mail to Russell as he always did, whether Shum had any letters or not.

"We had us about ten drops, didn't even wet the roof," Russell told him.

"Well, it was raining there," said Foster.

Shum giggled some more and his foot bobbed up and down.

Ordinarily, Foster would make some remark about his own mail—compare their electric bills, perhaps. He'd say something about Vinnie, maybe, and how she'd treed a coon, and then, when the uncles got bickering, he'd turn again and head back.

"Dog couldn't trap a coon if she was sittin' on it," Shum might say. "Nothin' like the setter we used to have when we was little."

"Wasn't a setter a'tall, was a golden retriever," Russell would answer.

"You think I don't know a retriever from a setter?" Shum would snap. "I'm talkin' 'bout old Ned, not Goldie."

"And it was Goldie that treed the coons, not Ned," Russell would continue in the same silvery voice as before. It would be about then that Foster would slip away.

Today, however, when the weather had been dispensed with, Russell turned his pale blue eyes directly on Foster and said straight out, "You lost your mind or what?"

Foster looked at his uncles and saw that today there would be no arguments between them at all, because they were like-minded when it came to him. Within twenty-four hours of April's saying yes, word had gotten around.

"Mind's as clear as it ever was," Foster answered.

"Well, now, that ain't sayin' a whole dang lot," Shum put in.

Russell's eyes looked beyond Foster and out across the yard as though he were seeing more problems than there were people to take them on.

"You marry that Bates child and you got folks thinkin' you ought to be put away," he said.

"Why's that?" asked Foster.

Shum stopped smirking and stared in astonishment. "Why,

Foster, those Bates're a mean-minded bunch with the morals of a chicken."

"April's not," Foster defended.

"She's just two years shy of when Thomasine went wrong," Russell told him. "You bring that girl here, you're going to have troubles you never even heard of."

"So much trouble you'll think that drownin' yourself's a blessing," added Shum.

Foster thrust his hands in his pockets and looked the other way. "April needs a guiding hand," he told them.

"Well, it sure ain't yours," said Shum.

Russell's face seemed, for just a moment, to soften. "Foster, you're thirty-two and past the marrying age, you want the truth. You got a quiet life here with Vinnie and you don't know the first thing about women. I'm only laying the facts before you. Last thing in this *world* you need is a child who's got the town so worried that Sara Dawson and those confounded women took out after her."

Foster felt his face redden. "Well, that sure weren't April's doing, and you can't judge her by her sisters."

Shum leaned forward, his long bony hands on each knee. "Your brother wouldn't have looked twice at a girl like that. You marry her, Foster, she'll be no relation to me."

"Hush up, Shum," Russell told him. "Listen, Foster, a man can get lonesome living by himself, I know that, but if you've really got your mind on marrying, you can do a lot better than April Bates."

"I already asked her," Foster said, stretching the truth. He stood up, slapped his thigh, and Vinnie trotted after him.

Foster's feet struck heavily on the dirt path and his jaw ached with tension. What Russell knew about women you could fit on the back of a matchbox, and they were as rare in Shum's world as turkey at a ham-and-oyster supper. Still, Foster's own experience wasn't so extensive. He talked to them when necessary, and had even slept with a few, but except for a fumbling anatomy lesson, he had felt more estranged from them afterward than he had before. Especially a young woman named Ramona Wheeler.

What had happened with Ramona was that nothing had happened at all. And when she ran off the next week with a man from Baltimore, Foster was the only one in Medbury glad that she was gone, taking his humiliation with her.

It had always seemed to him that some people were born knowing what to say and how to act. Foster never caught the cues. Not with women. They always took him by surprise.

It had been Lloyd, five years younger, who was the Golden Boy, the extrovert. Born to aging parents, Lloyd was like a pet to the family, and Foster carried him around on his shoulders, showing him off. Foster saw his parents transformed from cautious elders of few words to a more relaxed couple bent on enjoying their second child. Egged on by Foster, Lloyd would toddle up to strangers, who never failed to exclaim over his blond hair. Foster would watch in devilment as his brother raised a general ruckus around relatives, something Foster had never been allowed to do. It was no surprise that when Lloyd reached high school, there were always friends in the house, a girl in the picture, or that when he left for Vietnam, he was engaged.

Foster had assumed somehow that Lloyd's freedom would free them both. The clever quips and meaningful glances that came so naturally to his younger brother would rub off, eventually, on him as well. He was startled to discover that, if anything, the opposite was true. His own shyness seemed to stand out even more in contrast; compared to Lloyd, his own feet felt more leaden, his words unsure. Foster went from feeling inexperienced to believing himself over the hill.

Something about April Ruth Bates, however, stirred him up again. The clumsy conversational groping that they recognized in each other made Foster feel, when he was around her, that he was safe from ridicule, if nothing else. The subtleties of romance at which women his own age were so adept had not yet crossed her mind. She accepted Foster's reticence as something that just was.

Back in his own house, Foster looked at the clock and saw that it was a little after three. April Ruth probably wasn't home from school yet. If he put his mind to it, he could clean the kitchen before dinner and go visit April for an hour or so afterward.

He took off his light jacket and one of two flannel shirts. With a rag and a can of Ajax, he started in on the stove, whose grease-caked burners rested heavily on several years' accumulation of food spills. He had barely begun when his eyes drifted to the chili spots on the wall above, and when he had wiped those clean, he turned his attention to the salt and pepper shakers, greasy with fingerprints, gray with use. The coffee can of bacon drippings sat sordidly there on the counter in congealed grease, and when Foster attacked the grease, he noticed the pot holder that had not been laundered at all that he could remember. There was no stopping. Before he realized it he was wiping down the doorframe that led to the hall, and he knew if he wasn't careful he'd be in the spare bedroom with its broken window and squirrels and the mice nesting in the dresser. The panic swelled and receded inside his chest with each swipe of the wet rag.

His uncles had said no more than he expected, yet still their words stung. Some folks in Charles County talked about the Bates girls as though they were afflicted with a hereditary moral disorder. Others attributed their wild behavior to the old man's drinking and the way he had neglected his daughters. Mrs. Dawson, however, was of the opinion that it was the death of Opal Bates, the mother, that had turned Earl to the bottle and made the girls seek the affections of whomever they could find. Opal, said Mrs. Dawson, had been a fine Christian woman who would have raised those girls with a firm hand. The worse Thomasine and Dorothy carried on, in fact, the more virtuous the dead woman became, the only woman on record, for all Foster knew, who was brought close to sainthood by the carryings-on of her daughters.

Over the years, Foster had listened to the stories going around, and from time to time he had wondered whether April would follow Thomasine in the diner. But it wasn't until he heard Mrs. Dawson and the others talking about a court order to take April away from Old Man Bates and send her to the juvenile home that he had mentioned, in passing, that perhaps, if there were no other solution, he might, for a time, maybe, take April in. One week later he found himself engaged.

Foster gave up trying to clean the whole kitchen and concentrated on the stove. He used steel wool to clean the oven and the burners, and by dinnertime, it was his sole accomplishment for the afternoon. He would have gladly gone on scrubbing for the rest of the night rather than face what he had to do next; but April had to be courted, there was no getting around it.

At seven o'clock, he dialed Earl Bates's number. The phone rang four times, then five, and Foster was just about to hang up when he heard a voice saying, "Hullo?"

"Is this April Bates?"

"Yeah."

"Well, this is Foster Williams."

There was a pause. "Yeah?" she said again.

"You going to be home tonight? I was thinking of coming by."

One second, two seconds, then three seconds passed before she answered.

"Nobody's stoppin' you," she told him.

TWO

When I come back to bed from using the commode, Thomasine was over on my side. She always does that way. Like a cat, seeking out every little bit of warmth. Just once in my life, I thought, I'd like to have me a bed all to myself, but seeing as how I was marrying Foster Williams on Saturday, didn't look like that was about to happen.

"Thomasine, get your legs over," I said. She only purred.

I rapped her knee hard with my knuckles, and this time she slowly started to unwind herself. She rolled over on her back, stretching her legs full out, toes all pointy, then gives this little grunt and flops over on the other side, drawing her knees up close to her chest.

I got in beside her and yanked on the blanket she'd pulled with her. I was trying not to think about Foster Williams, but he kept coming to mind. Dorothy says the worst part about sleeping with a man is all the grunting and rooting about under the covers like they do. Had to admit I was curious, though. Wasn't hardly one single song on the radio not moaning about it. I tried to imagine Foster Williams, the covers up over his head, making hog noises, and I laughed right out. Thomasine stirred, then grew quiet again.

You'd asked me a week before would I be married the next Saturday, I'd have said you got the wrong number. That was before this car pulled up back of the diner at ten-thirty of a weekend morning, and these women got out, every one of 'em wearing a hat. There's this woman calls herself Sister Perry from up at the church, goes around all the time in white. I thought she was a hairdresser or something, but Thomasine says no, she does that way to show her spit's holier'n yours. Sister Perry had on a white felt hat, her hair all tucked up inside it like a shower cap. Sister Perry's a great big old woman. I could fit in her dresses twice.

Then there was a little tiny woman with feet that pointed out at the sides. She looked like a sparrow coming up the path toward the trailer. She walked sort of stooped over, clutching her purse in front of her like it was about to get away. She had on this little fuzzy hat—a beanie, I think it was.

And then there was Mrs. Dawson. She walked as straight as a broom, her brown coat buttoned right up to the chin, a hat that looked like a rowboat. All the way up the path she's smiling, like they come to a tea party or something.

Thomasine was doing her nails over at the table, and I says, "Thomasine, we got company."

"Who?" says Thomasine.

"Looks like a nurse, a misfit, and a undertaker," I says, knowing full well who they was.

Thomasine puts down her cinnamon coral nail polish and saunters over to the window to have her a look, scuffs flopping on the floor.

"Oh, great Jesus!" she chokes. "It's the Decency Committee!" and she grabs Daddy's coat, throws it over her slip, and goes out the back door.

Those three women been on Thomasine's case since they give up on Dorothy. Used to be they was always trying to send her away to summer camp or get her to join the Girl Scouts—find some nice young man to invite her to church. What they going to try now? I wonder, when Mrs. Dawson knocks and I let 'em in. That's my problem; I'm curious.

I had to put the sofa bed back together so's there'd be a place for them to sit, and every one of those ladies walk over and set down so straight it was like they was wearing a stovepipe round

their middles. First I figured they'd come about Thomasine, but
when Mrs. Dawson finished her speech, I knew it was me they
was after. Never so scared in all my life.

"I want to be kind," Mrs. Dawson says, "but I'm going to be
honest as well. We all knew your mother, April—the sweetest
woman God ever put on this earth—and after she passed away,
we told ourselves we'd keep an eye on her girls, the way she
would have wanted. Well, we didn't keep as close a watch as we
should have. Everyone knows what your sister Dorothy is doing,
and it doesn't take much imagination to figure out what Thomasine is up to with those truck drivers. Of course, Dorothy and
Thomasine are over eighteen, and unless they make the effort,
there's not much we can do to help them; but it's not too late
for you."

Sister Perry leaned forward. "April Ruth, you haven't been to
school more than five days in the last three weeks." She opened
her purse and pulled out a paper, then lifted her glasses a little
off her nose so she could read it: "Last semester you failed En-
glish, United States history, typing, and business math—"

"Did *not!*" I said hotly. "Got me a D in typing."

Mrs. Dawson reached over and put her hand on my arm. It
felt like a dead chicken foot, all cold and clammy. "You're sixteen, and no one can make you go to school if you don't want,"
she said, "but you're still a minor, April Ruth, and you're still
the responsibility of the community. We've seen two girls in this
family go bad and we're not about to watch it happen to you."

I wondered right off if they'd ever found out about me fooling
the truck drivers back when I was nine. I'd picked me up a lipstick
once in a drugstore without paying for it, and I'd slipped in the
movies three or four times, but I sure hadn't done nothing lately.

"Haven't done *nothin'*!" I said aloud, and I didn't know how
mad I was till I heard my own voice.

"We didn't say you had, dear." Mrs. Dawson kept on squeezing
my arm. "But when a home is obviously a bad influence on a
child, the only thing to do is find a better place for that child to
live."

I felt just like somebody had punched me square in the stomach. I wanted to yell for Thomasine, but I knew she was sitting back in the woods in our daddy's coat and wouldn't come out for anything in this world. Daddy hadn't been home the night before, and wherever he was, he wasn't in no shape to help me. Neither was Dorothy. I'd been left to myself for most of my sixteen years, but I never felt so alone as I did right then.

"You don't got the right," I says in this little bitty voice that hardly had any breath to it.

"My dear, I'm not threatening you, but believe me, I have friends in the courthouse, and I will do whatever it takes to get you removed from this place," Mrs. Dawson tells me.

"Like where?" I says, almost a whisper.

She looks straight into my eyes. "We're considering a number of possibilities, and to be honest, the juvenile home is one of them."

I sprung up off my chair like it was hot and leaped around behind it, keeping the chair between me and the ladies.

"I'm not going to the juvenile home!" I says. "I ain't done *nothin'!*"

Mrs. Dawson sighed and exchanged looks with the other women.

"Of course, the *ideal* arrangement would be a kind family that would take you in," said the woman who looked like a sparrow, and the other women nodded, "but truth to tell, April, we just can't find one that will have you—because of your sisters, you see."

A great big lump worked its way up my throat. Felt like a baseball. Seemed to me I was growing smaller and smaller till finally I was just this little speck behind the chair and the women was all looking down at me like hens about to scratch. They had me, I knew. I tried to think of one single, solitary person I could ask to help me. The men at the Amoco station were nice, but they wasn't about to take me home. And Tillie, at the Laundromat, was okay, but I think she'd had a crazy spell sometime in her life and I didn't want to get mixed up with that. I felt my chin start to tremble and I pressed my teeth together hard to keep from crying.

And then Sister Perry's face lights up like a Coca-Cola sign, and she says, "But we've got good news for you, April Ruth, if *you're* willing."

I felt like I was hanging suspended and the committee had hold of the ropes.

The women were smiling at each other. "It's quite romantic, really," says Mrs. Dawson, and she gives a little giggle. "Somebody wants to marry you."

I could feel my teeth pulling away from each other as my jaw dropped. Buddy Travis, from typing, I thought.

"Somebody who has watched you grow up and wants to give you a home," added Mrs. Perry.

"And take care of you," said the sparrow.

I looked quickly from one woman to the other. I tried to think of the mechanic's name over at the Amoco station. Was it him?

"Foster Williams," said Mrs. Dawson.

I come back around the chair and sat down on it hard. Just couldn't get it through my head. Foster! The bridgeman! And before I could say anything, the women all starts in again, about how he's lonely and he's a good hardworking man, got this house all to hisself, don't drink much to speak of, and he'd be good to me. They used the kinds of voices that have violins playing in the background, and every one of 'em made it sound like if Foster Williams had asked for them instead of me, they would've left their husbands and run right off.

"Well," says Mrs. Perry finally, "what do you think, April Ruth?"

What was there to say? I had the choice of going to the juvenile home with wire over the windows or living with Foster.

"I guess so," I said.

Oh, but they was proud of themselves, then. All started beaming and pinching at me and the sparrow says she's going to get together some clothes for the honeymoon, and the next day Mrs. Dawson's back with a paper for my daddy to sign saying it's okay I get married.

"You sure you want to do this?" Daddy said to me, holding the pen over the paper. He come in around noon stinking like a goat, way he sleeps in his clothes.

"Yes," I told him, and Mrs. Dawson sticks the signed paper in her purse and leaves me a sack full of dresses.

"My Gawd!" says Thomasine, peering down in the sack and pulling out something that looks like it was made to be wore by a missionary. "Why'd you go and say you'd marry Foster?"

"Well, you sure didn't stick around to help out," I told her. And just thinking 'bout that later was what made me roll over in bed and give her a good hard kick.

Thomasine woke up.

"What's *that* for?" she asked, angry, rising up on one elbow.

"For all the times you wasn't here you should've been," I told her, and then I turned my back and left her staring after me in the darkness.

***

The day Foster called, I said to Thomasine, "Don't know why he asked to come over before the wedding."

"You talk like a crazy person," said Thomasine. "Hardly even knows you. Got to get acquainted."

"*He* knows me," I said.

"Not like he's going to."

"Embarrassing is what it is," I told her.

I put on a clean shirt.

"Tuck it in, so he'll see you got a waist," says Thomasine.

If I'd known I was going to marry Foster Williams one day, would have paid him more attention. He was just an ironworker who ate at the diner and hung around sometimes with Jed and Wallace Harley who, if they was to die this very minute, I would dance on their graves. If I had anything at all against Foster, it was the company he kept—the Harleys, anyway. They got this tobacco farm couple miles from our trailer, and I never liked 'em one bit more than I do now.

When I was seven or eight, Wallace used to come roaring up to the Amoco station in a old Pontiac, back hitched way up, and if Thomasine and me was playing there on the concrete, he'd always act like he was going to hit us, put the brakes on just in time. Then he and Jed would step out, laughing their fool heads off, spitting tobacco ever' which way. Howard, man who runs the Amoco, he'd tell 'em to stop, but they'd laugh in his face. Fact is, nobody messed much with the Harleys.

So one day Howard gave me his old bicycle to ride, and I'm doing pretty good at it, I ride around the corner of the station and there's Jed and Wallace standing near the pumps.

"Git outa my way!" I yell, but they don't move, and I swipe Wallace good with the pedal as I go by, scrape the skin off his leg. He's cussing to beat the band.

"I *told* ya to git!" I call back over my shoulder.

Next time I see the Harleys down at the Amoco, I get on Howard's bike and head for 'em again, and this time they see me coming they scatter! Miss Jed by a inch.

"You *crazy*, girl?" Jed hollers after me, and it's all I can do to keep a smile off my face.

They never come roaring up to Thomasine and me again after that, and ever' time they see me on the bike, they move over quick. All the time I'm dressing for Foster to come visit me I'm thinking about the Harleys, how I hate 'em.

'Bout quarter to eight, here he comes in the pickup, driving around the Amoco, and parks right outside the trailer.

"Oh, Gawd," says Thomasine, and goes into the bathroom and shuts the door. Too painful to watch, she says.

Daddy's got the TV on, and he's been drinking since four o'clock. He drank right through dinner and now he's crying. Sitting there watching the TV with tears just pouring down his cheeks. Even cries at the commercials.

I put on my coat, figure I can get out the door before Foster come in, but soon's I open it, Daddy says, "That Foster Williams, April? I wanna meet the man going to take my baby away." Weren't nothing to do but invite Foster in.

He was taller than I remembered. Had to duck his head to get in the door, and soon's he come in, I could smell his after-shave. That was one thing I always liked about Foster. Some of the men in the diner, they always smelled of sweat. Foster smelled of sweat and after-shave.

"Evenin'," he says, nodding to my daddy. Strangest feeling in the world to have him standing not two feet away, hands hadn't ever touched me hardly, and know that on Saturday we was going to lie down together in bed. There was little wrinkles where his eyelids sort of sloped down. Them blue eyes just looked out from under the bushy brows like they was back in a cave or something. Hair was curly and come to a V in front where the scalp showed high on either side.

Daddy was still bawling. He leaned forward and stuck out one hand toward Foster. "I jus' wanna shake the hand of the man what's goin' off with my baby," he says again.

Foster walks over to the couch and Daddy grabs his hand and starts blubbering on it and says how Foster's got to be good to me or he'll have the law on him and Foster says he never intended to be anything else.

"Sweet Jesus!" Thomasine says from the bathroom.

Then Daddy says what a hard life he's had and starts telling Foster all the things he like to did but didn't, and then I saw his trousers were growing dark in front where he was peeing in them, and I says to Foster, "We got to go."

Foster leaned down and shook Daddy's hand again and Daddy don't even know we're leaving, just jaws on, wiping his eyes at his own story.

We got outside on the step and I said to Foster, "Bet you're the only person in the state of Maryland whose father-in-law peed hisself when you shook his hand."

Even in the half-light from the Amoco station, I could see Foster's face turning all shades of pink.

"Where you want to go, April Ruth?" he says.

I shrugged. "You're the one who asked to come over."

Foster sticks his hands in his pockets and looks at me sort of sideways, then smiles a little. "Want to go to the diner?"

"We just ate," I tell him. I step down and start up the path to the Amoco station, Foster alongside me, few feet away. The station's shut up tight, only one light burning there over the desk. All the while we're walking, we're not saying a word.

We get up to the gas pumps and Foster walks on one side of 'em, I walk on the other. Don't know what come over me, but suddenly I stop walking and hang back behind a pump. Foster's footsteps go right on. He don't even know I'm missing.

Then I hear his feet stop too. There's silence for a couple seconds, then he takes a few steps more and stops again.

"April?" he says.

I'm leaning back against the pump, my lips all tucked in, trying not to giggle. I hear Foster laugh.

"What'd you do, April? Fall in a hole?"

He starts 'round the left side of the pumps and I move over to the right. He knows I'm hiding then, but he don't know behind which one. He comes back around the first pump and I go behind the second. Then it's quiet, quieter than the woods on a Sunday morning. I start counting off the seconds. I get up to twenty-three, and there's still no sound at all. My heart starts thumping. Suddenly a big old hand reaches around the pump and grabs my jacket and I give a scream bloody murder, and then he's chasing me 'round and 'round the pumps and we're making plumb fools of ourselves right out there by the highway.

I lean back against a pump out of breath and Foster's laughing 'gainst another one. When we stop laughing, it gets quiet and embarrassing all over again.

"Where you want to go, April? The movies?" he asks again.

Don't want nobody seeing me at the movies with Foster Williams just yet. "No," I tell him. "Just set down somewheres, I guess."

I start walking toward the diner and then I see the chairs inside the Laundromat is empty, so we set down in there and proceed to get acquainted.

"How you doin' in school?" Foster asks me right out.

"I don't wanta talk about that!" I tell him. I'm picking at a cigarette burn in the vinyl cushion, not looking at him, you know. So Foster tries again.

"I'm cleanin' up the house real good for you," he says.

I go on picking at the hole. "How many rooms it got?"

"Five," he says, "countin' the bathroom."

I think about how the three of us—four, when Dorothy was home—lived in that trailer all these years, two rooms and a bath, and I says, "Five rooms for one man is a whole lot of rooms."

I could tell he was smiling the way the words come out. "Need somebody else to fill up the space, I guess."

"What happened to your family?" I'd heard it once but I forgot.

"Lost 'em all in a car crash up on 50."

I looked over at him. "How many of 'em was there?"

"Mom, Dad, and Lloyd. He was five years younger than me."

I didn't even have sense enough to say I was sorry. Just kept on picking at that hole.

"April, stop messin' with those cushions," Tillie yells at me from over by the dryer where she's folding sheets, and I slouch down in the chair and slide my hands under me. It's warm in the Laundromat. Smells like Clorox and Tide. Thomasine and me, when we was littler and sometimes there wasn't any heat in the trailer, we'd come over to the Laundromat and play. Tillie used to let us pour the detergent in the washers, but last few years she's been crotchety. She always wears an old dress nothing under it—can see right through it in the summer when the doors is open—and she's got a old saggy body you wouldn't hardly believe.

Some man come in and pulls his clothes out of the dryer. He's got a cigarette hanging out the side of his mouth with ash a inch long, and all the while he's folding his clothes, head turned to one side, I'm waiting for the ash to drop.

"Gonna burn right through his sheets, he's not careful," Foster says, and we both laugh to ourselves.

While Foster's watching the man and his cigarette, I'm studying Foster. He's got funny ears, for one thing—they're great big old ears, but they end in a sort of point. You could see on his face where he was going to have to shave next day, so he must have splashed the after-shave on over his whiskers. His nose come down sort of straight and then squished out at the bottom. He wasn't bad-looking for thirty-two, but when I thought on how he'd been alive twice as long as I have, made me feel creepy. I ever live to be thirty-two I'll be a old woman for sure.

"What do I got to do after we're married?" I ask him.

Foster wrinkles up his forehead and just looks at me.

"I mean, I got to wash and iron or what? Dorothy took the iron with her and I never did learn it."

"Haven't had my shirts ironed for seven years, don't see no reason to start now," Foster says, and smiles at me. Then he goes back to watching Tillie swipe at the floor with a mop and once, when she couldn't get a machine to start, he went over to help her. Foster sure talked nice to me. I didn't love him, but I supposed I could do a lot worse.

He asks me later should he come back the next night, and I tell him I don't see the need. I don't fancy sitting in the Laundromat ever' night this week, and no point asking him in if Thomasine's going to lock herself in the bathroom and my daddy's going to cry. Foster says that's okay, then, 'cause he's got the rest of the house to clean, so he'll pick me up Saturday morning, eleven o'clock, and drive me to Denton to get ourselves married.

Thomasine's waiting for me in the trailer.

"Help me get him to bed," she says, motioning toward Daddy, who's sprawled out on the couch, smelling of pee.

She takes one arm and I take the other, and we pull him off the couch and drag him back to the little bedroom at the end. He gets half awake and cusses me up a storm. Not a name in the book he don't call me, and we just leave him there on the bed, pee pants and all.

Thomasine unfolds the sofa bed.

"Well," she says, "how'd it go?"

I shrug. "Okay, I guess."

"What'd you do?"

"Nothin'. Just talked."

"What about?"

"Everything," I tell her, but we didn't talk about nothing. I lay there in the dark, wondering what it'll be like Foster's next to me 'stead of Thomasine. And all at once I get this big scared feeling inside me, like a balloon blowing itself up, that Foster and me, we won't never have anything to talk about; we got two different lives completely.

***

I didn't go back to the high school after I was engaged to Foster. Wasn't no point to it I could see. The teachers must have all thought I was just dumb, and I know I'm not brilliant, but it wasn't that so much. School just didn't agree with me. Back in sixth grade, for example, when we was studying bugs, all I wanted to do the rest of the year was catch 'em in my jelly jar. Wasn't *ready* to read the next chapter on frogs. Teacher didn't take that into account at all.

Spent the next couple days figuring what to take with me over to Foster's. Soon's I'd take my stuff out of a drawer, Thomasine would have hers in it. She got on my nerves the way she'd go pawing through the bureau ahead of me.

"Thomasine-put-that-down-I'm-gonna-hitcha," I hollered when she held up the little pink monkey with big eyes that Buddy Travis won for me at the carnival. "Seems like you can't git rid of me fast enough."

"Just helpin' out," she said, and started fingering the blouse that Dorothy gave me.

I'd got me a box that buns come in from behind the diner, and I folded up most of my clothes and laid 'em in there. Then I filled a cloth bag with OCEAN CITY writ on the side of it, and what was left over I stuffed in a paper sack. Didn't seem like there was all that much to me when I saw how easy I could get all my things together.

"Looks like you just got off the boat," says Thomasine when I tied up the box with string. "It was *me*, I'd call up Buddy Travis and have myself one last fling before I got to be an old married lady."

"Never had my first fling, so no sense in havin' the last," I says, and put my box by the door.

"Well, I'd go anyhow," says Thomasine. "You git married now, April Ruth, you're goin' to wonder all your life what other men are like."

"Buddy ain't no man yet."

"The hell he's not." Thomasine just smiles and lights a cigarette, then tips her head way back and blows smoke toward the ceiling.

I felt hot back by my ears just thinking that maybe Thomasine and Buddy Travis had sex with each other, but I wasn't going to give her the satisfaction of asking right out.

About seven o'clock Friday evening, Dorothy come over. She's got eyebrows drawn on her face high up on the forehead and you can see where the real eyebrows had been pulled out down below, all naked. Dorothy's the pretty one in the family, and she's got on this little skirt so short she'd be arrested she ever leans over.

"Well! Well!" says Dorothy, looking at the box and sacks there by the front door. She shakes her head. "If it was me," she says, "I'd put my stuff on the first Trailways bus goin' through and get as far away from Foster Williams I could get. You aren't pregnant, are you?"

"*Course* not!"

Dorothy sighed again and flopped herself down on the couch. "Where's Daddy? He going to be here tomorrow to see you off?"

I shrugged.

Dorothy grabs my hand and pulls me down beside her. She's wearing some kind of expensive perfume 'cause it still smells good even when you get up close. "April, you be careful or you're going to find yourself with a mess of babies before you're twenty."

I wanted in the worst way to find out just how careful I had to be, but I didn't want Dorothy to know.

"Maybe I *want* a mess of babies. You ever thought about that?"

"Oh, Gawd!" says Thomasine.

"He don't wear a rubber, you will," says Dorothy.

I couldn't believe that's all there was to it. Rubbers all over the place. See 'em lying by the side of the road, even. If there's so many rubbers how come there's so many babies?

Dorothy stopped preaching then and smiles. "You want me to give you a pedicure? Fix your toes up pretty?"

She and Thomasine laughs and then I got the giggles, and next thing I know I got my feet up on the magazine table, little wads of newspaper stuck between my toes, and Dorothy's painting my toenails with dusty rose while Thomasine's giving me a haircut.

That night, when Thomasine and me lay down in the same bed for the last time, she says, "April, there's something you better know. About Foster."

"What's that?" I ask. Anything Thomasine got to tell me, I already don't want to hear.

She don't tell me right off, and that's not like Thomasine. Most times her mouth going so fast you have to run to catch up with it.

"You remember Ramona Wheeler?" she says.

Whatever Thomasine got to say next ain't about to cheer me, I know that for a fact.

"Well, she and Foster went to bed together a week before she run off, and Foster . . . he couldn't get it up."

I turned over on my side. "That's a lie, Thomasine! How come I never heard about it?"

"Because Ramona never told nobody but me and I never told anyone till now."

"Ramona's been gone six years!" I say. "You couldn't keep a secret that long if it was tied to your body!"

"She told me last year when she come back to visit her aunt. There's *some* things, April, I got sense enough not to tell."

Just the way she said it, I knew it was true. Never in my life give Thomasine credit for that much decency.

"I just don't want you married up with a man can't do nothing," Thomasine said. Scared the living daylights out of me.

"Don't necessarily mean he'd be that way with somebody else," I said.

"Of course it don't," says Thomasine. "Least little thing get a man upset, and that's the first place his trouble shows up. Just wanted you to go into that marriage with your eyes open, that's all."

My eyes were open, all right, till about three the next morning. Then I decide that if Foster Williams didn't think he could be no husband to me, he wouldn't be marrying me in the first place, and he ought to know that a whole lot better than Thomasine. Went right off to sleep after that.

Next morning Thomasine went off to her shift at the diner and Daddy's still sleeping off whatever he was doing the night before. I put on the white blouse Dorothy give me last year and the gray skirt with the blue flecks from the Decency Committee and the shoes Thomasine loaned me for the wedding.

Marie, over at the diner, said she'd give me a wedding break-

fast, so after I was dressed, I put on my coat and went around
to the Amoco station to tell the men goodbye.

Howard and James were hosing off the concrete in front of the
lift when I come around. James give a whistle that goes up high
then drops like the edge of a cliff.

"Well, lookee here!" Howard says, and turns off the water.
"April Ruth must be fixin' to get herself hitched today." Howard's missing half his teeth, and he says, "April, honey, if Foster
proves too old for you, you just come see me." He laughs. James
laughs too.

"I just come to say goodbye," I told them. What I was doing
really was practicing walking in Thomasine's high-heeled patent
leather pumps with the little bows on the sides. They was a bit
too long and slipped some at the back.

"Your daddy's gonna let you do it, huh?" James asked me.

"Don't hardly even know I'm gone," I answered.

"Well, you come back and see us now, hear?" Howard says.
"Shucks, I knowed you since you was no higher than my belt
buckle, April Ruth. I been too long in one place when it gits to
where the children's goin' off to git married."

I clacked over to the diner, Thomasine's shoes dragging on the
cement.

Marie was stacking little boxes of Rice Krispies on a shelf when
I come through the door, and she sings out, "Ta . . . ta . . . ta
ta!"

Truth to tell, I was beginning to feel just a little bit like a bride
after all. First time in my entire life anybody paid the least bit
of attention to me when I walked in. Maybe you had to be a
married woman, I thought, before people treated you any different.

Used to think that the Meadow Diner was 'bout the closest I
could get to heaven. Earliest memories in this world is of Dorothy
carrying me in when I was about three, and she herself only eight.
Place always smelt good, even when they was having cabbage,
'cause they cooked it with ham. First thing you see, you walk
through the door, is the way the silver metal wall behind the
counter has got this sunburst pattern on it. Starts down near the
grill, then the rays shoot out in all directions, like fingers pointing

to the stainless steel refrigerator off to the right, up to the Pepsi clock near the ceiling and down the other side to the glass case of Mrs. Smith's pies.

"She looks real pretty, don't she, Thomasine?" Marie says, cleaning the grill with a big metal scraper. "Sit down right there in that booth, April, and we'll give you the best breakfast you ever ate. Can't have you riding to Denton on an empty stomach."

I sat down in a booth just like a paying customer and let Marie serve me. Thomasine's sitting on a stool by the counter smoking a cigarette, waiting for the noon customers, her fanny bulging out over the back. First thing Marie gives me is this big mug of coffee, which I don't drink much, but I fill it about half-full of sugar and cream. Then she brings me this fresh-squeezed orange juice, would have cost a fortune.

I always liked Marie. If I'd thought she would have took me in, I wouldn't be marrying Foster, but Marie always said she only liked children from a distance; couldn't stand 'em close up for more'n five minutes. A good thing, she says, she never had any. She's got red hair, you can tell it's dyed, and freckles all over her face. Arms too. Looks like a speckled egg.

"She's takin' away our best customer, Jake," Marie says to the cook when he brings out the Good Morning Special. Platter was hot, too.

"Oh, no she's not," says Jake, winking at me. "One taste of her cookin' and Foster'll be back again every evening draggin' her with him."

There was just about everything in the world on that Good Morning Special. Two eggs sunnyside up, big piece of red ham, biscuits, milk gravy, and some home fries. I tried to eat it real slow, sloshing it down ever' so often with the coffee.

Thomasine got up after a while and began filling the sugar containers from an old bent metal pitcher while Marie does the catsup bottles. When Marie gets to my booth, she turns the handle on the jukebox to the oldies side and puts a quarter in. When the music starts in she says, " 'Cherry Pink and Apple Blossom White'," and hums it while she swipes at the lid of the catsup.

Maybe I was going to like being married, I thought, feeling real good with a second biscuit in me. Got to thinking how Foster and me once sat in that very booth when I was in seventh grade having trouble with fractions. Used to bring my math homework to the diner and do it on the table after school—Marie didn't care long as she didn't need the table. She'd try to explain fractions with a coconut cake. I got that part all right—halves and fourths and eighths and sixteenths. It was when you went to multiplyin' four thirty-seconds by nine-sixteenths that my brain just rolled over. Couldn't imagine any time in my whole *life* I'd ever want to do that, and that's when Foster come over to the table and shows me real patient-like how you got to change the numbers underneath the lines. Still never used it, but Foster got me through fractions. You'd told me I would up and marry him someday, I would've said, "Yeah, and I'm Miss America, too."

By the time I finished the Good Morning Special I wasn't feeling quite as good as I did when I walked in. Pepsi clock says a quarter of eleven, so I figured I'd better get my things on down to the highway so's Foster wouldn't have to come up to the trailer. Daddy was still sleeping and I didn't want any kind of scene between him and Foster.

I thanked Marie for the breakfast.

Thomasine comes over and kisses me on the cheek. "Good luck, April," she says. "It don't work out, you can always come on back."

The words didn't exactly fit with the good feeling I had before, and I wished she hadn't said it. Marie did better, though. She hugged me and says, "Goodbye, sugar. I don't care how good your cookin' is, I want to see you and Foster in here once in a while."

I went on up to the trailer and brushed my teeth, then put on lipstick again. The coffee was gurgling around in my stomach like it didn't have no place to go. I picked up my things and with Daddy snoring up a storm, closed the door and went down to the highway.

I sat down on a stack of tires that Amoco keeps out there, with a sign stuck in the middle saying RETREADS. Got the box of clothes by my left foot and the bag from Ocean City by my right, and the paper sack there on my lap, all ready to go.

This is my weddin' day! I thought over and over, trying to see if I felt any different inside other than the coffee. Up in the sky, the wind's pushing the clouds on ahead of it—gray clouds with pink around the edges—pink as the polish on my toenails. March ain't such a bad month for marrying, with clouds looking like that, I'm thinking.

Seemed to me I was sitting on them tires a little too long for comfort, though. Ever' so often I'd look up at the Amoco, and see Howard or James peeking at me, then ducking their heads like they hadn't looked. When I heard a car slow down, I figured it was Foster, rented hisself a car, but it was some man asking did I want a ride somewheres, and you could just tell by his small eyes that he wasn't fixing to drive you anywheres but back in the woods.

Thomasine and Marie was watching me from the window of the diner, and my face begun to feel hot. I got up and walked over to look in the window of the Laundromat to see what time it was. Eleven twenty-six, it says.

I stuck my head in the door.

"That clock right, Tillie?" I asked her.

"No more'n a minute or two off," she says. "What's happened to Foster Williams?"

"Supposed to pick me up at eleven," I said. "Guess he'll be along any time."

"You're as big a fool I ever did see," says Tillie, "sittin' there by the side of the road waitin' for misery."

"He'll come," I told her.

"Foster Williams ain't goin' to come for you, girl, and if he do, goin' to wish he hadn't. Or you going to wish it. Or both together, you're goin' to wish he had drove his pickup right on by. He's too old, too smart, and you don't know nothin' beyond the woods on one side, the highway on t'other. Don't know about nothin' a'tall."

I went back to the road and waited about fifteen minutes more till my face was so hot I couldn't stand it. Everybody's watching now—Howard and James there at the Amoco, Thomasine and Jake and Marie at the diner. My throat felt so tight I couldn't hardly swallow. Finally I picked up my box and my bag from Ocean City and my paper sack, and with the patent leather pumps making blisters on my heels, I went on back to the trailer.

THREE

Foster had been up since five. He had spent the previous night boarding up the broken window in the spare room and, as it turned out, he had penned something in. Whatever it was, a squirrel or raccoon, began chewing through the wall about daybreak and finally made its exit through a hole up under the eaves. Vinnie was half-dead from carrying on.

Russell walked down about seven.

"That dog's fixing to get itself shot," he said, standing out on the grass.

Foster was fitting a piece of tin over the hole under the roof. "Got me a squirrel or something worked its way out, and Vinnie was just helpin' it along," he told his uncle.

Like a sentry, Russell stayed where he was, feet together, back stiff. Despite his baggy overalls and torn jacket, he could have been standing at attention in full uniform. He fished in his pocket.

"This is everything I owe you on last week's groceries," he said, holding out a few bills. When Foster made no move to come after them, Russell walked over and thrust the money in Foster's pants, then stepped back. "Want everything clean between us. I'll be doing my own shopping from now on."

"There's no need," Foster told him. "I got the truck. April and me can pick up five sacks of groceries easy as we can pick up three."

"I'll tend to it myself," Russell said again. He turned and walked resolutely back to his house at the end of the lot.

As a rent-free boarder in the spare house, his uncle could make no other protest, Foster knew. It was all a matter of land. When the property reverted to him after his parents' death, he and his uncles, never close to begin with, had grown even further apart; Shum and Russell were beholden to Foster in a way that did not suit them at all, and Foster took no pleasure in it.

It was land again that allowed Earl Bates to keep Medbury at bay. The tract there by the highway had been passed down from one Bates to another, and by the time it got to Earl, he simply hauled a trailer back behind the Amoco, and there wasn't a thing anyone could do about it. Earl had just enough rent money coming in from the gas station, the Laundromat, and the diner to pay his taxes and keep his daughters alive, with money left over for drink.

Land, to Foster, had been something you came home to after a day on the bridge, a place to turn Vinnie loose, to park the pickup. Nothing to make a fuss over.

He went back inside and set to work cleaning the skillet from breakfast. His uncles didn't know how close they'd come to getting the place themselves. More than once Foster had thought about throwing a few things in the pickup and taking off—becoming a boomer like Jack Tulley—living in motels and rooming houses, never knowing from one year to another where he'd be next. He hadn't done it because of Vinnie. Couldn't picture himself walking out on a lame dog that Shum would as soon run over as not.

It was nine o'clock before he even thought it was eight, and Foster leaped into the truck to pick up April's corsage. For the first time in his life, Foster had made a list. Up until now, there hadn't been anything much worth remembering.

Monday night, he had courted April.

Tuesday, he'd mailed off the forty-dollar check for the marriage license to Denton, accompanied by the signed consent form from April's father, which Mrs. Dawson had obligingly brought by. Being a notary public in addition to the public's conscience, she had imprinted her seal on the spot.

On Wednesday, Foster had purchased the ring, a plain gold band that could be reduced or expanded, and had tucked it in the pocket of his blue suit.

Thursday, he had taken his shirts to the laundry and Friday he'd picked them up. Now he strode quickly into the florist's and waited as a heavyset woman waddled in from the back room.

"Today's the day, huh?" she said as she handed Foster the corsage box. "Listen here now, you be good to that little girl, you hear?"

"Won't beat her more'n once a day," Foster said dryly.

"You keep them flowers in the refrigerator, they'll stay fresher," the woman called after him.

Ten o'clock, and the suit, the shirt, and the ring lay on Foster's bed while he quickly polished his shoes. He went over the plans again. Denton was just across the state line. Clyde Sheldon had told him about the Denton Marriage Chapel. No blood test, no physical. All you had to do was apply for the license twenty-four hours in advance, and you could do it by mail. If Foster picked up April by eleven, they could reach Denton by one.

Little flecks of black polish dropped onto the newspaper as Foster applied the brush to the heels of his oxfords. Vinnie ambled over, sniffed, and lay down on the floor, thumping her tail. It was not the thought of the ceremony that bothered Foster so much, nor even what would happen later, but rather what he was supposed to do with April all the time in between.

Most folks went somewhere. He knew that. But most folks had more than a Saturday and Sunday for their honeymoon. There was no time off when you built a bridge. He couldn't just drive April to Denton and home again, however, and Foster had decided that morning, lying in bed listening to the squirrel chewing up the wall, that after the ceremony he would drive April to Ocean City. The more he thought about it, the more pleased he was with himself. There was always something to do at the ocean. They could walk up and down the boardwalk till it got too dark to see, and they wouldn't have one bit of trouble getting a room in the middle of March.

By the time Foster packed and showered, it was already ten

forty-five. He dressed quickly, interrupting himself from time to time to throw another item, almost forgotten, in his bag. It wasn't until he'd tied the knot that he discovered he'd put on his brown tie instead of the blue. He started over, one eye on the clock, his pulse ticking off the seconds.

He did not get out of the door till five after, and then he remembered Vinnie. If he took April to Ocean City, there would be no one to feed the dog, and he wasn't about to ask Shum. Russell either.

"Vinnie," he said, coming back inside and pouring a bowl of dry food. "This is for tomorrow."

The black dog looked at him and took a step forward.

"No!" Foster raised one hand. Vinnie stopped.

Foster went around the corner to the living room and dialed April's number. He let it ring six times . . . seven. . . . In the kitchen, Vinnie munched her Ken-L-Ration.

Nine rings and still no answer. Foster rushed out to the truck. A small seed of uneasiness grew in his chest. He imagined driving up to the Bateses' trailer and finding it locked, April gone. Imagined one of the younger men at the Amoco station grinning over at him, Thomasine laughing from the doorway of the diner. *What's wrong, old man? April gone and stood you up?*

He got as far as the K-Mart before he remembered the corsage back in the refrigerator. Veering off onto the shoulder, Foster swore under his breath and made a U-turn, tires squealing. . . .

At home, he dialed the Bateses' number again. One ring . . . two . . . three . . . four . . . five. . . . There was a clatter from the other end, the sound of the receiver being dropped, retrieved, and dropped again. Then a string of profanities from April's father for being awakened—a dozen cusswords without a single repetition. Even the bridge crew would have been impressed.

"Is April there? I've got to tell her I'll be late," Foster pleaded. But the old man added Foster's name to the list so effortlessly that he didn't even stop for breath. Foster hung up and charged back out to the truck.

Twice on the way to April's, Foster was tempted to call it off.

The more he thought about it, the more certain he was that April was only playing with him, that when he drove up, she'd be watching from back in the woods, laughing up a storm. Something carried him forward, however—a feeling so new he hadn't a word for it yet—and when the Amoco station came into view and Foster circled behind it toward the pines, he strained for a glimpse of April Ruth.

She was standing in high-heeled shoes on the stoop of the trailer, a coat thrown over her shoulders, one hand on the door-knob. Two bags and a string-tied box lay at her feet. She turned when she heard the pickup and watched without expression as Foster brought it to a stop.

"April, I tried to call," he said, springing out quickly and walking over. "I saw I was going to be late. . . ." He searched her face for some sign of forgiveness.

"I got to go to the bathroom," April said, and went inside.

Foster looked around uneasily. There was no one else in sight, yet he felt he was being watched nonetheless, felt that a dozen eyes were looking at him from the service door of the diner. He walked over to the stoop, picked up April's things, and put them in the truck.

She came back out at last and, without a word, walked around the pickup and got in.

"Didn't think you was comin'," she said, and sat with her head pressed back hard against the seat, eyes staring straight ahead.

"I told you, April, I tried to call. Didn't get any answer the first time; got your daddy the next."

"I was sittin' out by the road," she said.

"Well, then!" He waited for her to understand. April sat tapping her fingers on her patent leather pocketbook. If you ain't the stubbornnest! Foster said under his breath.

Aloud he told her, "You look real pretty, April Ruth," and reached around behind him for the corsage box, placing it on her lap. It teetered there on top of her purse.

"What's that?" she asked, without touching it.

He smiled. "Open it up."

The lid came off, and April's fingers gingerly picked up the corsage of white carnations and purple violets.

She glanced at Foster in surprise, then back at the flowers again.

"You like them?" Foster asked, starting the engine.

April held the corsage to her nose, sniffing the scent. "The purple flowers look like they come from that pot Marie keeps on the window ledge in the diner," she told him.

"Well, they didn't," Foster said, unsmiling, and hunched over the wheel.

They rode for several minutes without speaking. Out of the corner of his eye, Foster could see April giving him sidelong glances, and finally she said, "It's real pretty, Foster. Thank you."

The knot inside Foster's chest seemed to loosen, and he relaxed his grip on the wheel.

"I'll pin it on you when we get to Denton," he said.

She was studying him, he could tell. "Never seen you in a suit before. You look like an insurance man," she said.

Foster laughed and April leaned back again, her legs crossed, one foot jogging up and down. Foster began to feel better and better all the time.

She was curious about what she would have to say during the ceremony, and Foster tried to put together every line from all the weddings he'd ever attended, which weren't too many.

"Probably got to say something like 'I, April, take you, Foster, to be my lawful husband. . . .' "

"Can't remember all that in the right order," April insisted.

"Preacher'll say it first, a few words at a time."

"What else?"

" 'Poor or rich, in sickness or in health . . . uh . . . forsaking all others, till death do us part.' Somethin' like that, anyway."

Like the alternating patches of sun and shade that fell on the windshield as the clouds skidded by overhead, the conversation inside the pickup went by fits and starts. For a few minutes Foster would find himself and April talking as easily as if they had been cousins all their lives, and then just as suddenly, they would both lapse into silence. Nothing Foster could think of would seem worthy of saying aloud.

Now and then April's stomach rumbled. Foster tried hard to ignore it. He thought of turning on the radio, but that would be embarrassing. The rumble became a chronic, rhythmic gurgle. Every time she took a breath, the gurgle came again. He saw her hands press her pocketbook down more firmly over her abdomen, but it didn't help.

When it was too obvious to ignore any longer, Foster said teasingly, "Didn't have any breakfast this morning, huh?"

"Had me some coffee I shouldn't have drunk," she said.

Foster drove on and tried to distract her. He had planned to keep Ocean City a surprise, but decided it was best to tell her now.

"How many times you been to the ocean, April Ruth?"

She shook her head.

"Never did? Says so on that bag you got back there."

"Dorothy give me that," she told him.

"Well, I just thought we ought to go somewhere special tonight. Once the ceremony's over, I'm taking you to Ocean City. You like that?"

There was no answer. April was leaning back against the seat with her eyes closed, lips pressed tightly together. Foster studied her. She didn't look too good. Despite the red lipstick, her face seemed more pale than it had before.

"You okay?" he asked.

She made no response. Foster drove on, his eyes traveling back and forth between April Ruth and the road.

"Foster," she said suddenly. "We got to stop."

"There's an Esso up over the hill," he told her, and pressed his foot to the gas.

She bolted forward. "We *really* got to stop!"

The pickup swerved off onto the shoulder and April, flinging the door open, leaned out over the seat and retched.

Foster sat motionless on his side of the truck, one hand hovering above her back, wanting, but afraid, to touch her. Just when he thought she was through, she vomited again.

"It's okay," he kept saying. "It's okay."

She rested at last on her elbows, head bobbing weakly, and finally sat up. "Now that feels a *whole* lot better," she told him. Then she noticed the stains on her blouse.

"Foster!" she cried. "I'm not going to get married like this!"

"I'll stop at the Esso, you can change," he told her, pulling out onto the highway again. "You sure you're all right now?"

She nodded.

At the gas station, she took one of her bags in with her and emerged some time later wearing a T-shirt with REDSKINS on the front. She had washed the blouse and stood wringing it out beside the pickup.

"Didn't have nothin' else," she told him. "It'll dry."

Foster stared as she climbed back in beside him. "It's soaked through, April!"

"How long before we get there?"

"Hour, maybe."

"It'll dry," she said again, and as the truck picked up speed, she held her arm out the window, the blouse flapping in her hand like a headless chicken.

Foster began to feel uneasy about the time. In his wallet, he was sure, was the address of the marriage chapel in Denton as Clyde had given it to him. But on a separate slip of paper, he was equally sure, were the hours that the chapel was open.

He could see this second piece of paper lying back home by the telephone after he'd made the call. No matter how hard he imagined himself putting it in the pocket of his suit, the paper remained by the phone. Or perhaps he had last seen it buried beneath the pile of unsorted socks on his dresser.

Methodically, Foster went over the hours in his mind, trying to see them as he had written them down. He remembered a five and a nine. Yet a ten and a two and an eight flashed before him as well, along with "Monday to Thursday." Why had he wanted to be in Denton by one? He couldn't remember. The uneasiness grew.

When they reached the parking lot at last, Foster was relieved to see three other cars near the chapel and a bride and groom passing out wedding cake and champagne from the tailgate of their station wagon. Assorted relatives stood about in polyester suits and teased the bride, who kept one hand on her veil to prevent it from blowing away. April watched in fascination.

Foster rested one arm lightly about her shoulder. "Well?" he said. "We ready to go get married?"

April pulled in the blouse that dangled outside the window. "Turn your head," she commanded.

Foster averted his eyes while April slid down out of sight and changed clothes.

"I'm ready for that corsage now," she told him.

The blouse was still damp and gently outlined her breasts. It was the first time Foster's hands had been so close to her skin, and as he thrust his fingers inside the collar of the blouse to pin the corsage, he felt a rush of protectiveness toward the young girl there beside him, the closest he had come so far to love.

The marriage chapel itself was a converted railway station to which a porch with white columns had been added. April's heels clacked on the concrete paving, and when they reached the steps, Foster paused, holding out his arm, and April took it. Together they started up. On the top step, however, Foster came to a dead stop. A wooden stand stood in front of the white double doors. CLOSED, said a sign on the stand.

At first Foster's eyes did not seem in focus. Numbly he dropped April's hand and went over to read the small decal on a side window:

HOURS

Monday through Thursday:	3 PM to 6 PM
Friday:	5 PM to 8 PM
Saturday:	10 AM to 2 PM
Closed Sundays	

He looked at his watch. Twelve minutes past two. He tried the door but it was locked. Shielding his eyes, Foster peered through the glass, but the room was deserted.

His neck grew hot, then cold. It was his habit of not looking to the future that was responsible. It was the way he lived, papers and socks and candy wrappers strewn all over. It was the years he had spent alone, responsible for no one but himself.

"Well," he said, turning to April. "I guess we've got to go find us a justice of the peace." Scarcely were the words out before panic struck again. The application had been sent here to the Denton Marriage Chapel. Somewhere inside, in a desk, sat his forty-dollar check and the license.

"I've got to think this out," he said, and lowered himself onto the steps. Forget the forty dollars, he told himself. Apply somewhere else. Go to another town, fill out an application, wait twenty-four hours, and be married tomorrow. Panic Number Three: they could not be married anywhere without Earl Bates's consent. The signed and notarized paper was also inside the marriage chapel behind the locked door.

April plunked herself down beside him on the steps and took off her shoes.

"April Ruth, I don't know what to do," Foster said at last, and explained the problem. "I am as sorry as I can be. Not every day I get married, but you'd think when I did, I could do it right."

"Well, I'm not goin' back home to git sick all over again," she declared, examining her heels where the shoes had rubbed. "You said we was going to Ocean City and I never seen the ocean, so let's go."

"We aren't married!"

She smiled, the corners of her mouth turning down ever so slightly. "*I* know that, and *you* know that, but don't anyone else know it."

Foster stared at her dumbfounded.

"We'll have our honeymoon this Saturday and git married the next," she said, as though it were all settled. "License be just as good then as it is now, won't it?"

Foster felt his blood begin to flow again, his muscles relax. Here was a girl who was totally sensible about it. There was certainly no point in delivering her back to her father to go through it all over again the following week. Instinctively he put his arm around her there on the steps where she sat dangling her shoes in one hand. She did not pull away from him.

"I guess that's what we'll do then, April," he said. "It'll be our secret, won't it?"

She nodded. "Foster, you git me a ring?"

"Yes."

"I'd like to see it."

Foster reached down in his suit pocket and produced the small, ivory-colored box. He opened it and held it out. April looked at the ring, but didn't touch it.

"I'm goin' to Ocean City with you, I want to go like a married woman," she said, and held out her finger.

Smiling, Foster took the ring from its velvet slot and slipped it on her hand. It went on a little too easily, but his guess hadn't been off by much.

"Now say them words you told me," said April.

Foster held her small hand between the two of his. "I, Foster, take you, April, to be my wedded wife. Uh . . . to have and to hold, till death do us part."

She frowned. "That wasn't the way you said it the first time."

He tried again. "I, Foster, take you, April, to be my wife." He paused, fingering her ring.

"Somethin' about sickness," she coached.

The lines came back to him now: "For richer or poorer, in sickness and health, forsaking all others, till death do us part."

"Now help me say it."

Still holding her hand, Foster repeated it phrase by phrase, and April said it after him, her little pointy chin tucked under, eyes serious. When she'd finished, Foster leaned over and kissed her very lightly on the lips.

It was a festive drive to Ocean City. There was a shared experience between them that was theirs alone, and now that they had a plan, Foster could joke about it.

"Where'll we say we're goin' next Saturday?" April asked mischievously.

"To do our laundry," Foster deadpanned.

"All the way to Denton?" she shrieked.

"Sure do like that Denton water," he said, and they broke into laughter.

It would take several hours to get from Denton to Ocean City, but already the Bay Bridge was visible far off against the horizon.

"You want to see where I work?" Foster asked her.

"Where?" She looked around.

"Ever been to the bay?"

She shook her head.

"Never? April, girl, you got some travelin' to do. Look up there straight ahead—far down the road as you can see."

Everything was a new experience for her. The toll booth, even. The curving edifice out over the water, the gulls, the choppy waves below.

"Over there," Foster said, pointing to the second span, where derricks and barges sat waiting for Monday morning.

"Don't take your hands off the wheel!" April cried in alarm, grabbing at him as they started over the bridge. "Where, Foster?"

"See up there on the tower? That's where I'll be standing come Monday."

She studied it without speaking, turning her head so she could follow it with her eyes even after it passed behind them. Her small chin was tucked under again. "Get yourself killed!" she scolded.

"Haven't yet," Foster laughed.

They reached Ocean City around five, when the sun had given way to a cold twilight. Most of the motels were shuttered, their signboards reading CLOSED. As he pulled into the parking lot of the Marvel Oceanfront Hotel, Foster realized he should have told April in advance where they were going. It would be cold along the boardwalk later.

The wind grew stronger as they walked up the concrete ramp gritty with sand, April several steps ahead of him. The ocean, dark in the fading light, lurked just beyond the beach, where breakers slapped and hissed against the wood pilings.

April stopped in her tracks and stared, completely captivated. There was not a soul in sight except an old man with a metal detector. Everything was gray as cold ash, yet there could have been sun and surfers and beach umbrellas for the look in April's eyes. Foster stopped and let her stare, one arm about her shoulder.

"*Never* seen the ocean before?" he asked incredulously.

"Daddy says I did when I was so little it didn't even count," she told him. "Just think, Foster, if I was to go right straight across the water, far as I could, I'd hit China."

"Hit a couple other countries first." He smiled.

There was a light lit on the porch of the hotel, where the empty rockers, all in a row, tipped back and forth in the evening wind. Two teenagers, in jeans and ponchos, hurried along the boardwalk carrying a large boxed pizza to some rendezvous.

Foster left April to amuse herself in a rocker while he registered. He had never slept in an oceanfront room himself. He had never, in fact, stayed in a hotel here by the water. Up until now, trips to Ocean City had been fishing expeditions with the Harley brothers; they stayed in a musty-smelling cottage on the inlet, and the mosquitoes were fierce. In the last few years, the Harleys' tastes had turned more to the racetrack than to fishing, and Foster had stopped coming to the ocean at all. He was unprepared for the rates, even off-season, and asked for the smallest double room.

"I got us an oceanfront room on the third floor," he told April, when he came back out.

She got up reluctantly from the chair and followed him through the dimly lit hall and up the carpeted stairs.

There was barely space inside for the double bed and dresser, and Foster wondered if he'd done right. But April did not even notice. She scrambled across the bed to get to the windows beyond and crouched down by the sill, yelping with delight when she saw the lights of a ship far out on the water.

Bemused, Foster sat down on the bed behind her. It occurred to him that, except for the peck there on the steps of the marriage chapel, he had never really kissed April Ruth, never held her in his arms. Tentatively he reached out and ran one finger up and down her arm where it rested on the sill. She did not shy away, but seemed oblivious to it, to him. The ocean took her full concentration. Foster decided that the embrace could wait.

"I'm going to change into something warm, April, then we'll go have dinner. We can walk the beach after," he told her.

In the bathroom, he laid out his shaving supplies, discovered he had put out his condoms as well, and dropped them back in his shaving kit. He changed to a pair of twill work pants, a plaid shirt, and hooded jacket.

"Here," he said, coming back to April and handing her his sweater. "You put on the warmest clothes you've got."

It was almost worth marrying, Foster decided at dinner, just to see April enjoying herself. She was probably the only patron in the dining room of the White Marlin who had never smelled the salt air. She would rise from her chair and exclaim aloud over a chartered boat pulling up just outside, its deck strung with lights, or run over to the window to see what someone was carrying in a bucket.

"You hardly touched your shrimp," Foster told her.

"I'll take 'em with me," she promised.

"What about this baked potato, April? We didn't have any lunch, remember."

But the potato went begging and the salad as well, and after a few bites of cheesecake, April was fidgeting to go back out.

On the boardwalk, the wind took her by surprise. Each time a new gust smacked into her, bringing with it the sting of sand on her cheeks, April would turn sideways, burying her face against Foster's chest. She came into his arms naturally now, drawing out his warmth, and Foster welcomed the wind.

It was a new experience for him as well. Not that he had never walked the boardwalk with a woman. There had been other times that he and the Harley brothers—Jed and Wallace—after a day of crabbing, would come over to the amusement park at night and try their luck at the shooting gallery. Guns made Wallace mean, however. The chipmunk with the target on its belly, the piano player with the bull's-eye on his back, the frog, the clock, the skunk, the beer can—all became mortal enemies in the sights of Wallace Harley's gun. From there he would move on to the ringtoss and the bottles, mad as a demented rooster, and Foster and Jed would go talk to the girls who stood outside the french fry stand, just around the corner from Ripley's Museum.

There the air was pungent with the smell of hot grease and watermelon rinds, perspiration and cheap perfume, and sometimes—twice, maybe—they had talked some girls into going back to the van with them, parked on First Avenue. After Jed and his girl had taken a turn inside, Foster would crawl in with the woman he had found, groping around in the dark on an old mattress. He would taste the salt on her lips as he'd struggle to get her blouse up over her breasts. There would be wet stains under the sleeves where she perspired, and he'd wonder how he was supposed to get her clothes off with her bouncing around and moaning and clawing at him before he hardly even knew her name. If the girl was wearing a bathing suit under her clothes, Foster didn't think he would ever find the right hooks to undo her, ever get the skintight suit down over her hips. And finally, while she lay there impatiently, knees spread, he would desperately conjure up images of other girls he had seen on the beach that day, girls who were completely beyond his reach, who would never allow themselves to be picked up outside the French Fry Palace and taken back to a van.

But this night, with April, was different from the others. Whatever lipstick she had started out with that morning was gone now. Her high heels had been exchanged for penny loafers, and she was all but swallowed up in Foster's old navy-blue sweater. With her small face pressed against his chest, her yellow-brown hair blowing wild about her head, fingers clutching at his jacket, Foster had never felt the way he did now—a mixture of longing, tenderness, and the something else he couldn't yet name.

"April, you take my jacket," he said, feeling her body shiver. "You got ice cubes for ears."

"What you going to do, Foster?"

"This old shirt's like a horse blanket. I'll be fine."

Snug in the jacket, April broke free of him and ran ahead, simply crowing, arms outstretched to embrace the wind. Foster, several paces behind her, laughed aloud. The sound of it startled even him, but it felt so good that he laughed again. Laughed at nothing.

They stopped in a store along the way, one of the few that was open, and Foster purchased a small Naugahyde suitcase for April.

"A wedding present," he told her. "You aren't going anywhere no more with your clothes in a cardboard box."

She stood dead still, studying him. "We supposed to give each other presents, Foster?"

He ignored the question. "Just something I wanted to do."

"But I don't have nothing for you."

"You're marrying this old man, April. That's enough."

They walked back to the hotel, her head leaning against him, his arm around her waist, and despite the cold, Foster felt that if only this moment could go on, stretched out forever, exactly the way it was now, he would want nothing else for the rest of his life. He thought how incongruous it was, really—he and April Ruth—the skinny-legged nine-year-old he had scolded once in the diner. Yet here they were together, on the verge of being married, and as the hotel loomed up before them and he could make out the light they had left on in their room, he would have preferred to keep walking. Here they were alone yet not alone. When they chose to be quiet, the ocean filled up the silence.

Once in the room, April went immediately to the window again but it was too dark to see, and Foster knew she was disappointed.

"Well," he said, "we just got to come back here in the summer, is all. We'll come as much as you want, April."

She backed up to the edge of the bed and sat down, her hands in her lap, shoulders hunched high, then let them drop. Foster looked about for a radio, a television—anything to break the stillness. There was nothing and the room was cold.

"I guess we'll have to go to bed to keep warm," Foster said. "They don't heat these places unless they have to." He waited. "You want to use the bathroom first, April? Take a hot shower or something?"

"You go first," she said.

Foster took pajamas out of his bag, pajamas he hadn't worn more than once since his mother gave them to him ten years before. He showered, shaved again, then put on the after-shave that smelled of musk and slipped the package of condoms in his pajama pocket.

April was still on the edge of the bed wearing his jacket. She rose obediently, picking up one of her bags, and avoiding his eyes, went into the bathroom, locking the door behind her.

Foster turned down the spread and slipped the condoms in the bedside table. In the single act of opening the drawer, however, he had a vision of his secret—his and April's—traveling down the streets of Medbury, from one house to another, like the scattered pages of a newspaper. He lay woodenly between the sheets and stared unblinking at the ceiling. He realized April would be home alone while he was at work, and in that first week, there would be visitors. Thomasine and Dorothy would both be by. Possibly April's father. Mrs. Dawson could be counted on to show up with a gift, and Marie, from the diner, as well. There were women in Medbury who lived for weddings and would want to know all the particulars: What kind of chapel was it up in Denton? Were there flowers? Music? Was it a real preacher or one of those justices of the peace, and if so, did he know his Bible?

Could Foster count on April to give the same answer every time? Not to fumble? If it were any woman other than April Foster wouldn't have cared whether the community found out or not. But this was serious. Getting to Denton too late for the ceremony was one thing; taking her to Ocean City afterward instead of home to her daddy was something else. What would matter to Medbury was that Foster Williams, age thirty-two, had carnal knowledge of April Bates, a minor.

The bed felt colder to Foster than the room. Earl Bates, as shrewd drunk as he was sober, would smell a lawsuit. At the last count, April's father, in cahoots with a lawyer down in La Plata, had three lawsuits going simultaneously. Anybody look at Earl Bates cross-eyed, he was like to get himself a summons, Foster thought. Not that any suit had been successful so far, but one of these days, that lawyer was going to come through. It wasn't the summons that worried Foster; it was losing April.

The bathroom door creaked open and Foster turned his head. April stood hesitantly there in the doorway holding her clothes. She was wearing a short see-through nightie of red chiffon with matching red satin panties beneath. A ruffle about the neck dipped halfway down the front.

"It's Thomasine's," she said by way of explanation, and made a dash for the bed.

Each lay on his own side. The light on the nightstand did not make the room more cheerful, but seemed, in fact, to make the shadows grotesque, the silence even more pronounced. Foster longed for the noise of trucks going by on a road outside. For Vinnie's barking, even. April quit fidgeting and settled down, then lay so still that Foster knew she sensed something. He had to speak—couldn't just lie there.

Tentatively, his hand reached out and touched her knee. The boniness of it startled him—like a boy's kneecap there under the blankets. It was still warm and moist from her bath and he let his hand caress it gently, going no further than halfway up her thigh.

She turned toward him then, knees bent, and brought her second leg down gently on top of his hand, so that his fingers were imprisoned between her thighs. His pulse pounded against the pillow and reverberated inside his head.

"April Ruth," he said finally, carefully withdrawing his hand and placing it on her hip. "We got us a problem I didn't think on before. To do this right, we ought to go to Denton Monday, but I already told the men I'd be in. We're floating in another deck truss, and they're going to need me. We wait till Saturday, though, with folks asking questions, there's a mighty big chance one or the other of us is going to slip up, and people are going to know."

April scrunched down a little further, edging over in his direction. "I don't care." Her face was so close to Foster's he could feel her breath on his cheek.

"April, if even one person gets an idea that the wedding didn't come off, it'll go right back to your daddy."

"So what he got to say? The chapel was closed!"

"He might could say I planned it like that. Didn't mean to marry you a'tall. Just wanted an excuse to have my way with you."

April lay absolutely still. Even her breathing seemed to stop. Finally, after a long pause, she asked, "So what we going to do?"

He patted her hip once more, a paternal pat this time. "I'm goin' to take you back the way you were when I brought you here. No one will be able to do anything if I don't touch you."

He could tell she was smiling without even looking at her. "You're touch-*ing* me," she sang out softly.

"You know what I mean, April." Foster withdrew his hand. "Next Saturday, we'll go back to Denton and make it legal. I just want to do right by you, that's all."

He reached over then and turned out the lamp. He imagined them lying there talking the night away, telling funny stories, maybe. Getting to know each other a little better. Laughing the way she had laughed on the boardwalk. It would be still another shared secret, the kind of thing you talked about for years to come.

But she did not talk. April lay so long without moving that Foster wondered whether, conceivably, she could be asleep. Then, so carefully that Foster could almost see her body turning in slow motion, she rolled over, away from him, and sighed. And the sound of her sigh stayed with Foster half the night.

He did not rule out the possibility that he was afraid. Every time he thrust the idea from him, Ramona Wheeler appeared the way she had that night—sliding in beside him on the car seat and asking what did he think she had on beneath her sundress, the answer being nothing. And she had taken his hand and guided it up her thigh.

It was an act of charity, he knew. For three months after Lloyd's and their parents' accident, Foster had left the house only to go to work. The deaths were so unexpected, and Lloyd's so ironic, so robbed of glory, that they seemed to demand a sacrifice of sorts to give them meaning. If Lloyd couldn't live, then Foster paid his respects by simply marking time. The community called it grieving, but Foster knew better.

Ramona had asked him out, and after the movie they ended up at her house, with her parents gone. Foster came too soon— came even as she was lifting her dress up over her breasts. She had labored on for an hour to arouse him again, but every sigh, every squeeze on her part seemed to Foster more like resuscitation. He had felt dead—flat and cold and empty—and that was the way he was supposed to be.

Now he struggled to rid his mind of Ramona, to fill it with April instead. Toward morning, he fell asleep for an hour or so, waking once to the sound of April's deep, steady breathing, grateful that she had not left him; glad that she had not lain there feeling hateful. Dreams came fitfully, and when he woke again the room was barely light.

Foster was lying on his side, one arm up over his face. Gradually, as he became aware of the room, the walls, the windows, he was aware too of something resting on his thigh. Slowly he lowered his arm to peer at April.

She was lying on her back, head turned away, arms bent at the elbows, her hands on either side of her face. The red chiffon nightie was askew and one small breast was exposed. Foster gently raised himself on his elbow. One of April's knees protruded from the blanket on the far side of the bed, while her other leg rested lightly over his own.

Foster put his hand beneath the covers and stroked April's bare leg. Her lips made a popping sound and she stirred, then dropped back into sleep. He brought his hand up and let it touch her arm, his fingers moving on to her bare shoulder, the collarbone, one finger touching the side of her neck. He marveled at the feel of April's skin against his finger. It was as though he were bringing the girl to life, *giving* her life. . . .

Suddenly April swallowed and her lips closed. For a moment her breathing stopped altogether and then she opened her eyes. She lay perfectly still, her head still facing the bathroom, then, slowly, turned toward Foster.

He pulled her to him, burying his head on her pillow, reveling in the scent of her hair.

"April," he whispered, "I don't care what people got to say. Don't want you goin' one more minute thinking maybe I don't want you, 'cause I do."

Sleepily, April lifted her two skinny arms and wrapped them loosely about his neck. Foster dwelt on all the months and years he'd lived alone, all the nights he had missed holding her small body as he was doing now, and wondered what bridge there was in all the world that could possibly compare with this.

FOUR

The road from Pomonkey to 301 dipped and rose and dipped again. Even Foster, riding high behind the wheel of the pickup, could see only the crest of each hill, one after another, stretched out in a line before him. He let the truck fly over the rims, catching his stomach in midair as he bounced down the other side. The landscape was gray, the color of early morning.

Now and then the trees opened abruptly to reveal a tobacco field or a small house with CHAINSAWS SHARPENED or FRESH BROWN EGGS on a hand-lettered sign in front. Just as suddenly, however, the trees closed up again, and the mist thickened on the road ahead. A county sign warned of deer crossing and another warned of floods, but the thing that concerned Foster was not painted on any sign. One minute he thought he should ask for Tuesday off and drive April to Denton. The next he saw no need for that at all—no need for the questions it would provoke or the delay it might make on the bridge; Saturday was soon enough.

He had left April that morning playing with Vinnie there in the kitchen. He had not thought the girl would get up. When the alarm went off at five, in fact, Foster had gently disentangled himself from April's bare arms—from their two days at the ocean as well—and headed for the shower. But when he came into the kitchen, there she was, sitting languidly on a chair at the table, wearing a lavender kimono over her red chiffon nightie. Foster proceeded to make breakfast.

"I'll fry you some sausage too while I'm at it," he had offered, sliding the skillet onto the burner and dropping in a dollop of grease.

April yawned, her head tipping back further and further, then suddenly jerking forward again as her jaws snapped shut. "Don't see how any living person can get hisself up at five in the morning and think of sausage," she had said.

"You got to make a habit of it, that's all," Foster laughed. "Should eat a regular breakfast; put some meat on your bones."

Immediately April straightened and drew her feet back under the chair. The eyes which had rested half-closed only seconds before popped wide open and stared at Foster. "You wanted a woman with dimples in her butt, you should have run off with Dorothy," she told him.

The spatula in Foster's hand suddenly felt like a shield raised in self-defense. April's answer seemed to be coming at him from all sides, and he hardly knew where to begin.

"Didn't want Dorothy, didn't run off, and I wasn't saying I didn't like the way you look, April. Only trying to keep you healthy. You look fine to me, and you ought to know that by now." He managed a smile.

They had eaten breakfast together then, and when Foster noticed the sausage gone on April's plate, he rose to fix her another. Then he discovered Vinnie resting her head in April's lap. He sat back down.

"That dog's so fat already she can't run she don't grunt."

But April had her face close to Vinnie, her long hair hanging down around the dog's ears, arms encircling its thick body. "You ought to see the way she's lookin' at me, Foster," April purred, and the dog made soft pleading noises in its throat.

"Huh," said Foster, holding back a smile. "Could get herself an Academy Award, way she carries on. You start feeding her at the table, she won't give you a moment's peace." He lifted his coffee mug, heard the contented thump of Vinnie's tail against the floor, and it was at that precise moment—five forty-seven by the kitchen clock—that Foster knew he was in love. One minute he had imagined himself walking over a mine field that could be detonated by a single word, and the next moment he loved the girl. It made no sense.

He lowered his cup and considered for a moment. It was more than the tenderness he had felt earlier, more than lust. He would have liked to get up, lift April to her feet, and say those words— words he hadn't said to any woman before in his life. Foster rehearsed it once in his head. Then he saw himself pulling April toward his gray undershirt that probably should have gone in the wash last week, and decided to wait for a better time. That evening, perhaps.

"You and Vinnie have a good day now," was what he said as he pushed away from the table.

She went on patting the dog.

Foster made a left turn onto 301 and edged into the northbound traffic. Past the Brandywine Saddlery. Past Chew Road, the Cadillac Motel and the sprawling tobacco warehouse of white corrugated metal, its doors open wide for the merchants who gathered early for spring auctions.

He flipped on the radio and got a local evangelist with a voice like Mickey Rooney's, concluding his *Spiritual Sunrise Program*: ". . . no patience at all with that tired old argument that when a person dies, it was because God needed him in heaven." The preacher's voice cracked with indignation: "God's got fifty million angels up there, what's he need another for? No, my friends, when a good person dies, it wasn't because God called him home. It was because Satan robbed him of his Christ-right; Satan, the worst con man of them all. . . ."

A fuel truck passed Foster on the left, then cut suddenly in front of him. Foster slowed, swearing softly. A swell of organ music came from the radio and the evangelist began talking faster before his time ran out: "If you want to be remembered in prayer just write to me in care of this station, if you want to send a love-gift to continue the work of Jesus Christ just send it here, any amount at all. . . ."

Foster turned the radio off. *A love-gift.* The pickup seemed to leap again, though the road was level. Always before, Foster had looked forward to work each day. That was where his life was centered, there at the bridge. But now, for the first time he could remember, he was already thinking about coming home.

As he pulled onto the deeply rutted road near the landing, he found himself behind Juju's ancient Plymouth filled with bridge-men. The Plymouth parked and the pickup parked. Foster opened the door and put one heavy boot down in the dirt.

Juju stood sideways, collar turned up, and grinned steadily as Foster approached. He was grinning and humming both at the same time, knees dipping, fingers snapping to some inner beat. His eyes traveled slowly up and down Foster's large frame. "Um *um*mm!" he declared at last. "Here he come, boys, old Brother Bridegroom."

Foster smiled, walking on toward the change shack, and Norris followed along behind, the other men trailing in turn.

"So how you doin', man? How your weekend go?"

"Went pretty good," Foster said, not looking around.

"She feed you right?" Every word came out a chuckle. "Make you a good solid breakfast this mornin'?"

Foster opened the door of the shack. "Made it myself," he said. He reached for his heavy jacket and hard hat and put them on.

"She fill that lunch bucket for you?"

"Filled it myself," Foster said, laughing, and went down to the landing where small groups of men stood waiting, their life jackets making them hunchbacked, silhouetted against the water. As they climbed into the boats, Foster slid onto a seat between Clyde and Jack. Juju and the others sat across from him. Clyde was smiling.

"Sure must've been hard to get yourself out of that warm bed this morning," he said knowingly.

Juju and the others grinned, waiting.

"Hard every morning," Foster replied.

"*It* be hard, all right," Juju added, and the men exploded with laughter as the boat roared away from the shore.

"At least she don't make you late for work," Jack Tulley said.

"I can forgive a gal being sixteen if she don't make you late."

Clyde shook his head. "Well, now, we got us another old married man. Crew's gettin' old, Tulley, when half the men go home at night to a missus."

Foster smiled again, even more broadly, and was smiling still when they reached the barge.

Like a small amphibious army in their fiberglass helmets and bright orange life jackets, the men swarmed up over the side and onto the deck of the barge. Foster swung his arms to warm himself while Tulley discussed the day's work with the deck foreman. Another span would be floated into place as planned, but until it had reached its slot, Foster and Clyde were to help a second crew with the roadbed.

Clyde got the word first that they were going up, and passed it on. "You're goin' to hang out by your ass this mornin'," he told Foster, "and you better take good care of it now, get it back home safe again for the little missus." His smile was friendly. The men crowded into the cage.

It was the first time Foster had ever thought of his own death as affecting anyone other than Vinnie—precious few times he had thought of dying at all. Dead was dead, and the idea of being maimed was a far greater threat. He would imagine his uncles getting a call that he was in the hospital—imagine them walking down to his house, stone-faced, and feeding Vinnie for a few days before hauling her off to the pound. That was as far as his fantasy went.

Now, as he stepped out onto the working platform and adjusted his tool belt, he wondered who—should anything happen to him—would come for April. Surely not Russell and Shum. There was a new caution in his step as he started across the beam, and it bothered him. The thing he never thought about—never allowed himself to think about—was fear. He deliberately did not "tie off" when he could have—ignored Tulley's admonition—and worked all morning guiding the steel into place.

Each time a beam was lifted, dangling on the end of the derrick, the men called out to each other across the gridwork, keeping one eye on the tag end.

"Over here, Frenchy."

"Easy down."

"Watch it, hillbilly."

"Hey, Bigfoot! Move it this-a-way."

Once the beam was in place, Foster secured it with driftpins, and when they wouldn't go, pounded a bull pin in first, then the driftpin, and left it for the bolt-up gang to do the permanent fastening.

By noon, the air had warmed, the wind had calmed, and the surface of the water glazed over with sunlight. Foster tipped his helmet to shade his eyes and opened his collar.

"Wrap it up, it's lunchtime!" Tulley called.

"Goddamned boats," the signalman said, looking out over the bay at the fishing boats, which seemed to have sprung up out of nowhere. And then, over his radio to the deck below: "Dave, get the Coast Guard out here this afternoon, will ya?"

Foster settled down on the working platform with his lunch bucket and unzipped his life jacket. The platform swayed and Foster rode with it. The jib of the crane, just beyond the tower, danced against the sky. For every inch that the barge moved at its base, the crane could be moving in feet at the top. The fishermen, oblivious to the wake of their boats, could cost the crew several hours if the fittings wouldn't mesh.

Jack sat down beside Foster, pouring the hot coffee from his thermos into the cup. "So you got yourself hitched," he said, squinting out over the water. "It's the boomers who stay single. You local men all run off and settle down with some woman." He chewed thoughtfully at his sandwich, the small knobs of his cheekbones sliding up and down as he ate.

"Beats goin' home to an empty bed," said Bigfoot, at the other end of the platform.

"Maybe," said Tulley. He chewed some more. "Thing about me is . . . when I want a woman, I want her now. But when I don't, don't even want one around the place. Can't treat 'em like that."

"Nope. Can't just whistle, expect 'em to come," Clyde agreed.

Foster said nothing at all, and finally Clyde glanced over and asked directly: "So she going to be good for you, Foster?"

"Seems that way," Foster told him, smiling.

"A long and happy life, then," Jack said, raising his cup in the air.

A Coast Guard boat arrived about one and warded off the fishing boats as the prefabricated section was maneuvered into position. While water was pumped into the barges on which it rested in order to lower the span into place, Foster prepared for the linkup. Ordinarily he enjoyed the connecting of two large spans, but this time every hour that passed seemed like two. April was on his mind.

When he walked in the house that afternoon, however, she was gone. His first thought was that the girl had run off with Vinnie. Then he saw her sweater on the sofa. Checking further, Foster found April's clothes, neatly on hangers, all huddled together at the far end of his closet, three pairs of shoes in a row beneath. The bed was made. The towels in the bathroom hung straight from their racks. Foster smiled to himself and his breathing returned to normal. He took off his clothes and showered.

When he dressed again beside the bed, it seemed to Foster as though it weren't the same room with April's things in it. The wallpaper, the spread, the rag rug in front of the old, scratched bureau appeared alive, almost—waiting for her return. He hesitated as he reached for a shirt from the closet, then touched the sleeve of her kimono instead. Furtively he brought the silky cloth toward his face and sucked in the scent. A sweep of desire came over him. Embarrassed, he let go of the kimono and turned his back, but wherever he went in the room, the sleeve seemed to follow, tapping him on the shoulder and stirring him up again.

He remembered the two drawers he had given her in his bureau and stood before them transfixed. Foster opened the top drawer only one inch, just enough to glimpse the red chiffon of her gown. Then, heart racing, he slid the drawer out. There were a few pairs of panties, not quite new. SEARS VELVET TOUCH, SIZE 4, the labels said. Two small brassieres, carefully folded, their elastic worn, nestled beside the panties. Several pairs of knee socks, an old purse, a pink acrylic monkey with big eyes, a hairbrush. . . .

There was the sound of April's voice outside, talking to Vinnie, then the latch of the kitchen door as it clicked. Foster quickly closed the bureau drawer, combed his hair, and started toward the kitchen, his body warm beneath his jeans. Vinnie came skidding down the hall to meet him, tail wagging, nails clicking on the bare boards.

"Hi." Foster stood in the doorway and smiled at her.

"Hi." April plunked a box on the table and took off her coat. FINGER LICKIN' GOOD, the box read. "Supper," said April. Her long yellow-brown hair was windblown and her cheeks fiercely pink.

"You walk all the way to Gino's and back?" Foster questioned.

"Couldn't git the stove lit." April opened the cupboard and carefully took down plates and glasses. "Every time I turned the handles there'd be this gas smell. Afraid I'd blow the house up."

Foster chuckled. "You got to strike a match first. It'll light."

"Well, I ain't used to a stove like that." She opened the refrigerator and poured herself some milk.

"What'd you do for money?"

"I had some."

Foster looked in the box. There were three pieces of chicken, two envelopes of fries, and two white rolls. He lifted the chicken to see if he'd missed anything. "This it?"

She nodded.

"April, this isn't enough to feed my right foot. I eat this whole thing myself I'm just gettin' started."

"You can have my roll," she told him.

Foster went to the cupboard. "I was fixing to make supper myself when I got home. Go on, sit down, and I'll put on some beans and franks. You like corn? I'll open a can of that, too."

He had thought of several things that day to talk about over dinner, but somehow they all escaped him. April took the smallest piece of chicken and ate silently. Foster thought maybe she was riled because she'd had to use her own money at Gino's, so he pulled out his wallet.

"Here," he said, pushing a ten toward her plate.

She stiffened. "What's that for?"

"The chicken."

"Oh." She slumped and went on eating.

If you ain't the moodiest! Foster thought, as he spooned down the beans. Then, aloud: "What'd you do all day?"

April shrugged again.

"Get lonesome all alone in this old house?"

"Vinnie was here," April answered. And then: "Foster, who's those two men live back of here? I was outside with Vinnie and they come past for their mail lookin' daggers at me. One did, anyways. The other marched on by like he was goin' to church, lookin' neither right nor left."

Foster grinned. "Two old men jealous as can be, that's who. My uncles."

April played with one of the fries, bending it between her fingers, then stuffed it in her mouth. "Seems like no one wants me here."

"What you talking about, April? *I* want you here! Could hardly wait the day out to get home."

The eyes across from him brightened. "Really?"

"Really."

April smiled shyly, then leaned down and scratched Vinnie's ears.

Foster smiled too as he cleared the table. Just needed a little reassurance, this girl. She offered to wash the dishes, but he remembered the silverware drawer with a seven-year accumulation of crumbs in the corners. So he sent her out in the yard instead and wiped out the drawer as April raced around the shed, Vinnie barking at her heels.

Foster thought of all the evenings and weekends he had spent drinking with male friends in some deserted bar, all the holidays he had walked back to Russell's and listened to his uncles trade complaints. He laughed as he watched Vinnie skid to a stop when April changed direction, then go tearing off again, as fast as her lame leg would take her. It still did not seem possible to him that his life had changed so radically—that he had considered and courted and near-married the girl in the same amount of time it would take him to buy a truck. If Lloyd could see him now. . . .

That night, when Foster made love to April, reaching tentatively for her under the blanket, she came willingly as usual and wrapped her arms about his neck. When he had come, however, and was on the verge of telling April that he loved her, he saw—by the dim light from the window—that her eyes were wide open. It unnerved him. So he held her close and said nothing. But he knew now what it was to love a girl. He remembered something his brother had written to him from Vietnam: *Knew I'd miss Carol, but didn't know how much. Didn't know that lonesomeness could hurt, the way it sticks to you. . . .*

Foster had never thought of lonesomeness as pain, exactly—more like a dull, flat feeling that whatever you did didn't matter one way or another. He imagined himself separated from April, coming home at night to an empty bed. His arms tightened around her body.

On Tuesday, when Foster had fixed the dinner and washed the dishes, April said, "How 'bout you teachin' me to drive, Foster?"

"*Drive?*" Foster turned and looked at her, then laughed. "What the dickens for? You don't have nothing to drive. I got the truck all day."

"I know, but I just want to learn it."

"April honey, there's any place you want to go, you just say so. I'll drive you there myself."

April watched until Foster had dried the pans, then she put them away in the cupboard. "What am I supposed to do around here, Foster?" she asked finally.

Her question, like her eyes, always caught him off guard.

"What do you mean? You make the bed in the morning, don't you? Straighten up the place? Feed Vinnie?"

"Takes all of fifteen minutes," April declared. "All I got to do afternoons is sit and watch the soaps."

"You could go back to school."

"Foster, I'm not goin' back; I told you that. Don't keep at me." She plopped down on the other end of the couch.

Foster's stomach felt like a load of wet clothes at the bottom of the dryer. Four days together, and already she was restless. He'd known, when he took her in, that he would have to feed and clothe her, pay her bills, but not once had it occurred to him that he would have to keep her entertained. She was bored already. My God, he thought, we won't last a month.

When he spoke again, his voice was flat, disguising the turmoil in his head. "Well, what'd you do back home all day?"

April picked at a thread on her shirt. "At least there was somebody to talk to."

"You're pinin' for your family, you can always ask 'em over," Foster told her.

She turned. "I can have 'em here?"

"Of course you can, April! It's your house too."

It pleased her, he could tell. April crawled across the sofa and leaned against him, her hand on his knee. Foster felt passion mounting in his loins as he put one big hand down on top of hers, covering it completely. She tilted her head up toward him, and with her other hand ran a finger over his Adam's apple.

"You missed shavin' here," she said playfully. "You ever notice how the hair grows all crazy here, Foster? Goes around in a circle."

"Never noticed." He smiled and continued stroking her hand, his hardness extending down one leg of his trousers. At the same time, however, Foster knew that her boredom could not be remedied forever by inviting her family over. Nor could all problems between them be resolved by carrying her off to bed.

The next morning, as he left for work, Foster said, "How about you making supper tonight? There's pork chops in the freezer. And anything else you find to go with 'em."

She nodded.

Her restlessness bothered him all day, however, and on the way home that evening, he stopped at a Drug Fair and purchased a five-hundred-piece jigsaw puzzle of a mountain with a lake in the foreground.

When he reached the house, Earl Bates's Buick was parked in the drive, and Foster steeled himself as he got out of the pickup. Not already. The old man couldn't have found out. . . . As he entered the kitchen, however, he heard giggling. A low murmur from the other room, then the giggling again. Vinnie's toenails clicked on the bare boards and Foster turned as the dog trotted in. She was wearing a pair of April's blue panties and a bra.

Foster dropped his packages on the table. "April!"

The giggles erupted into laughter. Foster marched into the other room.

Thomasine was sitting on the couch, one arm thrown over the back, a cigarette between her fingers. Her mouth was stretched in a wide smile. April's smile was more cautious.

"Get them things off Vinnie."

April's smile ended abruptly and she immediately reached down and undid the knot in the bra.

"Jesus' sake, Foster, it's only a joke!" said Thomasine, crossing her legs high and showing her crotch when she did so.

Foster felt instantly aged by her rebuke, and forced a smile as Vinnie slipped out of the bra and ran around in circles, one foot still caught in the waistband of the panties.

"Dog don't like to be messed with," he said, taking off his jacket.

"Was *you* doing the minding, not Vinnie," said Thomasine, tilting her head and blowing a cloud of smoke toward the ceiling.

Foster struggled to stay cordial. "So how you doing, Thomasine? Like to stay for supper?"

She drew in another lungful of smoke before she answered and ran her hand through a thick mass of curly bleached hair showing dark at the roots. "Just come by to see how you were treatin' my little sister." She smiled sweetly at April Ruth. April went on patting Vinnie.

"Well, what'd you tell her?" Foster said to April, sitting down across from them. "Tell her how I beat ya every morning, got you scrubbing floors day and night?"

April smiled just a little but didn't look up and didn't answer.

"I got to get the car back to Daddy before he has a fit," said Thomasine, rising. Her short skirt rose with her and she tugged it down. She wore a nylon blouse with only a bra beneath, and every stitch in the seams of the brassiere was visible. "Come on by the diner once in a while, Foster," she said, throwing on her coat. "Jake's chicken's good as it ever was."

"We'll be by one of these nights," Foster promised. But when the door closed behind her, he turned to April in exasperation. "Why didn't you say something, April Ruth? Thomasine asks how I'm treatin' you and you just sit there with your mouth closed."

"*She* knows," April told him. "She already asked me before you came."

Foster waited some more. "Well, what'd you tell her?"

"You treat me good. What'd you *think* I'd tell her?"

Foster slid down in his chair, legs extended, and poked at April playfully with one foot. "Sure would be nice to hear you say it once in a while."

She edged away from his shoe. "Just said it," she told him, then scowled. "You sure don't have no sense of humor, Foster. You didn't have to get so mad about Vinnie. Thomasine and me was only looking for something to do."

"*You* lookin' for something to do is one thing," he told her. "You and Thomasine together looking is something else. You got dinner to make anyway. That's something to do."

"Old Sourpuss," said April, and went off to the kitchen.

Foster retired to the shower. He had just applied the shampoo when he heard banging from down the hall. Damn! he thought. April's gone out and locked the door behind her. He rinsed quickly, turned off the water, and wrapped a towel about him.

She was standing in the kitchen with a hammer, hitting away at a cellophane package on the counter.

"April, that meat's already dead. Don't have to kill it!"

"They won't come unstuck, Foster. How am I supposed to cook 'em?"

"My God, girl, you got to defrost chops ahead of time. Didn't you think of that?"

"You never told me."

"Well, I figured you had sense enough to know." Foster checked himself. "It's okay," he added. "We'll just keep 'em in the refrigerator overnight, and have 'em tomorrow. I'll make up some hash with that leftover ham."

"You shoulda told me," April said again.

"Well, you shouldn't wait till the last minute to find out."

He made the dinner himself, but afterward set April to work on the dishes. She turned on the radio above the sink and listened to her favorite station. Foster, meanwhile, opened the jigsaw puzzle and silently began sorting through the pieces, looking for those with straight edges, checking them against the picture on the front.

"What's that?" April stood curiously behind his left shoulder, drying the saucepan.

"Oh, just picked me up a puzzle. Like to see if I can get it together. Lloyd and me used to do puzzles sometimes—get a big old puzzle going, could work on it for a week." Foster whistled to himself.

April's hand shot out in front of him and produced a piece with two straight sides. "Here's a corner, Foster. Look. It's all dark here with a little blue speck right on the end. Bet it goes in that corner there."

"Probably right," Foster told her, and went on whistling.

April put the dishes away, then came back to rest one knee on the chair next to him, watching. Every so often she would reach around to find another piece. By bedtime they had the border and part of the sky.

"Foster," she said, when they'd finished their lovemaking, "how many girlfriends you have before me?"

The question stopped him cold. "Well, now . . ." he said.

"I only had one boyfriend," April went on, "and he was Buddy Travis, but I only went out with him three times."

"You don't have to tell me about it if you don't want to," said Foster.

"Nothing to tell," April retorted, and waited.

"Well, I've had some women, I won't lie to you, April," Foster said, stroking the side of her breast, then circling his big hand around one shoulder and running it down her back.

"Anybody I know?"

"Mostly women I met at Ocean City—went down there sometimes with Jed and Wallace Harley."

"They the only friends you got?"

"Only friends I got who aren't married—them and Jack Tulley."

"Any more? Women, I mean?"

"Went out with Ramona Wheeler once . . ." Foster's voice trailed off.

"And after her, who'd you go with?" April questioned.

Foster was quiet a moment. "Guess I didn't go out with anyone after her," he said, and his hand circled once more, gently caressing her buttocks. "Then I met you," he told her.

The next evening they worked on the puzzle again, even though Foster would have preferred a basketball game on TV. He counted up the days they had been together, the years that were yet to come, and had a vision of babysitting April for the rest of his natural life. There was a moment of uneasiness—panic, even— and then he told himself he'd think of something.

Get her in the family way, she'll stay, Clyde had told him, but Foster dismissed it as soon as it came to mind. He wanted April to stay of her own accord, not because she was tied here.

He had made the dinner again himself. April had insisted she could do it, then stood at the stove frying every last bit of moisture from the pork chops she had beaten to death the day before. When Foster realized that she was planning to cook them, then set them aside while she tackled the potatoes, he took over the kitchen once more.

"How'd you come to learn cookin'?" she asked him.

"Watched Mother do it."

"Then I'll watch you," April said.

Foster laughed. "You just have the table set when I get home nights, clear the dishes up afterwards, and that'll be fine," he told her.

On the way home from work Friday, Foster filled the gas tank for their trip the next day to Denton, but when he reached the house, April announced that she was spending Saturday with Dorothy. Foster turned and faced her there in the hallway.

"You forget, April? We're going to Denton."

She had not forgotten. Her forehead scrunched up and she pressed her lips together. "I don't think I'm ready for that yet, Foster."

A chill swept over his body. "Why not?"

"I don't know. Don't push me."

Foster's lips seemed frozen to his teeth. "Something wrong?"

"Didn't say that. I just got to see if I'm going to take to this."
The cold in Foster's body crept into his voice as well. "Seems to me you should have thought of that before."

"Wasn't time to think about it. Only had a week."

Foster moved into the kitchen, sat slowly down in a chair, then got up and went back in the hallway again where April was leaning against the wall, tracing a crack in the plaster with one finger, her ankles crossed.

"Now look here, April. You and me made an agreement we were going to Denton. You just tell Dorothy you can visit her some other day."

"I'm not going to Denton, Foster, and you can't make me."

"Well, then, maybe you should just get yourself back home to your daddy."

She looked at him, surprised, and studied him for a moment. Then, disentangling her feet, she started down the hall. "All right," she said.

Foster grabbed her arm, but she broke free. He followed her into the bedroom.

"This what you want? You want to leave me?"

"No."

"Well, why you acting this way?"

"Foster, I wasn't never married before. I got to have time to get used to it." She plopped down on the bed.

Anger and exasperation took over once again. "Thomasine put you up to this? Tell you to back off this way?"

"Thomasine thinks we're married. Didn't tell her nothing."

"Jesus Christ." Foster leaned against the door, arms folded over his chest. He stared at her hard. "You do this a lot? Make up your mind to do one thing and go off and do another?"

"You don't want me to stay, Foster, just say so."

"Goddamit, I'm asking you a question, April! You do this a lot?"

"I never lived with a man before, I told you! How do I know what I'm going to do?" she shot back.

Foster let out his breath, turned away, then looked at her again in disbelief.

"I swear to God I don't know what to do with you."

"Want me to go?"

"*No*, damn it! Of *course* I don't!"

"Then I'll stay," she said, and went back out to the kitchen.

He worked outside Saturday morning, raking the last of winter's leaves toward the brush heap, then set about transferring the pile of used lumber to the back of the shed. Make things look nicer. Come summer, he and April would have something to look at from the porch besides a stack of old boards that should have been carted away years ago.

He had just hauled some concrete blocks behind the shed and was going back for the lumber when he saw Russell coming across the yard in his one good suit.

"Mornin'," said Foster. He went on over to the lumber pile, picked up the longest plank, and carried it back, dropping it across the cement blocks.

Russell, standing off to one side, took a small step forward as though an invisible line had been drawn in the dirt and he had just crossed it. "Foster," he said, "you're an even bigger fool than I thought."

Foster stood up slowly, edged the plank in place with his foot, and started back for another. "Never figured you thought any different," he said. He dragged the second piece over.

It was the first time either Foster or Russell had said these words aloud, but now that they were out, Foster knew the truth of them. It was Lloyd who had charmed his uncles and dazzled his friends, not Foster. Lloyd had dreams of making it big in real estate, and there was grandiose talk of buying the property west of the house for a cattle farm—Lloyd and his father and Shum and Russell all going into it together. When Lloyd graduated from high school, however, and the dream was up against the reality of ready cash, he joined the Marines, and by 1963 was a helicopter mechanic in Vietnam.

I know Carol's sore that I put off the wedding, he wrote a month later to Foster, *but I couldn't see working at the Amoco or something. When I'm feeling good, I figure I'll learn mechanics and come home to start my own shop—have us that cattle farm on the side. When I'm not, I think how I got my helicopters and you've got your bridges, and maybe that's as high as either of us will go . . .*

People talked about the sacrifice that Lloyd was making. Every time the comment was made aloud, and it was made often, it carried with it the unspoken accusation that it should have been Foster who went and Lloyd who stayed—Lloyd with his wit and charm and a girl with his ring on her finger.

Russell took still another step, close enough now for Foster to see the Chesapeake crab and Maryland flag pins planted firmly on his lapel. "I was down at the bank this morning," he continued, "and I heard the full story of why you married April Bates. How Mrs. Dawson could hoodwink you into believing April was headed for the juvenile home is beyond my understanding. That Decency Committee of hers can't do nothing but make noise."

"Wouldn't say that," Foster said. "Made enough noise four years ago to get the slot machines out of Charles County."

"Wasn't just them doing the complaining, that's why," Russell declared. "Slots are one thing, but a young girl's another. Why, Foster, Thomasine and Dorothy could set themselves up in neon lights, and that still wouldn't be reason enough for anyone to take Earl Bates's youngest away from him. You got yourself stuck with a girl don't have no idea what marriage is about, and Earl is mad as a hornet that he let her go."

Foster heard the words but they did not seem to register. He stared at his uncle blankly, and Russell went on:

"He says Mrs. Dawson got him to sign that paper when he was drinking, and nothing in this world would have made him sign away that girl. He says the first hint you give of mistreating her, he's going after you with a lawyer."

With that, Russell turned and strode back to the house where Shum stood listening, and both uncles marched inside and shut the door.

Foster moved behind the shed and lowered himself down on the lumber. The syllables aligned themselves into words and the words into sentences. He had known long before his uncle opened his mouth, even before the drive to Denton. While the thought was still nebulous in his head, however, he had blown it away, like smoke: Mrs. Dawson had not used Foster, Foster had used her. It was easier to pretend that he was saving April Ruth from the juvenile home, it seemed, than it was to admit that he had loved that girl since she was nine—that her isolation there in the trailer had reached out and caught hold of the loneliness in himself. Caught hold and held on.

FIVE

Only been at Foster's for a week, but it sure felt good heading down that driveway with Dorothy. Passed his uncles on the way, coming from the mailbox. Russell, he keeps walking, pretends he don't even see us at all, but Shum stops, his jaw dropping, head turning right along with the car.

"Hey, mister, put your teeth back in your mouth," Dorothy yells out the window, and when we reach the road, we laugh. "Sure hope Foster doesn't turn out like them when he gets old," she says.

Dorothy don't bleach her hair like Thomasine, lets it hang long and black around her shoulders. She's shorter, too, and you know she's got hips, but her eyes are big and blue and she always smells like cinnamon or something.

"Mrs. Foster Williams," she says, rolling the window up again. Then she gives me the kind of look that means she's going to ask something personal. "So what's he like, April?" I knew she didn't mean how good a talker he was.

"Like most men, I guess," I told her, studying the road ahead.

She watches me a moment, then sighs. "Well, sometimes it's better than others," she says, and shuts up.

Wouldn't know it by what she said to Shum, but Dorothy's more polite than Thomasine. Daddy always said Thomasine got the manners of a moose. When she was by to see me, first thing she said was, "So how was Foster, April? He get it working?"

"Shut up, Thomasine," I told her. "You got a mouth like a slop jar."

Thomasine just laughed. "If you can't talk about it to me, honey, you can't talk about it to anyone."

"There's not a thing wrong with Foster, that's what you're thinking," I told her.

"Well, I sure am glad to hear that," she said. "He hurt you?"

I really didn't want to tell her anything, 'cause Thomasine's the kind that'll hold on to something you tell her and give it back when you least expect it.

"Hurt some," I said, and pressed my lips together tight to show I wasn't going to say any more.

She laughs again. "Should have done like I told you, had a romp with Buddy Travis first. He's only half as big as Foster."

"Thomasine, I'm gonna hit you, you don't shut your mouth," I told her. "You don't know a thing about Foster!"

"Relax," says Thomasine. "I'm talkin' about body size. Don't have yourself a fit." Then she went on smiling like now that I was a woman we'd have us all kinds of things to talk about, but I never give her the satisfaction.

Now Dorothy's little white car flies over the hills like there was wings for doors. She's wearing jeans and a jacket and high-heeled alligator shoes.

"Foster sure does live back in the sticks," she says as we cross the railroad tracks down by Old Woman's Run. DRESS-MAKING; LAMPSHADES, says a sign in somebody's yard. LAUREL RACE COURSE, says a bumper sticker on a car beside the house. You never see no people back here—just signs saying what they do and where they been.

I watched the trees whoosh by on either side of us, big old sycamores looking naked, deciding how much to tell Dorothy if she asked any more. I was thinking about that morning Foster and me had sex for the first time. Didn't think we were going to try it because of what he said the night before, and it just didn't seem right. Here I'd borrowed Thomasine's chiffon nightie and Dorothy's kimono, and then Foster's telling me he's not going to do nothing. I'm worried to death he couldn't. Guess he couldn't keep hisself away, though, because next morning there he was, wanting me. Made me feel good to think I could get him to do something Ramona Wheeler couldn't.

"Foster," I told him, "my teeth's not brushed." But he didn't even care.

He says, "April, I think this is going to hurt you some, but I'll go gentle."

He was right about that. First I wanted him 'cause I wanted to see what it was like, then there I was, pushing at him, trying to get him off. Nobody ever sings about that on the radio. Afterwards he tells me it wouldn't hurt so much the next time, and he was right about that, too.

Dorothy been chattering away for the last five minutes. She'd promised to take me out, buy me some shoes as a wedding present, but now she's talking how she got five pairs back home she never even wore, so she don't see no reason to buy me any.

"I got bigger feet," I told her. "That's one reason."

But Dorothy's got her mind on something, there's no stopping her. Twenty minutes later we pull up outside her apartment; it's two rooms over a pet store, and belongs to the man she's been living with since Christmas. You go through this door at the side and up the stairs, and there's a living room with a stove and sink at one end and a bedroom. Looks real nice. Dorothy's got plants hanging down from the ceiling, and a fake tigerskin spread on the bed. Only thing I don't like is when the heat comes on you can smell the parakeets from below.

"Sit down and look what Max gave me," Dorothy says. She opens the closet and takes out this long gravy-colored dress with only one sleeve in it so's the other shoulder will show. There's a slit up one side you could run a bicycle through. Dorothy shows me the gold bracelet Max gave her to wear high up on the arm. She kisses it before she puts it back in the box. "He calls me his Egyptian princess," she says.

"You serious about Max?" I ask her.

"We're crazy about each other," she says. She kneels down on the floor, rump in the air, and drags this big flat box out from under the bed. It's got about fifty million shoes in it, all of 'em with heels so high you'd fracture yourself you ever turn an ankle.

"Dorothy," I tell her, "you couldn't wear out all these shoes if you had four legs."

"Here," she says, shoving a silver pair at me with butterflies for buckles. I try, but my heel won't even go down inside.

We sat there trying to squeeze on yellow patent leather wedgies and transparent shoes look like cellophane, but my toes scrunch up so tight I can't walk.

"Okay," Dorothy says at last. "We'll go shopping."

The thing about going around with Dorothy is that she knows just about everybody, and every twenty feet or so, we have to stop. Man sweeping the sidewalk outside the dry cleaners gives her a big hug. So does the man at the drugstore. Outside the bowling alley, the Coca-Cola man makes a grab for Dorothy and she laughs and grabs back. Dorothy's embarrassing to be around sometimes, but not as bad as Thomasine.

We were heading for the Shoe Barn at the end of the block, when suddenly here comes this woman out of the A & P, grocery receipt in one hand, keys in the other. I recognized her hat first, then the rest of her, and there we were, walking right into Mrs. Dawson. Her eyes went from me to Dorothy to me again, and from then on she pretended Dorothy wasn't there.

"Why, April! How nice to see you!" she says. "I suppose you're out shopping for your new home."

Dorothy clacks to a stop in her sling-back alligator pumps and waits with her hand on one hip, chewing a piece of Juicy Fruit.

"Not exactly," I say. "Dorothy here's buyin' me a pair of shoes."

"That little house is as cute as it can be," Mrs. Dawson goes on. "Just needing a little wife to fix it up."

You ever have the feeling you could be saying anything at all, wouldn't make a bit of difference what?

Mrs. Dawson's words are coming out sugar-sweet, but all the while she's jabbing holes in her grocery receipt with the car key. Every few words, another jab.

"I'm spending the day with Dorothy," I say again in case she missed it the first time.

"A nice house and a good husband and a fine reputation you'll want to keep," Mrs. Dawson says.

"Piss off," says Dorothy.

Mrs. Dawson's face turns the color of cherry Kool-Aid and she gives me the kind of smile goes straight out at the corners but don't turn up. She marches right out into the parking lot, not looking either way, could have got herself killed.

Dorothy jerks my arm like I'm slow-minded. "How did you let her talk you into marrying Foster Williams? She sure must have scared you something awful."

"You'd be scared too if you thought you were going to be sent away," I said. "She wouldn't have come over in the first place if you and Thomasine hadn't got her attention."

Dorothy glared after Mrs. Dawson. "If she doesn't quit holding herself so stiff some dog's going to figure she's a fire hydrant. Every time I think of you married at sixteen and all the fun you could be having instead, it makes my skin itch."

I yanked my arm away. "Well, maybe I just happen to like Foster Williams. You ever think of that?"

"Yeah, you settle for tea, too, till you've had coffee," says Dorothy.

I'm beginning to feel mad at her, the way she's trying to make it sound like her life's so much better than mine. I walk out of the Shoe Barn a half hour later holding a pair of red suede shoes with little straps around the ankles and four-inch heels. Wasn't what I would have picked if I was by myself, but I was too angry at Dorothy to say much. By the time we're back in her car and riding around, though, I'd cooled down some. Always did like to be out riding. Like to feel the road moving out from under me, *going* somewhere, always a surprise around the next corner.

We had lunch at McDonald's and rode around some more, and I could see that Dorothy was running out of ideas. Middle of the afternoon we went by the trailer to see Daddy. Dorothy promised him she'd bring me by, but first we stop at the diner.

"April, honey!" says Marie, and come around the counter to

give me a big hug. "Just this morning I said to Jake, 'Wonder how April's doing?' and here you are."

The cook grins at me. "Where's the mister? Don't tell me the honeymoon's over—you out runnin' around with the girls."

It's strange, because I liked the folks at the diner, but all at once I began to feel small again, like the time Mrs. Dawson had me cornered behind the chair, talking 'bout the juvenile home. Everybody seemed to have some idea of what I was supposed to be like as a married woman—where I was supposed to be going, what I was supposed to do—everybody but me.

"Foster and me will be by some night for supper," I promised, and was glad when Dorothy said we had to go.

When we got to the trailer, though, Daddy was asleep and Thomasine's in the shower. The TV's going full blast, nobody watching.

"Shit," says Dorothy, and sinks down on the sofa to light a cigarette.

The way she kept looking at her watch, I could tell I was getting to be a burden.

"It's okay," I said. "I can visit Daddy another time. You can drive me back home if you want."

"Max is meeting us for dinner at the City Chicken," she says. "Might as well wait here as go riding around using up gas."

She went out in the kitchen and came back with some cheese and Ritz crackers. From the open door of the bedroom, we could see Daddy flat on his back, snoring to beat the band. In a little while the shower cuts off and Thomasine starts singing. Only thing worse than Thomasine's jokes is her voice. Sings so bad almost makes your eyes water. She opens the bathroom door and steps out with a towel around her head and nothing below.

"Great Jesus!" says Thomasine when she sees us. "Foster here too?"

"No," I told her. "We just come to see Daddy."

"Take a good look, then," says Thomasine, and flounces on by toward the closet, her breasts jiggling. Grabs a robe and puts it on. "Puked all over one side of his bed last night, and I'm not cleanin' it up. Can sleep in it a month for all I care."

I can tell both Dorothy and Thomasine's in bad moods. Seems

about the way it was when we were all living together. Living together but separate—everybody looking out for herself. Thomasine goes on down the hall to Daddy's room and bellows, *"April's here!"* Daddy's arms flail about, looking for something to grab, but Thomasine don't wait, just comes back to the living room, bends over, and proceeds to shake her hair from side to side.

It suddenly occurred to me that I didn't live there no more. The drawer where I used to keep my stuff had one of Thomasine's stockings hanging out of it. The closet where I'd hung my things, Thomasine's dresses went all the way across. Leaving the trailer and going to live at Foster's was like getting out of a bathtub. Water closed in where you'd sat and it was like you hadn't been there at all.

"You'll never believe who come by yesterday," Thomasine says to Dorothy. "Your old police boyfriend." She plops down on the couch beside Dorothy. "Come to give me a warning. Says he got a complaint from one of the truckers."

Dorothy laughs, her skinny penciled-in eyebrows shooting up on her forehead. "The *truckers?* What's the matter, Thomasine? Don't you treat 'em right?"

Thomasine hit at her, laughing. "Some old man complained when I knocked on his window, woke him up. Police sent your old boyfriend over to give me the warning. And all the while he's talking, you know where he's got his hands."

"Not his pocket, that's for sure," Dorothy says, and laughs some more.

"Thomasine," I say, "you know the only reason Marie hired you is because of it being Daddy's land. Seems like you'd have the sense to stay out of trouble in her parking lot."

There was the sound of bedsprings squeaking and then Daddy comes down the hall. Looks right at me and don't say nothing about me being there 'cause he'd already forgot I was gone. He goes in the bathroom and pees with the door open, then comes out, zipping his pants.

"Look who's come to see you," Thomasine says.

Daddy looks at me hard, then shuffles on to the bedroom again, pulls on a T-shirt, and comes back.

"You run out on him, huh?"

"Course I didn't! Dorothy said you wanted to see me, so we come by."

Daddy hawks the phlegm from his throat, goes into the bathroom to spit, then sits down at the table.

"Listen to me, April. I got taxes comin' up next month, 'bout to wipe me out. Got to have a new refrigerator—this one sours the milk. Buick needs a new clutch and Thomasine's wanting a car of her own."

"What's that got to do with me?" I asked him. "Don't have me to feed anymore, do you?"

It was another case of saying words and nobody listening.

"Saw a lawyer day before yesterday," Daddy says. "Told him how Foster Williams took my baby away. He says all you have to do is come home, say you didn't want to marry him in the first place, but he talked you into it. We got a good case for him corrupting the morals of a minor, and could get us something off'n him."

"That's pure crazy talk," I said. "Foster's been good to me. Why would I want to do that?"

Daddy turned on me then. "Foster raise you the last sixteen years? Foster pay your bills? You got any obligation, April Ruth, it's to me."

Then Thomasine jumps in with both feet, like she and Daddy been talking this out already. "Any thirty-two-year-old man marries up with a sixteen-year-old girl with no experience of life whatsoever has got to have his reasons," she says. "He ask you to do any kinky kind of stuff, April?"

"Don't know what you're talkin' about," I said.

"Anything straaange," says Thomasine, drawing out the word.

"I haven't got no complaints at all against Foster, and you sue him, Daddy, I won't show up to say nothing against him."

Daddy belches and scratches at one knee. "Don't know how in the world I'm goin' to buy Thomasine a car and pay taxes too."

"Thomasine's got on this long without one she can wait some more," I said. "You're not takin' it out of Foster's pocket." Now I had 'em both mad at me.

Dorothy, though, she's about as bored as I am, so after a few more rounds with Daddy, we go on out to the car.

"Don't worry about him," she says. "He'd never keep himself sober long enough to go to court. Sell us all down the river if he had a chance." Now that it's close to the time we're meeting Max, Dorothy's feeling better. Always got to have a man around her, giving her things, talking how pretty she is. It's like if she don't hear it from someone else, she might not believe it herself.

We get to the restaurant about five-thirty, and Dorothy swings into the parking lot, sending the gravel flying up under the fender of the car. THE CITY CHICKEN, WHERE COUNTRY MUSIC'S KING, says a neon sign in pink and purple.

"Max'll be here about six," she tells me. "We can have something to drink while we're waiting."

There's a bar just inside the door with this big chicken on the wall behind it—feathers made out of plaster that turns up at the ends, and over the years everything folks has left behind is stuck up on that chicken for them to recognize next time they come by—gloves, keys, eyeglasses. . . . The restaurant was in the next room, and on Friday and Saturday nights, the tables was all pushed to one side for dancing. Dorothy and me took a booth by the window to watch for Max. I was drinking Coca-Cola and Dorothy had herself an old-fashioned. I'd just got the soda up to my nose, fizz in my nostrils, when I saw this bunch of boys from school come in, heading for the pinball machines near the back. They was halfway to our table when I noticed that one was Buddy Travis.

Buddy's got a nice face, even though there's acne scars on both cheeks. He sees me the same time I'm looking at him, and he grins.

"Look who's here," says Buddy, stopping by our booth. "Is it true, April, you an old married woman? Haven't seen you in school the last month."

"Yeah," I said, lifting up my straw and watching the Coke run out the bottom. "I'm living out at Foster Williams's now."

Buddy shook his head. "Whew. Can't handle it. April Ruth

Bates married." Then he grins some more. "How you like married life?"

"Like it fine."

"Your old man good to you?"

"He treats me fine," I said again.

Buddy studies me. "You remember the time we went to the carnival? You still got that pink monkey I won for you?"

I could feel my face starting to color. " 'Spect it's around somewhere."

"Heck," he says, sticking his hands in his pockets. "I thought you were savin' yourself for me."

I stared up at him. Didn't know if he was serious or not. He never said one little word about marrying to me. Then I could see he wasn't talking about marrying at all. He and Dorothy started laughing.

"See you around," he says, and goes back to join the others.

"That's what you could have married you didn't let them old ladies scare the pants off you," Dorothy says, getting up. "Come on. Let's dance."

Dorothy always did like to dance—always pestering Thomasine and me to try out some new step. Wanted to be a dancer up at Atlantic City, but it never worked out. I wasn't comfortable out there on the floor with Dorothy, even though there wasn't hardly any other people around. She wanted me to lead, so I moved her about the floor while she sung along with the music:

> *Oh, wh . . . ah do I miss you . . .*
> *You treat me . . . so low . . .*

Her eyes was half-closed and her breath sweet, like a cow in clover. Dorothy's got skin like a china plate, I can't keep my eyes off it. Even when she gets her periods her chin don't break out the way mine does.

> *Oh, wh . . . ah do I love you . . .*
> *I'd just like . . . to know.*

Over her shoulder I see this man come in, about twenty-five, maybe. Tall. So tall he has to bend down some to get through the doorway. He's got a jacket on with some kind of writing over the pocket. He comes down the aisle slow and when he reaches our table he just stands there, leaning against it, watching Dorothy and me. HOTPOINT, it says over his pocket. I turn Dorothy around so she can see him and immediately her arms go limp.

"Max, baby," she says, and then she's all over Max like some kind of sheepdog, licking the side of his face.

"This the married sister?" Max says to Dorothy, holding her off.

"Yeah," says Dorothy, like she just remembered, and turns around. "April, this is Max."

"Hi," I say, sitting down and picking up my Coke again.

Max slides in across from me and his knees scrape against mine. I pull my legs back as far as I can. His knees go away.

"You just get here?" Max says to Dorothy.

" 'Bout twenty minutes ago, love."

"What'cha been doing?" Max is studying the boys back by the pinball machines.

"Dancing with April. Haven't we, April?"

I nod.

If Max ever smiled, I hadn't seen it yet. I try to imagine going to bed with a man who never smiled. I look at the clock at the back of the room. Ten of six. I wonder what Foster's making hisself for supper.

When the waitress come by again, Max orders a beer, then turns his attention to me.

"How long you been married?"

"Week," I tell him.

"One of the bridgemen, huh?"

I nod again.

Buddy Travis come walking by and Dorothy puts out her hand and stops him. "We're about to order some dinner," she says. "Sit down and eat with us."

"I'll have a Pepsi, that's all," says Buddy. He looks at Max, who don't look too happy, and slides in beside me.

"Max, honey, this is Buddy Travis, used to go with April."

Buddy grins. "Went out all of about three times," he says. "Never got to first base."

Max merely tips his glass. Don't even smile at Buddy.

The supper platter at the City Chicken's pretty good, so that's what we had while Buddy drinks his soda.

"This is April's wedding present from me," says Dorothy. "A day on the town." She just can't resist telling everybody. "Bought her a new pair of shoes, too."

"To the bride and groom," says Buddy, lifting his Pepsi like a toast or something.

He and Max start talking—Max wants to know what he drives— and Dorothy's eyes sort of glaze over. She's running one finger up and down the sleeve of Max's jacket, just waiting it out. I'm looking at the clock back on the wall. Six forty-five. Suddenly there wasn't any place in all the world I wanted to be but home with Foster and Vinnie.

I try to catch Dorothy's eye. Every time she looks in my direction I frown and nod toward the clock. She pretends she don't see me. Finally, though, she says, "April, what's wrong with you? You got a tic or something?"

"I just thought maybe I ought to get home," I say. "I never told Foster when I was coming back."

"Then why worry? You sure know how to ruin a nice wedding present."

"Let's dance," Buddy says to me.

I just didn't know how I felt about that.

"Go on, April," says Dorothy. "He's not gonna bite you."

I get up and move out on the floor. Singer's moaning about "just one more kiss, just one more night together. . . ."

I start to put my hand on Buddy's back, then remember I'm not leading. Buddy laughs. "What's the matter? You forget how to dance?" He's holding me a little too close for comfort. We start moving around the floor. "They'll have a live band in here later," Buddy says. "Why don't you stick around?"

"Got to get home," I say.

Buddy just laughs. "After couple of months, it'll be Foster thinking up ways to slip off. Should have you a good time while you can." All the while he talks his hand is sort of caressing my backbone. Hand's not nearly as big as Foster's. Feels puny against my shoulder blades. He pulls me even closer, though, and dances his cheek against mine. My skin's burning up. All kinds of strange feelings down there where Buddy's pressed hisself against me. When the song's over, I wrench Buddy's fingers from around my waist and march back to the table.

"Dorothy," I say, "it's time for me to get home."

"I'll drive her," offers Buddy.

I didn't even look at him. "Dorothy!" I says again.

She's kissing Max's ear, got her hand I don't know where under the table. "So let Buddy drive you," she says, and her tongue flicks in and out.

"I'm not goin' home with Buddy," I say, and my voice is low and firm as I can make it.

"I'll take her," says Max, and starts to get up.

I wasn't going home with Max, neither.

"Dorothy!" I says, like I'm about to make a scene. "You brought me here and you're takin' me home."

Suddenly she turns on me. Dorothy get a couple drinks in her, she turns mean. She grabs her purse and stands up, wobbling on her alligator shoes. "Put on your damn coat and let's go, then," she says, and heads for the door. "I'll be back," she says to Max, and pushes me on ahead of her.

We roar out of the parking lot like the devil's after us, and Dorothy hardly speaks to me all the way home.

I lean back and try to get my own self straightened out. Have to admit I'd felt like a woman out there on the dance floor with Buddy, the way we were moving together. Wonder how much of a woman I've been to Foster so far. Then I think of Dorothy and her alligator shoes and the way she danced, eyes half-closed, breath all sweetness. I decide that the minute I walk in the house, I'm going to fix my eyes on Foster the way Dorothy did on Max, and I'm going to say, "Foster, take me to bed." Just like that. Very soft.

I can feel my face color even thinking about saying those words out loud. I practice them in my head. *Foster, let's go to bed.* No. *Foster, will you take me to bed?* No, I had it right the first time. Have to sound like I'm in pain, almost. *Foster, take me to bed.*

The car's going up and down the hills on Foster's road like a crazy person driving. If there was any little animals in the way, we hit 'em for sure. Ten minutes later we tear up Foster's driveway, barely missing the lilac bush there by the mailbox. Dorothy squeals to a stop by the house, motor still racing.

I get out. "Thanks for the shoes and the lunch and everything," I say.

Dorothy just grunts. "Knowing you, you won't have any place at all to wear 'em," she says. The car takes off again and skids when it comes to the road.

I start across the yard. The kitchen's dark, but there's a light in the living room. I can hear Vinnie yipping up a storm of welcome. Putting one foot before the other, I open the kitchen door. *Foster, take me to bed.* . . .

Vinnie almost knocks me down she's leaping up and licking at me, but I don't even pet her, don't want to break the mood. I set my new shoes on the kitchen table and head for the other room.

Foster's sitting in his chair watching the TV. I stand there waiting to say my line. Soon's he looks up, I'll say it.

"April," he says, not even moving his eyes in my direction, "I'd have thought if you were going to be this late you'd have called." His voice don't have no curves to it at all—flat as a stick of wood. "Kept your supper long as I could, then stuck it in the refrigerator. It's there, you want it."

My voice came out all small and scratchy, not at all like Dorothy's voice when she was singing there on the dance floor: "I told you I was spendin' the day with Dorothy. . . ."

"Well, maybe we got different ideas about day and evening," Foster says, "but when folks go home to supper, that's my idea of evening."

He still won't look at me. Won't even say if he'd worried about me. I could've been raped back there in the parking lot by Buddy Travis. Dorothy could've had a wreck out there and me with a broken leg, but he never asks me that—never asks if anything went wrong.

I try to catch hold of how I felt coming home, how it was out there on the dance floor with Buddy, but I can't get it back. Not even the words will come.

I go on into the bathroom and take a shower. Wash my hair with balsam shampoo and pat myself all over with the dusting powder Marie gave me. Then I lay down on the bed in Dorothy's kimono and wait for Foster. It's only eight-thirty. I sniff at the skin on my arm and it's all fragrant-smelling, and I begin to feel just a little like I did with Buddy, but I'm angry some at Foster for not looking at me. I roll over once to make sure the springs squeak so Foster'll know I'm in bed, not going to come out to him, and wait some more. But Foster's watching a movie and it goes on and on, and finally I crawl under the sheet and go to sleep.

He come to bed about midnight. The dusting powder gets to him, I guess, 'cause he reaches over and puts his hand on me. I let him do it, but neither of us says nothing, and it's not one bit like I wanted it to be coming home.

SIX

Mrs. Dawson and Sister Perry come by one day and give me this book of recipes by the Women of the Mount Olive Baptist Church. I was learning to make things out of Cool Whip. Foster would always fry the meat when he come home, do the potatoes, but I'd have us a dessert of some kind. We'd eat at it till we got tired, then give the rest to Vinnie. First week of May I made a white cake from a mix, punched little holes all over the top, poured hot strawberry Jell-O in the holes, and covered it all with Cool Whip. Lasted from Monday to Friday and I don't think Foster liked it much, but he ate it all down.

On Saturday, Foster goes out to the pickup, won't say where he's going, and an hour later Vinnie's barking and running around in circles like a chicken with its neck wrung. I hear this noise like an engine, go outdoors, and here come Foster on a tractor. I figure he's lost his head—traded in the pickup for a old green tractor tearing up the driveway. Vinnie's acting so crazy she's almost sick.

I just stand on the steps and stare as Foster pulls up to the house grinning, engine roaring.

"Take off your shoes, April!" he yells.

"What?" I shout back.

"Get your shoes off. We're going to have a garden."

Didn't make one bit of sense to me. I walk over to the tractor and look Foster square in the face. "You crazy or what? Why'd you trade the truck for somethin' like this?"

He laughs. "Just renting Jed Harley's tractor to plow up the land; we'll have us a garden right where Mother used to grow one. If you want to feel something nice, walk barefoot behind the tractor. I used to do that myself, me and Lloyd."

I can see Russell and Shum standing out on the porch up at the other house, eyes popping out of their heads. Foster's grinning at me and I grin back. I take off my shoes and follow Foster over to the big patch of land between his house and Russell's. It's all sunlight and covered with weeds. Foster lowers the plow at the back of the tractor and it digs down in the ground, turning over a wide heap of purplish dirt. The heap grows longer and longer as the tractor moves on. Vinnie won't go in the dirt, just runs alongside on the grass, barking, but I put out my foot and step in.

Never felt anything so soft in my life—warm at the top and coolish and damp at the bottom where the clay's still packed. Next thing I know I'm running along behind Foster, each foot sinking down, squishing up earth between my toes, best thing in the world next to bubble bath. Every time I see a worm I scream my head off, and Foster laughs, and I expect, looking back on it, I'd have to say that it was one of the happiest days I ever knew. There was dirt under every single one of my toenails but I didn't care.

May was just the nicest month! Every couple evenings, Foster and me would get in the pickup and go buy something else for the garden. There was plants already started and all kinds of special soil packed in bags. Never in my life knew you could walk in a store and buy dirt.

"You got to help me plan this now, April Ruth," Foster says. "What you like to eat?"

We come home with sweet corn, peppers, tomatoes, and just about every other vegetable I could pronounce.

I'd get up with Foster every morning, and by the time he was off to work, I was outside in my garden, looking for weeds. Dig 'em up with a teaspoon. The day the first shoots come up, I was down at the mailbox when Foster drove up, yelling to him before he even turned in the drive.

When Foster told me how I had to thin the plants—pull some of 'em up right out of the ground to give the others room—I didn't think I could stand it. Waited till he went to work one day, then went out and carefully dug 'em up, laid 'em in a box, and planted 'em somewhere else. Went all around the yard, and everywhere there was a bare spot, I dug a hole with my spoon and stuck one of the plants inside. Seemed to me that anything make the effort to work itself up through two inches of dirt ought to have a chance to live. I was going to wait till they got bigger, then tell Foster where they were. Next morning, though, all the seedlings I'd replanted was lying on their sides like limp spaghetti. Poured water on 'em, but all they did was drown.

Weekends, Foster would teach me how to take the hoe and break up the clods so's rain could get through. Vinnie would lie off on the grass, panting, enjoying the feel of sun on her lame leg, and the bees would be buzzing around the big red azalea bush over by the shed. I think the closest I come to loving Foster Williams that summer was Saturdays, when we'd work the garden.

Ever' so often, though, Foster say to me, "Well, April, you ready to go get married yet?" Once I almost said yes, but I just wasn't strong enough yet. Strong inside myself, I mean. Figure once we're married, Foster's stuck with me no matter what, and one of the worst things in all the world is somebody stuck to you like flypaper. So far it was just Foster doing things for me, trying to make me happy. Every time *I* try, just make more work for Foster. After I get a sense of myself, I tell him—of what I can do—then maybe I'm ready to marry. He don't like it, but he don't keep at me.

Worst days were when it rained. I wanted to go weeding in my boots, but Foster said you can't work a garden when it's wet, so all I could do was sit at the window and watch the puddles gathering round the sweet corn. Even when the sun come out, you couldn't work the ground till it was dry. So one time when it rained, Foster and me set about cleaning the spare room.

"You don't want to go in there," Foster been saying ever since

he brought me home. "Biggest mess you ever saw." He sure had
that right. Newspapers, magazines, and boxes almost to the ceiling. Broken lamps and window shades. Foster sets to work tying
the papers into bundles and packing up his mother's clothes for
the Salvation Army. Everywhere I tried to help, though, I got
sidetracked. Liked to hold up his mother's dresses, see how big
she was. Could have fit in them twice, myself. Three times, maybe.
Found a box of tablecloths, too, napkins pressed flat with an iron,
folded so the tips come perfectly together. Take all day to iron
me napkins like that, I'm thinking. Everywhere I look, there's
something I can't do.

Over on the stepladder there was a box full of pictures. Foster
told me who they all were. There was his dad standing out on
the porch in his Sunday suit, his ma holding Lloyd when he was
two, Foster and Lloyd sitting in a wagon pulled by Shum, who
looked like he had lots more brains than he does now. Picture
of Lloyd in his uniform, too. I started to open another box, could
see there was a flag in it, but Foster says, "Put that back, April.
Don't mess with that one."

"Just a flag, Foster," I said.

"Just put it down," he tells me, so I did, but nothing makes
you want to see in a box as much as somebody saying not to look.
Next day, when Foster's at work, I look anyway, and it's a flag
all folded up and a uniform underneath. Don't see anything so
strange about that.

Finally had most of the stuff cleaned out. Never could have
known there was a bed underneath. Seemed sort of nice to have
us a guest room, case anybody dropped by. Made me feel rich,
have us a home with so much room we don't even bother to use
all the beds.

That night I was thinking about how good Foster been to me—
planted me a garden and give me this house with a guest room—
and I had this feeling I wanted to be a better wife to him. All I
ever did was lay there, let him come to me. It was warm for a
June night, and we had all the covers off. I had on one of Foster's
T-shirts, but Foster lay there on his back, not a stitch to cover
him, one arm across his forehead, telling me how the bridge
wasn't going to be done that summer, lucky to be done the next.

I turned on my side, listening to him talk, and slowly put out my hand. I laid it on Foster's chest. He stops talking for a moment, then goes on: "Tulley, he's already put in his name for the new bridge going to be built in Baltimore when this one's done. Clyde, too. Think I might as well sign up. Longer way to drive each morning, but sure would take workin' on a bridge to workin' a building. . . ."

I moved my hand down, and when I come to it I just took it real gentle in my fingers. First time in my life I ever did something like that. Just lay there, holding it in my hand, and it moved. Felt like a bird, something live with a will of its own.

Foster sucks in his breath. "April . . ." he says, and puts his hand over mine.

I didn't hold on long because Foster rolled over pretty soon and took me, but I'd learned something about pleasing him I probably should have known before. Foster was especially nice to me that night and all the next day, too. Trying to let me know he liked it. In all the time we'd lived together, though, he'd never once said he loved me, and I'd never said it to him neither. I think maybe he did love me. It was just that we didn't start out that way—talking about it—and now if either of us was to say it, would sound like we hadn't loved each other all the months before.

I should have been happy, I know, but there was a fearfulness inside me wouldn't let up. Fear of losing Foster. Fear of messing up so terrible he'd turn me out. Sometimes the fear get so big it's like I can't stand waiting for the worst to happen—got to run out to meet it. Get it over with.

***

It was the second Saturday in June that the Harley brothers come over. Foster's working on the spare room, replacing the window frames the squirrels have chewed up. I'm outside in the yard watching while he lays a long board across two sawhorses. When he goes over to the truck for more lumber, I climb up on the board to see if I can make my way across without breaking my neck.

"This 'bout as wide as the beams on the bridge?" I call over at him, putting one foot on the board.

"Little wider than that," Foster says.

Carefully I pick up the other foot and put it down in front of the first, almost leaning too far, my arms out at the side for balance.

"What's it like up on the bridge, Foster, when you walk a beam?"

"Well, you see three things," he says, "the beam, the sky, and the water. Four things. Your foot. Got to keep your eye on where you'll set it down."

"How high up am I, Foster, if I'm working on a bridge? How high at the very top?" I close my eyes halfway. I can feel the board begin to bend a little under my weight.

"Couple hundred feet. Three hundred, maybe."

"How high's your house?"

"Twenty feet, I suppose."

I look over at Foster's house and figure it out in my head. Try to see myself up in the air fifteen times higher than Foster's house. Next thing I know I'm leaning off to the side again, my arms going like windmills.

"Steady up! Steady up!" Foster yells, laughing, but I'm on the ground.

I try it again. Climb up on the sawhorse and put my foot on the board.

"You just come up in the cage," Foster says, "and you're steppin' out on the platform, wind hittin' you square in the face, your jacket blowin'. . . ."

I put out my arms again.

"Now you're starting across the beam, heading for a corner," Foster says. "Got a big old belt of tools around you, slapping at your leg every step you take. Can't go too slow or you'll lose your balance. Go too fast, you might misstep. Just keep yourself a steady pace, your eyes on your feet in front of you."

I walk a little faster this time.

"That's it . . . don't look right or left, April Ruth, you'll get the wobblies. . . ."

I almost made it across that time when I heard a car engine down the lane, and I stopped just long enough to see who was coming, lost my balance, and then I was down. Didn't even have time to pick myself up when this old panel truck come bursting into the clearing. Vinnie's losing her mind again, barking.

Wallace Harley gets out first, then Jed. You want to see ugly, you should see the Harley brothers. Not face-ugly so much as sheer ugliness oozing out from inside. The way they walk, the way they hunch up their shoulders, the wet way they say their words.

Faces weren't exactly the kind you'd want hanging on your wall, though—like pulled rubber, big space between their noses and mouths, no mustache to take up the slack. Puffy lips and dirty-yellow hair. Jed's the thin one, got on this T-shirt cut off along the bottom, tatoos all up his arm clear to the shoulder, where there's a pack of tobacco rolled in the hem of his sleeve. Wallace has a stomach on him like a bed pillow. When he turns his back on you and leans over, his pants ride down so far you can see where his butt divides. Harley brothers ever come by you're about to eat supper, you won't want nothing at all.

They saunter over to where I'm picking myself up off the ground. Each got a big plug of Red Man tobacco in their mouths, and when they smile it shows black between their teeth.

"Got the garden goin', did you?" Wallace says, and spits sideways.

"Yeah, it's doin' all right," says Foster. "We'll have us more than we can eat, you want to stop by this summer and help yourselves."

"Got you a wife, too," says Jed, leering at me. I turn my back on them and go on about my work, which is picking bean beetles off the plants and dropping them in a jar of kerosene.

"Yep. Got me April Ruth," says Foster, and smiles at me as he goes back to the pickup for another board.

"How she treating you?" Jed asks.

"Don't hear me complaining, do you?" says Foster. I figured he could have said a little more than that.

"Truck running okay?" Wallace wants to know.

"Running good," says Foster. He stops and opens up the hood. "Got a Holley double pumper on it."

Wallace gives a whistle. "Sumbitch! That is sure a clean-lookin' machine."

"Yeah," says Jed. "He's got dual exhaust, too."

"With headers and glass packs," says Foster, beaming.

Men get talking about trucks, they don't make one bit of sense. The Harley brothers jaw on and on, Wallace seeing just how close he could spit to where I was. I wished they'd go. Didn't care if they *had* rented Foster their tractor.

"Going out to Rosecroft this afternoon, play the horses," Jed says. "Thought you might want to come."

"Well, now . . ." says Foster, and he wipes his arm across his forehead.

I stayed where I was, squatted down in the dirt, a beetle between my fingers. Why didn't Foster just say no? What was he waiting for?

"Don't think I can leave the garden," he says finally.

" 'Pears like April can handle it okay," says Jed.

Foster looks over at me. I just stare back, don't give him no sign one way or the other. Want to see what he'll do on his own.

"Not today," says Foster again. "We've got a lot to do."

I don't know why it bothered me the way Foster said it, but it did. Don't suppose a man can come right out and say no, but there was something in Foster's voice told me he might would like to go sometime, and maybe if it was with anyone but the Harley brothers, I wouldn't have cared.

"How about poker one of these nights, then?" Jed says. "You going to give us a chance to win back that four hundred dollars you got off us last year?"

First time I'd heard of Foster playing poker. He sort of smiles.

"How you know I won't walk off with another four hundred?"

"Well, I'm bettin' you won't," says Wallace. "You play us a whole weekend, don't quit after one night, I'm bettin' *we'd* be the ones got a Chevy truck with a 454 big block in it, sittin' in *our* driveway."

"I ever find me a whole weekend with nothing to do, I'll prove you wrong," Foster laughs.

Jed and Wallace stand around a couple minutes longer like maybe Foster will change his mind, go to the races. I pick up my jar and go over to the steps, Vinnie trotting along behind me.

"Dog's still limpin'," Wallace says to Foster. "Wouldn't have a dog like that around the place if I was you. Take her out and shoot her. Get me a real bird dog, a Bluetick."

The words boil up out of my mouth. "People go 'round shootin' misfits, you and Jed woulda died long ago," I tell him.

Wallace stares at me, but Jed grins. "Hey, Foster, you married yourself a hotbox."

"You got nothing better to do than pick on a lame dog, why don't you and Wallace just get on your way?" I tell him.

Wallace grunts. "You ain't changed one bit since you was eight years old, April. Feisty as a rooster."

"Well, you ain't changed neither, and I'm sorry to see it," I tell him, and go into the house, letting the screen door slam.

When they were gone, Foster comes in for a drink of water. Thought he'd take my side, but he's quieter than I'm comfortable with.

"You mad about what I said to Jed and Wallace?" I ask.

"You can at least be civil," says Foster. "When Thomasine shows up, haven't I got the decency to ask her in for a meal?"

"You wanted me to have 'em to lunch?" I screech. "The way Wallace was talkin' about Vinnie?"

"He wasn't going to shoot her, only shootin' off his mouth. If you don't like the Harley brothers, April, just say so."

"I don't like 'em," I says.

"Okay, you said it," says Foster, and goes back out.

***

Shouldn't have opened my mouth one peep about Jed and Wallace, 'cause the last day of June, as if to test me, Thomasine and Dorothy come by. It was Dorothy who got there first. I was straddling the row of bush beans, picking our first crop. Once I'd got the hang of it, the garden was the thing I could do good. Seemed like I had a natural sympathy for anything trying to grow, make something of itself. I was just having myself a time, dropping 'em in the bucket by the handful. When Dorothy got out of the car, though, and come over, I figured she was mad at somebody the way she lit into me.

"You look like Alabama trash, April Ruth, spreading your legs over a row like that," she yells.

All kinds of smart answers come to mind, but then I see a bruise the size of Texas on her cheek. I stand up, wiping my hands on my cutoffs.

"What happened between you and Max?" I ask her.

Dorothy's chin trembles and she comes over and sits on a sawhorse. "Goddam bum," she says, and sniffles.

"He do this a lot, Dorothy?" I ask. "Hit you like that?"

She sniffles again. Wouldn't answer, so I go back to picking beans, and Dorothy says, "Can't even *talk* to another man, Max thinks I'm up to somethin'."

"Are you?" I ask.

Dorothy lets loose with a string of cusswords, make your head rattle. Vinnie lies down, nose on her paws, ears flat against her head.

"Just askin'," I say.

"Oh, he's not particular about the ones *he* arranges," Dorothy says, reaching in the neck of her blouse to pull up a strap. "Just don't want me taking on anyone without his knowing about it. So goddam scared he's not going to get *his* cut."

I wished Dorothy hadn't said that. All these years I knew what she and Thomasine were up to, I wished I didn't. Kept hoping maybe they just had them a lot of boyfriends that gave 'em stuff. Didn't really want to believe they did it for money, though any fool could plainly see.

This time I straighten up and look right at her. "Dorothy," I says, "how come you spread yourself around like that?"

"You think I want to end up like you, stuck out here in the dirt picking beans?" she screeches. Her voice was like a rusty saw. "*Look* at you, April. Dirt on your legs. Haven't had a decent haircut since I don't know when. I swear, Foster come home at night, I don't know what in the world he sees in you."

"I take a bath," I tell her, and carry my pail of beans over to the porch, hurting inside. Feel uglier than a old rag mop. Dorothy follows after me and plops herself down on the side of the porch, legs crossed high over the knees. I can tell she's wearing a new pair of shoes, 'cause the soles are hardly stepped on. "Want a glass of Hi-C?" I ask her, trying to be civil.

She guessed so, so I come back out on the porch with two glasses. Hadn't even sat down before here come Thomasine up the drive in a bright yellow Ford.

Dorothy turns and stares. It's a later model than Dorothy's, and Thomasine's wearing a new pair of sunglasses too, curved around the edges, her hair freshly bleached. She steps out in a pair of pink shorts and pink shoes, and sidles up to the porch, grinning like a cat.

"Daddy bought you a car, huh?" I says to Thomasine.

"Weren't Daddy," she says, giving her halter top a yank so's her breasts fall back into place. "Found me a real nice trucker from Illinois."

Dorothy plunks her glass down and sneers. "What'd you have to do to get it, Thomasine? Sit on his face?" And before I can blink my eyes, Thomasine's purse goes flying through the air and hits Dorothy right smack on the bruise.

Dorothy, she leaps up from the porch and goes for Thomasine, and with Vinnie hightailing it around the house, they're scratching at each other, arms flailing, high heels digging down in the dirt. I seen Daddy pour a pail of water over two dogs once that was fighting, and I just grab up my bucket of beans and give 'em a toss. Biggest mess you ever saw—beans flying ever' which way and Vinnie howling out behind the house like someone's getting killed.

"Look what you did to my shorts!" Thomasine bellows to Dorothy, backing off. She's pointing to where the seam's pulled open at the side.

"Gonna take them off anyway, first chance you get," Dorothy says, and they would have gone at it again if I didn't say I'd sic the dog on 'em.

"You just get out of here, both of you, you're going to carry on like this," I told them, knowing Shum and Russell was hearing the commotion and enjoying every little bit.

Dorothy sits back down, licking at one of her fingernails got broke. "Bloody bitch," she says.

Thomasine turns to me. "Wouldn't have come if I'd known *she* was going to be here," she says. Then, remembering what she come for, "How you like it, April? This Illinois man got it for me secondhand from his cousin. Towed it all the way to Maryland on the back of his truck. Give me the papers on it this morning."

I followed her over to the car.

"Got blue-tinted glass on the windshield," says Thomasine, "AM–FM radio, cigarette lighter, four-speed wipers. . . . Come on. I'll take you for a ride."

I look over at Dorothy.

"She can come too, she keeps her mouth shut," says Thomasine.

"Wouldn't ride in that if it was the last car leavin' hell," says Dorothy.

"I'm going to try it out," I say. "Be back in a little while."

Dorothy just folds her arms and looks the other way, so I slip in the front seat beside Thomasine. She turns around in front of the house and we're off down the drive, tires squealing, dust blowing back on Dorothy.

I worry sometimes there's a bad streak in me. Had no business getting in that car with Thomasine only a half hour before Foster come home. Dorothy was there first, after all; she was company, and I had the beans to put on for supper. There's just something about a car—about heading out for anywhere in the world you want to go, nobody stopping you—that turns my head. Don't even have to know where you're going, just follow the road.

"Don't go far, Thomasine," I tell her, knowing all the while she will. "Got to get dinner on."

"Foster was cooking for himself long before you come along," says Thomasine.

We must have drove over half of Charles County with the radio going full blast. South through Pisgah to Poor House Road, on to Port Tobacco, Bel Alton, and Faulkner, till we get to the crab house down at Popes Creek. We get out then and buy us a Pepsi, drink it leaning against the car—me with dirty legs, Thomasine in her torn pink shorts.

By the time she gets me home again, drops me off out on the road, it's a quarter past six.

Foster's pickup's there by the house. So is Dorothy's sports car. Seeing them two side by side done something to my stomach. The string beans was all picked up off the ground, and I walk in the house feeling small and scared. Here I am, trying to be a wife, got no more sense than I had back in sixth grade.

They were sitting at the table—Foster and Dorothy—having supper, and there was an empty plate waiting for me. I could feel my face burn. Dorothy's got herself all prettied up best she can, and she's holding her pork chops in her fingers, all dainty, licking the grease off her lips, hanging on to Foster's every word.

"I'm sorry, Foster," I say, sliding into my chair. "Thomasine had a new car and wanted to give me a ride. Once she turned south, couldn't hardly get her home again."

Foster smiles at me but I could tell he didn't mean it. "Should have asked her to stay for supper," he says. Knew he didn't mean that neither.

I forked some beans into my mouth. They were only half cooked. Problem with me was I didn't have no road map, no model of what I was supposed to be. Didn't know what I was supposed to do till after I hadn't done it.

"Don't *worry*, April," Dorothy says, her voice as sweet as a Hostess Twinkie. "Foster and me have been having the nicest talk."

Foster's got his eyes on his plate, and I can imagine all kinds of things I didn't want Dorothy talking about to him.

"I know when I'm in the company of a gentleman," she goes on, and looks right at him. "Foster says I can come here the next time things get bad with Max."

Foster helps himself to the bread, not saying a word, and goes on eating.

"Things get bad with Max you can always go home to Daddy, too," I said. I shut my mouth after that, but soon as dinner's over and Foster's in the other room, I say, "Dorothy Bates, you ever try to spend the night here you'll be sorry you did. You don't wear no nightgown, and I can just see how you turn up at the breakfast table."

Dorothy laughs. "You think I came by to steal your bridgeman from you? What's the matter, April, can't you keep him?"

My chest was getting tight. "Don't want to embarrass him, that's all. You just get yourself on back to Max."

"I'm just staying long enough to make him worry," she says. "I'm not about to spend my life back here on this godforsaken place straddling a row of beans bare-legged. Not *this* girl."

She goes in to Foster then, her voice all silky, saying how he was her port in a storm, and it was nice to know there were men like him around, the world so full of scum, and on and on. Finally I give her a bump from behind and she leaves. Gives a little tap on her horn before driving off.

I was still so mad I couldn't see straight. Mad at Dorothy, mad at Thomasine for making me late, mad at myself. Didn't know whether to be mad at Foster or not. I stood at the sink scrubbing the fat from the skillet, wondering if he was interested in Dorothy or just being polite out of kindness. Then I hear his footsteps behind me and he's got his hands around my waist.

"Foster," I says, scrubbing even harder, not even looking at him. "Don't know what got into me. I get in a car, I just want to ride and never stop."

"Figured that's what happened," he says.

Suddenly I started to cry. Not so's he could hear me, but I could taste the salt in my mouth. Next time I said something, my nose was clogged up. "Didn't mean to leave you here with Dorothy."

"It's okay," Foster said, and now I could tell he was smiling. "Got Vinnie here to protect me."

I laughed then, and wiped my arm across my eyes, and after I finished the skillet, we went in and lay down side by side on the sofa to watch television, only we didn't watch nothing. Person could have walked right in on us.

***

By August, the whole garden was ready for picking—something every day. I got a little book at the A & P told how to freeze vegetables, but I still got more than I could fit in the top of our refrigerator. Every Wednesday, Foster and me would go to the Meadow Diner, and we'd always have some vegetables with us. Thomasine see us coming, she'd say, "Well, look what the cat dragged in," but Marie was glad to have the sweet corn and lettuce, and always give us supper on the house. Take along enough vegetables for Howard and James at the Amoco and Tillie at the Laundromat and Daddy at the trailer and still have enough tomatoes for the whole of Charles County. Once we passed Russell on the way to the mailbox, and Foster leans out the window of the pickup and says, "Anything you want from the garden, you and Shum just help yourself." But Russell don't even blink, just keeps walking.

From the day I moved in, Shum and Russell hadn't said one word to me. Nor to Foster neither, far as I could tell. To be truthful, I hadn't said one word back; if looks could kill I'd have died the first day I come. All summer long, anything go wrong down at the garden, I could hear Shum's little laugh drifting down from their porch. The tomato cages fall over, Shum would laugh. The dog dig up the peppers, Shum would giggle. Two old men sitting up there on the porch waiting for the worst to happen.

One afternoon they was propped up there again like they was at the circus or something. I'd loaded up my basket with all I could carry and was starting toward our house, but every few steps, something fell off. First it was a pepper. I reach down for that and a squash fell off on my foot. Time I set the basket down, picked up the squash, and started off again, a cucumber hits the ground beside me. Tomatoes rolling every which way. Shum's laughing to beat the band.

Don't know what got into me, but all at once, instead of going to our house, I turn and march up the slope to Russell's. Shum's laughter cuts off short. I can hear the rockers stop dead, hear the old men breathing, almost. I just walk on, one foot in front of the other, right up their steps.

"Hope you all enjoy our garden," I says, setting the basket down between 'em, and take myself on home.

Get inside Foster's house and can't stop laughing. Nothing kill a mean man quicker'n kindness. They was so surprised they didn't say one word. I look out of the window and they're still sitting there, scared to touch it. After a while Russell gets up and goes inside, then Shum, leaving the basket where it is.

Okay, I says to myself, basket can sit there a month for all I care. They can eat the vegetables while they're fresh or throw 'em out once they're rotten, but one way or another, they got that basket to reckon with.

Hour goes by. Two hours. Then, when I'm passing by the window, I see Shum come out, take a look around, grab up the basket, and take it inside. I laugh some more. Trouble with accepting a basket is it's got to be returned. I sure had 'em there.

Next day, if Shum and Russell come to the mailbox at all, I didn't see 'em. Day after that they didn't come neither. Knew I had 'em worried. Scared to death if they come out of the house and see me, they'd have to say something.

Third day, though, they come out and get in Russell's car and take off, and after they get back, here come Russell carrying my basket all filled with peaches.

"Shum and I went to the orchard and got more peaches than we can use," he says. "Thought you might like to have some."

"Why, thank you very much," I say, the kind of voice I used at school. "We will most surely enjoy them."

Russell nods and turns around like a windup man and goes back up the hill.

After that it got easy. Every day I'd take up another armful of vegetables, whether Foster's uncles was on the porch or not, just leave 'em there. And every few days, Shum come out and say something civil, or Russell give me something to take back home. Once he tells me to wait, he's got some plums we can have, and while I'm there at the door, I can see a photograph hanging on his wall inside, same picture we got in the shoebox: Lloyd in his soldier's uniform.

There was something between Foster and his uncles I didn't understand. Knew the old men were mad he brought me there to live, but once they started speaking to me, they still weren't speaking to Foster.

"Foster," I says one night while he's frying the meat, "what in the world is it between you and Russell and Shum? They got a picture on their wall of Lloyd, but they don't give you the time of day."

Foster peppers the meat and turns it over. "Just liked Lloyd better, is all," he says. He sure wasn't telling me something I didn't know.

"How come they don't like you?"

"Lloyd's the one that got killed," he says.

I set the forks on the table. "If there's any sense in that, I surely can't find it," I tell him.

"Never said there was any sense to it. Russell had his heart set on him and Lloyd starting a cattle farm, but Lloyd was one of the first Marines to go to Vietnam. Elks Club give him a big send-off—guest of honor at their Thursday lunch. Russell and some of the Elks brothers drives 'im to Union Station the day he leaves. Figure dead or alive, he's going to come back a hero from Charles County."

"So what's that got to do with you?" I ask him.

"Two years later Lloyd was home on leave, and next day, out on Route 50 with my folks, they're hit broadside by a gasoline truck. Shum and Russell, I guess they figured I'd go take Lloyd's place in the Marines, but I didn't sign up and I wasn't drafted. The uncles didn't get their cattle farm or their hero neither, and they never forgive me for that."

"Two dead nephews is better than one?"

"Think I'm a coward," Foster said, and his voice is low and flat like maybe I'd hear it, maybe I wouldn't.

I'm setting the plates on the table and all of a sudden I look over at Foster's back and it's like I'm looking through the layers—like I can see through his shirt and his skin and on into his chest and see it still hurts, what his uncles think of him, whether he says so or not.

"Foster," I says, "your uncles ever fight in a war?"

"No," he says, and lifts out the meat to make gravy.

"They ever work on a bridge, three hundred feet in the air?"

"No. . . ."

"Well, then," I said. And we had our supper.

SEVEN

What Foster remembered most about that summer was the way April walked through the sweet corn at the south end of the garden. The tassels rose inches above her head, and she would move slowly, palms turned outward so that her fingertips brushed against the stalks, the long rough leaves scraping her bare arms. Halfway through the rows, she would turn and start off in another direction, examining a leaf here, an ear there, running the silk through her fingers as though it were the hair of an old friend.

Foster, shovel in hand, would pause by the potato mounds and watch her, pleased that the garden delighted her so much. It didn't matter that, in one thrust of the shovel, he dug up more potatoes than April could eat in a week, or that most of what they grew was carted off each morning in the pickup and divided among the bridge crew. The rectangular patch of purple soil and sunlight had brought him and April closer together, in some ways, than they were in bed, and though April managed to work off what little weight she gained, her skin was tan, her eyes bright, and she looked better to Foster than she ever had before.

Sometimes, when he arrived home from the bridge, he would find her sitting in the shade of the pole-bean trellis, Vinnie beside her—the dog stretched out with her belly against the damp earth.

"April," he said once, bending over and looking in, "you look like a broody hen sittin' under there."

She grabbed at his trousers and pulled him down beside her. "Feel how cool, Foster!" she said. "It's like my own little summertime house."

He crawled in with her, leaning back against the fence he had built for the squash, surrounded on three sides by vine with a canopy of leaves on top. He tried to look out at the world as April saw it low in the garden—a jungle of green, far as the eye could see. She took pleasure, it seemed, in spaces, as though once leaving the confines of the trailer, she saw each new vista— a room, a house, a garden—as a place to be occupied. She had even explored beneath Foster's porch on her hands and knees, wondering what use she might make of a six-by-eight patch of darkness. It seemed inconceivable that the small cubicle of shade beneath the bean vines should go uninhabited.

"What's this?" she said once when he crawled under the trellis and handed her a jar filled with a colorless blob.

"Present," said Foster, setting his lunch bucket on the ground.

She stared in bewilderment, turning the jar around in her hands.

Foster grinned. "Sea nettles," he said. "Bay's full of 'em this time of year. The men hang off the barge by a rope and scoop 'em up, take 'em home to their kids to look at."

"You hung out over the water to pick up somethin' as ugly as this?" April asked incredulously. "Foster Williams, you like to get yourself killed!"

He laughed. "I'll bring you an old octopus next time."

By September, most of the corn had been picked, and now, when Foster and April worked the garden, they were accompanied by the constant rustle of dry leaves against dead stalks. The sun was still bright, Saturdays were still hot, but the pepper plants had begun to wither, the leaves of the tomato plants were yellowing along the edges, and the squash had rotted in the last rain.

April was dismayed. "It's still warm out, Foster!" she said in protest. "What's got into 'em?"

"The garden's got its own timetable," he told her. "It knows September, warm or not."

April behaved as though she had not heard, as though by sheer will she could keep the garden alive. She staked up plants that had begun to droop, watered those that were yellowed, and spent hours rearranging leaves and stems so that the plants that remained had their full share of sun.

The garden, however, was shrinking. Every day, another plant had withered beyond repair and was finally pulled up. The lifeless cornstalks were carted off to a heap among the walnut trees. The emptiness they left behind was too big to be ignored.

"Foster," April told him one Sunday, "I've been thinking some about it, and I want us to have a baby."

The words seemed to settle themselves untidily there on the table between the butter and the Safeway jam.

"What do you mean, you've thought some about it?" Foster asked when he realized the words couldn't be brushed aside like crumbs. "You haven't said nothing to me."

"Well, I am now."

"April, we're not even married."

"I get pregnant, I'll marry you," she said.

"You got to do it the other way around. You've got to marry me because you want to, not because you got my child. What set you thinking about babies?"

"Be something I could raise. Didn't I do okay with the garden, Foster?"

"Sure you did!" Foster grinned across the table. "Worked like a hired man! Just thought you'd like some time to yourself before thinking about a baby."

"Had all the time to myself I need."

Foster slowly spread his toast with butter, then realized he was buttering the other side as well. "You marry me, we'll talk about children," he told her.

She did not answer.

They went on about their routine of Sunday chores, but the thought stuck inside Foster's head like gum on the sole of his boot. Nothing he did would dislodge it. The idea tantalized and terrified him in turn. He knew by the set of April's lips that she was too stubborn to give the idea up, and he was not sure that he wanted her to. A pregnancy, at least, would get them married. Would he, could he, should he risk it?

Each afternoon when he walked in, he could feel her gray eyes on him, waiting. As diligently as she had put her mind on the garden that summer, she would fight for her right to be pregnant.

"April," he announced on Friday, "we're going to the ocean tomorrow. It's to get up to eighty over the weekend, and I always said we'd go back. Pack your bathing suit this time, because we'll go in the water."

She looked at him curiously. "Haven't got one."

"We'll buy one, then."

Perhaps he had thought he could distract her. He realized that as they made their way across the Bay Bridge the next morning, April marveling again at just how high the towers rose, then looking across the open water at the second bridge, half-finished, silhouetted against white sky. Or perhaps he simply wanted her to taste something of what other girls her age were enjoying, he decided. More than once, arriving home in the pickup, he had sat there a moment watching April Ruth in the garden, back bent, scrawny arms picking at the plants like a little old woman. She shouldn't be here doing this way, his conscience had told him then. Should be out having herself some fun. Well, he was giving her that chance now. He was going to force upon her the realization that she was still young. Foster felt as though he were driving with one foot on the gas, the other on the brake.

He paid fifteen dollars more for a larger room this time. There was more space to put their bags, and April did not have to crawl across the bed to reach the window. On this trip, the windows were open, and the salty tang of the sea blew in. April knelt down, arms on the sill, and watched in the same fascination as before.

"Look at all those people!" she said. "Oh, Foster, I can't go down there."

"Why not?"

"Just can't. Don't know how to act."

The sound of his own laughter against the four walls cheered him. "April, honey, you don't act any way but natural. You get out there in the water, you'll know what to do."

They went shopping for a suit for April, and found most of the suits on sale—heaps of orange and red and purple—and set to work finding one that would fit.

"Size five, maybe," the saleslady guessed, and April went into a cubicle at the back to try them on.

Foster, on a chair outside, could see her feet beneath the partition, one lifting at a time, then both on the floor tilting outward, and finally coming to rest with the toes pointing toward the mirror at the back.

"April, how you doing in there?" he called when the procedure had been repeated four or five times without apparent success.

"Come to the door and look," she mumbled.

He opened the door a crack, shielding it with his body. April stood in front of the mirror in a green two-piece suit. There were wrinkles around the fanny, and the top gaped beneath her armpits.

"Only trouble is you got the wrong size," he told her, and went back to search for a size three, his big hands pushing the hangers along the rack. He found one in yellow and returned.

"Don't *watch,* Foster," she insisted.

Foster closed the door. The bare feet danced their routine again beneath the partition.

"Foster," she called at last.

He went to the door again and studied her with mixed feelings. The suit came up high on the legs where it was held together with laces, showing a naked expanse of flesh. The bra top was also laced at the front.

"I don't know, April," he told her. "You go out on the beach like that, you're liable to get yourself pawed."

She laughed delightedly. "But don't it fit good, Foster? *Now* can we go in the water?"

It was three before they got back to the room and changed. Both laughed at the untanned parts of their bodies—Foster's legs, April's torso and the tops of her thighs.

"We're going to be two funny-lookin' people out there," she said self-consciously as they went down the back staircase with their towels, but she hurried nonetheless, pulling Foster along.

Outside, the temperature had reached a record ninety. April yelped when her feet hit the hot sand.

"It's burnin'!"

Laughing, Foster carried her to the shore and set her down on the cool, smooth surface of wet sand. April squealed in delight as the first breaker cast its foam around her toes.

She clung to him as they moved in knee-deep, acclimating themselves to the cold. When the water reached her suit, April shrieked and covered herself, and some young men nearby laughed.

Foster taught her to stand sideways when a wave came, jumping up to escape its force. She hooked her arms tightly about his neck, cheek pressed hard against the matted hair on his chest, keeping a lookout. Once however, when their attention was diverted by a young man on a belly board, they missed a high breaker rolling in from the side. A moment later, Foster felt April's hand wrenched from his, and then he was head over heels himself, the hollow thrubbing of water in his ears—elbows and knees scraping the bottom, the sting of salt in his nostrils.

He was on his side then as the wave went on. Staggering to his feet, laughing, he looked around for April and saw her yellow suit. Before he could reach her, the boy on the belly board had grabbed her by one arm and was pulling her to her knees. She clung to the boy's leg, thinking he was Foster, and the young man relinquished her reluctantly when Foster picked her up.

She was coughing up water, hair down over her eyes, shoulder bruised.

"I'm sorry, April, should have kept an eye on you," Foster said, trying to halt her march to the shore, but April high-stepped her way back to the sand again, and they spent the next hour walking along the beach, picking up bits of shell.

Foster was aware of the eyes that followed April's body as they passed. Some were old men—older than Jack Tulley, even—smiling appreciatively at the young girl who stopped every so often to dig furiously for a sand crab that had burrowed down in a wake of bubbles. But others were young men her own age, and out of the corner of his eye, Foster could see their heads turn as he and April passed, their eyes caressing the back of her legs, her fanny.

Later, when the tide was out and the breakers were calm, Foster and April went in the water again. This time she rode on his back, arms wrapped around in front of him, clutching him so tightly he thought he might choke. But she eased her grip when she saw that she rode well above the surface, and Foster lightly stroked her legs under the water, enjoyed the feel of her small breasts and stomach against his back. It was at this moment that Foster knew he would do whatever necessary to keep her. These unexpected pleasures were the things that did him in. Since March, he had never ceased to wonder at how recklessly he was leading his life. Walking a six-inch beam above the bay did not seem half as foolhardy as what he was planning to do next, yet he knew, even then, he would do it.

They stayed on the beach long after the lifeguards had gone off duty. The crowd thinned as harried mothers shook out their blankets, folded their towels, and gathered up children and cups and sandals for the sandy trek to the showers on the boardwalk.

"If you had children," Foster observed, in one last effort at reason, "you couldn't stay out here like this—have to be worrying about getting them cleaned up for supper."

His words seemed carried away on the wind; if April heard, she made no response.

That night, however, when she came to bed beside the open window, still warm from her bath, her hair smelling of balsam, she said, "Foster, I still want that baby." And this time he took her with nothing between them, skin against skin. He did not think about babies again until morning.

The room was flooded with sunlight, and the walls that had appeared soft in the flow of the lamp now seemed harsh and unyielding. Foster rolled over on his back and studied the corners where the walls came together, wondering, quite consciously, if he were going to feel trapped. What had happened the night before could not be undone. Not only the single act itself, without precautions, but his silent acquiescence in the matter. The decision, as far as April was concerned, was made.

Surprisingly, this particular fix in which Foster found himself did not upset him half as much as he expected. It seemed more an extension of the original predicament, further defined and distilled. Once the decision had been made to take April into his house, he was borne along on the current, and each successive problem was merely a wave to jump over, through, or under.

They sat together on the sand before starting home, watching a small child totter bravely toward the water, then run screaming back to the safety of his mother's arms, just out of reach of a wave. Once, when the child stumbled over his own feet and fell, April half-rose to pick him up. Maybe, Foster told himself, motherhood came naturally to some women, and April was one of them. She was not oblivious to the young men who admired her on the beach, he could tell. There was something about her smile, about the way she carried herself, that let him know she enjoyed it. At the same time, she seemed willing to give all that up to bear a baby, and never mind that she had only been talking about it a week. Foster simply could not bring himself to deny her.

She sat close to him in the pickup going home, legs thrust out and crossed at the ankles, elbows resting on the seat where she slumped, her head on his shoulder. The afternoon sun came in the window at a slant, warming her small hand, which lay languidly in Foster's lap.

> *I'm nothin' without you,*
> *So please understand . . .*

crooned a singer over the radio.

Foster thought for a minute that April might have fallen asleep. Then he felt her hand move against his leg, lazily outlining his testicles with one finger. A shiver went up his back and settled between his shoulder blades. She didn't know her power, this girl of less than a hundred pounds.

> *. . . I can't live without you,*
> *So say I'm your man.*

In the weeks that followed, Foster had to admit that he enjoyed sex more. He sometimes pulled April onto his lap soon after he got home, played with her like a kitten, and sometimes barely made it to the shower before they were off to the bedroom, even before supper. He anticipated long months of leisurely, spontaneous lovemaking without worry, so he was unprepared for April's tears one morning when she announced her period. His laughter did not help.

"April, honey, Rome wasn't built in a day. You can't expect to get pregnant the first time."

"Told us in school you could."

"Don't mean you *would*."

"But why didn't it work?" She sat on the edge of the bed, blowing her nose.

Foster shrugged helplessly, lost for words. "Just didn't, that's all. Maybe it isn't the right time or something."

She concentrated once more on the garden. When October brought an early frost, April was still out after dark, covering the shriveled tomato plants, protecting the peppers with over-turned boxes.

For several mornings, when Foster went to work, he could see his breath in the air. By noon, on the bridge, the sun was warm again, and sometimes the men took off their jackets, but the wind had a crispness that bespoke the fall. The deep-lobed leaves of the sweet gum tree had turned crimson, and each afternoon, when Foster returned home, the garden seemed to have shrunk even more. Once, looking out, he saw Shum come down from Russell's house with bushel baskets to help protect the plants that were left. Foster marveled at the power April had over his uncles as well.

But she did not conceive in October.

They were washing windows together one Sunday, Foster doing the panes, April scrubbing the sills.

"Foster," she said, without looking at him, "I want that baby. Maybe we're not doing it right."

Foster suppressed a grin. "We're doin' it right," he told her.

"Well, maybe there's something more we should be doing we aren't."

The grin inched its way across Foster's face in spite of himself. "Might be you could close your eyes," he said, and regretted it instantly when she reddened. "Just kidding, April," he said. "You do it fine."

By November, the garden had given up. April carefully picked the last of the green tomatoes, wrapped them in newspaper as Foster instructed, and had them ripening in a box in the kitchen. Only a pumpkin vine remained outdoors, making its solitary way over the deserted rows where the corn had stood, wrapping its tendrils around the stakes of the bare bean trellis before moving on.

The landscape was gray again—gray fence and house, gray trees and sky—the color of nothingness. When Foster stepped outside in the mornings there were no bird songs now to greet him, only the death rattle of dry leaves. The grayness extended to the road, the bay, and the bridge.

It was a November, too, when Lloyd had come home on leave to be with the family on Thanksgiving. The Elks Club was having a Patriot's Day parade to honor the pilgrims, the Founding Fathers, and every war fought thereafter. Servicemen were invited to participate. Lloyd was to ride on a float along with a soldier and sailor, and they were to sit at the base of a howitzer, each holding a weapon, frozen like statues. For five-and-a-half miles, at ten miles an hour, Lloyd was to sit without moving a muscle, his face glazed over with love of country, Mom, and pie.

"Tell the truth, I'm like to fall asleep," he had joked to Foster Thanksgiving morning. " 'Stead of holding that rifle, I ought to have it propped inside my shirt to hold me up."

He and his parents had left the house early to visit with friends in Prince Georges County before the parade, and Foster had just put a new Gillette blade in his razor when the police called to say that there had been an accident up on Route 50. It was left to Foster to tell Carol, Lloyd's fiancée.

There were some things Foster remembered doing that morning and others he had no recollection of doing at all. He hadn't remembered shaving, yet when he examined his face later, it was done. He remembered leaning over the sink in the kitchen heaving and nothing coming up. He did not remember crying, only an overwhelming sense of loneliness, mixed with last remembrances of his parents, of the dress his mother wore that morning, the tilt of his father's hat, Lloyd's joke about the parade. . . .

He had sat for several minutes in the car outside Carol's house before he went to the door, and she had come downstairs in her robe.

"Good grief, Foster, what are you doing here?" she had said. "Dad's already gone to help out at the parade, and there was nobody left to answer the door." She looked at him curiously as he stepped inside.

Foster remembered thinking that in a matter of minutes, he was going to rob that woman of her happiness. Like a rapist, he would damage her in a way that could never be put right. One minute she was standing there as she was then, studying him with mild annoyance, and the next she would be inconsolable. He struggled to find the words.

There must have been something about his face, his pallor, perhaps, that cued her, because her mouth twisted strangely. Foster saw her body stiffen.

"What's happened?" she asked, and her voice came out raspy, loud. She was clutching the neck of her robe.

Foster didn't know what to do with his hands. Cautiously he reached out and touched her elbows.

"What's happened to Lloyd?" she said again, her pitch rising.

"Carol," Foster told her, "there was an accident."

"No!" It was as though he had hit her in the stomach. Carol doubled over and leaned against the wall, head turned to one side, the uncombed curls on her head bobbing strangely. She held one hand to her mouth.

"Is he dead?" she asked.

"Yes."

She sucked in air and held it, like a small child holding her breath, and then the sobs began—strange and jerky, her eyes tightly closed. Foster's own grief came back in waves as he told her about the accident, about the gasoline truck, and how it wasn't Lloyd's fault. Carol moaned.

Foster wanted to hold her, rock her, comfort her the way Lloyd would have wanted him to do. Awkwardly he gripped her arms and tried to pull her toward him.

She cringed as though in revulsion and pushed him away. "What are you *doing?*" she screamed.

"I just—"

"Don't you ever put your hands on me!" Tears streamed in rivers down her face. "Lloyd's *dead,* and you trying something like that!"

Foster drew back, confused, hurt compounding the pain he felt already. He flushed, then wheeled about there in the hallway and bolted out the door.

Now, at the construction site, Foster parked, still thinking of Lloyd. Inside the change shack, the men warmed themselves at the oil stove while waiting for the others. His wife, Clyde told them, was expecting again, and Juju had become a father for the first time.

"Looks like a little old man," Juju said, passing out cigars. "Wrinkled-up face, puffy old eyes. . . . I ask my wife, 'Who you been messing with?' "

The others laugh.

"They all come scrawny," Clyde told him. "Takes 'em a month or so to fill out."

Juju smiled with satisfaction. "Nothin' like it," he said. "Norris Wainwright, Jr. Could sit and hold him all day and never get tired lookin'." He punched Foster playfully on the shoulder. "When's April gonna make you a daddy?"

Foster laughed. "Got plenty of time for that."

She didn't conceive in November, however. This time her period made her irritable. When Foster toyed with her Angel's Delight—cubed bits of store-bought cake covered with Cool Whip and frozen solid—she got up suddenly, jerked the rest of the dessert from the refrigerator, and turned it upside down in the sink.

"What the hell was that for?" Foster asked.

"Can't stand watchin' you just pick at something," she said.

"Could be I'm not too hungry," he snapped. "Could be I'm just dog-tired and need to rest. You ever think of asking first?"

She calmed down then, and silently cleared the dishes, but flared again later when Foster turned on the TV after they'd started a new jigsaw puzzle.

April whirled around in her chair. "I'm not workin' any more of these puzzles," she said. "You haven't got one bit of interest in them yourself. You sneak off ever' chance you get."

"Just watching the news, April! What's got into you?"

She left the room, however, and the puzzle remained on the card table untouched for the rest of the week. Finally Foster put it back in the box, folded the card table, and put them both in the spare room.

Their lovemaking did not change. April accepted him as soon as he touched her, and sometimes reached out for him. It was the silence afterward, that bothered Foster—his own as well as hers. He didn't know what to talk about anymore; all kinds of things could set her off. Sometimes, he knew, they both lay on their backs staring at the ceiling, both awake, neither saying a word. He did not like to admit, even to himself, that perhaps it was a good thing they had not married; good, too, that she had not conceived.

It was on a Friday when Foster came home and found April with her long hair in a huge mass of tight curls that surrounded her face like a ruffle.

He stood motionless inside the door, holding his lunch bucket.

"My God, what happened to you?" he asked finally, then realized he had said the wrong thing. Trying desperately for humor, he added, "Something's different here, wonder what it could be?"

She turned halfway around to show him the back, and her body stiffened as she completed the turn.

"Thomasine come by and give me a permanent," she said.

Slowly Foster set his bucket on the table. *"That* it, huh? Well, now. . . ."

"You like it?" she asked.

Foster could not hold back his chagrin. "Permanent don't mean forever, does it?"

"You don't like it."

He was too tired to continue the charade. "Hell, girl, I liked your hair before. Thought you had *pretty* hair, April! Why didn't you ask first?"

"I got to ask can I fix my hair? I got to ask every little thing I do around here?" she taunted. April rushed angrily down the hall to the bathroom, slamming the door.

"Goddam," Foster sighed, and leaned against the wall. Another evening shot.

"It looks okay, April," he called. "I just have to get used to it. Makes you look like a big old sunflower." He waited. "Can go out in the rain like that and every hair will spring right back into place," he continued, hoping for a laugh. "C'mon. If I can still run my hand through it without it gettin' caught, I won't have no complaints."

In the quiet that followed, he heard a soft, steady disconcerting sound from the bathroom. He tried to decipher it. There was a pause, and then it came again.

"Jesus!" he said suddenly, and flung open the door. April stood at the mirror with a pair of scissors, her mouth set, eyes narrow slits of determination. The sink was littered with curls.

"April!"

He wrenched the scissors from her, but one side of her head had already been shorn, leaving behind a wavy inch and a half of curl. April beat against his chest with her small fists, then suddenly leaned against him and cried. Foster wearily kneaded her shoulders, rubbed her back.

She sat forlornly on the kitchen table with a sheet around her while Foster tried to undo what had been done. The only possible remedy was to cut off the rest of her hair to make it even. Each lock that came off in Foster's hand was like a stab in the arm.

"Don't know what's wrong with you lately, girl," he said finally. "Just seem to have a splinter in you somewhere, making you mean. Everything I say sets wrong."

A silent tear rolled down April's cheek.

Foster pretended not to see it and reached for the broom, sweeping up the hair on the floor. "You got something on your mind, I wish you'd say it. I'm tired of coming home feeling like I got to step over eggs to make it to bedtime."

April said nothing, but a second tear followed the first.

"If I knew what it was in this world would please you, I might could get it for you, but I sure don't like having to guess," Foster continued. "You missing your family?"

She didn't answer but he could tell that wasn't it.

"Missing your friends?"

Still no answer.

"You want that baby."

She turned her face away, lips pressed tightly together.

The next morning Foster tried not to look at April's hair, but his eyes, in their perversity, would look at nothing else. Her ears stuck out on either side of her head, and there were several uneven places he had missed in the trimming. She moved about the kitchen like a shorn lamb. And then, as though there were not trouble enough, a yellow Ford pulled up and Thomasine got out. Foster thrust his hands in his pockets, braced himself, and waited for the scream.

"Jesus Mary Mother of God!"

Thomasine stood in the kitchen doorway holding a bottle of conditioner in her hand, mouth slack. Slowly she turned her face toward Foster.

"*I* cut it," April said, her voice flat.

"She started, and I finished the job," Foster corrected.

Thomasine drew in her breath. "You bastard. I spent three goddam hours on that permanent."

"Well, April and me unpermed it," Foster said.

Thomasine continued to stare at April's head in disbelief. "Swear to God, April, you look like a choirboy in the Roman Catholic Church."

"That's one hell of a lot better than lookin' like a . . ." Foster stopped himself in mid-sentence.

Thomasine thrust the bottle of conditioner back in her purse. "Well, you sure won't need this, April, seeing as how you haven't got hardly any hair left."

"You got any more to say?" Foster inquired coldly.

Thomasine rested one hand on her hip and studied him. "Why, thank you very much, Foster Williams, for invitin' me to sit down." Then, turning to April: "I don't know how you can stand him." She went back outside and drove off.

"Foster," said April, "you can at least be civil."

Her words mocked him. For several seconds Foster and April stood there eye-to-eye, straining—Foster felt—to see some trace of warmth or humor in the other's face. But April's eyes were as gray as the November landscape, and finally, almost in unison, each of them turned and went about his solitary business.

Foster was deep in his own thoughts when he parked the pickup the next day, but when he walked down to the landing where the men were waiting, he could see the merriment in their eyes.

"Well, you still in one piece," Juju observed.

Foster looked around the circle. "What are you talking about?"

Clyde chuckled. "Why, Foster, the whole town's talkin' how you cut off April's hair."

Foster swore under his breath.

Juju shook his head, eyes laughing. "You in the thick of it now, old married man," he said. "You git the women against you, have to paddle twice as hard just to keep yourself up."

"You don't see me worrying, do you?" Foster said, and led the way to the boat.

It seemed to Foster as though April deliberately bungled her share of the chores. Dust balls beneath the bed, which had never bothered him before, bothered him now. When he and April took their clothes to the Laundromat, Foster would discover later that April had forgotten the bath towels or dishcloth, and hadn't even included the sheets.

"I got to do this, too?" he would ask her. "I got to work all day and come home to your jobs as well?"

She answered only by silence. It would turn out that she had spent her time covering Kleenex boxes with contact paper she'd found in the spare room, or putting decals of vegetables and fruits on the door of the refrigerator.

Christmas, however, brought a truce. Foster suggested they cut a tree on their own land, and April put on her coat and boots and went with him. They found a small spruce back behind the walnut grove, and after putting on the ornaments, April continued trimming it with whatever she could find—small aluminum stars cut from milk bottle caps, buttons, a cookie cutter in the shape of a rabbit. . . .

Carols filled the space between commercials on the radio, and a few Christmas cards arrived in the mail—from Marie, from Sister Perry, from the First National Bank of Charles County, and from a hardware store in La Plata. April pinned them to the windowsill above the sink with thumbtacks.

Foster and April went shopping together. Foster turned his

back and April bought him, with his own money, a pair of navy socks—one size fits all—and a bottle of Hai Karate men's cologne. While April stood watching a demonstrator fry eggs on a Teflon skillet, Foster went over to lingerie and bought her a robe-and-gown set of blue nylon with fake white fur around the wide sleeves of the robe.

She stared at the garments in wonder on Christmas morning, running her fingers over the fur, examining the lace on the bodice of the gown, thanking Foster again and again.

"Go put 'em on, let's see how you look," he told her.

"Now?"

"Got to make sure they fit," he said.

When she returned, all shimmery in the nylon, covered only by the transparent blue of the gown beneath, she found Foster sitting naked except for his new socks, rubbing a splash of Hai Karate across his chest.

Her eyes crinkled in laughter. "What are you *doing?*"

"Just tryin' on your gifts for size." He grinned and pulled her down beside him. Vinnie lay contentedly by the hot air register, looking on.

The spell of Christmas held over into the next few days. April went about the house with the red ribbon from one of her packages stuck in her hair like a flower. But when December gave way to January, and a 1973 calendar took its place on the wall, the grayness returned and Foster's worries were never far from his mind. He had tried secretly charting April's periods, making love to her nightly when he deemed her fertile. But her sullenness the second week of January told him their timing had been off once again. He didn't know if he was glad or not.

He had only been on the bridge an hour the next morning when a light drizzle, not expected till afternoon, turned to sleet. The men were sent home with the usual two hours of pay just for showing up, plus one for the wasted hour on the bridge.

April was sitting on the couch with Vinnie in her lap, watching TV, when he walked in. The legs of the large dog spread out in four directions, and any other day, Foster would have smiled at the sight of it.

"What you doing home?" April asked as he passed her on the way to the bedroom.

"Take a look out the window, you'll see for yourself." Foster pulled off his clothes and climbed back into bed.

When he got up around eleven, April was still where she'd been before, and it irked him. If she was bored, let her find something to do. Sit around all day watching television you were bound to be bored. He heated up the breakfast coffee and ate his lunch from his bucket. April came in later and poured herself a bowl of Cheerios.

"That all you have for lunch?" he asked, looking over.

"Eat a banana sometimes."

"No wonder you don't put on any weight, girl."

She made no answer but continued eating, eyes on the table.

They seemed to be in each other's way all afternoon. When Foster needed the bathroom, April was washing out bras in the sink. Just when he had settled down in his chair with the paper, in she came with the vacuum.

"April, you could have done that this morning," he snapped.

"You were sleepin' this morning."

She had him there. He threw down the paper, put on his jacket and gloves, and went out to the truck with Vinnie, taking her to La Plata with him to have the front wheels realigned on the pickup.

He stood in the drafty door of the garage while they worked on the truck, anger boiling up inside him. Vinnie limped around slowly, sniffing at grease spots on the floor. He had no business bringing her out in this weather with her lame leg. He blamed that on April, too. At the same time he was worrying about Vinnie's leg, however, he was thinking how the autumn had slipped by without once taking her coon hunting. His life, before April had moved in, took on a retrospective sweetness.

Give him a crisp November night anytime—a night so black that the men wore miners' headlamps. The Harleys would be out there in the woods, Clyde maybe, a couple of men over from Indian Head, and another from Welcome, and long before Foster's pickup turned off the narrow dirt path to go as far as the underbrush would allow, Vinnie would whimper in anticipation.

There was something about the smell of trees at night, the feel of heavy boots, and the deep, faraway bawl of dogs already gathered that claimed Foster's soul the moment he climbed in the truck. Never mind that Vinnie was a wide hunter, would go off after a fox—a "trash dog," Jed called her. She was a belly-rubber, would hug the trunk where a coon was treed, barking her brains out, and Foster wouldn't trade her for love or money. How could it be that April had distracted him to the point of neglecting hunting altogether?

He rode back from the garage with Vinnie that afternoon, one hand resting protectively on her leg, and turned up the thermostat a degree or two when they got inside the house.

When he settled down in the living room after dinner, however, Vinnie asleep at his feet, he was feeling more mellow, ready to chalk up the antagonism with April as simply an off day. If she made even the slightest effort to be pleasant, he'd put down the paper and talk to her—turn on the TV, anything she wanted to watch.

April, however, clattered and clanked about the kitchen as though there were a sore festering somewhere inside her. Twice Foster was on the verge of yelling to her either to let the dishes go or put them away quietly, and just when he thought she was through, the bang of a cupboard door would make the house rattle.

She came in at last and sat down across from him where she proceeded to look quarrelsome. Something about the tilt of her chin, the way she sat with her elbows stuck out over the arms of the chair.

"C'mere, Vinnie," she coaxed.

"Leave her be, April," Foster said. The dog slept on.

There was silence for a minute or two. Then: "C'mere, Vinnie! Here, Vinnie!"

The dog raised herself and looked sleepily around.

Foster lowered his paper. "Don't mess with her, I said. She was out this afternoon. Needs her rest."

"Wasn't me that had her out in the rain," April snipped.

Foster glared at her. April glared back and went over to sit on the couch, as far away from him as she could get. She sat with knees crossed, swinging her foot up and down, jiggling Foster's paper, then got up and turned on the TV. The sound was too loud, and Foster knew that she knew it. He reached over finally and lowered it some, but later, when he left the room momentarily and returned, he could tell that she had tinkered with it again. The air seemed charged with resentment, yet Foster could find no words to draw it out. He simply hoped that he and April could sleep it off and start in fresh the next morning. It had happened before that they had gone to bed angry but had somehow come together in the night, waking the next morning with their arms around each other. It could happen again.

They avoided each other until bedtime. As Foster was hanging his pants in the closet, however, April came in from her bath and tripped over the work boots he had left lying in the middle of the floor.

"Damn it, Foster!" she yelled. "Keep your boots where they belong!"

Her words seemed to clap him over the ears, reverberate inside his head. This was his house, his land, his bed, and he wheeled around in fury, hand raised.

He faced a steely-eyed girl, her chin thrust forward, balancing precariously on one foot, holding her toe. Slowly Foster lowered his hand, chagrined. He picked up his boots, flung them into the closet, and climbed into bed, heart thumping.

It was raining again. The drops pinged against the window and thrummed on the roof. Foster lay there, eyes on the wall, back toward April, remembering the nights they had lain in each other's arms, listening to rain. He was tempted once to roll over and hold her that way, but anger held him back.

They said very little at breakfast the next morning.

"Got a call in for a plumber," he told her. "The bathroom sink's about to stop up, and I did all I could on it. You tell him when he can take a look at it."

April took small, snapping bites of her toast. "I'm goin' out with Thomasine," she said.

"Well, he calls if you're *here,* tell him when to come by," Foster said irritably. "Or you goin' off tomorrow too?"

His sarcasm was not lost on April. "No, I'm not going off tomorrow too." She put down her toast and left the table.

Outside, the sun was a brilliant white glare in the sky, and the air had warmed, the typical January thaw. Foster was glad for a full day's work, glad to occupy his mind with something he could manage. He found the other men in a jovial mood, and Foster spent his time between fittings thinking of how he and April might work things out.

It occurred to him that there was something about women he had not taken into account. From what he could deduce, listening to Clyde and Juju talk about wives, women took a lot of pleasure in what was about to happen. They needed something to look forward to, whereas men took their pleasure in the moment. They were always looking ahead, women—always thinking about what lay in front of them. Why, it was as clear as the nose on his face. And hadn't that been Foster's trouble all his life, practically—his habit of not looking to the future? Had to stay a jump ahead of April—be talking about what they were going to do long before it was time to do it.

At the same time, Foster was weary of being the one who worried over the relationship, tired of coming home to a girl who wanted things done for her when she could do them herself and who wanted to do things herself that she didn't have any sense for. One minute she was complaining she didn't have enough to do, and the next she was running off somewhere without doing the jobs she should.

In any case, by the time he started home that afternoon, Foster had a plan. They would be celebrating their first anniversary, of sorts, in March, and he'd let her decide where to go. Maybe another trip to Ocean City. That would give her something to think on through February. After that, it would be time to look to the garden again. Last year, hadn't she wished they'd planted a melon patch? He'd let her pick what kind. Do the whole garden in melons if she liked.

Then, at the turnoff from 301, the anger surfaced again. Here he was thinking up ways to make April happy, while she'd spent the day with Thomasine. One-sided, that's what it was. He had thought that taking her in would make her see what a chance he was giving her, somebody to care for her, treat her right. Seemed like she was running off every little chance she could get.

His feelings played tricks on him, though; by the time he pulled in at the mailbox and made his way up the drive, he had already thought of taking the old lumber out behind the shed and building a little vegetable stand for April to sit in out by the road come summer. Now *that* was an idea that had never even occurred to April. The stand would be hers, too, her very own business. He always had to have an idea in his pocket, ready to pull out.

As he neared the house, Foster saw April kneeling on the porch. He parked and hopped down out of the truck, smiling to himself.

The angle of April's shoulders, however, the way her hands rested, palms up on her knees, got his attention. He paused. Something lay there on the porch in front of her. Foster took a few steps closer. And then he saw that it was Vinnie. His throat tightened.

April turned and faced him, her eyes swollen with crying.

"Foster, I'm sorry!" she cried. "I'm really s-sorry!"

He stopped on the path, his heart pounding, chest cold. Then he dropped his lunch pail and broke into a run.

"What happened to her?"

April turned her face toward the wall, eyes squeezed shut. "Thomasine accidentally hit her when she c-come for me." Her nose was clogged, shoulders shook. "Oh, Foster, I'm so sorry."

Foster stared, then sank to a crouch beside Vinnie. The dog lay on her side, legs stiff, eyes half-open, congealed blood in the corners of her mouth. Dirt from an automobile tire was caked in the short black hair below her ribs.

Foster couldn't speak. His own mouth filled with rage, hard and cold against his teeth.

April went on weeping. "*You* know how she's always throwin' herself at cars when they turn in, Foster—right down by the wheels. Thomasine hit her and we both of us looked her over, but she just come up here on the porch and we figured she was all right."

"You left her?" Foster asked incredulously, his voice husky. "You just went off then and left her here?" There were tears behind his own eyes, but anger held them back.

"We didn't think she was hurt! We didn't see any blood. She looked all right to us!" April lurched forward and clutched his arm, anguish pulling at her face. "We were tryin' to make the two-o'clock movie, but I wouldn't *never* have left her if I'd known she was hurt. *I* loved her too!"

Foster swallowed and pulled his arm away. For just a moment he covered his eyes with his hand. Then, jaw clenched, he gently picked up the dog's body without a word to April and rose to his feet. He carried Vinnie across the yard toward the shed, tears stinging his eyes.

It was after Lloyd's funeral, after the fiasco with Ramona Wheeler, in fact, that Foster had first seen Vinnie. The dog had been rooting around the shed, backing off when Foster went out to investigate. He held out his hand to her, and she had come then, all skin and bones—a stray, Foster figured, that folks sometimes brought out on a country road and left. She had come at a time he needed her most and she'd stayed. For seven years she had seen him off every morning, welcomed him home at night. And now, beside the shed, Foster buried her. Each time he put his weight on the shovel, slicing through the frozen ground, a thought reoccurred: April was here, but she wasn't his, and he had lost Vinnie in the bargain.

He did not want to look at April, to talk to her, to have her around him, but anger propelled him back to the porch. She was standing now, leaning against the doorframe, her face still wet, watching him come. When he reached the top step, he paused and said tersely, "Maybe it's a good thing you *didn't* get pregnant, April. If you can't even care for a dog, I sure wouldn't trust you with a baby."

She seemed almost to reel from his words. Her face colored, and for a moment she looked as though she could not catch her breath. Foster felt a rush of regret and tentatively reached out for her, but April pushed him roughly away.

"Don't touch me!" she screamed. "Don't you ever put your

hands on me again, Foster! You never wanted no baby. You just took me in to have sex, see if you could do it." Her pointy chin was thrust out toward him, eyes flashing. "Don't think I don't know about you and Ramona Wheeler!"

Foster startled, but April plunged on, eyes blurred with tears, face screwed up, the veins on her neck standing out. "You just better go look up Ramona, tell her you can do it now, 'cause I don't want you to do it to me. Not ever!"

***

There was no supper in the house that night. April went in and lay down on the bed, still dressed, and Foster sat in a chair in the living room, the TV silent. Once or twice he dozed off, but around four in the morning, awake again, he shaved, made his lunch, and set off for the bridge early.

He did not trust himself to speak to April. Whether he still loved her, *could* love her, was uncertain. He knew from experience that when the hurt had dulled, he would feel more charitable toward her. Perhaps when the fury had played itself out, they could both sit down and talk.

When he reached home that afternoon, however, Vinnie's absence cut him again. For a long while, Foster sat in the truck, hands on the wheel. He would have to say something to April; wouldn't allow himself to go the whole evening without speaking. He ought to apologize for what he had said, he knew, yet there was still anger inside him that craved a target.

He got out and walked toward the house at last. In the kitchen he placed his lunch bucket on the counter and rinsed his thermos. The few dishes he had left in the sink had been washed and put away, and Foster found a measure of reassurance in that.

"April?" he called finally, glancing around and going on back to the bedroom. She wasn't there either, and he was relieved. He didn't feel like talking anyway.

At five-thirty, after he had made chili for dinner and April still hadn't come, the anger bunched up under his skin like a boil. Was she going to walk in late again? Didn't even get home in time to set the plates on the table? She think she could just go

out like this without even telling him where she went or what
time she'd be back?

He walked on into the bedroom, but there was an uneasiness
now that accompanied him, making him swallow, making him
walk over to the closet and open the door.

It hit him like a wave of water in the face, and he staggered
inwardly although his legs remained rigid: April's clothes were
gone. The hangers were askew along her half of the closet, only
a few dust balls on the floor where her shoes had stood.

Whirling around, Foster moved to the dresser and yanked open
a drawer. Empty. He opened the one beneath. That was empty
too, except for a piece of blue ribbon from one of her bras.
And then his eyes fell on a small piece of notebook paper on top
of the dresser, folded so small he had overlooked it completely.
He held it for several seconds before he got up the courage to
read it.

Dear Foster:

   Both of us knowed it wasn't going to work so I have left and
   don't try to come for me. I should have done something else
   except move in with you, I know that now, and it wasn't just
   what happened to Vinnie.

EIGHT

All I did when I got to Dorothy's was sit on the bed and cry.

Dorothy was throwing the stuff from my suitcase into one of her dresser drawers and wasn't too gentle about it, either. She wasn't all that glad to have me.

"For God's sake, April, you were crying when you called this morning and you haven't stopped yet. Max hear you carry on like this, he'll put you right out on the street." She picked up the blue robe with the fur on the sleeves. "Foster give you this? It's *pretty!*" She held it up in front of herself there at the mirror. "Why'd you leave him, April, he give you nice things like this?"

I was bawling again. Whole pile of Kleenex there on the bed beside me. "Just had to," I said.

Dorothy looks over and then she comes and sits down beside me. "April," she says, without a blush of shame, "it wasn't because of sex, was it?"

"No," I said.

She was still looking at me funny and I knew an even worse question was about to fall out of her mouth. "He want to do it different, sometimes? Nothing strange about that. Lots of men like to—"

I clapped my hands over my ears. "Wasn't *sex*, Dorothy!" Knew there was all kinds of things Foster and me hadn't tried, but I didn't want to hear about them.

She just sighed and let her arms dangle down between her knees, turning one foot sideways to admire her new ankle-strap shoes. "Well," she says, "you just wouldn't listen, April. I *told* you not to get yourself tied up with Foster, you only sixteen."

"Seventeen tomorrow," I told her.

"Well, what are you going to do? I don't know why you didn't just go home to Daddy."

"I am *not* goin' there and have everybody looking at me, asking questions," I told her. I blew my nose and wiped one arm across my eyes. "I got an appointment this afternoon at the City Chicken. They had an ad in the paper for a table girl, and I'm supposed to see Mr. George Hollander at three o'clock. If I get that job, I'll just stay here long enough to save up money for a room somewhere. Then I'll go."

Dorothy smiled at me then and her face went soft. "I swear, April Ruth, you've got guts, I'll say that for you. You walked out of Foster's house this morning with nothing in this world but a suitcase, and already you've got plans."

It was the nicest thing Dorothy ever said to me, and my head just soaked up the praise like a washcloth.

"Come on," she said. "You clean yourself up. Wash your hair and put on stockings. I'll drive you over when it's time."

For the rest of the afternoon Dorothy and me was as kind to each other as the Waltons on TV. She took a comb and teased my hair so it would stand out away from my head, and let me wear a dress of hers that come down a little far over the shoulders, but it still looked pretty good. I put on stockings, careful not to snag them, my fingers all rough, then the red suede shoes Dorothy give me, and finally we set off in Dorothy's car to the City Chicken.

It was about two miles down the road on 301, and I still had the want ad in my hand when I walked in, trying hard to keep from breaking my neck in those four-inch heels. Dorothy said she'd be back in an hour and I was glad, because I didn't want her coming along. Soon as I stepped in Mr. Hollander's office, though, he says, "April Bates, huh? Are you one of Earl Bates's daughters?"

I nodded and sat down where he was pointing. But he kept on

looking at me, and then he says, "Excuse me, Miss Bates, but I thought I heard you married Foster Williams last year. Is it Mrs. Williams, then?" I could tell he was looking at the ring I still hadn't figured out what to do with yet.

"I left him," I said. "I'm ready to work now, and I'd like this job, you just give me the chance."

"I see," he says, and sits down on the edge of his desk. "Where are you living?"

"Right down the road," I told him. "Won't be one bit of trouble getting here a'tall." And then I figured he knew I was at Dorothy's, and I wanted to put his worries to rest. "I'm only interested in a job, Mr. Hollander. I swear I haven't got nothing else on my mind, in case you're wondering."

He raised his eyebrows a little in surprise, and then he smiles at me. Seemed like a nice man—taller than Foster, with all his weight going to height. Deep-cut lines on either side of his mouth— looked something like Abraham Lincoln without the beard.

"You ever work as a waitress?" he asked me. I was afraid he'd ask that.

"Mr. Hollander," I said, "I worked a garden all last summer. Weeded, hoed, and carried those vegetables around in a bushel basket. Figure I can carry a tray."

"There's a lot more to it than carrying a tray," he says, but he's still smiling. "Tell you what: we've got a one-week trial period here. If you can't do the job, we let you go, no hard feelings. If you do good work, the job's yours. You want to start tomorrow?"

I could have jumped up and kissed him, but I tried to think what my typing teacher would have done. Keep her ankles together, for one thing; not let 'em lean out at the sides like mine was doing. I straightened up and told him thank you very much, and he give me a form to fill out.

"You'll be working the four-to-midnight shift," he says. "That okay, now?"

"Any time a'tall's fine with me," I tell him.

"Okay, you get yourself here each day, I'll see you get home at night. Irene!" he calls. "Come here and meet April Bates; she's going to start tomorrow."

A woman comes in, looks just like him in the face—sort of washed-out eyes and thick eyebrows—but she was plump in the bust and about the hips. Find out they're brother and sister, run the City Chicken together. At first I didn't think she liked me, way she was frowning, then I see it's my shoes she didn't like.

"You won't be working in *those!*" she laughs. "We furnish the uniforms, but deduct them from your first month's pay. You give me your sizes before you go, and I'll have some clothes here for you tomorrow."

I was happier than a bug in June when I walked out of that office. First thing come to mind was how I was going to tell Foster, and then I remembered. By the time I'd passed the bar and the man who was mopping the floor, I could feel the tears hot behind my eyelids. I stood inside the two sets of doors and watched out the little glass window for Dorothy. Everything's blurred and I'm swallowing one swallow after another to keep the tears back. Didn't want the Hollanders seeing me bawl just after they give me a job. Outside, the sign's blinking on and off like a Christmas tree—CITY in pink, then CHICKEN in purple.

It was about the first time I'd had to myself since I left home that morning, and I tried not to think of Foster, but it was Foster Williams kept coming to mind. I look across the highway at the big clock on the savings and loan. Another half hour and Foster would be heading home down this very road. I wondered what he'd think when he find me gone. Glad and sorry both, I figure. I knew from the way the both of us been acting lately we'd only get worse. I was mean to him as I could be, just seeing how much he'd take, I guess—see if he'd like me even then. But after Vinnie . . .

Keep thinking how much Foster must have loved that dog. Any other time he see me cry like that, my eyes all swoll up, he would've had his arms around me right quick. I wanted to tell him the rest—how all through the movie I got this feeling about Vinnie, how maybe she's not all right after all—and when it's over, I tell Thomasine I got to get home. She lets me out at the end of the drive and I run all the way to the house.

I couldn't believe that Vinnie was dead. Couldn't believe the blood in her mouth—that she'd just gone up there on the porch and died, not even a cut on her body. Guess she was bleeding somewhere on the inside, but it's like Foster and me were hurt on the inside too. What we said to each other, wouldn't neither one of us ever get over it that I could see.

The tears come in spite of the swallowing, and when Dorothy drives up she says, "Son of a bitch, you didn't get the job!"

"Yes I did," I tell her. "I'm crying for Foster now."

"Oh, Christ!" says Dorothy, and now she's sorry she's got me on her hands, all I do is cry.

I get hold of myself then and tell her how I'm on the four-to-midnight shift.

"Now all we've got to do is figure how to tell Max you've moved in," she says. "Don't expect him to jump up and down, April. You going to tell Daddy you've left Foster?"

"No, and don't you either."

"April, he's going to hear! It'll be all over town this time tomorrow if the Hollanders do any talking."

"Well, I don't want him looking for trouble."

"Daddy doesn't even have to go looking," says Dorothy. "Trouble comes and sits in his lap."

Didn't take me long to find out I was about as welcome at Max's apartment as a cat mess behind the sofa.

"Don't have a fit," Dorothy says to Max when he comes in from work, "but April's left her husband and she's got a job at the City Chicken. She's only staying with us till she saves up enough for a room somewhere."

Max looks at me and his expression don't change the slightest bit—cold as a piece of ice—and Dorothy goes on, "She's cried her eyes out all day, Max, so please don't give her a hard time. Okay?" All the while she's talking, she's massaging the back of his neck.

So Max don't say nothing to me at all. Got a face that always looks like there's a shadow on it—dark hair and eyes, little black mustache, and cheekbones that stick out like doorknobs, dark spaces underneath you could almost get lost in. Not one word to me all during supper, which was take-out chicken from the Red Barn and three fried-apple pies. Not saying anything at all to a person is worse than saying the meanest thing on your mind.

About ten o'clock, there's a phone call and my heart travels up my throat and sits there, like maybe it's Foster asking me to come home. It wasn't. Max did the talking, giving directions how to get to his place, and after he hangs up he tells me I've got to go out for a while, company's coming.

"Where am I supposed to go at ten o'clock at night?" I ask him.

"That's your problem," says Max. "Go to a movie or something. But don't come back till midnight."

I put on my coat, cross 301 to the bowling alley, and sit back there by the Coke machine till they close.

"Thought I told you not to come back till midnight," Max says when I reach the apartment.

"Just so happened the bowling alley's closed and I was outside freezing myself to death," I tell him. He goes back to the TV. The bedroom door's shut and I hear somebody moving around in there. I sit down on the couch, and after a while here comes a man about as fat as a barrel, zipping up his jacket, his shirt tail hanging out in back. He don't even look at Max, just leaves the apartment, and then Dorothy walks out of the bedroom wearing the blue robe Foster gave me with the white fur at the sleeves.

I felt all hollow inside. Wasn't one thing I could say. I was eating their food, sleeping on their couch, no way in the world I could ask Dorothy what she was doing wearing my robe. Dorothy goes out to the kitchen.

"I'm going to make some cinnamon toast, April," she says. "You ought to taste it with the sugar on both sides. Want some?"

I sit down at the table. Dorothy's hair's all mussed up and she smells of sex. She got this big hickey on one side of her neck, and I try to imagine what it's like having a man on top of you so fat it's like he's rolling, and all the while Max sitting in the next room listening.

"Well, I guess I'll go to bed now," I said when I finished my toast. "You don't care, do you?"

Sure they cared. I was lying there on the sofa under a blanket and they had to sit on the kitchen chairs to watch TV, and after they turned if off, I could hear them arguing in the bedroom.

My bawling started all over again, but I did it quiet. Down

deep where I never suspected, I guess I hoped Foster would have come after me, even though I told him not to. And all the while I was telling myself it wouldn't have made no difference, I could see myself climbing back in his truck.

Guess I had to live with a man before I found out how much I didn't know about him. Longer I lived with Foster, the more mysterious he got. Never understood why he wanted to marry up with me in the first place, and then the way I got moody and everything, why'd he put up with me at all? Why did he buy me that bathing suit showing me naked at the sides if he wanted to keep me? And why did he put all that work in a garden, most of which we never ate? Look at Foster sometimes and think he's a whole book I never read.

He probably feel the same way about me. Here I am wanting a baby, thinking how if I got pregnant, me and that child going to grow up together. I wasn't ready for it, and Foster knew it, but I went on wanting babies just the same.

Only other boy ever appealed to me was Buddy Travis. Once he was kissing me in his car, putting his hands up under my sweater. Wasn't much under there to interest him, probably why he didn't ask me out after that. Just never felt comfortable with boys. Never felt comfortable around Thomasine and Dorothy, neither, come to think of it. If I was to pick one time and one place I felt the best I'd have to say it was sitting under that pole-bean trellis last summer with Vinnie.

The tears really come pouring out now—slide down the sides of my face and into my ears. Back at Foster's whenever I'd cry, Vinnie would come right over and prop her head on my thigh, look at me all mournful. Sometimes she'd cry too—a whine at the back of her throat. Moment I'd stop, though, and stand up, Vinnie would dance around, her toenails clicking on the floor, like now that she'd cheered me up, what were we going to do next? Wondered who I was bawling for most—Foster or Vinnie.

Made my own breakfast the next morning. Dorothy and Max sure didn't keep around much to eat. Found some bread, some syrup, a jar of mustard, few cans of soup, and a half gallon of mint chocolate chip ice cream. Fixed me some toast and then ate some ice cream to celebrate my birthday. Hope Foster wouldn't remember about my birthday. Only make him feel worse, if he was feeling bad at all.

Max got up and drove to his job at Hotpoint, but Dorothy goes on sleeping. So at three o'clock I put on my coat and walk the two miles to the City Chicken. Wanted to be there on time. Cheeks and hands were as red as raw meat when I walked in.

"Good heavens!" says Irene Hollander. "Haven't you got any gloves?"

She had my uniform waiting—it was black nylon with short sleeves, two red aprons, and white nurse's shoes with soles one inch thick. I put those on and it's like I'm walking on marshmallows.

There were three of us on the four-to-midnight shift—me and a big-fannied, red-haired woman around thirty named Pearl and a scrawny little waitress, somebody's grandmother, by the name of Loretta. It was Loretta put in charge of me, going to show me the ropes. I liked her right off.

"You look real nice, April," she tells me when I come out of the rest room in my uniform nice and tight over the front which shows I got breasts. "You've got to remember to wash that every night, now. Nylon smells under the arms, you know. Don't want to reach across a customer to collect his dishes and him smelling your armpits."

First couple hours all I did was go along with Loretta to the tables and see how she made small talk, make the customers feel comfortable. Listened how she took the orders and told 'em what was good on the menu, then followed her out to the kitchen to see how she turned over the orders to Chub. First time I see her load a tray, though, I go weak in the knees. She puts all the plates on first, then she puts a platter of barbecued chicken on top the plates, and all up and down one arm she's got three different orders of onion rings.

"Loretta, I can't never learn to do that," I tell her. "First time I try lifting that over a customer's head, it'd be in his lap."

She takes me aside and says, "One thing you got to remember, April: You ever spill a tray, you go down with it."

"What?" I ask her.

"Right on the floor," she says. "The minute you feel that tray start to slide, you just let your legs go."

I stared. "Why?"

"Look. Let's say you bump into this man and you spill a platter of gravy over his shoulder, him wearing a good suit. First thing he's going to do is call you a name you won't repeat. Right? Stand up and make a scene. But if you're down on the floor, first thing that customer's going to do is ask if you're okay. Nobody's going to make a scene over a suit when a woman's half-dead on the floor."

We laughed then, and I said I'd remember. Customers liked Loretta, I could tell. She knew what they needed even before they did. Baby in a high chair can't even fuss before Loretta's got a cracker in his fist. Old people, they come in and Loretta seats 'em far away from the door, they won't get a draft.

"I want Loretta's table," some folks said the minute they walked in. Made Pearl mad sometimes—she'd be standing around with no customers while Loretta's got all the tables she could handle.

Business slacked off about eight, and we had a chance to eat a little, but around nine-thirty folks were coming in from the movies or bowling, and they'd play country songs on the jukebox, have a drink at the bar. Some of 'em even ordered a complete dinner.

By eleven that night, I still wasn't carrying onion rings on my arms, but I was moving a bit faster with the trays, weaving in and out among the tables, watching out for Pearl's behind every time she bent over. So tired by midnight, though, I could hardly crawl. Too tired to eat. Too tired to think about Foster, of which I was glad. We didn't get things cleaned up till about twelve-thirty, and Mr. Hollander drove me home.

"Loretta says you did okay," he tells me. "I'll say this for you, April, you hang in there. If you sat down even once, I didn't see it."

When I walked in the door, Dorothy yells, "Happy birthday, April." She's over at the table, already cut a piece of store-bought cake with green roses on top. Max is smoking on the couch, don't even look up.

I sit down at the table.

"Swear I'm too tired to even chew," I say to Dorothy.

"Could at least appreciate the fact I spent six dollars on this cake I'll have to eat myself," she says.

"I'll have me a big piece for breakfast," I tell her.

Went in the bathroom and washed out my uniform, then curled up at the other end of the sofa from Max. Drew my feet up so's I wouldn't bother him. Last thing I remember thinking is how tired I am.

Second night, Buddy Travis come in the restaurant with his friends, and when he sees me, he stops stone-still. Then he makes his way through the tables, his eyes smiling.

"April, what are you doing here? Foster got you out working, huh?"

"I'm not livin' with Foster anymore," I tell him, and fill four glasses with ice.

Buddy looks serious for a minute, then smiles even broader. "Where you staying?"

I fill the glasses with water and set 'em on a tray. "Living with Dorothy till I can get a room of my own," I say. "You better move along, Buddy, 'cause Mr. Hollander's watching."

He goes back to the pinball machines, but after I take the orders at table six, he's back again, standing just inside the hallway to the rest rooms where Hollander can't see. I'm making up four salads, pretending he's not even there.

"Need a ride home?" he asks me.

"Got one."

"Another night, maybe?"

"Maybe," I tell him.

When I come home, Dorothy's out. Visiting, Max says. I know that some man's paying for Dorothy to come to his place, that's all. I wash out my uniform and stockings, hang them on the shower rod, and take a long soak in the tub, water dripping down, splashing on my face. One-thirty and Dorothy's still not home. She's got my robe with her and I won't go around in my gown, Max there, so I put on my jeans and a sweater and go out to the couch to read a magazine. Only ones they've got are about racing cars or movie people. I'm reading about how many women Warren Beatty has made love to and suddenly I realize Max isn't reading anymore, he's looking over at me. I sort of tug at my sweater in case something's showing that shouldn't. He keeps on looking, though, and I can feel my neck is getting pink. Finally I just can't stand it anymore.

"Max," I says, "would you kindly take your eyes off me? Gives me the creeps."

He lifts one foot real slow and sets it on the coffee table and keeps right on looking. "How much you make tonight in tips?" he asks.

"Haven't counted yet."

"How much yesterday?"

"About fifteen dollars, maybe."

Max reaches into his shirt pocket and takes out a cigarette. Pulls out a lighter and lights it up and all the while he doesn't take his eyes off me once. "You know how much Dorothy's making tonight?"

I put my face back in the magazine. "Don't care one bit what she's making."

Out of the corner of my eye I can see him start to smile. "She makes more in twenty minutes you can make all night running your legs off."

"Rather be on my feet than on my back," I tell him.

A cloud of smoke comes rolling in my direction. "Pretty face," he says. "Nice bod. You'd bring in twice what Dorothy can do."

"I appreciate the compliment, but I'm not interested," I say, making my voice as cold as it can get. Still not as cold as his.

"You work for me, you can keep half," he says.

This time I turn and stare him right in the face. "Huh! And what do *you* do, I'd like to know? Dorothy out there, could get herself killed, and you getting half."

"You're a little bitch, you know it?" he says.

Something about Max's eyes stops me dead. He wasn't smiling anymore.

"Bitch," he says again, and no one in all the world could say that word with as much hate and malice in it as Max. "Think you can get a free ride, don't you?" He leans forward and mashes the cigarette right on top the coffee table, don't even use the ashtray. "Well, you thought wrong. Long as you stay here you turn your tips over to me, starting today. You want to work for me on the side, that's a different story."

I put down my magazine and go over to my purse. Reach down in the corner where I'd stuffed all today's tip money and pull it out—dollar bills, quarters, nickels—and dump them all in Max's lap. He counts it out. "Twelve seventy-five," he says. "You said fifteen."

"I said fifteen was what I made the first night, Max. Don't make the same every night."

"You give me fifteen," he says.

I went back and got three dollars from my wallet and give it to him just as Dorothy comes in. She sees me handing money to Max and her face goes purple.

"What the hell is going on?" she says, and turns on me. "You little whore! I step out the door for one minute and you're taking my place!"

"Dorothy," I tell her, "I haven't the energy or the inclination to mess with Max. He wants my tip money for rent, he's got it."

So Dorothy turns on him. "What'd you take her tips for, you bastard? She's *never* going to get out of here if you take her money."

Max moved so fast my tips went spilling all over the rug. Like some big dog he springs up off the couch and whacks her one side of the head. I'm backed up against the wall, scared to move.

Dorothy drops her purse and starts whimpering, holding her head, and Max sits back down.

"One more word," he says. "One more word and you get it again."

I didn't know what to say. Figure Dorothy must have been brain-damaged, because the next minute she's down on the couch beside him, asking will he forgive her, she's so sorry she's so jealous, that all the while she's out working all she's thinking about is him, and someday they're going to have enough money to go to Hawaii, just like Max promised.

I didn't sleep much at all that night. Too scared. Never saw a man get mad so quick or settle down so soon afterwards. Wasn't natural. If Foster had drove up right that minute, I wondered if I would have gone home with him. Maybe I would.

But he didn't. Next day I waited till Max got up and went out and then, while Dorothy's still sleeping, I take all my clothes out of their closet and all my underwear out of her drawer, and put 'em in the suitcase Foster give me. All but the blue robe, which Dorothy's got on. Then I set out along 301, the suitcase banging against one leg, looking for that hotel I passed each afternoon on my way to the City Chicken.

The entrance was off on a side street, but you could see the little sign from 301. ADAMS HOTEL, it says. ROOMS DAILY, WEEKLY, MONTHLY. Was a Maytag store behind.

I walked inside. There wasn't much of a lobby to speak of, just an old sofa along one wall, then the desk and, behind it, the stairs going up to the two floors above. Place smelled old. Man behind the counter's old too.

"How much is a room a week?" I ask him.

Name on an old yellowed sign says he's Mr. Cody. He's got liver spots all over his head, and when he talks the spit gathers on his lips in a sort of foam. He says it depends on whether I want a kitchenette or just a bedroom, and it's cheaper by the month. I ask can I pay him a deposit and the rest at the end of the week. He says the only way is to leave a deposit and something of value, so I give him what's left of my tip money from the first day and my wedding ring, and he gives me a key to 207, cheapest room he's got.

Had two windows, both of 'em facing an alley. Nothing to see outside but a brick wall. Had to bend down and twist your neck to see the sky, even. But it was okay. Single bed was covered with a pink chenille spread looks like Thomasine's old bathrobe. Red and yellow flowered drapes, a vinyl chair, a dresser, a closet, and a little table with a hand-lettered sign that says:

Coffee makers permitted
NO hot plates
NO electric irons

Only thing was I didn't drink coffee.

There's this television set but you had to put a quarter in to turn it on. Behind a curtain there's a little cubbyhole with a toilet and sink, but no bathtub. You want a bath, Mr. Cody told me, there's a public bathroom down the hall.

I hang my clothes in the closet, put my underwear in the dresser, and set the fuzzy pink monkey Buddy Travis give me on top of my dresser. Then I sit down in the vinyl chair and look around.

It wasn't much, but it was the first time in my life I was on my own. Had me my own job and my own place. Didn't have to depend on Daddy or Foster or Max.

I prop one foot up on the dresser and then the other foot on top of that—pretend I had a cigarette in my hand, blowing smoke up at the ceiling like Thomasine. Then I laugh. Hardest part's over, I tell myself, all the while not believing one single word of it.

NINE

Foster lowered himself down onto the bed, staring at April's note. He felt as though a noise were rising in his chest, swelling his lungs, gathering force as it rushed up his throat. But when it reached his lips, nothing came out. Nothing at all.

His first impulse was to leap in the truck and find her. The second was to let her go.

"Now just get hold of yourself and think this out," he said aloud finally, when he could speak. "No use both of us acting like fools."

She had not, he realized, left her ring. He scanned the dresser again to make sure. April had taken everything he'd ever bought her—the suitcase, the bathing suit, the robe, the gown. . . . He knew for a fact that she did not take them out of greed. If she hated him, she would have left them behind. The one thing Foster knew for certain, then, was that April did not hate him.

There were only two places she could have gone—back to the trailer or to Dorothy's. She had no money of her own to speak of. Other than a ten-dollar bill Foster handed her occasionally in the drugstore, he never gave her any. She never asked. They were too far away from the shops for April to get there on her own, and when they needed something they went together.

He strode rapidly down the hall to the kitchen and stared out the window, shoulders tense, hands thrust woodenly in his pockets, then went back to the bedroom again. *Don't try to come for me,* the note said. Okay, he wouldn't. One night back in the trailer or over at Dorothy's and she'd be ready to come home soon enough. Give her a little taste of what it was like back with a drunken daddy if she thinks she's so put upon here.

The phone rang loudly in the kitchen, echoing along the empty hall. Foster smiled wryly to himself and let it ring twice more before he answered. Maybe it didn't take April even a whole night to change her mind.

It was Thomasine.

"April there?" she asked.

The question seemed to collide with the answer that had formed so carefully on the tip of his tongue. Was she playing with him?

"No," Foster said. "She's out."

"Well, when she gets home, you tell her Drug Fair's having a sale on that shampoo I was tellin' her about. Supposed to be good for hair what's been mangled, cut, and messed with." Thomasine's voice put its own exclamation point at the end, like the bang of a hammer.

"I'll tell her," Foster replied coldly.

"Seventy-nine cents a bottle," said Thomasine, and hung up.

Slowly Foster moved over to the stove and dipped up a bowl of chili. Then he sat down at the table and looked at it. So she wasn't with Thomasine. The anger dissipated somewhat and a trace of worry moved in.

It would have been embarrassing for April, of course—going back home to her father; everyone would know, but at least she would be safe. At least she would be at the other end of a telephone number that Foster could reach. He did not know Dorothy's number or the last name of the man she was living with. The only way to reach April there was to drive into Medbury and ask around, and any man asking where he could find Dorothy Bates had only one thing on his mind.

At seven, Foster was still sitting at the table and the bowl of chili was only half-eaten. Now it was the last line of the note that bothered him. If it wasn't just because of what had happened to Vinnie, it meant that there was an accumulation of problems, and while he knew that this was true, it bothered him that April thought so. Now he was getting closer to the source of the pain, as if searching out the bullet in a wound. How had he expected, really, to keep her—a young girl like that? At the same time, Vinnie's absence fueled his anger and he thought that maybe, when all was said and done, it was better that April had left; it would keep a bigger quarrel from happening later on.

He even wondered, sitting there at the table alone, his eyes on Vinnie's supper dish against the wall, whether it was Vinnie he missed the most. Missed the way she came skittering down off the porch when she heard his truck and lunged lopsided across the yard to greet him. Missed the way she followed him on into the bedroom while he changed his clothes and waited outside the door when he showered.

Foster regretted that he had not taken her hunting one last time. She wasn't a Redbone or a Walker, but she was a good hard tree dog nonetheless. Didn't squall the way Clyde's dog did—didn't boohoo on a tree where a coon was trapped. Foster could tell from her racket whether she was following a fresh track or an old one; whether she was running, swimming, or was down in a hole. The memory of Vinnie was achingly sweet, and anger toward April throbbed once more in his chest.

"Well," he said, getting to his feet, "I'm not going to go after her begging. She decides to come back, she can get herself home the same way she took off."

He decided not to shower, however, just in case the phone should ring—just in case it was April wanting him to come after her. He would, he supposed, but he wouldn't be too quick about it. And he'd have plenty to say when he got there.

Foster put the dishes away and sat down with the paper. Headlines about Watergate danced before his eyes. There were problems everywhere, and Foster's was insignificant in comparison, he knew, but all he could think about was what it would be like to go to bed without April.

He woke about two, certain that she was there—sure he had heard her breathing. Somehow she must have slipped back during the night and crawled in beside him. Tentatively he reached out to explore her space. The bed was cold and empty. He rolled over on his back, arms folded across his forehead, an ache in the pit of his stomach that wouldn't go away.

For the first time he thought about the possibility that April was hitchhiking. He imagined her walking along the tarred road with her suitcase, pointy chin thrust out. Just like her, too. Then he imagined her reaching 301, tired, and the truckers who would be only too happy to pick her up. She could be anywhere right now. Raped in Raleigh. Dead in Savannah. His back bathed in perspiration, Foster threw off the blankets, pulled on his trousers and an old sweatshirt, and went out to the kitchen to make coffee. Then he took the cup and sat down in front of the TV, muting the sound, wanting the company of people without their intrusions into his head. Figures moved about on the screen with their mouths opening and closing like goldfish. Foster was struck by the seeming helplessness of people who could make no noise.

Having considered rape and murder, he was left with the bedrock fear that accompanied the first sentence of her note: *Both of us knowed that it wasn't going to work. . . .*

Had she known it before Foster permitted it into consciousness, even? At the ocean, maybe? At Christmas, when she wore her new robe? Anger closed in once more, and he felt better. Anger he could deal with. At the same time he knew that all she had to do was walk in that door and he'd give her as many chances as she'd need.

He was cautious the next day as he approached the bridge, bracing himself for the men's questions, for the humiliation he would feel if they discovered he didn't know where April had gone. When he reached the landing, however, he could tell from their banter that no one had heard, nobody knew. Not yet. Foster rode silently out to the tower.

Standing in a gridwork of steel beams that stuck out in all directions like giant Tinkertoys, the raising gang lowered cables to pick up sections from the barge below. The pneumatic wrench of a workman above them drowned out all conversation, and when the rat-a-tat-tat ceased, there was nothing left but the whistle of wind. Foster preferred the noise of the wrench and was grateful when it began again. He did not want his silence to be noticed.

Halfway through the afternoon, he laid his eight-pound sledge on the beam, and the cuff of his jacket spun it around as he reached in his bag for a bull pin. Juju, working a few feet away, steadied the hammer before it could plunge off onto the men below.

"*Watch* yourself, Foster!" he chided, frowning, a questioning look in his eyes.

Foster, straddling the beam, cussed himself under his breath and set his mind once more on his work.

At quitting time, he fought against the growing hope that April would be there when he reached home. She won't have come, he told himself, yet at the same time he was thinking of what he would say when he walked in and found her. He tried to imagine his father in the same predicament. Tall, big-boned, and silent, his father, Foster decided, would say nothing at all. Perhaps "Well, you're back, then . . ." and let it ride. Let the feelings go underground again, and he would be cautious ever after not to spade too deeply lest the problem be unearthed once more. No, Foster decided, he would let April know he was glad to have her back, but after supper they would talk.

When he turned into the winding dirt lane, he passed Russell walking down to pick up his mail. He gave the usual wave of his hand, and Russell, in turn, the cursory nod that, had it been a half-inch less in either direction, would have been no nod at all. Not a word was exchanged between them, both Williamses to the last.

April, of course, was not there.

It wasn't until Foster picked up the paper after dinner that the date seemed to jump out at him, and fill up the page. January 10. Her birthday. It struck so quickly that when his eyes misted over it took Foster a moment to realize that there were tears. April was seventeen, and he didn't even know where she was. He tilted his head back, but the tears leaked down one side of his face.

"*Damn,*" he said, and wiped his eyes on his shirt.

Thursday was the same, but Foster had made up his mind: If he heard nothing more by Friday, received no tips, got no news, he would drive into Medbury and look up Dorothy. Just to be sure that April was all right—nothing more.

Friday evening, he drove the pickup into a Texaco station.

"Looking for Dorothy Bates," he told the attendant. "Anyone here know where she lives?"

"I'll ask." The young man went into the garage. "Anyone know where Dorothy Bates lives?" he yelled above the din of the air ratchet.

The noise cut off.

"Dorothy Bates?" The mechanic smiled. "Hey, Smitty, somebody wants to know Dottie's address."

A second man stepped up out of the grease pit, wiping his hands on a rag. "Looking for Dorothy, huh?" He sauntered, grinning, over to Foster's window. "Well, now, you go back up 301 to the second light. Row of shops there on the right. You'll see a stairway between the paint store and the pet shop on one side. It's the door at the top of the stairs."

As Foster drove off, the man called after him. "Tell her hello from Smitty," and the other men broke into loud laughter.

Foster tried not to think about what he would say to April when he found her for fear it would sound stilted, rehearsed. For once in his life he would let the words come naturally, whatever it was he felt when he saw her; for once he would trust himself.

He turned in at the shops and parked. The concrete stairs at the side of the building had rust stains where water had leaked down from the metal flashing on the roof. A wad of pink gum, brittle with age, still clung to the brick wall halfway up. Foster's pulse quickened when he reached the top, and he listened for the sound of April's voice. It was dark in the entryway, and there was music coming from behind the door. He knocked—cautiously, at first—then more deliberately.

"Hold your horses!" came Dorothy's voice.

The door flew open and she stood there in a long blue robe, a little too snug over the shoulders and bust, with white fur around the cuffs. Something tightened in Foster's chest.

"Well, look who finally showed up," Dorothy said, stepping aside for him to enter, but Foster remained rooted to the mat. A well-rounded knee showed where the robe did not quite come together. "Wondered when you'd get here."

"Where's April?"

"You're too late."

"I just want to talk to her is all. She don't have to go back home with me if she don't want to."

"She's not here, Foster." Dorothy's voice softened.

"Where is she?"

"You find out, you tell me," Dorothy said. "When I got up this afternoon, she was gone. Took her suitcase with her. No note, nothing. After all we did for her, too. Gave her a place to sleep, fed her. . . ."

He was up against a question mark once more, and Foster had not come prepared for that. He let out his breath and leaned one shoulder against the doorframe. The blue robe had pulled open a little over Dorothy's breasts but she made no effort to close it. A man loomed up in the background.

"You suppose she went home to the trailer?" Foster asked.

Dorothy shook her head. "Told me she'd never go back again to Daddy. I don't know where she's staying, but she's got a job at the City Chicken—four-to-midnight shift."

"April's working?"

"She just said so, didn't she?" Max stepped forward, tamping a cigarette on the back of one hand, then sticking it between his lips.

Foster studied him. "Why'd she leave here, you're so good to her?"

"Max don't know any more than I do," Dorothy chirped.

"I'm askin' Max," Foster said. "You touch that girl?"

Max drew a long breath on his cigarette, looking past Foster's shoulder. "Not my type," he said.

"Oh, for God's sake, Foster, she's not hurt," Dorothy said. "You want to see her so bad, go look her up."

Foster clattered down the stairs, got in the pickup, and drove the two miles to the restaurant. So April was there. He had an address.

The parking lot filled early on Friday evenings. The pickup scrunched across the gravel and skidded to a stop. Foster got out and walked toward the entrance, the hickory smoke of the charcoal grill thick in his nostrils. Once inside the first set of doors, however, caught in the lusty whine of the country singer's lament, he paused. He had wanted to know if April was all right and had been assured that she was. So what was he doing here? If she wanted to be found, she would have come back, wouldn't she? If he could just see her face, he thought, see how she looked at him, he'd know whether it was all over between them or only a temporary setback, April trying her wings. Did he *want* her back? he asked himself. He postponed the answer.

Opening the inner door, Foster stepped inside. Most of the tables were full. A space had been cleared in the center of the large dining room, and a few couples were dancing. A woman in a long purple dress with puffy sleeves was holding the microphone as if it were some little animal she was breathing life into, and she swayed from side to side, her eyes half-closed. Two guitarists nodded their heads along with the beat. Foster sat down at the bar.

"Schlitz," he said. Then he leaned his elbows on the counter and watched the dancers. A heavyset waitress appeared with a coffeepot and filled the cups at a corner table. Foster waited, his eyes on the swinging doors to the kitchen.

> . . . and darlin', I tell you,
> it just . . . isn't right,
> My bed seems . . . so empty,
> without you . . . tonight.

A black nylon uniform passed behind Foster and he jerked his head suddenly as a waitress came from the small room on the left, carrying a tray full of dishes. It wasn't April. She was a woman of fifty in support stockings with thin, muscular arms that held the tray aloft. Gliding effortlessly through the tables, she disappeared through the swinging doors.

The song ended and the people at the tables clapped.

" 'Rosie'!" called out one of the men at the bar.

The singer smiled and fondled the microphone again. Her voice was husky. "Just had a request for 'Rosie,' " she said. "I love it, honey. That's one of my favorites, too."

The man grinned gratefully as the guitarists started the introduction.

And then, at the far end of the room, Foster saw her. She had come around the corner from the service area near the back. Foster's eyes took in the uniform, the red apron, the white shoes—watching her every move. April was picking up clean silver and setting it on a tray. Then clean napkins, a cloth. . . .

Someone was walking over from the pinball machines, a young man, possibly a year or so older than April. Foster's eyes took him in as well. He wondered why the boy didn't go on by; there was room. Then he realized that the customer was talking to April, making it appear he was only passing. All the while he was talking, April kept her head down, her hands busy on the tray, but Foster could see the smile. She left the tray and went to fill the water glasses, then returned. The boy was still there, still smiling, still talking, looking furtively around as though they might be observed.

Get your ass out of there before she loses her job, Foster found himself thinking. As if on cue, the young man looked up at the clock and turned to leave. He said something else, starting back toward the pinball machines, but this time, when he moved around her, rested his hands lightly on her waist, the way a person might pass another on a train.

Foster's arms felt numb. He looked down at his own hand there on the bar. It seemed far too large, too scarred, too old. There was dirt beneath his nails. An ugly, brutish hand that had never had the sophistication to rest lightly on a girl's waist in passing.

He stood up suddenly, pushed his way through the two sets of doors, and strode quickly across the gravel toward the pickup. Once there, he felt he had no breath. He squatted down beside the truck, his jeans tight across his large thighs, and rested his forehead in one hand. It was as though his knees had given way.

Old man, Juju called him there on the bridge. He and April

Ruth were now both a year older, but April had tried living with him and ended up here at the City Chicken with friends. Foster had tried living with her and was right back where he started.

All Saturday, Foster worked determinedly about the house, reluctant to stop for a minute. His mind, however, ignored the jobs at hand and fastened itself on April. One minute Foster was ready to leap in the truck and go see her regardless, and the next he told himself that they'd simply go at it again. Painful as it was, better to have it over and done with than drag it out any longer.

Whenever the question entered his head as to where April Ruth was staying nights, Foster drove it angrily away, knowing that if he gave it space, it would fill his head. The visions were already there, waiting for permission to play themselves out— April Ruth on her back, her skinny legs wrapped around a boy's buttocks . . . April's breasts, her thighs. . . . Foster attacked the brush pile outside with a hatchet, chopping dead branches into smaller and smaller pieces, kicking at the chips and sending them flying.

By Monday, at the landing, the men had heard. Foster could tell by the way their voices stopped when he appeared on the path, then started in again, more loudly. He could feel Juju's eyes on him there in the change shack, see Clyde glance furtively in his direction, then look away—noticed how Jack Tulley and some of the others avoided looking at him at all. They knew.

Once they were in the boat, Jack said right off, "Foster, we heard about April. We're sorry."

Foster nodded curtly and stared stonily out over the water, hoping that Jack had summed it up for all of them.

Clyde, however, couldn't resist. "Well," he said, "we give her six months and she lasted ten, so *we* wasn't right about her neither."

Juju, this time, said nothing. Foster, catching his glance, saw pity in his eyes, and Foster could not tolerate being pitied. He swung himself up off the seat and was the first one out of the boat when they reached the barge.

The cold was penetrating there on the water and seeped through Foster's clothes no matter how many layers he wore. He found himself longing for spring, when—if the weather was good—the men sometimes put in ten hours. He wanted as much time as possible on the bridge; the less at home, the better.

The raising gang was working toward the day that the center span would arrive. In another two months, its 540-foot length would be floated into place, connecting the bridge in the middle. The construction site was like a small city in the bay. Foster's world was bordered on the left by a derrick that bobbed up and down on the connecting beams of two coal barges, on his right by the first Bay Bridge, from above by the Sikorsky chopper that carried the concrete or moved a derrick, and by the water below. During peak periods there were a thousand men employed on the bridge, and more than seventy-five barges anchored at the site. The men, however, worked in close-knit groups. Those that stayed with the same company year after year developed their own in-jokes, and some even chewed the same tobacco as their pusher. They were a special breed, and if a man did not feel particularly useful back on shore, he had only to don his safety helmet and life jacket to know that he worked on a job few others even dared to attempt.

It was uncertain work, however. Water on the bay could change almost instantly from calm to six-foot waves. When a northeaster came slashing in off the ocean, a dozen cumbersome pieces of floating equipment had to be tugged into harbor through a violent sea. Hundreds of men had to be snatched up from trestles and towers and catwalks, dropping down onto bobbing decks from rope ladders that whipped in the wind. Caught in the fury of a storm at sea, an ironworker could ignore, temporarily at least, the turmoil in himself.

It had been cold but calm when Foster went to work that morning, but by early afternoon the wind gusted to thirty miles an hour. Three years before, a storm had overturned a barge bearing a pile driver. The year after that, high winds knocked the boom off one of the huge floating derricks. Tulley ordered the men down.

"Damn it," Foster exploded, "we've been up in worse than this!"

"Foster, get your ass off here," Jack said.

"We can finish this plate!" Foster argued loudly.

Jack did not answer, simply turned to the signalman and motioned the steel back down. Sullenly Foster climbed down after the others, dreading the free time he would have to think.

They sat in the crew shack at the base of the tower, waiting for the boat.

"When's opening day?" Tulley asked the deck foreman.

The foreman grunted and lit his pipe. "Nobody's pinned it down yet. Governor wants it by the Fourth of July. I said, tell the governor we'll make him a deal; he holds off the rain and snow, we'll have it done by Memorial Day."

The men laughed.

"And may be he could do a little something about the wind while he's at it," said Juju.

"You make up your mind yet about that bridge going up in Baltimore?" Jack asked Foster, setting one booted foot on the oil-burning stove.

"I'll put in for it if the rest of you are going," Foster said. "Won't be that much further to drive in the mornings."

"Good," Clyde told him. "Wouldn't want no other partner."

They stopped at the Sandy Point Bar on their way back to Route 50. For a few minutes the four of them sat hunched over a small table in one corner, relaxing in the warmth of the room. Then Jack brought the subject up once again: "You know, Foster, you've got a clear-cut case of desertion. All you have to do is wait a year and file for divorce."

"Could get it sooner if the charge was adultery," Clyde put in. "Don't take much imagination to figure out what April's doing at the Adams Hotel."

Foster lifted his head, his brain spinning. "The Adams Hotel? Where'd you hear that?"

Clyde stared back. "You mean you didn't know where she was? Sue and I went to the City Chicken Saturday night and saw her there, and Sue gets it out of her where she's staying. I was in the Adams couple years ago, and it's a fleabag of a place, I ever saw one."

Juju tried for a joke. "And what *you* doin' inside it, Clyde, it's such a fleabag?"

"Now *that* ain't any of your damn business." Clyde grinned.

Foster stared down at the table, turning his beer around and around in his large hands. The men shifted uneasily in their chairs.

"Maybe you don't *want* to divorce her," Jack suggested. "Didn't mean to push it on you, Foster."

"I don't push easy," Foster replied, and turned the talk to other things.

All the way home, the Adams Hotel floated before his eyes, first one place, then another. He thought he had seen it near the Edelen warehouse on 301 going south. Then he seemed to see it on the other side of the highway a mile from the City Chicken. Or perhaps it was that basement hotel down below the pool parlor.

He drove twice through Medbury before he saw the sign. Then he drove by the hotel itself and parked a block away. A bald man with age spots on his scalp looked up from his ledger.

"You got an April Williams registered here?" Foster asked.

Old Mr. Cody studied him, wiping the saliva from his lips. "Nope."

It took Foster by surprise. "You're sure?"

"Got a April Bates in 207 but no Williams."

Foster rested his palms on the desk, supporting his weight. April had chucked his name so quickly, then.

"She had many visitors?"

"Who's asking?"

"Her husband."

"Oh." Mr. Cody took off his glasses, looked at Foster, then paused to wipe them with his handkerchief. "Well, now. . . ."

"I don't want to bother her," Foster said. "Just want to be sure she's all right."

"Saw her not more'n an hour ago on her way to work, and she looked healthy enough to me," said Mr. Cody. "Don't know if she's had any visitors or not. Leastways I haven't seen any."

Foster hesitated. "She have enough money to pay for her room?"

"Well, now, the fact of the matter is she don't." Mr. Cody turned back a page in his book and ran his finger down the columns. "Paid me a deposit of twelve dollars and left her ring."

"Left her ring?"

"Only till she can pay the rent. It's the rule. Something of value."

"How much she owe you?"

Mr. Cody told him. Foster pulled several bills from his pocket and asked for a receipt. "She's paid up now," he said. "And you see she gets her ring back."

"I most surely will," the man said.

Driving the rest of the way home, Foster wondered whether he should have left a note for April, should have left his number with Mr. Cody, in case April were in trouble. Did he *want* her back? The question rolled over and over in his head. He missed her in bed beside him, across from him at the table, sitting next to him in the pickup. . . . Did he need her aggravation? No, but he missed that too. He gave up trying to explain it, even to himself. Beneath all the wanting, however, the words they had had between them hardened like a rock in the pit of his stomach. He had hurt her, he knew, and she had struck back with a ferocity that caught him off guard. Thomasine might have said those words to him, possibly even Dorothy, but he had never expected it of April. The anger returned. Then the remorse. He thought of Vinnie, and the anger came again—a roller coaster, all the way home.

When he got there, he found aggravation of a different sort. Earl Bates was waiting for him, sitting in the front seat of his old Buick, the motor running for warmth. He got out when the pickup pulled in beside him.

"Foster Williams, you and me are going to have us a talk," he said. He was sober, for once.

Foster stepped down. "Come on in," he said, and held the door for him.

Foster motioned toward the couch. "Want some coffee?"

"Got anything stronger?"

"No," Foster lied.

"Don't want no coffee," Earl said, and sat down, resting one foot on the other knee. He wore no socks, and his thin ankle looked like a dry white bone that had been left in the sun to bleach. "I hear my little girl up and left you."

"Looks that way," Foster replied, without emotion.

"What you do to April, that's what I want to know." Earl scratched at his ankle, then closed his fingers around it as if for warmth.

"Seems like we both want an answer to that," Foster told him.

"You'd best talk to April."

"You mistreat my daughter?"

"I never laid a hand on her in anger. Ask her yourself."

Earl sat silently, moving his gums. His shaggy gray hair hung down around his eyes, and with his free hand he kept pushing it back off his forehead. The purple veins in his nose seemed to darken, then lighten, with each breath that he took. "Well, I want her back," he said finally.

Foster studied him. "That's between you and April."

"Now see here, Foster." Earl put both feet on the floor and leaned foward, his eyes narrowing. "That girl's still a minor and she ought to be home where I can look after her."

"That is sure some joke," Foster said sardonically.

"Damn it, she shouldn't be off in some hotel where anything could happen. You know that as well as I do. She's not gonna live here, I want her home with me."

"Well, why don't you just get in your car then, and go tell her?"

"I did, damn it! Drove right over to the City Chicken and tried to talk sense into her. Wouldn't come. Mr. Hollander, he told me to keep my hands off her, she's a married woman can do whatever she wants."

"Well, I guess that's about the size of it, too," said Foster.

"They said once I signed that paper that April could marry, I signed away all the rights I had to my daughter. I tell you, if someone was to put a gun in my hands, first person I'd go after would be Sara Dawson and her damned committee."

"Well, it's done now, and April's on her own, and I can't see that either of us has got any choice but to wait and see what's on her mind," said Foster, wishing the man would leave. He slid forward in his chair, but April's father didn't budge.

"Look here now, Foster. We're both of us in the same boat.

April won't come home to neither of us. What I want you to do, what I'm asking, is for you to file for divorce. Then she'll be an unmarried child again, and I can make the girl come home where she belongs."

Foster let out his breath. "Anybody files for divorce," he said, "it's got to be her."

Earl Bates grabbed his jacket and got to his feet. "This is some sorry life," he said. "I got three daughters don't give a hoot whether I'm livin' or dead. Got nobody to look after me in my old age but Thomasine, and she ain't home long enough to blow her nose." He swore as he left the house, letting the door slam after him.

Foster sat back down. The whole of Charles County would soon be on his back to divorce a girl he had never married in the first place. Russell had been right. Once he brought April here, he had troubles he'd never even heard of.

TEN

Buddy Travis was hanging around the third night, too.

"Buddy," I told him, "Mr. Hollander see you talkin' to me, I'm going to lose this job."

"Just tell me what time you get off and I'll drive you home," he says.

"Midnight, but Mr. Hollander takes me hisself."

"Ha! He's got eyes for you, that's why."

"Does not!" I was making like I was real busy, hoping Buddy would go back to the pinball machines. It was always embarrassing when Buddy come over, because I could feel my neck turn red every time he took an interest in me.

"You still at Dorothy's?" he asks.

"No. I got me a room at the Adams Hotel," I told him, and just then Mr. Hollander looks around the corner of the bar, and Buddy makes like he's only passing by. He puts his hands on my waist as he moves around me toward the pinball machines. Marvina Sykes, the country singer, was moaning about love, and here's Buddy Travis with his hands on my waist, one finger brushing up and down.

Buddy and his friends left soon after that and I was glad, because here come this party of eight to celebrate someone's birthday, and my legs almost give way when they sat right down in my section. Loretta's tables was full, and Irene Hollander could have give those people to Pearl, but she didn't. I was glad there weren't no little kids with 'em. Party of eight's bad enough without having to mop up spilt juice.

There was five men and three ladies, and one of 'em was about ninety years old and wore a flower on her dress, so I guess it was her birthday. Sort of sad, too, because the rest of 'em was all making a fuss over her and her just looking off into space. Man at the head of the table slips me a dollar and tells me to ask Marvina to sing "Happy Birthday, Emma Wade," and I did, and all the while Marvina sings, the old woman's looking around like "Whose birthday is it?"

"It's okay," Loretta says to me while I'm fixing up their salads, "they want to do right by their mama, and they're giving her a birthday whether she knows it or not. Our job is to make them all have a good time."

Something about being a part of the City Chicken that made me feel nice, like this was my house and these people was invited. I was just as pleasant as I could be and it come natural because I wanted that old lady to know her children loved her. When I set her steak down I said, "Now this is for the birthday girl," just like Loretta would have said, and all the ladies smiled at me. I even cut up the meat for her like one of the men asked and brought out this little cake at the end with one candle on it. Woman just sits there and cries.

"Blow out the candle, Mama," the men keep saying, but she goes on bawling.

I go across the room and get this little boy, must have been about three, and ask his parents could I borrow him a minute, and bring him over and ask could he blow out the candle. And the old woman stops crying and smiles at the boy and he blows out the candle and the woman gives him a piece of the cake. Everybody's happy. I can see Irene Hollander beaming at me over by the cash register.

What made it hard for me that night wasn't the customers, it was Pearl. Everytime I went back to the kitchen for something and pass Pearl, she didn't give an inch. Big hips coming at me between the tables like a street sweeper. More'n once she pressed me up against a chair without so much as an "excuse me."

It was about eleven o'clock when I go out in the kitchen and hear Pearl telling Mr. Hollander lies about me. In front of Chub, too, the cook, and Loretta.

"Puts twice as much salad in the bowl for the man who's going to take the bill," she was saying. "Extra rolls, too. Table of eight, they should have had sixteen rolls, and she put in at least twenty. Just looking for that tip, that's all."

I couldn't believe my ears. Didn't think any of us had so little to do we could just stand around and count the other's rolls.

Before I could open my mouth, though, Loretta says, "Pearl, what you eat yourself in a week is more than any extra April gives the customers, so I don't see what you've got to complain about."

Pearl goes pink in the face, and I still can't find my tongue. Mr. Hollander just lets it slide—says something about how we all got to watch out not to waste anything, that any rolls come back in the bread basket he's got to throw out by law, and how he expects us all to get on good with each other—that if we're not happy working together, the customers won't be happy neither.

We all shut up then and went to clearing off tables. I was sorry Pearl was against me already, but I knew I had a friend in Loretta. Chub was nice to me too—tiny little man, smaller than Loretta even—but he could cook up a storm. Eat anything he wants and never gain an ounce.

I was afraid Mr. Hollander was going to give me a lecture when he drove me home, but he didn't. Not exactly. It wasn't the bread basket that was on his mind, it was something else.

"April," he says, "we're thinking about getting rid of those pinball machines. Think maybe they attract the wrong sort."

I knew then it was his roundabout way of referring to Buddy Travis and how he didn't want him bothering me on the job.

"That's a fine idea, Mr. Hollander," I tell him. "Noise of the machines don't mix so good with Marvina Sykes's singing anyway."

"Just what Irene and I decided," he says, but gives me credit for thinking of it too. He and his sister been real nice to me. When Irene found out I was living in a room without a kitchen, she saw to it that I always had a little something wrapped up in a napkin for breakfast the next morning. Chub would make me an egg sandwich sometimes. That would hold me till I got to work at four, and then we could eat most anything we wanted, so all my food was paid for.

Mr. Hollander always waits outside the hotel till he sees me go up the stairs. Mr. Cody turns off the front light at midnight and goes to his apartment right behind the desk, and I never know what I'm going to find on that couch inside the front door. Come in one night and there was a woman lying there with a man on top of her. Think they both was drunk but I didn't stay around to find out.

On Monday night, I'd just took off my uniform and had it soaking when there's a knock at the door.

"Who's that?" I call. Sometimes the men on this floor, they try all the handles when they come down the hall, so I keep my door locked.

"Company," says a man's voice, and I knew it was Buddy Travis. I pulled on this old Mexican dress of Thomasine's, made like a tent, and opened the door.

"What in the world are you doing here?" I ask him. "I was about ready to go to bed."

"So go ahead." He grins and invites hisself in. I close the door quick after him so nobody sees. Buddy looks around. "Seen worse," he says, and grins again like it's the only thing his face knows to do. And then he sees the fuzzy pink monkey on my dresser that he won for me at the carnival. I like to have died, him knowing I still hung on to it.

"Hey, look what we have here," he says, picking it up, and I'm turning all shades of red. He steps closer to me. "Listen," he says, "you want to go somewhere and get a sandwich?"

"Just ate," I told him. "Mr. Hollander always lets us eat before we go home."

"Too bad," says Buddy, and sticks his hands in his pockets, trying to think of some other reason to stay around. He walks over to the TV, sees the slot, and drops a quarter in. First time I'd had it on since I moved in. Right away there's this embarrassing scene on a late movie of a woman naked to the waist and this man watching her from across the room.

"Ummm!" says Buddy.

"Don't get any ideas," I tell him, and go over to rinse out my uniform. Next thing I know I've got my hands in the water and Buddy Travis has his arms around me. He takes my hands out of the sink and wipes them with his shirt and then he kisses me and I let him.

All kinds of things was going through my head—like how different his face felt from Foster's—not better or worse, just different. Way he pulled me up against him, too, was different, his hands pressing my bottom from behind. Right away I'm thinking about Foster, of him alone back in that house, not even Vinnie to keep him company, and me here in the hotel room with Buddy Travis doing this way.

"Don't, Buddy," I said, and pushed at him. "I got things to do."

"Well, do 'em and I'll sit here and watch," he says.

That gets me all rattled and I put soap in the water again, even though the uniform was ready to rinse.

"Where do you take a bath?" asks Buddy.

"There's a ladies' shower down the hall, but I never used it yet," I tell him. "Isn't any lock on the door. Anyone could walk in."

"Let's go take a shower," says Buddy.

I stared at him. "You are crazy, Buddy! It's for ladies."

"No ladies around at this hour."

"I'm not taking no shower with you."

"Why not?"

I figured it was time to set him straight. "Look here, Buddy, just 'cause I'm separated from Foster don't give you no right."

"Well, that's some kind of mess," says Buddy. His hand darts out to catch my dress, but I jerk away. "C'mere," he says.

"No, Buddy!"

He lunges for me, laughing, and I can't help laughing too.

"Buddy, I mean it!" I say, leaping up on the bed in my bare feet and down the other side, then running around over by the dresser. Buddy's in the center of the bed, his long arms reaching out for me first one way, then another, legs whirling. Looks like one of those water sprinklers that spins around. I figure we're making all kinds of noises and Mr. Cody's right below.

"Stop it, Buddy! Mr. Cody's going to hear!"

"Quit hopping, then, and be nice to me," says Buddy. "Can at least sit down beside me till my quarter runs out."

Figured that was the least I could do, him paying to watch the television. Once I sat down, though, he'd be wanting to lie on top of me and I just didn't trust myself not to let him.

I sat down couple feet away from him. Buddy pulls me over and puts an arm around me. On television, the naked woman is leaning back against the man now and he's got one hand on her breast. Buddy puts his hand on mine.

"Buddy!" I say. "Just because you and Thomasine—"

"What about me and Thomasine?" he says. With his other hand he takes hold of mine and puts it down between his legs, and I can feel his thing getting hard. And right this minute there's a knock on the door. I leap up, my heart thumping against my ribs, and go open the door. It's Mr. Cody. I know he can see all the way in to where Buddy's sitting on my bed.

"Just come up to return your ring," he says, and holds it out.

I knew he didn't come upstairs at one in the morning for that; it's because Buddy and me was making so much noise. My mouth is dry with shame. When I can speak I say, "I give you that for a deposit till I can pay it all."

"It's paid," he says. "Your husband come by and put up the rest."

My legs feel like they're about to give. "Foster come by? When?"

"Tonight," says Mr. Cody.

I can't hardly think. Maybe he come up and stood outside my door listening to Buddy and me. Him downstairs paying my rent and me doing this way to him.

"Mr. Cody," I say, "this friend here is just about ready to leave, so you can take him down with you."

Buddy stares at me. "Hadn't planned on leaving just yet," he says.

"Oh, yes you were," I tell him, and stand there holding open the door.

Buddy picks up his jacket and gives me a look that could stop a train. When he's gone, I close the door and lock it, and then

I lean against it, my eyes closed. I feel bad about Buddy, too. I was getting bad as Thomasine. Worse, even, 'cause I got Buddy all worked up and then turned him out. I wouldn't let him visit me anymore. He come here again, I wouldn't answer.

On Friday I cashed my paycheck, and first thing I bought was a plastic laundry tub, biggest one I could find. Bought me a saucepan, too. Then I come back to my room, set the tub on the floor, and filled the pan with water. Took twenty-five panfuls to get the laundry tub half-full and by then the water's starting to cool. Didn't care, though. I took off my clothes and climbed in. Sat there for an hour, maybe, and every so often I'd dip out some cold and add another pan of hot. Tub was just about big enough if I pulled up my knees. Wouldn't have to use the public showers at all. Everything I needed to start my new life was right there in that room.

I lift one foot and point it at everything that's mine. "*That's* mine," I say, pointing to the saucepan. "*That's* mine," and I point to my clothes. Sit there in my tub looking around the room like a queen on her throne, liking the feel of it.

Trouble with Foster Williams is he don't know what he wants. One minute he think I don't have the sense of a three-year-old child, then he turn right around and give me all kinds of directions what to do if the furnace don't work. Don't know one solitary thing about furnaces, I tell him. Might could keep your ears open and learn, he says back. Some evenings he like me to be all slinky in that blue gown he bought me, other times I curl up in his lap and he's so happy he just purrs. I sit there and he reads me aloud from the newspaper, like I'm back in kindergarten or something.

My mind's racing on ahead of itself now, getting to the real problem—what Foster said to me there at the end. I sink down in the water and it goes right over the side but I don't care. Nothing in my life anybody ever say to me hurt as much as that— how Foster couldn't never trust me with a baby. Seem like once those words were out, they pick up all the worries I ever had about myself, roll 'em up in a ball, and settle down inside my chest, can't never cough 'em up.

Foster cared about me, I know—wanted me to make something of myself, but he didn't want me back. Would have marched right upstairs here and asked me to come if he did. Instead, he just pays Mr. Cody my rent, like a father does a child, and takes hisself off again.

All at once I'm not a queen no more, and I close my eyes to keep the tears back.

***

Second paycheck didn't come to much because the Hollanders were still deducting the cost of my uniform, but when the third one came I was able to pay Mr. Cody in advance and still have some left over.

I was beginning to feel comfortable in that room. Sometimes people would leave newspapers and magazines on the couch down by the front desk, and Mr. Cody said anything I found when I come home at night I could take upstairs, 'cause he'd only throw 'em out the next morning. Got me a *Reader's Digest* that way and a copy of the Baltimore *Sun* and a sports magazine and a *House Beautiful*. Kept 'em on my dresser so folks could have something to look at if they ever come to visit. On the back of *House Beautiful* was this postage-free card you could send in for a seed catalogue, so I filled it out, and pretty soon here it was waiting for me, my name on it and everything. I never saw such pretty pictures in my life. Lady standing in a garden with roses growing in an arch over her head; melons so big you'd have to haul 'em in a wheelbarrow; there was even a tree that if you planted it would have five different kinds of fruit. Never even knew there was such a thing. Some days when I got up, wouldn't do nothing else but study that seed catalogue, think about what would I order could I have anything I wanted.

Buddy never come back to visit me. After Mr. Hollander took the pinball machines out of the restaurant, Buddy and his friends never came there neither, and Marvina Sykes was happy about that, I can tell you.

I was getting along pretty good at work. Was at Woolworth's one day and they had an engraver there carving your name on any jewelry you bought, so I bought three pins, kind you wear on your dress. They was each shaped like a heart with a rainbow painted on them and a space underneath for your name. Only

$1.98 apiece. Had my name put on one, Loretta's on another, and Pearl's on the third.

Next day, when I give the pin to Pearl, she looks at me like how can I give her something nice when she told Mr. Hollander lies about me? She puts it right over her left breast, which is already so big it don't need no advertising, and from then on we were sort of like sisters. All of us together were like sisters, Loretta and Pearl and me. When Pearl sees I'm not trying to take her tables or anything, and would help her clean off her own when she got busy, she'd help me back.

One thing Mr. Hollander never did was play favorites. Treated us all alike. If he give one girl a few extra minutes on her break, he'd give us all extra time. And so we was good to each other. One girl get behind in her work, the others would help out when they could—clear the tables for her, pour the coffee. She drop a plate or something, the others help clean it up. Never told the Hollanders this, but I would have worked at their restaurant for nothing, just to be a part of it. Somebody waiting for me to show up, a job to do. . . . First time in my life I had me some rules. Took to it like a duck to water. Felt more like I was going home when I went to work each afternoon than I did going back to the Adams Hotel.

All kinds of folks come in a restaurant, and you got to learn to get on with them. On Thursdays we had the Kiwanis Club in the small dining room. Fridays it was the Jaycees. Sometimes there would be something special going on, like the day the women arm wrestlers showed up for their annual convention, great big ladies walking around the room trying to stare each other down. Pearl said it was the first time in her life she ever felt small, and she and I had a laughing fit over by the bar.

I guess you could say I was pretty happy then, living at the Adams Hotel and working for the Hollanders. Even when they scold me for something, I see how I deserve it, and I put my mind to doing it right next time. Wasn't happy when I thought about Foster, though, which was mostly at night. Sometimes I'd pull the pillows down and pile 'em up against my back, like we was snuggled together. But I'd try not to let him enter my mind.

Every time I see a black dog remind me of Vinnie, I'd try not to think of her neither. One minute I'm mad at Foster, what he said to me there at the end. Next minute I wish I was back in his bed. Just shows how I wasn't even growed up halfway to where I was supposed to be.

First real company I had in my room, not counting Buddy Travis, was Thomasine. Come by to see me one Sunday wearing a fur coat of some kind, looked like rabbit, and I knew the only reason she come by was to show it off. I thought maybe she was going to take me for a ride in her car, it being my day off, but she says she's only got enough gas to get her home again, and how she wanted to drop in to see how her little sister was doing. I hadn't even talked to Thomasine since I left Foster's.

I say her little sister's doing just fine, thank you, and show her my stack of magazines, should she care to amuse herself. Thomasine only says how it's too bad I don't have a refrigerator because she is as hungry as she can be.

"April, honey, you're just starving yourself to death," Thomasine says, and sits down on my bed spreading her fur coat out on both sides making sure I get a good look. She says it's fox, and I don't know nothing about fur, but I never saw a fox look like that.

"I'm not starving at all!" I tell her. "Gaining weight! Look how round my legs are gettin'!" I stuck 'em out in front of me to show her. *Was* getting rounder, too. The Hollanders fed me good.

Thomasine just goes on stroking her coat.

"Thomasine," I say, "did you know that Vinnie died?"

"Foster's dog?" she says. "When was that?"

"The day you hit her with your stuck-up car, that's when."

Thomasine stares at me, and it could just be there was a little bit of sorry to her face. "She was *okay*, April! You and me checked her over. You saw her yourself!"

"Well, we didn't check good enough. She was bleeding inside somewhere, and I come home that afternoon to find her dead."

Thomasine's mouth still gapes. "Sweet Jesus," she says. "What'd Foster say?"

"So upset he couldn't hardly bear to have me around, which is partly how come I left."

"Well, I never meant to hit her," says Thomasine. "Next you'll be sayin' it was me that drove you apart."

"No," I said. "Wasn't you."

We was both quiet for a time, me thinking about Vinnie, Thomasine thinking God knows what, 'cause after a bit her foot starts wiggling, just a little at first, then faster and faster, and finally she says, "Guess you've heard what Foster's been up to since you left."

I feel something sort of turn over in my chest. "Don't come here telling me tales about Foster," I say.

"If I don't, someone else will," Thomasine says. "He and Dorothy been spending time together."

"That's a lie, Thomasine!" I yell at her. "You just keep your trash-mouth shut."

"Huh!" says Thomasine. "What do you expect? You walk out on a man through the front door and somebody else will be walking in through the back."

"He sure wouldn't take up with Dorothy," I say.

"It's Dorothy took up with him. She drove over to his house one night, didn't leave till the next morning. Everybody knows."

My throat's getting all tight like I'm going to throw up. Can't believe it, Foster taking Dorothy in my place. Then I think about it some more and I believe it. Didn't Foster say she could come by any time she was having trouble with Max? Wouldn't she be all over him with me not there? Dorothy's softer and bigger than I am everywhere on her body. Sleeping with Dorothy would be about like lying on a pile of pillows. I can feel my eyelids begin to sting, my lips quiver.

"Go on home, Thomasine," I say, and the sound can hardly get up out of my throat.

Thomasine looks at me. "Oh, for heaven's sake, April, don't go bawling over Foster. You wanted him yourself you shouldn't have left."

"Go on home," I say again.

Thomasine looks guilty then. "Hey, listen, April, I've got enough money for a chocolate milkshake. You want to go over to McDonald's?"

I shake my head, fighting to hold my chin steady. Thomasine gets up and buttons her coat. "Men are like that, April," she says. "You can't trust 'em one minute. Soon as you turn your back they got somebody else in their bed." She goes out and I close the door after her, and the tears start pouring down my cheeks like they come from a faucet.

I'm crying without making a sound. I take off all my clothes, fill my laundry tub, and climb in, hugging my knees. Sit there and bawl my eyes out. Never cried over anybody in my life as much as I've cried over Foster. No way in the world I could explain it to Thomasine 'cause I couldn't even understand it myself. Leaving him was just something I had to do.

Seemed to me that before I could do another thing in my life I had to live in that room like I was doing, work at the City Chicken, and do the way the Hollanders told me. Had to sit here in my laundry tub too, and bawl before I could ever go on to anything else, but I was as scared and lonely as ever I could remember.

Right in the middle of all this crying, there's this knock on the door and there wasn't any way in the world I could pretend I wasn't there. Had gone from crying quiet to just letting it all come out. Tears coming so fast I couldn't even ask who it was. Figured if I didn't go answer, it'd be Mr. Cody letting himself in with his key. So I climbed out and wrapped myself up in the bedspread, crossed over, and opened the door.

There's a woman standing outside all dressed in white. At first I think somebody's gone and sent for a nurse, and then I realize it's Sister Perry from the Baptist Church.

"April, honey!" she says, holding out her big arms, and next thing I know I'm folded up in them, my head on her big chest, just bawling like some little creature lost in the snow.

"Jesus knows! Jesus knows!" Mrs. Perry says, rocking me back and forth. She moves on inside and shuts the door after her. "Jesus sent me, that's why I came. The world is full of tribulation, honey, but the good Lord never gives us more grief than we can handle."

Leastways I think that's what she was saying. Didn't even care,

I was just glad I had somebody to lean on, even though she smell like Lysol. I let her hold me, sitting there on the edge of the bed wrapped in that chenille spread.

"I've been hearing it all, you taking a room in this place and that Travis boy coming by," Sister Perry says in her singsong voice. "I been hearing about your sister and Foster, too, and Jesus spoke to me this morning and says, 'Go minister to that girl, Sister Perry,' and here I am, to say you've got to take up the Spirit, April Ruth, and be born again."

"Don't I know it!" I wept. "It's like I *was* born all over again, right here in this very room."

"Oh, Jesus, we are thankful," Sister Perry says, hugging me tight. "We are thankful for Thy tender mercies to us Thy faithful servants. Where, April, honey? Show me right where you were kneeling when you began your life with God."

My nose was so clogged up I had to breathe through my mouth, my eyes all swelled up from crying. "Wasn't kneeling, was sitting right there in that laundry tub, and I said to myself, 'It's like I'm startin' my life all over again.' "

"*Praise* Jesus! Bless His name forever!" Sister Perry goes on, brushing the hair out of my eyes like a mama and squeezing my shoulder so hard it's like to break my collarbone. "You've got to become like a little child, the Scriptures say, to enter the kingdom of heaven."

"That's just the way it is, too," I tell her, "like I'm little again, and the Hollanders have took me in and give me sisters."

But Mrs. Perry's humming to herself, hardly listening, rocking back and forth with her big, warm arms around me.

I didn't understand half of what she was talking and she probably didn't know what I was carrying on about either. I figure we was just two lonely people on a Sunday afternoon. I thanked her for paying me a visit, and after she left I felt better. Got dressed and went across the street for a fish sandwich.

Next day when I get to work, I can tell they're looking at me funny, and finally Pearl takes me aside and says, "April, what's this talk about you being born again in a laundry tub?" Then I know how easy it is for two people to be talking face-to-face and still not hearing each other at all.

ELEVEN

There were three visitors to Foster's house the second week of April's absence.

The first was Shum. His tall, stooped figure appeared at the kitchen door one evening, arms dangling disjointedly from shoulder sockets, and he was carrying a mason jar of something green.

"We froze some of April's peas, and Russell made soup," he said. "Just wanted to give it to her."

Foster knew that his uncles had heard, that they could not help but hear, and this was their way of verifying the truth, of creating their own version of April's departure, so that when someone asked Shum in the Safeway, "Did you know that . . . ?" he could reply, "The look on Foster's face when I give him that soup!"

"She's gone," Foster said.

Shum contrived to look surprised. "Gone?" he repeated. That much he seemed to have rehearsed, but now there was the awkward problem of what to do with the soup. "Well . . ." he said, pausing. "I'm sorry to hear that." He started to tuck the jar back under one arm, then thrust it out toward Foster. "You might like it," he said. "Made with ham." He left, but he wasn't smiling.

The next visitor came on Thursday. Foster heard the sound of a car making its way up the lane, then the slam of a door. He glanced at the clock: nine-fifteen. There were footsteps outside, a knock, and then the sound of a woman crying. Foster sprang for the door.

Dorothy Bates stood on the step outside holding a towel to her face. One eye was swollen shut and her upper lip was split and bleeding.

"My God," said Foster, opening the door wide. "You been in an accident, Dorothy?"

She entered the kitchen, and the next thing Foster knew she was clinging to him, sobbing, her full breasts soft even beneath her coat.

Foster stood with his hands half-lifted, feeling the cautious obligation to provide comfort. Gingerly he grasped her arms and edged her toward a chair.

"Sit down and let me get a look at you," he said. "Max do this?"

She nodded. The paleness of her face contrasted strangely with the purple bruise over her eye. She pressed her lips together, but her chin puckered and the tears spilled out again.

"I'm going to put some ice inside that towel, and you hold it up to your eye," Foster said, glad for something to do. He took out the tray and dislodged several cubes. "Take that swelling down some so you can see out of it." He handed her the towel again, then pulled over a chair and sat straddling its back. "Listen, Dorothy, you're working for a man that ain't worth spit."

"Don't I know it," Dorothy sniffled.

"Well, why do you keep going back?"

"Why anything, Foster? Why'd April walk out on you? Why aren't you going after her? You can't answer with any more sense than I can. When Max is good to me, it's like there's nothing in the world that's better. Always the best after a fight."

"But you don't have to take this from him."

Dorothy blew her nose. "Where would I go, Foster? Max pays the rent, buys my clothes, bought me my car. . . ."

"Look here, now. You want to leave him, get yourself a new kind of job, I'll loan you money for a room somewhere. You don't have to stay with Max or go back to your daddy either. Get yourself a job like April did and start out on your own."

Dorothy sighed and shook her head. "Never could abide waiting tables," she said. "Max *loves* me, Foster. A man can't be jealous unless he loves you."

"Max so jealous how come he sends you around to other men?"

"Oh, Foster, that's different. That's not what I'm talking about at all."

"Well, you and me are talking two different languages here, that's for certain." Foster's eye fell on the coffee left from breakfast and he rose to heat it. "Why don't you have some coffee while you're waiting? Ought to keep that ice on your eye another fifteen minutes, at least." He helped her off with her coat.

"Don't know what I'd have done without you tonight," said Dorothy.

Foster felt his neck redden. He got out the milk and spoons and set them on the table. "Seen April a'tall?" he asked.

"No. She hasn't so much as called. That's gratitude for you. Hear she's doing okay, though. You talk to her, Foster?"

"No." He could feel Dorothy's eyes on him.

"Why not?"

"Maybe things are better like they are."

"You don't mean that, Foster." Dorothy sighed and thrust her legs out in front of her, resting her head on her shoulder, the towel wedged beneath her eye. "Don't know which of us is more mixed up, you or me. Love is shit sometimes, isn't it?"

Foster made no reply.

"It is," Dorothy said, answering her own question. "Men will do anything for money, but women will do it for love. You know who said that?"

Foster shook his head and poured the coffee.

"Me. I said it. 'Cause it's true. All I want in this world is for Max to love me, and he . . ." Her chin trembled. "He . . ."

"You want sugar, Dorothy?" Foster said quickly.

She nodded.

From across the table, Foster watched her. Dorothy had her eyes closed now, and for a while there was no sound in the kitchen except the clink of Foster's spoon as he stirred. Dorothy straightened up finally and reached for her cup, then held it under her chin, blowing away the steam with her swollen lips.

"Seems like your daddy would want you to come back home if he knew about this," Foster said at last.

He had meant it as an observation, a suggestion, even, but it produced instead a sardonic laugh.

"I could be at home a solid week and my daddy not even know it," Dorothy told him. "I stopped by the other night when he was drinking, and he says, 'Thomasine, you ain't no daughter to me; never around when I need you.' 'I'm not Thomasine, I'm Dorothy,' I tell him. 'Dorothy?' he says, like it's a name he can't recollect. And before the visit's over, he's called me April Ruth and my mama's name and a few more I won't mention." Just as suddenly as Dorothy had started to laugh her face grew sober again, and Foster detected a quaver in her voice.

"He's always been like that, then?" he asked her.

"Seems to me he has, but folks say it wasn't always this bad. Way back, when I was five, maybe, there was a time he'd sing to me. I remember that much. Had all kinds of songs—story songs, they were. There was one about a possum I liked the best, and every time he sang it, it was different, so maybe he made it up. And when I was nine I asked him to—" Dorothy swallowed— "I asked him . . . to sing the possum song again, and he didn't know it. Didn't even know what it was I was talking about, as though that little bit of fun we'd had together, him and me, hadn't ever happened at all." Dorothy turned her face away, and this time tears were visible on her eyelashes. "Thought maybe it was because I was getting older—there was Thomasine and April Ruth to take my place, but he never sang the possum song again, not even to them."

As Foster listened, sometimes responding, sometimes not, he realized that it was the first time in his life he had not felt any great discomfort talking with a woman other than April. He was able to listen to Dorothy without his mind rushing on ahead of itself, wondering what he would say in turn when she finished.

Just when he had begun to feel relaxed, however, Dorothy said, "Foster, can I stay here tonight? I don't want to go back till morning."

Foster swallowed and coughed. "Well, now . . ." he said.

"Please, Foster. It takes Max a whole night to cool off. If I go back now, I'll only get the other eye closed. By tomorrow he'll be all sweet and forgiving."

"There's a spare room," Foster said finally, when the silence had stretched on embarrassingly long. "I'll be up and off at six or so. You can help yourself to breakfast."

"Foster, I told you this before, but you are one nice man. And that's more than I can say for most of the men I know."

This is a mistake, Foster told himself as he laid out sheets and an extra blanket. What could he say, however? Couldn't just turn a woman out into the night, her eye so closed up she could hardly see to drive.

"If you want to take a bath or something, you can use it first," he told her.

He went into the living room and picked up the paper.

There was something faintly risqué about the sounds drifting in from the bathroom, he decided. These were not the quick, choppy sounds of splashing that meant that someone was simply getting on about her business, but rather an occasional slow, languid slosh of water, as though a leg were being lifted, a toe extended, a round calf luxuriously lathered. This was followed by a long, penetrating silence, which was broken at last by the soft slushing of water against the sides of the tub, conjuring up the image of a woman sliding her hips downward until only her head and neck emerged—her head and neck and two round breasts that rose like islands in the soapy water. Foster turned on the TV and raised the sound.

At last, above the music, he heard water running out of the tub. He put down the paper, ready for bed himself. At that moment, he was conscious, even without turning around, of Dorothy there in the hall.

"Foster," she said, "do you have an old shirt or something I could sleep in?"

Foster was fully aware that Dorothy could be standing there in the altogether and not even bat an eye.

"You decent?" he asked.

There came a soft laugh. "Nobody ever accused me of that."

Foster froze. The blinds were up. The lights were on. Shum and Russell could be sitting outside the window on folding chairs for all he knew. "Well, go put something on."

"Jesus Christ, Foster! I'm covered!"

Foster turned around and immediately flushed. Dorothy stood there with the bath towel wrapped around her, breasts ready to pop out over the top, her long dark hair falling down one plump shoulder. Her eyes, even the swollen eye, laughed at him.

He walked brusquely past her, pulled a pajama top from his bureau, and gave it to her. "That should do you," he said, and went back in his own bedroom, closing the door.

It was the first night since April left that Foster gave in to his physical wanting. He lay in the dark, touching himself, aroused by Dorothy's seminakedness, but when he came, it was April who was on his mind. He felt even lonelier afterward than he had before.

Dorothy was still asleep the next morning when he left, and all day Foster worried that she might still be there when he got home. That she might have dinner waiting, even—her clothes already hung in his closet. She was gone. Her bed was made, the towels straightened, and her breakfast dishes stacked neatly in the sink.

Russell, the third visitor, came down on Saturday.

"Mornin'," Foster said, opening the door.

Russell invited himself in. He walked over to the table, pulled out a chair, and sat down. "Foster, I'd like to talk with you," he said.

Foster leaned against the sink, waiting, knowing all the while.

"I'm going to say this straight out," said Russell. "You brought Earl Bates's youngest here to be your wife, and Shum and I were against it, I know, probably with good reason, since she's left you. Be that as it may, we came to like her, and I don't mind saying I'm sorry that she took off. But somebody's got to say now what your dad would say if he was here."

"What's that?" asked Foster.

"Confound it, Foster, what do you *think* he'd say? What do you suppose all of Medbury's talking about this very minute?"

"I can't imagine," Foster told him, "because I haven't told a soul that Dorothy Bates was here, and knowing the shape she was in, I doubt she's said anything either. So if all Medbury's talking it must be you and Shum have been some kind of busy."

Russell flushed. "I keep what I know to myself."

"Better put a muzzle on Shum, then."

"Foster, I tell you, people are talking! They know April's not here. They see Dorothy's car pulling out of your drive at eight o'clock in the morning, folks aren't stupid!"

"Well, they're sure talking a lot of nonsense they don't know nothing about," Foster said. "Didn't know she was all beat up, didn't know she needed a place to stay, didn't know I never laid a hand on her. They want to make up stories, I can't stop 'em."

Russell's face reflected his relief. "It's just the way I figured, Foster. *I* know what happened, and *you* know it, but nobody else knows it."

"Then they ought to quit shootin' off at the mouth, hadn't they?" Foster said, and moved toward the door.

As Russell left he looked about for a moment, then asked, "Where's that dog of yours?"

"I buried her," Foster told him.

Russell stopped in his tracks. "Sick?"

"Hit by a car."

There was sympathy in his uncle's eyes for a change, which Foster didn't expect. "Foster, you've got more than your share of troubles right now, and I'm sorry."

It was a move to make amends, Foster knew. He did not want sympathy, however. All he wanted now was to be left alone, to slide back into the kind of life he used to have. At least that was simple, certain—each day the same as the one before.

At the bridge on Monday, Clyde said, "Christ, Foster! Not Dorothy!"

"Word sure gets around," said Foster. "Don't need any Western Union here." He bent over the work at hand. "Give me a seven-eighths spud wrench, Juju, would you?"

Juju pulled one from his tool belt and handed it over. "Well, don't say you wasn't warned, old man," he told Foster. "Didn't

I tell you what would happen? Didn't I say if you married April, you lucky her sister didn't move in with you, too? Seem like I read it right."

It occurred to Foster that he did not have to justify himself to anyone. It would make no difference, one way or another. Even if he gave a running account of everything that had gone on between him and Dorothy, no one would believe that she had gone to sleep in his spare room and stayed there.

***

The longer they went without seeing each other, the more sure Foster was that April was not coming back—the more grateful he was he hadn't asked her, made a fool of himself.

Weekends were the worst, however, as February turned to March. The sun now fell on the table during Saturday breakfasts, and Foster could not help but think how he and April might be planting the garden. They would have started earlier this year, too, put in the sugar peas, at least. *Wait for the onion snow that comes in April,* was what his father used to say when Foster's mother agitated to plant in March. Now the garden waited indefinitely for April.

He knew he would have to see her sometime, clear up their status. No use going on pretending they were married if April was telling folks they weren't. It would make him out to look even more stupid than he did already.

He found out bits and pieces at the bridge. On the day they were preparing to float the last span into place, Clyde told Foster what he had heard over the weekend. The floor of the catwalk, on which Foster climbed, was chainlink fencing, and he could stare down at the whitecaps below. With each bouncy step, the angle grew increasingly steep, and the men kept tight hold of the wire railings on either side as they walked from one tower to another, 180 feet up.

"Was at the bowling alley Saturday night," Clyde said, talking to Foster's back, "and there was this kid there named Buddy Travis—nineteen, twenty, maybe—shooting off his mouth about how he scored with April. You know him, Foster?"

Foster made no reply. The words seemed to hang there in the wind that whistled around his ears.

"Fellas that age say they scored when all they did was get a hand up a girl's sweater," Clyde went on.

"Then what you repeating it for, Bigfoot?" Jack Tulley growled over his shoulder.

"Better he hear it from me than somebody else."

"How about better he don't hear it at all?" Tulley snapped.

They were speaking of him as though he weren't there, Foster realized. "I don't give a goddam one way or another," he lied, and he knew the men caught on, because they all kept still about it.

Tempers were apt to be quick on the day a span was floated in. The tides were right, but a stiff breeze had come up that the men hadn't anticipated, making the water rough. The final span would not be lowered into place as the others had been, but raised instead, from below. On either side of the open gap, workers lowered cables from the hoisting engines. The one-inch steel cables were hooked to the center span, and as it began its ascent, the crew on Foster's side made a dry run of the connecting procedure, checking bolts and equipment, then stood watching, their Porta-Powers and jacking devices ready as the span neared its place at the top.

"How much margin we have on that chord?" Juju asked.

"Eighteen inches," Jack replied, not taking his eyes off the iron.

"What we going to do if it don't fit?" Juju went on.

"Plane to Mexico, first thing in the morning," Jack told him, and the men's laughter broke the tension.

Inch by inch the span moved up, until at last the bridge framework was one long curved ribbon, connecting the two shores. A rowdy cheer went up, passed along from the raising gangs to the bolt-up gangs to the detail crews and on down to the men on the barge. They worked steadily all afternoon to join the sections before darkness fell, and had a beer to celebrate after work.

"Thought I might go take a look at a motorboat Saturday," Clyde said to Foster. "You want to come?"

"Not this Saturday. You don't buy one, I maybe could go another day," Foster told him.

He already had plans for Saturday, and Foster reviewed them on the drive home. He did not want to visit April in her room, not only because he was afraid of whom he might find with her, but because he did not want an open stretch of time in which, if he ran out of things to say, he might add something unintended. They had to be alone, and there had to be a fixed beginning and end to the visit. This decided, Foster got in his truck Saturday afternoon and parked a half block down the street from the Adams Hotel.

He saw her come out, the black uniform and red apron showing beneath her short coat. She stopped a minute on the steps to pull on her knit gloves, then walked briskly down the sidewalk and turned toward the highway. Foster started the engine and pulled alongside her.

April startled when she saw him.

Foster forced a smile. "Want a ride, April?"

She paused uncertainly, then seemed embarrassed.

"I can walk it all right," she told him.

"I know that, but what I got to say won't last more'n the time it'll take to carry you there."

April seemed to be thinking it over. Then she thrust out her chin and solemnly climbed up inside the truck, closing the door behind her. She sat looking straight ahead, one hand in her lap, the other on the door handle, as though ready to spring at any moment. Foster caught the familiar scent of her hair. He had made love to this girl, yet now they sat separated from each other like strangers on a bus.

Slowly he inched the truck forward toward 301. April had changed some in the two months she'd been away, however. Her hair was a little longer, knees rounder, and the calves of her legs were filling out. Looked good. Healthy. Older, too, more a woman. Foster swallowed and could not take his eyes from her knees, wondering if Buddy Travis had touched them, slipped his hand between her thighs.

"How you been, April? Things going all right with you?"

Her voice was so soft at first that Foster had to strain to hear. "I'm workin' now."

"I know that. They say you're doin' a fine job at the City Chicken."

She glanced in his direction, smiling a little, pleased. "Hollanders are real nice to me. Treat me good."

And I didn't? he wanted to ask. Not a word of appreciation for the ten months she had lived with him? She missed nothing? A sense of the old aggravation rose in his throat. The pickup had reached the intersection and delayed so long that the light turned red again.

April asked, "What was it you had to say to me?"

"Just wanted to get straight what it is you're telling folks about us."

From the corner of his eye, Foster could see her chin jut out another inch.

"Only saying we're not together no more, that's all. You can go find yourself a real wife now, Foster."

His heart seemed to clang inside him like a brass bell. It seemed incredible to him that she could not hear it, was not startled by the sound of it.

"What I'm getting at, April, is folks still think we're married."

"Can always tell 'em we aren't."

"Yes, but your daddy came to see me, and he wants you home again. He might could take you back, you still a minor."

April's hand dropped down off the door handle and landed in her lap beside the other. "Well, I sure don't want to end up in that trailer again with Thomasine," she told him.

"Then best maybe we just keep it to ourselves, how we're not married, until you reach eighteen. Unless, of course, you want to marry somebody else in the meantime."

"Don't want to marry nobody else," said April as the truck pulled into the parking lot. She pressed down the door handle as the pickup stopped, then hesitated a few seconds. "Thank you, Foster," she told him. "Hope you're okay and everything."

He wanted to say that he wasn't, but his tongue refused. "Why shouldn't I be?" he said.

"No reason a'tall," she answered. "You got on good before I come along, that's for sure, and you can get along now."

She stepped down, closed the door, then marched across the lot to the restaurant, gravel scrunching underfoot.

Foster sat several moments without blinking. Then he lifted his foot mechanically on the clutch and moved slowly out into traffic.

***

Ever since April left, Foster had been waking early in the mornings, unable to get back to sleep. He would dress, eat his breakfast, and be at the landing long before the others, as though he could push time along, somehow—give it a nudge. On Wednesday, however, he woke to the sound of rain slashing against the window glass, and after checking the forecast, knew it was useless even to drive in.

The phone rang about eight.

"Figured you'd be home today, in all this wet." It was Jed Harley. "Wallace and me sent our tobacco in yesterday, and it's up for auction this morning. Thought you might want to go along. Bidding starts at nine."

"Sure, I'll go," Foster said, glad for something to do.

"Pick you up in fifteen minutes."

He waited for them outside under the eaves. In the downpour, his Chevy pickup gleamed, cleaner than Foster had seen it for some time. The Harleys' old panel truck, in contrast, was repainted a flat gray, and the right front end was crinkled from too many close encounters. Foster climbed in the seat beside Jed, and with Wallace at the wheel, they went bouncing back down the drive, splashing muddy water out on either side whenever the wheels hit a rut.

"Auctions are early this year, aren't they?" Foster asked.

"A bit. Be glad to have it over with. We don't do better than last year, I'll think about puttin' those ten acres to something else."

"Well, I sure hope you left the green out of it this time. Surprised they let you back in," said Foster.

Jed laughed and spit into a plastic cup. "They went down two damn rows only pickin' hands from the top. Wouldn't you know, when they got to us, that Philip Morris man reaches down and pulls a hand out the center—all green."

"You should have known," Foster told him.

They pulled into the muddy lot in front of the warehouse. Flatbed trucks partially blocked the unloading areas where the roof overhung, where the round, knobby heaps of tobacco on their saucer-shaped baskets were wheeled in to the scale.

Several dozen men milled about between the shoulder-high rows calling out greetings to each other and to Foster.

"Mornin', Foster. How's it going?"

"Hey, Williams, haven't seen you for a spell. How you doing?"

The starter began the auction, picking up a fan-shaped bunch of leaves from the top of a basket and setting the selling price. "Ninety-five," he said, and the auctioneer took over.

"Ninety-five fi fi fi gimme six six six fi six got six gimme seben seben seben *sold* to R. J. for ninety-six dolla."

"Sumbitch!" Wallace swore to Foster, as they followed along behind the retinue of buyers and growers who edged down the aisle with the auctioneer between the heaps of better-grade tobacco and the dulls. "These are brights, too."

"Not the best brights I ever seen, though," Jed said.

Some of the tobacco got considerably less, and for these the auctioneer opened at the government support price, prepared to sell it to Uncle Sam: "Eighty-two gimme fi fi fi four four four gimme four gimme three gimme three, *sold* to Uncle."

It felt good being there, Foster realized—the familiar banter between the auctioneer and the men, the smell of tobacco dust, the choreographed rising and falling of the tobacco leaves as they were lifted and discarded again atop each pile—the cherry red of the brights, the yellowish gray of the dulls.

Wasn't this where he belonged, really, the world of men? Here in the warehouse? Up on the bridge? He would miss the passion, of course, and the tenderness, but he could do without the worry. The worry and the sass. Do without those just fine.

"Open one, dolla fi fi six seben seben got nine gimme ten gimme ten okay ten gimme 'leben 'leben ten, Liggett, ya got ten."

The Harley brothers got ninety-seven for their brights, worse than they'd hoped, better than they expected. Outside, the rain had not slowed. Wallace, however, was grinning. "You know what I'm thinking? When our money comes through, I'm takin' mine to the races."

Foster laughed. "Now that you got some money, you're fixing to lose it."

"Fixin' to double it," said Wallace. "How about Saturday? Want to go?"

"Sounds good," said Foster.

***

There was an accident on the bridge the next day. The rain had passed, and the men put in a few good hours that morning, but early afternoon the wind picked up once again and Tulley decided to pack it in. Clyde and Foster set to work securing the whip line of the crane. Each new gust shook the span, rolling along from one level to the next.

From this far out on the water, everything seemed painted in varying shades of blue—the shoreline, the clouds, the sky, even the mast of a boat on the bay. The water below, however, had a brownish cast, like the wrinkled skin of an elephant.

"I'm going on down," Jack called from the catwalk, and began his descent with long strides, the suspended platform bouncing beneath each step.

Foster could hear the blast of a pneumatic drill coming from the beams below.

"Let's go," said Clyde. "If we get the first boat going back, I'll have time to bowl a few games."

"Be there in a minute," Foster told him, slipping his wrench out of its holder and leaning over the last connection.

Clyde stepped around him, then walked along a support beam over to the catwalk. There was a clatter, a shout. The drill cut off. A clank. A thud. More shouting from below.

Foster turned around, grasping the beam with both hands. Clyde had reached the catwalk and was staring over the side. "Holy Mother!"

Foster crawled to the corner and looked down. The man who

had been drilling had lost his footing and gone over the side. Now he slumped limply from the safety line tied to his belt, blood on his chin and lips.

"It's Pod!" someone yelled. "Hit his chin going over. He's out cold." Already men from the third level down were moving toward the ladder to crawl up.

Foster reached out for one of the two heavy cables suspended from the main cable, and, grabbing hold, lowered himself down the suspender until he reached Pod. Workers had gathered now on the beam above, hands extended. Foster maneuvered Pod's body around so that he was closer to the gridwork, and held up one limp arm so the others could grab it. Moments later the man had been pulled to safety and Foster up behind him. Pod was coming around.

"Easy, man."

"Get him up."

"See that gash?"

"You're okay, Pod—you blacked out."

"Lost your drill, but you're one lucky cuss."

There was uneasy banter on the boat going back. No one had seen the accident, so it could not be dissected, laid out before them where they could examine it and discover what had gone wrong. That a man could go over the side so suddenly. . . . Pod himself couldn't remember. Was it a turn of the ankle? A gust of wind? A misjudgment?

"Maybe it's time for me to retire," Pod said shakily. "Pull the pin."

No, the men answered. Each asserted, in turn, that the work was really not as dangerous as it looked. As long as you followed the rules, they seemed to be saying, things would go okay. The rules said to tie in with your monkey line, and Pod had, and look what happened. A cut on the chin, that's all. Some told of accidents on other bridges, and for every fall there was a rule that had been broken; for every rescue, a rule that had been kept.

But Foster knew it was not that simple. A quick miscalculation. A moment's distraction. One inch too far to the left. There were dozens of things that could take you by surprise, throw you off course, change your life around so fast it would make your head spin. Take in a girl like April Ruth Bates, for instance, she'd get in your blood so bad you'd almost pay to forget her. And just when you thought you were over her, had your life back to where you could manage again, you come to find out you'd even choose trouble over sitting home alone without someone to worry over.

***

He went to Bowie on Saturday. The Harley brothers had been drinking some and arrived in a jovial mood, and Foster struggled to recapture the excitement he used to feel at the racetrack.

"Gandy Dancer's running the ninth race, and I'm going to bet a bundle," Wallace said. "Bet on her last month to show, and she come in first."

"I've only brought forty bucks with me," said Foster.

"You can do okay with forty."

It had been a year at least since Foster had gone to the track. Solemn faces read the tip sheets as though no problem were so bad it couldn't be dropped on the horses. Foster concentrated on the program. Maybe he was expecting too much of himself. Couldn't live with a girl for ten months and then forget her in a matter of weeks.

"Who you like in the third race, Wally?" Jed asked.

"Mr. Lil looks good. Going to wait till the last minute, though. Big money might come down then, and you can see it on the board."

Foster stood up and stepped by them.

"What horse you going to bet?" Wallace asked him.

"West Glade looks good to me."

"Not bad."

Foster walked down the wide stairs, past the bettors camped out on folding chairs by the video screen. He decided to bet both horses, putting ten dollars on West Glade to show, five on Mr. Lil to place. What the hell. If he lost all his money on the first couple races, he could just settle back and watch the horses, no feeling one way or the other. He didn't care.

"Whoosh!" Jed was saying when Foster got back upstairs. "Look at the odds on Mr. Lil."

"Eight to one!" said Wallace. "No, now it's six to one! What did I tell you? I'm betting fifty to win."

"One minute to post," the track announcer was saying. The Harleys went downstairs. Foster sat watching a bird that had been trapped somehow inside the grandstand and was flying back and forth in front of the huge glass windows, looking for a way out. Now that he saw it, the bird seemed the most obvious thing in his line of vision, impossible to miss. Wherever he looked, he saw the bird. He glanced around him. No one else seemed to pay the slightest attention. It sometimes occurred to Foster, when he passed a stranger on the street, that in a few seconds he would not remember that brief moment, as though it had never been. Then he would wonder why he even thought it, what possible significance it could have for him, except as a reminder of his own life's passing. By the end of the race, he told himself, he would have forgotten the bird.

"Heeeere they come!"

Jed and Wallace slid back in their seats as the horses broke from the starting gate.

"They're off! Shadow out front for the early lead, Frontier Gal on the outside second, Grand Illusion runs third. . . ."

Foster folded his arms across his chest and watched with a certain detachment.

". . . Out of the turn now, Grand Illusion a length, Shadow in second, Mr. Lil on the outside closing ground. . . ."

The crowd stood up.

"Come on!" bellowed Wallace. "Come on, Mr. Lil."

"A sixteenth of a mile to go and Mr. Lil gets the lead. Sullen Jane moves into second and on the extreme outside here comes West Glade."

Excitement rattled in Foster's chest, and he welcomed it. He might have a good time after all. This was part of his world too, something he probably couldn't have enjoyed with April. Pester him to leave before the last race. Women just did that way. You think of three good reasons why you shouldn't do something, a woman would think up four. He craned his neck to see the finish.

"Mr. Lil on the inside, West Glade on the outside, they're head and head, nose and nose. . . ."

The crowd was screaming. A shower of mud spotted the spectators below as the horses flew by.

"A driving finish! Tight!" the announcer cried.

"Who won?" Foster asked, wishing he'd bet more.

The track announcer again: "Ladies and gentlemen, the judges have posted number three, Mr. Lil, first; number eight, West Glade, second; number five. . . ."

The Harleys whooped.

"Didn't we tell you right?" Wallace grinned, taking another beer from his cooler, and they all laughed at their luck. After the second race, Foster realized that he had *not* thought about the bird, as he had predicted. After the third race, if the bird was there, Foster forgot to notice.

By the end of the eighth race, he had only twenty-five dollars left. The Harleys, however, had come with three hundred and were up to three-sixty.

"We're puttin' ours on Gandy Dancer," Wallace said, opening the last of the beer. His face was flushed. "What about you, Foster? Want to bet yourself a winner?"

There was something here besides money that attracted Foster, but he wasn't sure what it was. The willingness to extend himself, perhaps. To take a chance. To go against the grain.

"I'm betting mine on Battling Blue," he told them.

Jed stared at him, his long jaw slack. "You know something we don't know?" he asked. "Look at those odds, Foster, for crissake!"

"Good jockey," Foster said stubbornly. For only twenty-five bucks he could afford to be stubborn. The Harleys had already committed themselves, and wanted company.

Wallace just laughed. "We'll see," he said, and handed Jed the full three hundred and sixty dollars. "Go bet the winner to place," he told him.

Foster and Jed went down together and stood at separate windows. Jed looked over at him from time to time as the line moved up and chuckled derisively. At the window, Foster put his last cent on Battling Blue out of sheer mule-headedness and nothing more. He had liked the look of the gelding when it paraded before the stand, but then all the horses had looked good. Foster was feeling mellow.

"They're off!"

Back in the stands, Wallace coaxed his horse on silently. Jed started to say something, but Wallace cut him off. "Just shut up and watch," he said.

Now the track announcer: "Away from the gate slowly was Battling Blue. On the outside, Gandy Dancer takes the lead by a length and a half. Fury second by one. Rasputin third, a length and three-quarters. Then it's Wanda Lee fourth a neck, but moving up on the outside is Battling Blue, fifth by two lengths. One length. The field heads toward the clubhouse turn."

"*Go*, Gandy, goddamit!" yelled Wallace.

"They turn for home: it's Gandy Dancer, then Battling Blue, closing in. Stoker Six is third by a length, but that's Battling Blue neck and neck with Gandy Dancer. Gandy Dancer falling behind. . . ."

"Shit!" screamed Jed. "*Go,* you goddam sucker!"

"Jesus Christ!" bellowed Wallace. "Don't slow down now!"

"Into the homestretch, Rasputin moving into third, and it's Battling Blue out front by a nose, Stoker Six second, Rasputin third, and Gandy Dancer. . . ."

"Fucking sum*bitch!*" Wallace threw down his program and stomped it. Jed, his long face pale, stared at the board.

A strange sense of elation crept up Foster's throat.

"Come on, let's go!" Wallace yelled, stepping over the row of seats in front. "Get your goddam money, Foster, and let's get out of here." He elbowed his way through the crowd.

Foster collected his two hundred seventy-five dollars. The Harley brothers had already left, and by the time he reached their panel truck, Wallace was revving the motor, the truck rocking forward and back like a skittish horse. Foster got in and Wallace roared off, weaving recklessly in and out of traffic.

"You *happy?*" Wallace grumbled to Foster.

"Well, I sure wouldn't turn down two hundred seventy-five dollars."

"Sumbitch, if you didn't know something we didn't. We tipped you off on the first race, didn't we?" Jed complained. "How come you holding out on us?"

"Sheer luck is all it is," Foster told them.

"You're goddam *right* it's luck," Wallace sneered, and the harping and complaining continued all the way home. Wallace didn't even turn in the drive, just let Foster out on the road.

"Listen, Foster, you still owe us a poker game from last year, and don't you forget it. Only the lowest kind of snake takes his winnings and don't give the others a chance to win it back."

"Never said I wouldn't, did I?" Foster retorted, and went on up the drive to the house, chuckling to himself. Not bad for one evening. Sure could do something nice with that two hundred seventy-five. As he made a sandwich, however, and took it in on the couch, he could not seem to latch on to any one thing he wanted to buy. As if to taunt him, his mind jumped around from the bathing suit he had bought for April to the robe with the fur on the cuffs to the suitcase he'd purchased for her at Ocean City. Slowly he put the sandwich down beside him and leaned against the back of the couch, staring at the water stain on the ceiling. Was this what the ten months had done to him—got him to the place where he was so used to doing for someone else he couldn't enjoy doing for himself? Was this what April had done? Crawled inside his head and sat there?

TWELVE

I don't know just what it was I thought would happen once I left Foster. Back of my mind, I guess, I figured maybe we'd get together again after I straightened myself out, have me something I could do besides just sit around, waiting to set the table for supper. After I took that room at the Adams Hotel, I even imagined Foster and me might start dating—me a single girl with a job and him a bachelor. But after what Foster said to me the day he drove me to work, how we'll just go on pretending to be married till I'm eighteen, I could tell he wasn't going to ask me out; wasn't going to take me back, neither. Probably got hisself another girlfriend now.

Loretta, she's a widow lady, got children of her own all growed up, and I was telling her once about how Foster and I come to live with each other in the first place, how Mrs. Dawson was going to put me in the juvenile home, and Loretta tells me that the ladies couldn't have done that way—have to have a court order to take a child away from her daddy—and how long as I was fed and clothed and my daddy wasn't trying to have sex with me, not anything the court would do. I don't think I ever once in my life thought about my daddy trying to climb in bed with me. Tell the truth, couldn't imagine him sober long enough to make babies in the first place, but they say he was different when Mama was alive.

One thing I knew, though, was that Foster still had some kind of feelings for me or he would have just told everybody we wasn't married and let my daddy move me on back home. I decided to do like he said; once I was eighteen, we'd say we was divorced.

"That doesn't mean you can't have friends," Pearl told me. She said it was all right me going out with men long as Foster and me was separated, and every now and then she'd introduce me to some of the customers that came in, thought maybe I'd take a liking to 'em, but all of them was fat as Pearl almost, and I figure they're so wonderful, how come she don't go out with them herself?

One Thursday night, the third of May, the whole restaurant was took over by the Southern Maryland Tobacco Growers Association, having themselves a banquet. Every table, instead of them three plastic roses in a vase, we had to stick a couple tobacco leaves there instead, make 'em look like flowers. Beside every napkin we put a pack of Salems and a Winchester cigar, courtesy of the R. J. Reynolds Tobacco Company. Wives come too, all prettied up, and the Hollanders said be real nice because we wanted their business again next year. Me and Pearl and Loretta was running so fast back and forth between the kitchen and tables you'd think we would have wore out the carpet.

Loretta come out of the kitchen carrying this big tray in one hand, holding it up high, and a basket of rolls in the other, and just as she's about to go past this table, she bumps into this man's knee sticking out and the whole tray goes right into his lap. Before I could even swallow, I see Loretta's legs give way, and next thing she's on the floor, face scrunched up in pain.

Nobody moves. Man who's knee she bumped has got string beans and a parslied potato on one shoulder and a couple slabs of roast beef sliding down his shirt front with the gravy.

"Oh, my God!" the man says. First he's looking at his lap, then he's looking down at Loretta. Suddenly the whole table's standing up and the women are saying, "Is she hurt? Is she hurt?" and there's all these men reaching down to pick her up.

"I'm so sorry," she says to the man at the table, but he's talking about how accidents will happen, and just hope to God she hasn't broke a leg.

"Loretta," I say later, "you ought to go on stage." We all have us a good laugh. We look out for each other there at the City Chicken, got our own secrets, and back there in the kitchen we can say pretty much what we want.

Wouldn't be truthful, though, I said I didn't miss Foster. But I made my own bed and now I got to lie in it.

Sunday mornings was the worst. Now when I woke up the room was already light, and I couldn't help thinking about the garden at Foster's and how good the earth smelled after we plowed it up. I was like a big kid, I know, carrying on in the dirt that way, Vinnie barking up a storm. But I missed it. So I went out and bought me some flowerpots and seeds and started my own little garden right there on the windowsill, but the sun never shown on it directly and the shoots come up all yellow and sickly.

Once I sent away for that seed catalogue, I started getting more mail than I ever got in my life—something from the Save the Earth Foundation and a key chain from the Navajos and somebody wanting me to write a letter to my congressman about the whales. Most of the mail, though, was picture catalogues, and I sent away for some Gro-Rite fertilizer, promised to make your house plants big and healthy, but all it did to mine was drown 'em. *Some* day, I said, I was going to grow something by myself from start to finish, something I could really call my own.

At first I was wearing Foster's ring on a chain around my neck, but Pearl tells me to stop doing that way, 'cause it puts men off. So I dropped it in a aspirin bottle and kept it in my dresser.

"Anybody asks," Pearl says, "you tell 'em your divorce is coming up pretty soon."

That's what I'd told her; Loretta, too.

***

It was sometime in June that Gus Freeman come into the City Chicken and introduce hisself to me. It's about four-fifteen on a Tuesday afternoon, and Pearl and Loretta and me was standing over by the kitchen, folding napkins. I looked around to see a man sitting at a table in my section, his briefcase open on the table, papers all around. He's got on a brown suit and a brown-and-yellow tie, and I guessed he was somewhere between Foster's age and however old my daddy was. I filled up a water glass and walked over. Man smiles at me.

"You suppose I could sit here an hour or so with a cup of coffee?" he says. "Got some work I have to do."

"Sure," I tell him, and bring back the coffee with two creams on the side.

"Don't worry," he says, "I'll be gone by the time the dinner folks get here."

"Take your time," I say. "Tuesdays are slow anyway."

"Some kind of salesman," Loretta says, back in the kitchen. "They like a restaurant table 'cause they can spread out, have 'em some coffee while they write up their reports."

The next week, here was the man again in a gray suit, sitting at the same table.

"You must be a salesman," I say, going over.

"And you must be some smart waitress to figure that out," he tells me. Didn't know was he making fun of me or not. "What kind of pie you got?"

"Blueberry, strawberry, Dutch apple, and coconut," I say, and he takes coconut, so I bring it back with his coffee.

"Gus Freeman," he says, shaking my hand.

"I'm April Bates," I tell him.

"Work here long?"

Irene Hollander says to chat up the customers when you got time, makes 'em feel special, so I lean up against the table. "Since January," I tell him.

"Good place to work?" Gus takes a big bite of the pie and sort of grunts with pleasure.

"I like it real fine."

"That's important," he says. "I used to tell my boys, 'You're going to spend one-third of your life on a job, so you better get one you like.' "

"How about you?" I ask him. "You like being a salesman?"

"I wouldn't have any other work," he says. "There's a different city to go to every day of the week. Different state, even. Maryland today, Delaware tomorrow, Pennsylvania, North Carolina. . . . Always something new to see."

"I can sure understand how you'd like that," I tell him.

"Wife didn't," Gus says, and his voice is a little softer. "She died five years back, and she never liked me going out on the road. 'It's in my blood,' I tell her, but she couldn't figure how a man could like living out of a suitcase."

"Who's taking care of the children?" I ask him.

He smiles at me. "All grown," he says. "Twenty, twenty-one, and twenty-three—all out on their own. And two of them salesmen, just like me."

Third time Gus Freeman comes to the restaurant, he hands me a little leather case.

"Got something for you, April," he says.

I hardly know what to say. Real leather, too. CORBY-ELLIS COMPANY, it says in gold on the top. Inside is a little manicure set—scissors, nail file, clippers, cuticle stick—just as cute as they can be.

"If this isn't the nicest!" I tell him, and he just smiles.

"For my favorite waitress," he says.

"Chub," I say back in the kitchen later, "how old you figure that man to be?"

Chub looks out the little window into the dining room. "Forty, if he's a day. Probably older'n that."

"He's sweet on you, April," Loretta says to me when I show her the manicure set. "Don't care if it is just a sample." Then she says, "You aren't getting mixed up with another man twice your age, are you?"

"I don't know," I tell her. "Things just sort of happen."

Next time Gus came, it was a Saturday.

"What day do you have off, April?" he says, and I tell him Sunday.

"Well, it looks like I'm here for the weekend, so how would you like to go somewhere tomorrow?"

"Like where?" I ask him.

"Anywhere you'd like. Washington, maybe. Thought we might go to the boat show, then have dinner."

"I would sure like that," I tell him.

Sunday I put on that Mexican dress of Thomasine's and was

ready a whole hour before Gus come to pick me up. This time he gives me a little travel clock with CORBY-ELLIS on the side in black letters.

"What kind of stuff you sell, Gus?" I ask when we go out to his car. He's got this pretty red convertible, and he opens the door and helps me in, just like I'm a twenty-five-year-old woman.

"Advertising," he says, when he come round the other side. "We make things that companies can give their best customers— provide 'em the wherewithal to say 'Merry Christmas.' "

"Well, they sure are pretty," I tell him.

Car starts up and next thing I know we're moving down 301 and my hair's flying out behind me, wind just whistling in my ears. I could hardly keep from shouting out loud. Never in my life had a ride in a convertible. I laugh to keep myself from shouting, and Gus laughs too.

"Like it?" he says.

I just nod my head and go on laughing.

Couldn't say Gus was handsome, exactly, but he always dressed real sharp, handkerchief in his breast pocket. On the day we went to Washington he was wearing snow-white pants and a blue-and-white striped shirt. Every hair on his head was in place, even the little white hairs on the sides above his ears. Got crinkles around his eyes and a mole one side of his nose, but he looked okay, and he sure knew how a man's supposed to act when he takes a girl out.

We went to this big place where they got all kinds of boats indoors. You could go inside any boat you wanted—sit down at the steering wheel even. Boats so big they was like houses, with beds and everything. I keep my mouth shut, try not to stare, but every time I turn my head there's something else to look at.

"April," Gus says afterwards, "you sure are easy to please. Is there anything in the world that doesn't interest you?"

"Can't think of anything," I told him. We was sitting in a seafood restaurant across the Potomac River from the airport. Gus asks the waitress can we sit by the window, and every couple minutes we see a plane take off. Here I am, nothing but a waitress myself, getting waited on in a fancy place like I'm some grand lady. Almost makes my head swim.

Just about that moment, though, something sad swelled up in me and I couldn't talk for a second. I guess it was the boats and now the water and everything, but all at once I'm thinking about Foster and me at Ocean City. I must have stopped chewing because next thing I know Gus has his hand on top of mine there at the table and he says, "Something the matter, April?" And when I don't answer, I *can't* answer, he says, "You thinking about somebody, maybe?"

I wished he hadn't asked it like that, because it made me feel sorry for myself and I could feel my eyes start to cloud up, but just as sudden the tears went away.

"Just for a moment," I tell him.

"I heard somewhere you were married once," he says. "Is that right?"

I nodded.

"Divorced?"

"Not yet," I say. "Another six months I will be."

"Your husband doesn't give you a rough time, does he? Would he be angry if he found you went out with me?"

"No," I said. "Foster's not like that."

"Good," says Gus, and this time he sort of pats my hand like he won't ask any more.

It was a good dinner, and I realized how much I'd grown up since I was at the ocean with Foster. Turn red in the face when I think how much food I left on my plate back at the White Marlin, and Foster paying for it, too. This time I taste everything put before me, to show Gus I appreciate it, and I don't squeal and point every time a plane takes off, neither.

On the drive back, it's turned chilly and the wind is just whipping about our heads, so Gus puts the top up and turns on his radio. Then he reaches over and puts his arm around me and I sit close to him on the seat. The worst thing about going out with men is you got to figure out what you're going to say once they get you home. I figured Gus would want to come in, but when we get upstairs to my room he says, "Worth doing again, April, just to see you laugh. You'll go out with me again?"

"Sure, Gus," I tell him. "I had a really nice time."

"So did I," he says, and kisses me real light on the cheek, and then he turns and heads back on down the stairs. I just stand there staring after him.

Gus and me went out every time he came through Charles County on his way down to Richmond, where the Corby-Ellis Company got its headquarters. Sometimes we'd see a movie or maybe eat at a fancy restaurant in Annapolis. Once he even come bringing me a new dress, green and blue all mixed together, so thin you could see right through it almost. I was pretty as Thomasine in that dress. Almost as pretty as Dorothy.

I learned how to walk down the street with a man, too—him with his arm sort of bent at the elbow and me with my hand tucked through his arm, case I turn my ankle or something. Every time we'd cross the street and round a corner, Gus would fix it so's he's walking on the street side.

"Why do you do like that?" I asked him once, and he says it's so if cars splash up, it's the man gets wet, but Gus always walks on the outside whether there's puddles or not.

End of July, we were coming back from the movies one night, and something told me Gus was going to get into bed with me. Nothing he said, just the way he looked at me, way he rubbed his finger up and down my arm in the car. Well, I thought, it's got to come sometime. I didn't love him, but he was all right, and I couldn't see no real reason to say no. I'd been going out with him six or seven weeks, taking his presents, not seeing any other man. So when he asks can he come in my room, I let him. And when he sat down on my bed, I sat down too. Then he kissed me and laid me back.

"April," he says, "I don't want to get you pregnant."

"You don't have to worry about that," I tell him. "That was one thing wrong between me and Foster, I can't have babies."

"Lucky for me," he says, and kisses me again.

I guess every man does it different. Foster, when he want me, he'd just take his clothes off, let 'em drop wherever they landed. Gus, though, he folds everything up neat and lays 'em to one side. Don't do a lot of touching first either, like Foster done. Just kisses me, climbs on top, and goes about his business, and when it's over, he lays there, one arm around my waist, till he gets his breath.

Next time he come to Medbury we went to bed again, and then it was just a regular part of the evening. I was his girl, I guess. Pearl, though, she suspected we was sleeping together.

"You better watch out, April, you'll get yourself pregnant," she said.

I shook my head. "There's something wrong with me, I can't have children," I tell her. "Got my period right this very minute."

"You can't *ever* have children?"

"Tried everything but stand on my head," I told her.

Thomasine stopped by the City Chicken once. Got on a sundress with no bra underneath.

"Thomasine," I tell her, "you haven't got an ounce of shame. Your nipples is poking out that dress like erasers."

She just laughs and orders her a Diet Pepsi. "What's this I hear about you going around with some man in a red convertible?" she asks me. "How come you didn't tell me you had a new boyfriend?"

"What's to tell?" I ask her.

"You hear about mine, don't you?"

"Shoot, Thomasine, you got so many boyfriends I stopped counting." I tell her about Gus, though, and how he takes me to Washington sometimes.

"Well, you sure get a classier bunch of customers than Marie gets at the diner, that's for damn sure," she says. "Everytime I see Jed Harley walk in carrying that plastic cup to spit in, I'm like to vomit. This Gus Freeman give you any presents?"

"Sometimes," I tell her.

"Well, you hang on to him," says Thomasine, " 'cause Foster didn't hardly give you nothing but a suitcase to run away with."

"That's not true, Thomasine!" I tell her.

"What else did he give you, then?"

I started to answer, then wondered why I didn't just save my breath. What did I care what Thomasine thought? Presents wasn't what I remembered him for. Didn't tell her most of the things Gus give me had CORBY-ELLIS on 'em, neither.

"April," Gus says in August, "you are some nice girl, and I want to show you a really good time. There's going to be a sales conference in Baltimore the first week of December. How would you like to go over there with me? You have any vacation coming?"

"Get two weeks a year, but haven't used 'em yet," I said.

"Well, you save one of those weeks for me. We'll do the town."

Thing about Gus, he never asked was I going out with anyone
else. Never asked me any more about Foster. I figured that was
his way of saying I wasn't to ask him what he did when he was
in Richmond, and I didn't. Suppose he had other girlfriends, but
I didn't care. Gus was somebody to be with, to talk to, to learn
how to do in restaurants with, and it was just as well, when he
was making love to me, we didn't get to talking about Foster
anyway.

***

I always wondered what it would be like to have somebody
close to me die. Never been to a funeral in my life. Was only a
day old when Mama died, they tell me. I suppose I've got cousins
or uncles somewhere who passed away, but if we got relatives,
Daddy never talks about 'em and I can imagine what they say
about him. I always figured it would be Daddy hisself who'd be
the first to go—fall off the bed or something—but I was wrong.

It was a Friday morning in August, hotter'n steam from a
kettle, and I'm sitting in my vinyl chair, cutting my toenails with
the little manicure scissors Gus give me, when there's a knock
on the door. I figure it wasn't Gus, 'cause he was in Richmond
that weekend, so I slip on this big old shirt, used to be Daddy's,
and open the door.

It's Daddy. He's standing there looking grayer than a old pet-
ticoat. He's been drinking some, but he wasn't drunk.

"You sick?" I ask, letting him in. "What's wrong?"

His lips move a little but nothing comes out and then he lets
hisself down slowly on my bed. "April, it's Dot. She's dead."

I hear the words but they don't make no sense to me whatsoever.

"What you talking about? I just seen her last week in the five-
and-dime."

Daddy shakes his head and he's crying now, face all screwed
up, lips a-quivering, but not making one bit of sound. I sink right

down there on the floor, my back against the wall. Now I know it's true, but the shock ain't hit yet.

"What happened?" I ask him, and this time he takes a big gulp of air and then he tells me.

"Neighbors hadn't seen her for two, three days . . . then the woman . . . down in the pet shop . . . she tells police there's this stink comin' from somewhere, not her puppies, either . . . and police go upstairs and find Dot's body, dead since Wednesday."

I couldn't talk. Daddy's words come slamming up against my head. I'm trying not to let 'em in, but they slip inside anyways.

"Where's Max?" is all I can get out.

Now Daddy's eyes flash. "Max is gone. Dot was murdered, April. Her neck was broke. Arm was broke. Sheriff's got a warrant out for his arrest, but he's gone."

"Oh, Daddy." I crawl over to him and wrap my arms around his legs and then we were both crying. Daddy's got one hand on my head and we're letting the sobs come, neither one of us caring how it sounds.

To tell the truth, first thought that entered my mind when I heard Dorothy was gone was how she can't go spend the night with Foster no more. And then, that out of the way, it's like I'm crying for some little sister, not a big one at all—Dorothy and her baby-like voice, the way she'd snuggle up to Max. Like her body went ahead and growed up without the rest of her, and she's a little child all her life just wanting some man to be good to her. Could see why Daddy's blubbering on about what an awful father he's been and how he ain't raised us right and do I forgive him, and I tell him I do, but he don't believe it, just goes on crying.

Only a hour or so before the whole of Medbury knows. Irene Hollander calls me on the hall telephone and says how sorry she and George are about it. "Take today and tomorrow off, April," she says. "If you need even longer, you can have it."

I thank her, thank all the folks that call. Old Mr. Cody come up from downstairs asking is there anything he can do. Only thing you want when somebody dies is for that someone to be alive again so you can treat 'em like you should have, even though you know that if they was to walk in that very moment, you'd probably go back to your old ways inside a hour or so.

On Saturday, when the police have taken all the evidence they need, they let Thomasine and me in so we can collect Dorothy's things. Place still smells of death, like meat left to rot, and we open all the windows and turn on the fan. Thomasine's crying all the while.

"Coulda been me," she keeps saying. "Some of the men I've slept with only wanted to slap me around. More'n once I got me twenty dollars just for lettin' a man bruise me."

Didn't anything make sense to me anymore. How come she and Dorothy be like that and I'm not? A man bruise me once, it's the last chance he ever get to lay a hand on me. Still, how come I meet a kind man like Foster and walk out? Meet a nice man like Gus Freeman, and can't get up no feelings for him? Like all us Bates girls is bent somewhere inside.

Thomasine sets to work dividing up Dorothy's clothes, but I didn't have the heart for it. Dorothy's feet so small neither one of us could wear her shoes. Fifty-seven pair of four-inch heels with bows and sequins going to the Disabled American Veterans. Only thing I wanted from her closet was my robe back that Foster give me with the white fur around the cuffs. It was ripped under both arms and had a coffee stain on the front, but I took it anyway.

Thomasine finally packed me up two sacks full of dresses and blouses and things, but I didn't see how in the world I'd ever have the heart to put 'em on.

"Daddy catch Max, he'll kill him," Thomasine says. We knew it was Max 'cause his stuff was gone. Drawers pulled out and furniture overturned, trying to make it look like a robbery, police said, but if it was a robbery, how come Max didn't report it, and how come him and his clothes are missing?

When I got back to the Adams Hotel, I had me a long cry about Dorothy—about what kind of life she could have had for herself, maybe, if she was raised different. Wanted Foster's arms around me in the worst way. I knew, though, that what I said to him there at the last hurt him more'n he could ever forgive—

thrown something up in his face even Thomasine had the decency
not to blab. And if I was to go back to him now, with a job of
my own, money in my pocket, I could be a lot better wife to him
but I still couldn't give him babies. It was good, I guess, I walked
out when I did.

Funeral was Sunday afternoon, a little graveyard down the hill
from the Exxon station behind Medbury. Thomasine and me was
holding hands in the backseat of the big black car that followed
the hearse, Daddy sitting up front with the driver, blubbering
away. Whole long string of cars following us to the cemetery,
everybody wanting to hear just what the preacher's got to say
about Dorothy. Always get a big turnout for funerals in Medbury,
no matter who dies. Just not that much to do on a Sunday afternoon. Thomasine said a crew of women showed up day before
at the trailer with brooms and mops and say they come to get us
ready for the funeral.

"Take ten women scrubbin' all day just to get the toilet bowl
clean," I tell her, trying to make her laugh, but Thomasine's still
sniffling.

"Then this morning," she says, "they all come back again with
so many pies and cakes and hams there'll hardly be room for
people in the trailer."

I figure they was just looking for a chance to get their hands
on the Bateses' trailer and turn it inside out. Daddy have any
bottles hid, you can be sure he wouldn't find 'em again after they
was through.

Easier to say who wasn't at the funeral than who was. Sister
Perry's there in her white dress and stockings, eyes closed, sort
of swaying back and forth. Mrs. Dawson and the sparrow lady.
Marie, Jack, Tillie, Chub, Pearl, and Loretta. Didn't see the
Harley brothers about, but saw Howard and James from the
Amoco. Foster's uncles was there, too. Got on their best suits.

"April," Russell says, "it is one sad shame about your sister.
Terrible thing to happen here in Medbury. We are as sorry as
we can be." Shum is nodding his head he's sorry, too.

"Thank you," I tell them.

Russell starts to move on by, but Shum lags behind like he's something to say won't let him rest. "Anytime you want to come back and visit, April, you can come see me and Russell," he says.

I just give him a little smile, 'cause there's no way I can promise that.

And then, when I get up to the grave and the preacher starts talking, I see Foster standing right there on the other side, his eyes on me. I fasten my eyes to the ground. What's he thinking? I wonder. Can't help but have heard about Gus and me. A wonder he come to the funeral at all. Then I think about him and Dorothy. . . .

Minister goes on longer than Daddy paid him to do. Figures this is the one and only time he'll get the Bates family together for a sermon, he's going to do it right. It's Dorothy who's there in the coffin, but it's some woman in the Bible taken in adultery that the preacher's talking about. He says how these men bring her to Jesus and say she's been sleeping around and how the law says they're supposed to stone her to death, and what does Jesus think about that? And Jesus says anybody who hasn't sinned hisself can pick up a stone and toss it first. And how all the folks walked away.

I liked that story. Never heard it before. Liked the preacher, too, for reading it. Thomasine told me later she didn't think the preacher should have said that, but I said I didn't see the harm— everybody knew what Dorothy was up to. When they started to lower the coffin, Daddy gets down on his knees, crying, and puts one hand on it, his arm reaching lower and lower like he's goin' down there with Dorothy. The preacher takes Daddy by the shoulder and helps him up, and then Thomasine and Daddy and me each picks up a handful of dirt and tosses it down on the coffin and the funeral's over. Grave diggers standing off to one side with their shovels waiting for us to go so's they can fill the hole up. All those heaps of flowers at one end sort of makes me sick—smell just like the rose cologne Buddy Travis give me once.

On our way back to the cars, Foster falls in step beside me, and my heart starts banging around in my chest.

"I'm awful sorry about Dorothy," he says.

"So am I," I tell him. "They say she died on Wednesday, and I keep trying to think what all I was doing Wednesday, going on about my business and her back there at Max's getting her neck broke. If I'd just gone over, I might could have stopped it."

"Everybody thinks that way when something like this happens," Foster said. "Dorothy come over to my house one night after Max beat her up. I let her sleep in the spare room. Now I'm thinking how I should have gone to the police, reported it, but I suppose if she wouldn't press charges herself, they wouldn't either."

I was so glad to hear how Dorothy slept in the spare room I wanted to grab Foster's arm and say how I knew it all the time. Then I'm thinking how I'm standing there in the blue and green dress Gus give me. I was Gus Freeman's girl now, and no use pretending any different. Foster would know all about it anyway, and be glad I was worrying someone else for a change.

"Foster," I said, while I had the chance, "it don't sound right, I know, but I felt ever' bit as bad when Vinnie died as I do now. I knew how that hurt you, and I just didn't want you to go on thinking it didn't hurt me too." Foster's face looks sort of strange, so I keep talking to fill up space. "At least you did something kind for Dorothy and you got that to remember. I seen her last at the five-and-dime and didn't say hardly anything to her."

We'd reached the dirt road where the cars were parked, and folks stood about talking in low voices. Mrs. Perry had Thomasine backed up against a Buick, giving her the born-again speech, and from the look on Thomasine's face, it wasn't taking so good.

"You can't let your conscience do you that way," Foster said to me. "Can't go around all the time treatin' folks like it's the last time you'll see 'em alive. It's the whole way you got on together that counts. You and Dorothy had you some good times now and then, didn't you? Got to remember those, too."

I looked up at Foster and wondered if he was really talking about us. Wondered if most of what he remembered about me was good or bad. Bad, probably. I wanted to throw my arms around him, wanted to say how I'd missed him, wanted to say take me back, even though I can't make babies. Something kind

I saw in Foster I never saw in no other man, not even Gus, but, like I said, I was Gus's girl now and Foster knew it. He kept his hands off me, even though everybody else was hugging and touching. I could hardly stand it.

"How's things with you?" I asked, trying hard to keep him there, keep him talking.

"Fair," he says, his hands behind his back like he can't quite trust hisself. "Finished the bridge. Catwalks come down in May. The Skycrane took the derricks down, and we topped off the end of June. It's a good-looking bridge, too."

"You working that one in Baltimore like you said?"

He nodded. "Drive up with Clyde of a morning." He stopped and looked out over my shoulder, like he was seeing beyond me. "Been thinking some about selling my place."

Everything in my whole body froze when he said that. It's like all the hope I'd had that someday me and Foster would be back together had just dried up into dust. Like Foster and me were seeing each other for the last time, maybe, standing there saying goodbye. Couldn't hardly speak.

"Why . . . would you sell it?" I ask him after a minute, my voice so shaky it sounds all sick.

"Well, I've been thinking about bein' a boomer like Jack Tulley—travel around, see places. . . ."

All the way to the funeral dinner I'm curled up in one corner of the backseat crying like I couldn't never stop. Thomasine's patting my shoulder and Daddy's reaching around from the front seat, patting my knee, both of 'em saying how Dorothy's gone to her rest, can't no man beat her up no more. But it wasn't Dorothy I was crying over. Was Foster. Was me.

THIRTEEN

Since spring, the world had mercifully gone into high gear. Foster, and everyone he knew, was busy. Even the Harley brothers had been swept up by the needs of a new crop: the tobacco had to be sown in April, then transplanted, cultivated, sprayed for cutworms, and topped.

Foster rose a half hour earlier each morning in order to be at Clyde's by six. From there they'd drive to the construction site at Hawkins Point in Baltimore. Sue Sheldon had given birth to another daughter in June and sometimes, when Foster climbed in the front seat of Clyde's car, he detected the milk-sweet scent of a baby, whether on Clyde's shirt or the car seat, he wasn't sure.

When the weather was good, the men worked as long as daylight would permit, weekends too. By the time Foster reached home in the evening, he had little energy for anything more than watching a recap of what John Dean had said that day at the Watergate hearings. But it was what Foster had been hearing since June about April Ruth's new boyfriend that made him welcome overtime at the bridge, the numbing fatigue, and the unconsciousness of sleep.

"Shoot, Foster, April's going 'round with a guy older'n you are," Clyde said. "Saw 'em together at the movies the other night. He's got gray in his sideburns."

Foster tried to see where the satisfaction lay in this particular information. He lined it up first one way and then another, but it always ended up a rock in the pit of his stomach.

"I seen 'em outside the Drug Fair gettin' in his red convertible," Juju added. "She got herself a sugar daddy, that's what she got. Buy her things, take her places. Not the type to settle down, Foster. You well off to be rid of her."

"Maybe so," Foster said without conviction. The men had obviously thought that he would feel young in comparison. It only made him feel older still. If he, at thirty-three, could not hold on to April, but a man in his forties could, then Foster was over the hill.

"How's that divorce coming along?" Jack Tulley asked.

"Another six months—end of January," Foster said in answer, and climbed the ladder to the metalwork on top of the concrete reinforcements, which rose like stair steps out toward the Patapsco River and the sky beyond.

Tulley's raising gang was one of several at the southern approach to the bridge. Others were assigned to Soller's Point across the river. Each group worked steadily toward the day when they would meet in the middle and put the final span in place.

Lunchtime was more pleasant for Foster when a tall, lanky Swede was eating somewhere else. It may have been his youth—twenty-two at the most, younger than Juju, even—or the way he would strip to the waist as he worked, the yellow-white hair of his chest glistening with sweat. Foster, surefooted on the high beams, his sea legs sturdy, resented the studied bravado of the young man with the golden chest who would ride the headache ball when the boss wasn't looking, or go scrabbling up a thirty-foot ladder, the sun in his eyes, reach the top, and go on climbing a rung that wasn't there. Then he'd laugh after he'd teetered and caught himself in time.

"Jesus!" Jack Tulley told him. "Next time, you're like to go over backwards. *Watch* yourself!"

The Swede only laughed again. He was always laughing. Foster felt sure that if the blond ever fell, he would rise again, laughing still.

Foster watched him parade about the construction site bare-chested, and then he would picture the man named Gus Freeman sitting by April Ruth in his red convertible, think about April up in her room at the Adams Hotel with a young punk named Buddy Travis. Men seemed to be coming out of nowhere—young men, old men, reckless blond men without shirts—and every so often Foster felt overwhelmed by a sense of loss, as though life were passing him by—rolling by on wheels, rushing by on feet, dancing by in the sweaty embrace of a country dance hall, where it was also said that April and her Gus were seen occasionally, April with her arms around his neck.

On the bridge, however, there was no one better than Foster. When the wind shifted, he was ready for it, leg muscles locked, leaning just so far into the gust and no further. He could walk the shiny surface of a six-inch beam as effortlessly as he could walk in the web of a wider inverted length of steel, or step from one to another several hundred feet in the air, nothing but space beneath him, each foot knowing just where it was to go.

"Where he learn hand signals like that?" Juju observed, watching the Swede give directions to another man high aloft an anchor pier. "Look like one of them lifeguards down at the beach." The others laughed.

"Flagman on a railroad," added Clyde derisively.

When it rained and the men left early, Foster would sometimes stop at the 7-Eleven and browse through magazines there on the rack, maybe pick up a couple to take home. Once, as he turned the pages of *Motor Trend,* he saw the red convertible glide by outside, the top up, and park just beyond the Italian restaurant a few doors down. He watched as a man with gray sideburns, impeccably dressed in shirt and navy slacks, came around the car with an umbrella, opened the door for April, and helped her out.

Everything about April seemed different. Her legs seemed longer, hips rounder, her walk more womanly, and yet—the way she hopped across a puddle, the way she clung to the umbrella handle with both hands next to Gus's, the way she shook the water off before she entered the restaurant, something she and Vinnie used to do together when they came in out of the rain—

brought back more memories than he could deal with. Foster left quickly and drove home without looking back.

He'd talked at work about becoming a boomer, but Clyde hadn't thought much of the idea.

"We been partners for over twelve years," he reminded. "Hate to lose you."

"Well, you got more reason to stick around here than I do," Foster told him. "Don't want to go back to raising buildings if I can help it. I like the open water."

"Dang it, Foster, we're close enough to water there's always a bridge going up somewhere. One going up right now down in Calvert County."

Foster never answered.

There were times, he discovered, when he managed to go almost all day without thinking once of April. Maybe even get halfway home before she seemed to perch there on the seat beside him, or mug at him in the windshield. That was progress. And then, one Sunday in August, he found himself standing in a cemetery, across an open grave from April Ruth, and all the feelings he had so carefully packaged, taped, and put away seemed to rise again and surround him.

He knew that she was Gus Freeman's girl now—knew that the dress she had on, probably, was a gift from Gus—the dress and the little gold earrings in her ears that were now pierced, and the slim gold chain in a serpentine twist that lay delicately on the skin about her neck. But he wanted to talk with her anyway. He fell in beside her on her way back to the cars and they talked about Dorothy. At one point she said something about Vinnie— about how Vinnie's death had hurt her too, and Foster could see in her eyes that she meant it. But throughout the conversation she kept her distance, made no move to touch him, not even to shake his hand. *Don't you ever put your hands on me again, Foster.* The words had haunted him even there. *I don't want you to do it to me. Not ever!*

And so they talked of this and that, but just as she was about to get in the car, Foster said, "I been hearing some about your new boyfriend, April. He treat you all right, does he?"

She only nodded, eyes on the ground.

"Well, then, that's good." Foster swallowed, and held the door open for her. She looked up at him for just a moment, then climbed in, over Thomasine's legs, and curled up in one corner.

***

Foster had seen Jed and Wallace Harley only a few times over the summer—coming out of a hardware store, in the checkout line of the Safeway, or the self-serve lane at the Amoco—and each time their sullenness seemed to have settled in a little deeper, developed roots.

"You guys haven't got over that horse race yet?" Foster chided once.

"Race like that can catch anybody by surprise," Jed told him. "What we're on about is you still haven't give us a chance to win back the four hundred dollars we lost at poker."

"Well, I don't have me a solid weekend to spend at cards," Foster told him. "Got better things to do."

"Trouble is," said Jed, "everybody plays different. Wally and me, takes us six, seven hours to hit our stride. You play only three hours, you got the advantage."

"You want a long game, I'll play you eight hours straight. Sit down at four some Saturday afternoon and play you through till midnight, that'll stop your whining. Then see if I don't walk off with more of your money, set you sulking for another year."

"We got us a deal," said Jed.

Their tobacco crop had not gone well, Foster knew. Jed and Wallace hardly opened their mouths August through September without a cussword coming out. What crop there was had to be harvested, speared, dried, stored, striped, sized, and bundled— a sixteen-hour day, so the poker game was delayed still further.

In the fall, Foster's uncles condescended to sit on his porch occasionally when the weather was good, and their conversation took the same bickering tone as before.

"Bad year for tobacco," Russell might say.

"Got the blue mold," Shum would add. "That's what the fellas up at the Texaco told me. Your crop get the fungus, you only get half the weight.''

"Not that bad," Russell corrected. "Third, maybe, per acre, but not half."

"Way I heard it, it'd be down a half," said Shum. "Too much rain."

Foster looked out over the yard where April and Vinnie once played. His life had made a revolution and was back where it started. The squares on his calendar were empty again, the garden unplanted, and the seasons of his life seemed as predictable as spring and fall.

"Lloyd always said he'd never go into tobacco," Russell mused.

"Lloyd said it right," Shum added. "Lloyd'a lived, he would have made some fine cattle farm out of this property. Wouldn't have just let it go to seed."

***

It was November when Foster saw Jed and Wallace next. He had begun eating at Marie's diner again on the nights Thomasine was off. Marie always welcomed him as an old friend, never mentioned April.

"That is sure some fine bridge you fellas built," she told him, setting his stewed tomatoes and roast pork down on the table. "Think of you every time I go to the Eastern shore."

"Going to be so there's hardly a bridge you haven't put your hand to," the cook told him.

"Looks that way," said Foster.

Jed and Wallace came in when Foster was half through and slid directly across from him in the booth. They were both smiling.

"Must have got some good news for a change," Foster commented. "Last time I seen you smile was March."

Wallace laughed out loud. "Always smile after the tobacco's sorted and put away. Got time on our hands till spring."

"How about that poker game?" Jed asked, getting right to the point. "We can set it up for Saturday."

"Suits me," said Foster. "I'll see if Bigfoot don't want to come. Better when we've got four."

He talked to Clyde about it the next day.

"Sue will kill me, but I've got to get away from her bellyachin'," he said. "Got herself pregnant again, five months after Belinda was born, and she's throwin' up again every morning."

"Figure you had somethin' to do with it, too." Foster grinned.

Clyde grunted. "All you got to do is throw a pair of trousers over the bed and Sue's pregnant." He turned suddenly there on the high beams. "Jesus! Look at that!"

Foster looked over to where the Swede, carrying a basket of bolts, had reached a corner girder and was stepping across onto the right-angled beam on the other side.

Foster edged around to where the young man was standing.

"Let me tell you something!" he said. "You don't never cross a corner like that. You carry a basket of something, you carry it in the other arm out away from you so you got a hand free to grab that girder, case you need it. That basket happen to bump the upright when you step across, could send you down."

The Swede looked at him with laughing eyes. "Whatever you say, Pops," he retorted.

All afternoon, and well into the evening, Foster fought against the image of the Swede falling, in slow motion, the basket of bolts swirling about his head. . . . *Whatever you say, Pops.* . . . Head over heels, slow cartwheels in the air, the bolts sprinkled like stars against the blue of the sky. . . . *Whatever you say.*

At four o'clock on Saturday, the first of December, Foster sat in the Harley brothers' kitchen, waiting for the game to begin. The edge of the table was sticky, and the linoleum had that same worn look that seems to move in when men live too long in a house by themselves.

"Got plenty of beer now," Wallace was saying affably, opening the refrigerator and showing the cans. "Ham here for sandwiches, anyone gets hungry. Just help yourself. This is an eight-hour game; last hand at midnight."

"Hold on, now," Clyde said. "I didn't say nothing about playing that long."

"Well, you play as long as you can, but Foster here made us an agreement."

Clyde chuckled. "Why, Wally, you might could play Foster for eight *days*, be deeper in the hole each hand."

"We'll see about that," said Wallace, still smiling as Jed shuffled the cards. "Draw poker, gents?"

"Fine with me," said Foster. "What's the ante?"

"Dollar a round," said Jed. "Jacks or better to open."

The room fell suddenly silent except for the slap of cards on the table. Now and then a chair creaked or a foot shuffled as someone shifted position. Faces that had been smiling before now assumed the uniform look of practiced boredom.

"Ante up," said Jed, and chips were tossed to the center of the table.

For an hour or so, the men played routinely, getting a feel for each other's style. There were no large pots, no big winners or losers.

Well into the game, however, after four rounds had been dealt with no one able to open, Foster, dealing, found himself with a pair of jacks and three low cards. He opened with a bet of five dollars and the other players called. Foster mentally counted the pot: thirty-six dollars. He noted with satisfaction that each of the others had drawn three cards. He immediately decided upon a play he liked to use in such situations, particularly when sitting to the right of the dealer or, as he was, dealing himself. He kept the jacks and two worthless cards, and drew only one card, merely pretending to look at it. In truth, he didn't care what it was.

"Twenty bucks," he said, in monotone, tossing in a couple of ten-dollar chips. As he had hoped, the other players, figuring him for two pairs, folded without a second thought, although they probably had him beaten.

"Sumbitch!" said Wallace. "Almost hit an ace-high flush!"

Foster, however, said nothing. He perfunctorily showed the jacks to prove he had openers, and raked in the pot.

There were some things that Foster did well, and poker, generally, was one of them. He played well enough to make enemies from time to time of Jed and Wallace—won enough from Wallace a couple years back to make a down payment on his pickup. He didn't do as well at poker as he did on the bridge, wasn't as sure

of his hands as he was of his feet, but he had never lost more
than he could comfortably afford, and now he felt the old stirrings
of luck, the same as he'd felt at the track when he bet on Battling
Blue.

Clyde was a more cautious player. With a wife and four daughters at home, a fifth child on the way, he rarely bet a hand without
good cards. Sat and sat, waiting for the sure kill, irritating the
Harley brothers.

"What's it take to make you bet?" Wallace chided once. "Playin'
with you is about as much fun as layin' a dead whore."

"Just deal, Wally, will you?" Jed complained. The cards went
around again.

The hands went by and the hours went by, and at eight o'clock,
Jed brought in another case of beer from the back porch.

"Make yourself somethin' to eat," Wallace instructed on his
way to the bathroom. "Want my guests to be comfortable."

As Foster handed the mustard around, Clyde said, "Don't
know that I can stay past eleven. Sue's not been feeling too good
all day."

Jed laughed. "It's not Sue that's feelin' bad, it's you, Clyde.
Your wallet ain't gettin' any fatter."

"Well, it's not that much thinner neither," Clyde retorted, and
bit into his sandwich.

"More beer. Help yourselves," Wallace said, coming back in,
but he did not take any himself.

Despite their losses, the Harleys seemed to perk up after eating, and the cards were shuffled again. Having played rather well
in the early hours of the game, Foster found himself dealt a bad
hand, and passed. The room felt warm. He'd been drinking too
much.

"Jesus!" he said. "Get a window open in here. You got the
heat on eighty?"

Wallace reached over, opened the back door, but closed it
again after a minute.

From nine on, Foster's luck got progressively worse. Now and
then he was dealt a good hand, but when he lost, he lost heavily—
having bet more each round to regain his losses than he knew

was wise. It was Wallace now who was ahead, Jed next, Clyde holding his own, and Foster losing.

"Christ!" he said, as he lost sixty dollars to the pot, knowing he should have passed. He had to play more cautiously.

At eleven, Clyde announced he was playing his last hand. Sue had been threatening to miscarry, he said. She might need him.

"She needs that forty-five dollars you won, that's what," Jed said. "You scared to try doubling it, that's all."

"Well, win or lose, this is my last hand," Clyde told him. He stared hard at Foster from across the table.

" 'Nother beer?" Wallace offered.

"No," Clyde said irritably.

Wallace removed the beer from the table but put a dish of peanuts there instead. While he was dealing, Jed managed to knock the dish off. Clyde stared hard at Foster some more. Foster, holding a full house, with three kings, bet heavily.

"I'll raise you," said Wallace.

"Raise you again," said Foster.

"Reraise," said Wallace.

Foster, palms sweating, called, and saw Wallace take the pot with three aces and a pair of tens. Clyde picked up his jacket.

"Well, that's it for me. Thanks for the brew."

No one said much when he left.

Foster won a small pot on the next hand, and they prepared to play again. As Jed was shuffling the cards, however, the phone rang. Wallace swung around and lifted the receiver from the wall.

"Hello." There was a pause. Then, "He's busy." Another pause. Then Wallace thrust the receiver toward Foster. "Clyde. Somethin' about the bridge."

Foster took the phone.

"What's up?"

Clyde's voice was barely audible. "Foster, they got that game rigged."

Foster looked around the table. Wallace's eyes were on him. Jed did not move a muscle.

"Yeah?" he said.

"I'm telling you, they'll skin you alive. You bet one more cent, you'll lose your shirt."

"How do you know?" Foster stalled.

"I don't know how they're doing it, but every goddam time they deal, they've got the good cards."

Foster tried to remember. He was more tired, or possibly on the verge of being drunk, than he had imagined. He could not remember the hands the Harleys had dealt. Jed was dealing out the cards now, his fingers flying like a pro, his eyes on Foster still.

"Make some excuse," Clyde said. "Tell 'em we've got to work tomorrow—something's gone wrong at the bridge. Tell 'em anything. I felt one of 'em kick the other under the table—got my foot instead. Don't let on that I told you."

"Well, I'll drive if you can't," Foster said in answer, then handed the receiver back to Jed, who hung up.

"What was that all about?" asked Jed.

"Sue," Foster told them. "Might have to go to the hospital. I'll be driving on Monday, 'stead of Clyde."

Uneasily, his stomach in a knot, Foster surveyed his hand. He was instantly reassured; Jed had dealt him a pair of aces. Clyde was mistaken. By God, it was time he made a killing. He was $900 in the hole. He took the pot, reducing his debt by a couple of hundred.

Wallace dealt the next hand and Jed won the pot. Foster dealt the hand after that, but his luck was bad; Jed won that too. It was almost midnight, and Jed dealt the last hand of the evening. Wallace opened with a fifty-dollar bet.

Concentrate, Foster told himself. Don't you let them pull nothing. Palms damp, he stole a look at his cards. A pat flush, king-high! Take it easy now, he told himself. Don't raise too much—keep these guys in. Maybe they'll improve and I can really sandbag them. Lord, but I could get well on this hand!

"Call and raise fifty," he said, placing two fifty-dollar chips in the pot to cover the bet and the raise.

Jed called, too. Foster's pulse pounded as he waited to see what Wallace would do. If he raises again, I'll be damned if the

game's not crooked, he thought. Wallace and Jed would have
rigged it together. But how?

Wallace only called, however. There was $300 on the table,
plus the antes.

"Well," said Wallace, "no use bluffing now. Give me three
cards."

"Two cards," said Jed.

"I'll play these," Foster told them, his mouth dry with excitement. He'd make them pay through the nose. They were con-
vinced *he* was bluffing. He'd been drinking, he was losing, this
was the last hand. . . . Anyone would bluff in a situation like
this.

"Bet a hundred," Wallace deadpanned.

Foster felt a trace of panic. Jesus, could Wally have lucked out
again? Should he just call? Get out while he could? What the
hell, go for it! he decided. "I raise a hundred," he said aloud.

"Now wait just a goddam minute, Foster." Wallace leaned
back in his chair. "I don't know what you had on you when you
walked in here tonight, but you owe eight hundred fifty right this
minute. I don't recollect we said nothing about credit. When you
fixing to pay what you owe?"

"I got a CD for three thousand dollars coming due next week,"
Foster told him. "You'll have your money by next Saturday, soon
as I can get to the bank."

Wallace thrust his tongue in his cheek. "Well, now, I don't
know. What you think, Jed?"

"If he's got a CD, I suppose that's as good as money, he don't
run out on us or something."

"Goddamit, I'm goin' to walk out of here *you* owing me yet,"
Foster snapped. "Play!"

"Raise you fifty," said Wallace.

"Your fifty plus a hundred," Foster told him.

"That's it for me," said Jed, and laid down his cards.

"I raise *you* a hundred." Wallace was looking Foster square
in the eye. The cards felt damp in Foster's hands.

"Call and a hundred to you."

"Reraise," Wallace said.

Sweat broke out on Foster's forehead beneath his hair. "One more time," he said.

"Two more times."

"Call," said Foster, his muscles locked in spasm.

Wallace showed his four queens.

**

"Christ!" Clyde said on Monday as they drove to work. "Foster, you were had! Those Harleys are as crooked as a cowpath. *Jesus*, why didn't you go home after I called?"

Talking about it to Bigfoot made him feel neither better nor worse. Foster already felt as ridiculous as was humanly possible. "I looked those cards over good, Clyde. Don't see how they could have marked them I wouldn't have seen."

"They set you up. All that beer. You didn't see *them* drinking much, did you? Something about the way they deal. They been hanging out with that card shark up in PG County. I saw them together couple times over the summer. He's a card mechanic if I ever saw one, and you can bet he taught them a thing or two. You ever see them shuffle the way they was shuffling Saturday night? Fingers move so fast you can hardly see 'em. Way they dealt? Why, they let you win the first couple hours before they raised the stakes, get you betting high, then took you to the cleaners, right down to your socks. How much are they into you, Foster?"

"Twelve hundred some. . . ."

"Holy Mother!"

"Look, keep quiet about it at the bridge, okay?"

"Not the kind of news I like to spread around," Clyde promised.

By the time they reached the construction site there was a message waiting for Clyde: Sue had miscarried. Clyde turned around and headed back.

"I'll drive you home at four," Jack Tulley told Foster. "We'll have to take on another man for today. We're working up on the grid."

The derrick was just offshore, and when the crane swung them up, it was the Swede who faced Foster there in the skip box.

"Where's your buddy?" the blond man asked, a twisted hand-kerchief tied rakishly about his head, just visible beneath the rim of the safety helmet.

"Wife's sick," Foster told him, his words clipped. Just shut up, he thought. Let's just shut up, do the work, and go home. He held on to the edge of the box and stared out over the river. It was his own fault for going to the Harleys' so cock-assed confident. Eat their food, drink their brew, thank you, boys, just hit me again. They'd set him up, all right. Had a whole summer to work at it. He dimly remembered getting a card that seemed to have a bump in one corner—a pinprick. Why hadn't he brought his own deck? Jesus, he was dense! And all those distractions toward the end of the evening whenever one of the brothers dealt—Jed spilling the peanuts? Wallace pushing beer right up under his nose? How come *he* hadn't seen it? he wondered. You're over the hill, old man, Juju would say if he knew.

The skip box rattled as it swung around, and the Swede got out before it had even stopped—put one foot up on the edge and stepped across open air to the beam beyond. Foster swore at him under his breath.

Down on the ground, Jack Tulley and Juju were helping assemble the pieces they would put into place later, but the ground crew had already attached a cable to a two-ton piece of metal that Foster and the Swede were to guide into place.

Foster waited at one corner, the Swede at the other. Seventy feet below, the water took on the color of the sky, that special grayness peculiar to the weeks between Thanksgiving and Christmas. The wind was cold and damp. Out of the corner of his eye, Foster watched the Swede. The young man stood with his weight on one leg, hip thrust out, thumbs stuck in the top of his tool belt. It rankled Foster the way the Swede refused to wear the warm caps that the other men put on beneath their helmets, preferring, instead, that ridiculous bandanna.

It wasn't just the kerchief. The Swede ran when he should have walked, jumped when he should have stepped. Every time Foster thought for sure that the man was going over, he proved as surefooted as Foster himself and laughed at the concern on the others' faces.

The deck foreman, standing below, signaled that the steel was about to be lifted, and the Swede was signaling, in turn, to Foster.

"What the hell's he sayin' with a hand signal like that?" Foster muttered aloud. "Fuckin' show-off thinks he's directing traffic."

The beam, dangling from a single cable, swung around 360 degrees.

Should've had a tag line on that to steady it, Foster thought. Down below, he saw Jack Tulley walk over, gesturing to the foreman. Give 'em hell, Jack, Foster said to himself.

The beam rose higher, and the swinging never stopped.

"Crap," Foster said aloud again. "Clyde would have had one hand on it by now. Swede gonna wait till it knocks him in the water? Waitin' for me to reach out over here? I got two yards between me and the steel; it's him got to get a hand on it first. Come on, you son of a bitch, give me a sign! You going to bring it in or you waitin' for me?"

Now the Swede had maneuvered himself behind the swinging steel. Holding on to the corner column with one hand, Foster leaned out at an angle, but still could not see the Swede's face, could not tell what was about to happen. But he heard the thunking clang of metal against metal as the beam swung against the Swede's girder and bounced off. And then, the searing, smashing pain as the other end swung into Foster's column, against his hand. He let go.

He remembered only the stillness as his body began the plunge. Like a bird, his arms were spread out on either side of him, the injured hand heavy and numb. The air rushed by his face as yard after yard of concrete flashed by. Foster's body spun dizzily downward toward the water, which grew blacker and blacker, then swallowed him up.

FOURTEEN

Gus and me had our first quarrel on the way to Baltimore. I took the week off like he said, and had my best clothes there in the backseat of the convertible. I was telling him how good the Hollanders been to me, how every time one of us has a birthday there at the City Chicken, they give us a little party in the afternoon, and all our friends can come by for a drink, no charge.

"You got a birthday coming up soon?" Gus asks me.

"January tenth," I tell him.

"How old you going to be? Twenty?" he asks, smiling.

"Twenty!" I look at him, pleased. Guess I always did look older in my uniform. "Going to be eighteen," I say.

Car almost goes off the road. Gus grabs the wheel with both hands. "Eighteen!" he says. "You're only seventeen, April?"

I stop smiling myself. "What's wrong with that?" I ask him. "Weren't you never seventeen?"

Gus lets out his breath. "Well, you sure fooled me. Figured you working and all, you were eighteen at least."

Something in his voice didn't set right with me.

"I didn't try to fool nobody," I told him. "All you had to do was ask."

He must have drove a mile without saying nothing. "How'd you get married if you're not eighteen?" he says finally.

"Daddy signed a paper."

"Jesus Christ!" Gus shakes his head like he still can't believe it. "It's a good thing we're not leaving the state. Get me with the Mann Act."

I didn't have the least idea what he was talking about.

"Look," I tell him, "if this changes things, you can just take me on back home. You ain't obliged or nothing."

Then Gus pats my hand. "Sorry, April. Just didn't expect you to be so young. We're going to have a good time in Baltimore like I promised."

First thing I noticed about Baltimore was the buildings is a whole lot taller than they are in Washington. Figured this must be a little what New York City is like. Sidewalks full of people, all hurrying to go somewhere. It was our hotel room, though, I couldn't get over.

"Oh, Gus!" I says. There was two beds, each of 'em king-size. Could have put all the employees of the City Chicken in those two beds with nobody touching.

There was a desk looked like it belonged in a museum and two chairs with a lamp hanging down on a chain, but it was the bathroom you just couldn't never forget. All done up in red and black, it had a light in the ceiling you could get yourself a suntan without ever stepping outside, the kind of shower gives you a massage, and there on the sink, in a tray, all kinds of things you could take home and keep for your own—tiny little bottle of mink-oil shampoo, soap, lipstick, mascara—all wrapped up in fancy paper. I walked over to the window, feeling like a princess, and looked down at the street. Wondered if Foster hisself had ever been this high up, even on the bridge.

"Like it?" Gus asks, putting his arms around me.

"Almost get to heaven up here," I tell him.

We was to be in Baltimore till Friday. I knew Gus had to go to meetings during the day, but each morning he'd give me some money, tell me to go out and buy myself something, have a good time. Never knew what to do, though, and I was afraid I'd get lost I go too far. So I'd just walk a few blocks either direction, look in the store windows, then come back to the hotel and watch TV. Rode up and down the elevators and learned what a mezzanine is. In the evening, Gus would take me out to dinner somewhere, or to a club with a floor show—woman in veils dancing around barefoot, getting all sweaty or something. One thing I didn't like was Gus telling me not to answer the phone if it rang. Might be his boss calling, he said; better for him not to know there was a woman in the room.

"What am I supposed to do if somebody knocks on the door?" I ask him. "Crawl under the bed?"

Gus doesn't say. "Just don't answer the phone," he tells me.

Another thing I didn't like was Gus going to the big sales banquet Wednesday night and not taking me.

"It just wouldn't look good, April," he says. "The other men will be there with their wives. They'd think you were my daughter, and I'd have to explain to everyone." Then he reaches in his pocket and hands me a fifty-dollar bill. "This'll be your night to howl," he says. "That enough?"

"It's enough," I told him.

I didn't feel like going out by myself, though. I'm thinking how Gus isn't never going to take me someplace important. Isn't ever going to ask me to marry him, either. Long as I'm Gus Freeman's girl, I get to see him when he comes through Charles County, but I don't even get to answer his phone.

Couldn't figure what got into me, whether I was more mad or just feeling sorry for myself, but I got the room service menu out of the drawer, ran my finger down the list, and ordered the most expensive things on the menu. Didn't even know what they was. Grouse with truffles, white asparagus, a wine I couldn't pronounce, and some kind of cherries for dessert. Then I watched "The Odd Couple" till room service knocked on the door.

Thought it would just be one man come in, put the tray on the dresser, like he did at breakfast, but in come two waiters in white jackets with a chair and table. They cover the table with a white cloth, put on a vase with roses, and light a candle. I just stand there staring. All the dishes had silver lids on them, and when they pulled out the chair for me and I sat down, they lifted the lids like I can't even lift them myself. Most embarrassing thing ever happened to me. I wasn't even hungry. After they left, I ate a little of the grouse and one piece of asparagus. Didn't touch the wine or the truffles, which are about as ugly a thing as you've ever seen. Half hour later, one of the waiters comes back again with my cherries and right before my eyes he sets 'em on fire. Supposed to be fancy, I guess. Tasted to me like vanilla ice cream and canned cherries. I give him a five-dollar tip later to take it all away, and tell him just to put my dinner on the bill. Then I go down to the gift shop in the lobby.

Had all kinds of things, from little glass birds with skinny necks to silk kimonos and candy. And then, on a shelf over by the stuffed toys, I see this little porcelain dog, looks for all the world like Vinnie. Tail was a little longer than Vinnie's, but its hair was black and short and its ears were floppy, and in every other way that little figurine was Vinnie exactly. I paid for it out of the fifty dollars Gus give me and took it back upstairs, all wrapped in tissue paper in a little gold box.

It came to me all of a sudden what I was going to do next. Guess I was feeling sort of lonely and half-sick from those burnt cherries, but I sat down and dialed the outside line, like the directions said, and then Foster Williams's number.

Heart was pounding so hard it almost hurt. All I wanted to do was tell him about the little porcelain dog, ask him how was he doing, how the bridge was going. Nothing to say we couldn't be friends.

Phone rung three times, four, five, and I waited. Six . . . seven . . . eight. . . . I couldn't seem to put it down. Sat there holding it till I counted twenty rings, and finally I hung up. It was nine-fifteen. Foster always in bed by nine-thirty when he worked the bridge. I got to wondering had he already sold the house, already moved away, and I didn't even know.

Went to bed about eleven but didn't sleep much. Got to thinking about Dorothy and how she would have liked to stay all night in a room like this. Wondered if just thinking hard about a dead person put you in touch with them somehow—could you send them a message. So I put my mind on Dorothy and gave her the message that they caught Max in Ohio and was going to try him there first for some kind of charges, then send him back to Maryland and let Daddy have a crack at him. Daddy get through, Max going to wish it was him with the broken neck, not Dorothy.

Gus come in around one-thirty with whiskey on his breath, and I let him take me but I didn't wiggle or nothing. Still mad, I guess. Pretended I was dead, just to see what it was like. Gus must have thought I was asleep all the while and he was having himself a good time, too. I wake up the next morning about seven, but Gus was snoring his head off, laying there on his stomach stark naked. I poked at him once or twice, tweaked his ear, wanting him to wake up and talk, but he just went on snoring.

I went in the bathroom and come back with that tray of free cosmetics. Drew me a large face on Gus's back with the eye liner. Gus must've thought I was rubbing his back. Then I put in the eyes and color in the cheeks with rouge and the mouth with lipstick. Having myself a ball. When Gus wakes up and looks at hisself backward in the mirror, he don't think it's one bit funny. Makes me scrub him down and then he's afraid it's going to show through his shirt where I've rubbed.

On Friday, when the conference ended, Gus took me on a harbor cruise. Somewhere, I'm thinking, Foster is out there in the water building a bridge right this very minute. The tour guide points out where the new bridge is to be, but it's so far away we can't see nothing. We have us dinner in a restaurant with paintings all over the walls, and about nine o'clock, we head back home.

"You have a good time, April?" Gus asked me. I know he's spent a lot of money.

"I sure did," I tell him. "Thanks for taking me along."

Gus is smiling. "What the heck did you have for dinner the night I went to the banquet?" he wants to know. "The way you eat, I can't figure how in this world you could spend more than three dollars, but the bill come to thirty-seven fifty."

I tell him about the grouse with truffles and the wine and white asparagus. Didn't tell him that I ordered it because I was mad at him, though.

"Well," he says, "I told you to live it up, so I've got nothing to complain about."

I could see how things wouldn't never work out between me

and Gus any more than they did between Foster and me. My being mad at him and spending his money like that, and him being ashamed to take me around. What I liked him for, I guess, was the way he treated me like a lady, took me places in his car I never would have gone; what he liked me for, I guess, was sex. I couldn't see how I was any different from Thomasine and Dorothy, letting a man do that to me just so I could have me a ride in his car. Thinking about it made me sick at the stomach. There was too much I couldn't tell Gus. Too many things he didn't tell me.

When we got back to the Adams Hotel, Gus takes my bag upstairs.

"Well," I say, "first time in my entire life I ever been in a hotel like that one."

"Probably won't be the last, either," he says, and kisses me good night.

That's what I meant about Gus. If he really loved me, really saw a future with me, he wouldn't have said "probably." Asked me once where I'd go if I could go any place on earth I wanted, and I told him New York City where the big ball comes down on New Year's Eve. He just laughs, but he don't say nothing about taking me there.

Next morning it's snowing to beat the band, and I'm glad to be back in my own place. I unpack my things and take out all that free shampoo and lipstick. Figured I'd give some to Thomasine, save a little for Pearl and Loretta, too. Was dying to tell Thomasine about the hotel, so I go out in the hall and call home on the public phone.

Phone rings seven times before she answers, and right away I can tell I woke her up, even though it's almost noon. "Who's this?" she says, and don't sound all too friendly.

"Thomasine, it's me," I say. "Got back from Baltimore last night."

"Oh, my God," says Thomasine, and her voice is so soft I can hardly hear it. Something about the sound of it just stops me cold. "April," she says, "you talk to anybody yet?"

I can't figure out what she's getting at.

"You heard about Foster?" she asks.

My legs go weak and I sit down right there in the hallway, people stepping all around me. I'm thinking about the night I called Foster's place and nobody answered. Thinking about me being gone all week, nobody know where I'm at.

"What's happened?" I say, my voice as shaky as a three-legged chair. I'm crying already.

And then Thomasine's crying too. "He fell off the bridge last Monday, April. . . . They got him in a hospital there in Baltimore, and he still hasn't opened his eyes."

FIFTEEN

A tiny pinpoint of light. Noise. A rushing, gurgling. Pain in his throat. Strep, he thought, when he thought at all. Sleep thinned as it rolled over the edge of consciousness, then came in deep but fitful clumps as it tumbled about in the foam. Foster tried to extend his hand to catch the Swede, but the man went on whirling, turning cartwheels there in the sky. Smiling. He was always smiling. This time, when Foster reached out, he realized that two of his fingers were taped together. The pinpoint of light again. Shadows moving back and forth across the foot of his bed. So he was in bed, then. God, but his throat hurt.

He wanted to see who was in the room, but it took all his effort to lift his lashes. Struggling, as though moving a beam, he tried opening his eyes for just a moment, but the shadows were gone and the room dark once more. Foster was conscious, however, of being conscious. Even as a ceaseless parade of strangers passed before him, stopped dead center, and looked him in the face, Foster knew that they were imaginary. He was aware of the sheets over his feet, the splint on his hand, of pressure on his lower lip and tongue. The strangers, however, kept coming. For days, it seemed, weeks, they had stood before him one at a time for his inspection, faces without expression, yet—if Foster could talk— he could have described each one in detail: the long thin nose of one, the slack jowls of another, the chipmunk cheeks of a third, the old man with the flag tattoo. . . . Foster grew increasingly tired of these people and their solemn procession. He tried to raise his hand, to ward them off, then remembered the ache in his fingers.

When the stupor rolled away again, he felt warm. There was a sensation of sunlight falling on his bed. The parade of strangers had stopped. His mouth felt musty. This time, when he tried to open his eyes, the lashes lifted of themselves and the sun almost blinded him. He squinted.

A middle-aged woman in a white pantsuit and navy cardigan was adjusting an IV unit beside his bed. Foster focused on her, trying to keep her there. He watched as she ran her fingers along the tube leading from the bottle to his arm. Suddenly she stopped, staring at Foster. Then she smiled.

"Good morning, Mr. Williams," she said, and waited.

Foster realized that he could not speak. There was a tube in his mouth as well as in his nose, another attached to his arm.

The nurse moved slightly to the left, and Foster followed with his eyes. Watching closely, the nurse moved to the right. Foster's eyes again followed. The woman smiled even more broadly and pressed his bedside button.

"Yes?" came a voice over the intercom.

"Nora, page Dr. Sheer, will you? The patient in 403 is conscious."

"Wonderful!"

The nurse sat down on the chair by Foster's bed. "There was an accident, Mr. Williams, and you're in Baltimore City Hospital. Can you understand me?"

Foster tried nodding his head.

The noises surrounding him now were familiar ones, he realized—sounds that had intermingled with the noise of wind and water. Now, however, the pounding of waves and the rush of water in his ears had slipped away entirely, and he was left with the rattle of pans in the hall outside, the squeak of a cart, the jokes of attendants on their way to the kitchen. . . .

The nurse chattered on as though, if she stopped, Foster might slip away again. He wanted to tell her that he was all right, but the tube pressed against his tongue.

"Quite a snowfall we had yesterday. They say if it snows too early, there won't be a white Christmas. I can do without it altogether myself. . . ." The talk went on.

"Dr. Sheer, two-oh-one; Dr. Sheer, two-oh-one. . . ."

If Foster closed his eyes even for a moment, the nurse touched his arm or jostled the bed; Foster kept his eyes open to please her.

The doctor came at last, followed by an entourage of medical students, who stood with their hands behind their backs, trying to look professional without looking curious.

"Mr. Williams!" The doctor extended his hand and shook Foster's right hand. He smiled as he listened to the nurse's recitation of Foster's pulse and blood pressure.

"Let's remove those tubes and let this man have some water," he said.

The nurse and doctor hovered—white sleeves in front of Foster's face. The pressure on his tongue lifted as the oxygen tube was removed from his mouth. The doctor paused, studying Foster intently, then picked up a towel and, with a long, steady stroke, removed the nasal gastric tube. Foster gagged.

Hands reached out to help, and Foster detected a lemony scent as the nurse swabbed the inside of his mouth. A glass of water was placed in his free hand.

"Try just a sip," the nurse told him.

The stench of his mouth was awful, and the water hurt going down. Foster raised one hand to his throat.

"Just irritation from the tube—it will feel better in a day or two," the doctor promised. He sat down on the edge of the bed and looked Foster in the eye. "These are routine questions, Foster, and I won't make you talk more than you have to. Do you know what year it is?"

The doctor waited. The students waited. The fact was, Foster didn't know if Christmas had come or not. Then he remembered what the nurse had said about snow. The holidays were yet to come.

"Nineteen seventy-three?"

"Bingo." The doctor smiled.

"How long . . ." Foster stopped. His voice was merely a hoarse whisper. "How long . . ." he repeated, "have I been here?"

"The accident was last Monday. This is Sunday. Do you remember anything of what happened?"

"The Swede . . ." Foster began. "He fell. I tried to catch him. . . ."

The medical students studied him, their faces blank. Poker players, all of them, Foster thought.

"You fell off the bridge from seventy feet up," Dr. Sheer said. "And you are one lucky man."

"What about the Swede?"

Dr. Sheer was frowning slightly. "I don't think anyone else was injured. As far as I know, you're the only one who fell."

Had he dreamed it, then? Foster wondered. Was he brain-injured? He took another sip of water. "What's wrong with me?" he asked.

"Two broken fingers," Dr. Sheer said, opening Foster's chart. "A fractured rib, a dislocated shoulder, and what appears to be a brain contusion. We'll want to watch you closely for a week or so, but it looks to me as though you're going to be all right."

The nurse and the medical students smiled broadly, but Foster did not react, and this disconcerted them, he could tell. He could not understand why, however. He had not even known he was hurt, so why should he be especially joyful to know that he was going to be better?

"Do *you* have any questions?" the doctor asked.

"Have I been unconscious all this time?"

"Not entirely. But this is the first time you've had your eyes open. I'm very encouraged." Dr. Sheer patted his arm and prepared to stand up, but Foster grabbed his sleeve.

"Will I be able to go back on the high beams?"

This time the students frankly stared.

"If that's what you want," the doctor answered. "You should be able to do anything you did before."

When the room was empty at last, even of the nurse in the blue sweater, Foster looked slowly around, studying every detail. There was no one in the bed opposite, so for now he had the room to himself. Two bouquets with official-looking cards sat on a table opposite. Other cards were strewn about the window ledge, and the sun made rivulets of the ice outside the pane. On his right was a bedside table, with the obligatory pitcher, water glass, and pan. And then, just to the left of the pitcher, he noticed a little porcelain dog that looked for all the world like Vinnie.

***

Late Tuesday afternoon, the bridge crew paid a visit. Foster could hear their voices in the hall, turning soft and cautious when they reached his room. Then Jack stuck his head inside.

"I'll be damned if he's not eatin' fried chicken!" Jack exclaimed, and the others pushed through the doorway and crowded around the bed, faces expanding in wide grins.

"Foster, you old son-of-a-gun!" Clyde said, grabbing the hand that Foster held out to him. "*Jesus*, it's good to see you sittin' up!"

"Find yourselves a place to sit," Foster said, shoving his tray aside. "You been here before?"

"Come last Thursday," Juju told him, "but you didn't know it. Man, you give us a scare!" He thrust a package toward Foster, a large phallic-looking sausage, tied with a red ribbon, and the others laughed. They added Hershey's bars, huge red apples, and a *Playboy* magazine to the pile.

"Swede sent the apples," Jack explained.

"How's he doing?" Foster asked.

"Smart-assed as ever. Sorry about the accident, though. Think he means it."

"He didn't fall?"

The men looked at Foster. "Hell no, Foster. You're the one who fell," Jack told him. "Juju and me was working the ground, and saw you go over. By the time you hit the water, Juju was in there after you, holding your head up till the safety boat got around."

Foster reached up and squeezed Juju's arm. "Didn't know that," he said. "Thought the Swede fell too."

Jack removed Foster's presents from the bed and put his dinner tray in front of him again. The others settled back to let him eat.

"You should've heard the cheer went up this morning when we called in and they said you were eating, talking, walking the halls. . . . You're looking good, Foster. Be back on the high beams in no time, and that's not bull."

"It okay to ask you something?" Juju said. "About the fall?"

"Most likely I won't remember," Foster told him.

"What you think about on the way down? I always wondered about that—what goes through a man's head when he falls."

Foster held back a smile. "Well, fellas, I tell you; all the bad things I ever done in my life come running through my head, one after another."

"Why, Foster," Clyde told him, "you didn't fall near long enough for that to happen." And the room rocked with laughter.

*   *   *

A month, the doctor said, before he could go back to work. Six weeks before he could go up on the high beams. Foster went home the week before Christmas. The visiting nurse came every other day, and now and then Shum or Russell brought down a meat loaf for Foster's supper, a jar of soup, a pan of chili. . . . The sky almost cleared, then snowed again. Foster's only consolation was that the other men were off work too, weather like that.

The day before Christmas, he sat on a straight-backed chair in the kitchen, doing the exercises he had been given for the shoulder. There was the sound of a car coming up the drive. Foster turned stiffly to see out the window. A Dodge Dart pulled carefully over to one side of the clearing and parked. The door on the driver's side opened and April Ruth got out, pulled something across the seat toward her, then slammed the door again and started toward the house, carrying a large basket. My God, Foster thought, she's drivin' now!

He sprang for the door, one hand on his rib cage, then stopped, catching himself in time. It was a social visit, nothing more. The basket should have told him that. He watched her come, stepping high in the snow, car keys dangling from one finger. More confident of herself, it seemed. More sure. He let her knock before he opened the door.

She stood there in Thomasine's old red coat, which came down halfway between her knees and ankles, hiding the tops of her boots. Her hair was longer now, bunching up around her shoulders. Her nose and cheeks were pink and shiny.

"Well, look who the wind blowed by!" Foster smiled. "Come on in."

She fixed her eyes on him as she passed him there on the doorstep, and set the basket on the table.

"Foster," she told him, "it sure is good news about you!" She stared some more. "You really all right? I can't believe you're up and walking. Look just like you always did."

"Well, don't feel quite as good as I always did, but they say there's nothing broke that won't mend. Want to sit down a minute, or you in a hurry to get somewhere?"

April unbuttoned her coat but didn't take it off. "Just came by to bring the basket." She smiled a little wider. "Chub helped me fix it up. Go ahead. Look inside."

Foster walked over to the table and reached around the red bow on the handle. "What have we got here, now?" He pulled out a small cheesecake, some oranges, a sack of walnuts, a canned ham.

"Everything you need for Christmas dinner!" April said delightedly, reaching in herself to pull out a box of Whitman's chocolates that Foster had overlooked.

"Going to have myself a feast!" Foster told her. "Who I got to thank for this? The folks at the City Chicken?"

April flushed noticeably. "Well . . . mostly me," she said. "But everyone says to tell you how glad they are you're getting well." She sat down finally on a chair beside the table. "You don't know how worried everybody was about you. I didn't get the news till the Saturday after you fell, and Thomasine drove me over to Baltimore in a snowstorm. You didn't even open your eyes. . . ."

"You come to the hospital?"

The color in April's face deepened. "Once."

Don't tell me this girl don't care for me, Foster thought, hating himself for the way his heart took off. "I wish I'd known you were there, April," he told her.

"Well. . . ." She placed both hands on top her purse, eyes averted. "I didn't stay very long. Thomasine driving around out in the parking lot, having a fit 'cause she couldn't find a space." She let her eyes sneak another look at him. "You find what I left you, though?"

Foster frowned, trying to figure it out, then suddenly began to grin. "That little dog—look like Vinnie?"

She nodded, laughing, and Foster pointed. "I've got it right there on the window sill over the sink. Never knew who brought it. I should have figured it was you." His heart pounded even harder.

"Thought you'd like it. Saw it in a gift shop and told myself, That's Vinnie, even if the tail ain't right."

"Well, how you doing yourself, April? *Driving* now, I see!"

She nodded, but fixed her eyes on her lap again. "Yeah. Gus give me that car. An early Christmas present."

Cold flanked Foster's chest where it had been all warmth before. Couldn't he have figured that out himself? Had he really thought April could have bought a car on her own?

He struggled to keep the corners of his mouth from sagging. "That Dart's a nice little car. He teach you to drive it?"

"Him and Mr. Hollander."

"That's good. Now you can get you anywhere you want to go."

April laughed a little. "Well, I don't go far. It's just the feeling I *could* . . . if I *wanted*. . . ."

The room grew embarrassingly quiet, and suddenly April brought her feet together under the chair and stood up. "Well, I just come by to say Merry Christmas and how glad we are you're okay."

He nodded. He thought maybe, if he didn't stand, she would stay a little longer, but then she was crossing the room.

"About you and Gus. . . ." Foster got to his feet.

"Don't talk about that," she murmured, one hand on the door.

"I just want what's best for you, April, that's all."

She didn't answer—stood with her hand frozen to the knob.

"He give you a car, I figure he's pretty serious about you," Foster went on.

She leaned forward so that her head rested against the doorframe.

"April. . . ." Foster came over. "You love Gus, that's good. I won't do a thing against it. But if he don't love you . . . well, I *do,* April. I don't know why it took me so long to say it. You always got a home here, you ever want to come back." He hesitated. "Now I suppose I went and said too much."

April looked up, startled, and stared at him so intently that Foster wondered if he'd garbled his words—said something else. Then she turned her face away and he was chagrined to discover that she was crying. "*Don't,* Foster!" she said again, and her chin trembled. "I didn't come here to start that all over again. Just wanted us to be friends."

He only half-believed her. "You sure about that now?" He reached out for her, but she shoved him away and plunged outside, slipping and sliding as she ran.

Foster stood in the doorway, his heart racing. "Tell me you don't love me, April," he yelled after her. "I want to hear you say that."

She reached the Dodge and yanked on the door with both hands, crying visibly now.

"Everything's changed between us, Foster! Isn't nothing a'tall like it used to be," she said, then slid inside and closed the door after her.

***

Clyde and Sue invited Foster over for Christmas, and Jack Tulley took him out on New Year's Eve. Foster was eager to begin again at the bridge, impatient for his ribs to heal, for full mobility in his fingers.

It was time to make a new beginning. He had lain awake most of Christmas Eve, thinking about his encounter with April, and had decided at last that he did not understand her any better than he had when she first moved in. That she did not love Gus Freeman, he was certain. Whether or not she loved him was unclear. What was increasingly plain, however, was that it was time to get on with his own life.

He had said what he had to say and April had responded that things were changed between them. It was unusual that she should cry, but pity was all it was. She had come prepared to renew their friendship and he had tried to force it over the line. She had wanted simply to wish him well and he had made her reject him, something she had not anticipated at all. And when at last Foster had come to terms with it himself, he set his mind on selling the house when the weather warmed. He'd begin again.

There were, however, several business matters that had been left untended. How to tell Shum and Russell that he was putting the place up for sale, for one. His debt to the Harley brothers, for another.

Jed and Wallace came by shortly after New Year's and sat stiffly across from Foster in the living room.

"We were real glad to hear that you're doing so good," Wallace said.

"Full recovery, that's what they say," Jed added.

"Guess I was plenty lucky," Foster told them. "I know I owe you money, but right now I've got hospital bills, and it's going to take some time to pay you off."

Jed and Wallace seemed to stiffen even more.

"Well, now, that's what we come about," said Wallace. "We're not the kind to stand over a man on his sick bed, say he's got to come across, but you were bettin' against a CD, Foster, and that CD come through. Jed and me got our eye on a used Mustang, and we need that money."

"I already used it up," Foster said. "Few days in intensive care took it all and more besides."

"Come off it. You got insurance."

"Only eighty percent. I pay the rest."

"Well, I guess you should have thought of all that before you raised your bets."

"A lot of things I should have thought about before I even come over that day," Foster said in reply.

**

The week Foster was to go back to work, the weather turned perverse. The sun over the weekend turned to snow on Monday and Tuesday, then rain the next two days—cold rain, driven by a bitter wind.

Clyde called him Thursday afternoon.

"Bridge won't be built till '77 at this rate," he grumbled, "and I sure am sick of sittin' around the house. Sue and me are going to drop in on April's party this afternoon. Figured we might see you there."

"What party is that?" Foster asked.

"Didn't you know? Hollanders always give a little party when an employee's got a birthday. Sign's been up for a week. Free beer between four and six—everyone invited. Sue says we all ought to go for April's sake—buck her up a little."

"She been sick or something?" Foster asked.

There was a pause. "Jesus Christ, Foster, I thought you knew! April's pregnant. Gus give her a car, some money, and took off." And in the silence that followed, he added, "Now listen, Foster— don't you go soft and take her back. You gave her a good home, and look at the thanks you got. Let someone else look after her now."

SIXTEEN

I knew I'd have to tell Gus sometime. Wasn't till November, the way my breasts were tender, that I was sure, 'cause I'd skipped lots of times before. Never did get to throwing up the way they say. The same time I'm thinking what a mess I've made of things, I know that if I wait long enough, nobody can take it from me. Gus planted the seed, but it's me going to give life to that child.

All sorts of things going through my mind, like how long the Hollanders would let me work and whether I could keep a baby at the Adams Hotel. One thing at a time was all I could handle, and I figured I'd wait till Gus and me went on that trip to Baltimore, tell him then. But once I got in that hotel room, didn't tell him at all. If he's so ashamed of me he don't want anyone to know I'm there, how's he going to feel when I tell him I got his child inside me?

Anytime you don't know whether to be happy or sad, something comes along and decides it for you. We get back from Baltimore, Gus still not knowing, and next morning, in the middle of a snowstorm, I find out about Foster.

It's like I'm there at the top of the bridge with him, like I feel myself slipping over the edge, nothing to hang on to—just emptiness. There I am in the second-floor corridor of the Adams Hotel with the wall phone in my hand, and it's like I can't catch my breath.

"Thomasine," I say finally, "if you was ever a sister to me, you got to drive me to Baltimore right this minute to see Foster."

Thomasine gives a shriek. "There's five inches of snow on the ground, April, and more comin'!"

"You don't drive me there, I'm goin' to walk," I tell her, and she knows I would, too.

Half hour later Thomasine comes over and I slide in the car, my eyes all puffy from crying. She says if she gets killed on the beltway, it's me she's got to thank for it. And all the way there she tells me how it's pity I'm feeling for Foster, not love.

"You wouldn't never have walked out on him, April, if you loved him," she says. "You just got a soft heart for anything sick and suffering."

I just keep right on bawling and don't pay her no mind. Windshield wipers going so fast to keep the snow off make you dizzy. Thomasine looks over at me now and then and grunts.

"You got to quit going around with old men, April, and pay attention to the young ones," she warns. "People are startin' to talk about you."

"I don't care one small least little bit," I tell her. "What do they say?"

"Say you're looking for some kind of father, 'cause Daddy weren't no father to you at all."

"What's so surprising about that?" I ask her.

"Sweet Jesus!" says Thomasine. "It's sick, that's what." I could've said what kind of sick it is climbing in bed with a bunch of truck drivers, but it's Thomasine's car getting me to Baltimore, so I just go back to weeping again. Thinking how last Monday there I was in Baltimore with Gus when Foster was falling off that bridge. Then all week long, while I'm lying in that king-size bed in the hotel room, Foster's lying in the hospital between life and death, and me not even knowing.

At the Baltimore City Hospital, Thomasine can't find a parking space, and she is cussing something terrible. So I run up to see Foster while she circles around. And after all that, he don't even open his eyes.

Gus still around over the weekend, so he takes me out that

night when Thomasine and me get back. I don't tell him about Foster, 'cause I don't even like saying their names in the same breath, but I'm so worried I can't even tell you what we had for dinner; can't remember the movie afterwards to save my life. And then, when we get in Gus's car to go back to my room for sex, I decide to tell him about the baby, just to keep him off me. I say, "Gus, there's something I got to tell you." And I know by the way he don't move a muscle that he already has an idea what it is.

Afterwards he says, "Well, April, that's the second time you've fooled me."

I can hardly breathe. "What you mean by that, Gus?"

"First you had me thinking you were over eighteen, and then you said you couldn't have a baby. Well, like Barnum said, there's a sucker born every minute, and I guess I'm one of them."

"Only way I ever deceived you, Gus, was telling you I couldn't get pregnant. Fooled myself as well. All the while I was with Foster, it never happened, and I figured there was something wrong with me."

Gus turns around and stares. "You mean you never heard it from a doctor?"

"Never been to a doctor," I told him. "Not *that* kind, anyway."

"God Almighty," says Gus.

We must have sat there three, four minutes, not saying nothing, Gus just looking out the window.

"Well, you've sure got me in a fix," he says at last.

"I'm sorry, Gus."

"Sorry doesn't help," he says. We sat some more. "So what do you want me to do, April? Marry you?" he says finally.

I was ready for that one. "No, Gus. You been good to me, but I sure don't want to live the rest of my life with a man won't even let me answer his telephone."

He looks at me right quick. "Well, I'm willing," he says, now that he knows I'm not. I just shake my head.

"You want to go somewhere, then? Have an abortion?" he asks.

"Isn't *nobody* going to take this baby."

Gus puts one arm around me on the seat. "Now listen, April," he says, real gentle. "You're just a kid, really. You can't support a child. Can hardly even support yourself."

"I'm not gettin' rid of this baby, and it's too late anyway," I tell him. "Way I figure, it's due in May."

"Jesus Christ," Gus says softly, and leans back against the door like he don't know what in the world to do with me.

"Gus," I say finally, "before you ever walked in the City Chicken and seen me, both of us was gettin' along fine without the other, and we can get along just fine again. Why don't you go back to whatever you was doing before, and I'll manage. Something always comes along."

Now he's losing patience. "April, you can't go your whole life waiting for something to come along! You can't just let things happen to you! You think I'm just going to walk out?"

"Don't look like you've got much choice," I tell him.

I don't have to mention that Gus decides not to have sex with me that night. Takes me up to the door and I figure that's the last I'll see of Gus Freeman. Next day, though—Sunday—there he is, back at the Adams Hotel. He's bought me a used car, put five hundred dollars aside for me, and wrote down the names of three doctors so I can choose one to take care of me and the baby. And then, 'cause the snow had turned to slush, he takes me out for two hours and gives me a driving lesson.

"I figure that the money and the car should see you through till May," he says.

"They'll do just fine," I tell him.

"Well, then, April, I'll check up on you from time to time— see how you're doing," he says. "If the kid's mine, I guess I've got a responsibility to support it."

I would have liked Gus a whole lot better if he hadn't said that last thing. But what did he know of me when he wasn't around? And what did I know of him? I made up my mind right then that I wasn't never going to *let* him support that baby—Gus going all his life thinking maybe it was his, maybe it wasn't. When Sunday night come, the end of my vacation, and Gus takes off, you could just tell he's so happy being rid of me he hardly knows what to do.

Well, I say to myself as I see him turn at the light, sure didn't do much of a job planning my life up to now, but I wasn't licked yet. I'd figure out something. Maybe move into an apartment with some woman who has a baby herself, and she could look after mine too while I'm at work. Thing now was to go along like I always had and see how long I could keep the baby secret.

Wasn't very long. Couple days later I called the Baltimore City Hospital again and they tell me Foster's up walking around, talking—going to be all right. I was so excited I got in my car, didn't even have my license yet, and drove out to the diner to tell Thomasine and Marie. All the way there I'm planning in my head how when Foster comes home I'm going to go see him every day, take him soup and clean his house. For once in my life it would be *Foster* needing *me*. The very idea sends joy through my veins, and I go rushing through the door of the diner, hair flying every which way.

I guess the excitement was just too much for my stomach. "Foster's goin' to live!" I yell, half-crying, and throw up right there on the floor, which is the next to the worst thing you want to see on the floor of a restaurant.

While Jake mops up, Marie and Thomasine sit me down in a back booth, and all the while I'm telling about Foster, Marie's not taking her eyes off me.

"April Ruth," she says, "you going to have a baby?"

I suddenly get quiet and stare down at the table.

"Sweet Jesus!" breathes Thomasine.

"Is it Gus Freeman's?" asks Marie.

I nod.

Thomasine grabs hold of my arm. "He going to marry you when your divorce comes through?"

"*I'm* not going to marry *him*," I tell her. "He's gone, and he done what he could to help me. Now just don't you blab it around, Thomasine."

She says she won't and Marie says she won't neither, but the only secret ever kept in Medbury was about Foster and Ramona Wheeler. The very next day at the City Chicken, Loretta and Pearl know all about it, and Irene Hollander calls me in the office with her face sad and tells me how terribly sorry she is. Here is a baby going to get itself born and everyone's acting like a funeral. I start to feel ashamed of myself. Feel now that I done something cheap and low, Foster's wife getting herself pregnant by another man. Can see how it reflects on Foster. Everyone tries to put the blame on Gus, and I tell 'em how he asked me to marry him, but not a soul believes me.

"That poor girl," I hear Loretta say to Pearl in the supply closet. "What's she got left to do but move back in with her daddy?"

Couldn't stand people talking like that. I *wasn't* going to move back in with Daddy. I told the Hollanders if they'd just let me work as long as I could, I'd figure something out, and Irene says I can, so after George Hollander goes with me to get my driver's license, I drive myself to the City Chicken every day, but I don't go near Foster's place. All them plans about how I was going to take care of him, I can see they won't work out. What's he think of me now, I wonder, and I'm too afraid to find out.

Christmas comes, though, and I don't care what Foster says. He can slam the door in my face, but I'm going to take him a present, and just thinking about it makes me feel better. Chub helps me fix it up, and as soon as I get to Foster's and see how he smiles at me, I know he ain't heard yet, and then I realize what's happened: Nobody wanted to tell a sick man that his wife was havin' a baby by somebody else, whether they was living together or not. And then, when Foster says those words, about loving me, I'm sick all through my body at how I can't go back to him again, and I wished I'd never gone to his place at all.

***

Second week of January, I come to work to find a big sign above the bar saying HAPPY BIRTHDAY, APRIL RUTH, and a bunch of balloons. Underneath says how there will be free beer from four to six on January tenth, in honor of my birthday. I'm not sure, but that just might have been the only birthday party I had in my life, 'less you count Dorothy buying me a cake.

Everybody's trying to be nice to me, I know, now that I disgraced myself. Any day I expected a visit from the Decency

Committee, but Mrs. Dawson never come near me. Sister Perry neither.

Thursday was the darkest January day I can remember, with rain just pouring down, and I figure nobody's going to show up. George Hollander was ready just in case, though. Had big bowls of popcorn out on the bar and a jelly-bean jar with my name on it, case folks wanted to drop in some loose change or a dollar bill or something.

Daddy was the first to arrive, of course, and he's already red-eyed and weepy, hugging his beer like it's about to rise up and walk off, and telling everyone how he ain't got a baby daughter no more.

"Hush up, old man, you're going to have you a grandchild," Chub tells him once, but Daddy just goes on blubbering. Once he gets an audience, he don't never shut up.

Then Thomasine come in wearing a pair of leather pants look like they been glued to her thighs, and Marie stops in with Tillie from the Laundromat. One of Foster's friends showed up, too—Clyde Sheldon, with his wife, Sue—so there was enough people to make a party, and I could tell that the Hollanders was relieved.

Embarrassing part was that Pearl and Loretta went together and bought me a bassinet. They pull it out and set it right up there on the bar, full of rubber pants and bottles and things, so if anybody didn't know before, they sure did now. That starts Daddy blubbering all over again.

"Uh-oh," says Thomasine, and rolls her eyes toward the door.

I look around, and then I turn all shades of red, 'cause standing right there in the front entrance is Foster Williams.

I can't see his face so good because he's in the shadows and I just sort of go down on my knees, like I'm looking for clean glasses behind the bar. But I can't stay there forever. When I raise up, there he is not more'n two feet away.

"Happy birthday, April," he says to me, and he's looking awful serious.

I swallow. "Thanks, Foster," I say, and turn to go down to the other end, but Pearl's leaning over the bar talking with Sue Sheldon, and when Pearl bends over, can't nobody get past her fanny.

And then Foster's got one hand on my arm. "April," he says, "I'm not putting this off no longer."

I still can't look him in the eye. "I didn't mean for you to find out," I say real soft.

"Why didn't you tell me?" he says. "I *wanted* to know."

Now I look straight at him, but there's still hardly any breath to my voice. "I didn't mean for it to happen, Foster. Didn't think it *could*."

"Things happened to both of us we never meant to," Foster says. I swallow again. "April," he says, "I want to help you raise that baby."

Suddenly the restaurant's grown so quiet you can hear Daddy breathing all the way to the other end of the bar. He's got his head on his arms, sound asleep, but everybody else is looking off into space, not saying a word, like they been froze in a photograph. Every ear is tuned in on Foster and me. Foster's face starts turning pink. He didn't want anyone else to hear, but he barrels right ahead. "You don't have any feelings for me, you got to say so now, April. But if you do, we ought to get ourselves married."

Now people aren't polite no longer. *Everybody's* staring.

Clyde turns around on his stool. "Foster," he says, his voice low, "I think you still got some head damage from that fall. You and April are already married—till the end of the month, anyway."

"No, we're not," says Foster. "Chapel was closed when we got to Denton, and we just never went back."

People's lips open all at once like just before the National Anthem, only no sound come out. Daddy begins to snore. I'm thinking how if this was a movie, Foster and me would probably lean over the counter and kiss. But it's not a movie. I'm trying to speak soft, but there's not a soul who ain't listening.

"I tried to tell you, Foster. Wouldn't be like it was before."

"Don't want it to be like it was before. I want it to be better." Foster just don't let up. "Do you feel somethin' for me or not?"

Here I am, I'm thinking, in love with a man what folks say is too old for me, happy about a child not even his. Can tell by the looks on some of the other faces what they think about the idea, and then it come to me how can't nobody else tell you what happiness is. Everybody's got his own idea on that.

A smile creeps across my face before I can stop it. "I feel somethin'," I tell him, and now I'm smiling like one of those Hawaiian dolls on a rearview mirror.

"Sweet Jesus!" says Thomasine, and covers her eyes with one hand.

I'm remembering what Gus said about how I can't go on just letting things happen to me. And I can tell that Marie and some of the others is thinking how Foster and me just sort of fall into life, and whatever comes, that's what we take. Well, maybe so, I say to myself, but at least we take it. We make room in our lives for things we don't expect. We don't give up and we don't break down and, except for me leaving Foster the one time, we don't run away, neither.

"Foster," says Clyde, getting up and coming over, "why don't you go home and think about it some more. April will still be here tomorrow."

But Foster just looks at his watch. "We got fifteen minutes before the courthouse closes," he says to me. "I figure you can take a half hour off for us to go get a license."

I can't even talk 'cause my smile's took over my whole face. George Hollander sets the bassinet in Foster's arms and Loretta helps me on with my coat, and everybody picks up a handful of popcorn and throws it at us when we go out the door. All but Daddy. His baby daughter's getting married at last, and he don't even know it.

***

So I settle down in Foster's house once more, with a Sears washing machine, a subscription to *Family Circle,* and my Cool Whip recipe book.

I was more shy our first night back together than I was at Ocean City on our honeymoon. Shy about my body, I guess, with Gus's baby inside. Foster figures the reason I didn't get pregnant with him was that I had some growing yet to do. He says all that good food at the City Chicken helped fill me out, and we don't watch it, we'll have children crawling around all over the place.

Once I got between the covers with him where I belong, seem like everywhere Foster put his hand, my skin just rise up to meet it, it's so hungry for him to touch me. And when Foster come, I just want him to stay and stay, like I can't get enough of him.

"I love you, Foster," I tell him, and pretty soon he come all over again.

Foster go back to work each morning and I finish out the month at the City Chicken, short shift, ten to four, then I'm home all day like I used to be. We pick up our life like it was before—Foster come home, cook the meat, I'd set the table . . . same as always. Got something to do in the evenings now, fixing up the spare room for the baby—"Gussie," Foster calls it, till it's born and got a name of its own. Now and then I drive over to see Thomasine and Daddy, or take Shum to the Safeway. I miss Vinnie, but Shum sort of takes her place—way he dances from side to side when he sees me coming, glad to have me back. Russell's glad, too, I can tell, only Russell wouldn't never dance if his feet was on fire.

Life never goes like a storybook, though. Some days Foster and me would argue, then sit through a whole supper not saying a word. Or there would be cold and rainy Sundays, whole house feel damp, and nothing appeal to me at all. After a time, Foster and me come together again, and the good feelings would start all over, but there was something about being with Foster that made me miss the City Chicken, and that almost scare me to death. Didn't know what it was. The men customers, the way they'd tease? The cars, always coming and going, people on their way to somewhere? Was I settling down with Foster just to up and leave him again, I birth a baby, not even his? Wasn't nothing I could talk with him about, it's still so tangled up in my head. But it's just like Foster said once—a splinter in me, making me mean. And then, 'round the middle of March, something happened.

Shum and Russell had come down for supper and I'd just sent 'em off with some banana bread, Loretta's recipe, when more company arrives, this time the Harley brothers. I remember how I was rude to them before, so this time I invite them in, but when I hear what they say to Foster, I wished I'd turn the hose on 'em.

They don't even set down or go into the other room. Just stand over by the sink, 'bout as far away from me as they can get, looking nasty.

"Foster," Wallace says, "you owe us twelve hundred dollars at poker and we're tired of waitin'."

How in this world Foster could get that far in debt to those Harleys I can't even imagine, but I can tell by the look on his face that it's true.

"I've got four thousand yet in hospital bills, but I can pay you by installments, fifty a month," Foster says.

"That ain't the way the Harleys do business," says Jed, the tobacco in his cheek bobbing up and down, and I don't see no cup.

You spit on my floor, you going to get more than you bargained for, Jed Harley, I'm thinking, and he must have known it, 'cause he looks at me sideways, then spits in the pocket of his flannel shirt. Plain to see how come the Harleys never married. Jed's looking at my big belly like he hopes to God I stay on my side of the kitchen. Remembering how I use to ride my bike straight at 'em, maybe.

"Well, you want your money all at once and I don't have it," Foster says to Jed. "You got any ideas?"

Jed spits in his pocket again. "You got a Chevy truck out there and a Dodge as well. Could sell one or the other and pay us from that."

"That Dodge is April's, and you just leave her out of this," says Foster. "If I can get together a hundred dollars a month, I will, but I'm not sellin' my truck to do it."

"You play dirty, Foster," says Wallace. "Don't keep to your end of the bargain."

"You got it backwards," Foster tells him. "And I'd have to be brain-dead to play you fellas ever again."

After they're gone I say, "Foster, you *know* the Harleys were cheatin'! They ain't played straight in their whole rotten lives! You don't owe them nothing!"

"Clyde knows they were cheating too, but we can't *prove* it," Foster says. "Claiming I don't owe nothing because of cheating just looks like sour grapes."

"We can sell my car, then," I tell him.

It's as close as Foster comes to getting mad at me. "You aren't selling nothing and you're not giving them one cent, April. It was me who got in the mess in the first place, and me that's got to get out of it."

It was right then I get that feeling some more about Foster and me, about our marriage and would it last. Worries me all night and into the next day.

Next night, though, 'bout ten o'clock, Foster had just got in the shower when Thomasine calls up.

"April," she says, "I'm callin' from the diner. Where's Foster?"

"In the shower," I tell her.

"Well, listen. Jed and Wallace were here tonight, sittin' in the back booth, and Marie hears them say how they're going to go out to Foster's about midnight, steal his truck, and strip it down for parts."

My heart starts beating hard inside my chest. "Tonight?" I ask her.

"That's what she's not sure about. Didn't want to let on she was listening. You better tell Foster to take his shotgun and keep watch. Jake says a truck like Foster's worth a lot more stripped down than it is sold whole, and those Harleys could drive it off in the woods and have it apart before morning. Jed and Wallace are always talkin' bigger than their boots, but you better tell Foster anyhow. Hear?"

"Thanks, Thomasine," I tell her.

I sit there listening to Foster splash around in the shower, and I picture him sitting up all night with a shotgun. Maybe the wrong night, too. Maybe the Harleys have guns and somebody going to get killed. And even if Foster chased 'em off, the meanness would just hang around in the air, waiting for the Harleys to figure another way of getting their money.

The more I think about Jed and Wallace, the madder I feel. Madder I feel, the more set I am that Foster's not going to lose any sleep over it. A wild kind of excitement takes hold of me, and next thing I know, I got this plan.

Foster come out of the shower, wiping his back with a towel. "Comin' to bed, April?" he says. "It's late. Almost ten-thirty."

"Can't get this child to settle down," I tell him. "Kickin' somethin' awful."

Foster grins. "I could maybe shake him up a little."

I smile up at Foster and run my hand over one side of his body. "Better not tonight. He shaken up enough lately. I'm goin' to walk around a bit, see if I can't get comfortable. You go on."

Foster kisses me good night and goes to bed, and in five minutes he's snoring. I look at the clock. A quarter to eleven.

What I got in mind to do is some kind of crazy, but I couldn't think of nothing else. I put on all the clothes I can find—sweater, coat, boots, scarf, old woolly hat of Foster's—and then I pick up the laundry bag in the hallway. I listen once more at Foster's door to see if he's asleep, then I turn out all the lights and slip outside. Only one way the Harleys would be coming, so I set out for the clump of pines little way down the road.

There was so many things that could go wrong it make my stomach sink just to think of 'em, not the least of which was I might catch my death and die. Next thing could happen was Foster wake up, find me gone, and come looking. Or the Harleys drive by lickety-split and I miss 'em altogether. Could even be they was coming another night, or just spouting off, not coming at all.

At least I thought to bring a watch with me, and I never in my life saw time go as slow as it did then. Big old moon come flying out behind the clouds, then slide back under again, and each time it come out, seem to say, "*You* still here?" Would have felt better if Vinnie was with me.

Only two cars come by between eleven and eleven forty-five, and I'm thinking my feet are froze solid when far off I hear the sound of a motor. I just know it's the Harleys' panel truck. Sound as mean as they do, even though I could tell they was keeping it low. My heart starts banging again something painful. Staying close to the pines, I move right up to the edge of the road where the trees jut out, holding the laundry bag tight in both fists.

Here comes the truck now, slowing down to ten mile an hour as it rounds the bend. I get as close to the road as the trees will hide me and raise the laundry bag, all lumpy with clothes. Minute the front end of the truck goes by, I swing out the bag with all my strength—*whump!*—and give the most pitiful scream you ever heard. Could have woke Dorothy from her grave. I throw the sack far back in the weeds as I can get it and sink down to the ground, just like Loretta there at the City Chicken.

The truck skids to the left and stops and both doors fly open. Any other time, the Harleys would jump out for the pure joy of seeing what they hit. They're mean enough to run down a dog for the pleasure of it, but they wasn't so bad off as to hit a woman and leave her there.

"*Ho*-ly shit!" says Wallace, creeping towards me. "I didn't see *nothin'* in the road, Jed! Did you?"

They come closer and I can hear Jed's breath, all shaky.

"Oh, Jesus!" Jed stops short, making Wallace bump him from behind. "It *is* a woman!"

Then they're over beside me and the moon come out full on my face.

"It's April Ruth!" Jed says, and steps back.

Slowly I sit up, holding my belly.

"April, what the hell you doing out here?" Wallace says, and now he's lifting me under both arms. I let my knees collapse again for good measure. "What you doing out here by yourself?" he asks again when I'm on my feet.

I whack at Wally's hands to get them off me. "Just doing like the doctor said and gettin' in my bedtime walk," I tell him. "You run right into me, Wallace Harley! Bumped me right in the stomach!"

"Oh, Lord Jesus," Jed says again, and this time it sounds honest-to-god like he's praying.

"Where'd you *come* from?" Wallace says. "Didn't see *nothing!*"

"You couldn't see a elephant if it was comin' down the middle of the road," I bellow. "This child be born dead, Wallace Harley, I'm holdin' you and your brother fully responsible."

"Now wait a minute, April," says Wallace. "You're all right, aren't you? Ain't got nothing broke."

I back away from him, pain and misery on my face. "This child manage to get born alive, and anything's wrong with it, it's you that done it," I tell him. "He got a harelip or a club foot or some fingers missin', I'm goin' to tell the doctor how you run me down."

"Didn't even *see* you, did we, Jed?" Wallace says, but Jed don't even answer—just stands there shaking his head so hard it's like to fly off.

"This child gets to school and can't see the blackboard or be deaf in one ear or retarded anyway whatsoever, it's you Harleys got to answer for it," I tell them. "What *you* doing out here this time of night, I'd like to know?"

Oh, I got them now, I'm thinking. Any minute they're going to make me a deal. Any minute Wallace going to say, Listen here, April Ruth, we're sorry, and we're calling off that debt of Foster's.

"Got as much right out here on this road as you have," is what Wallace says to me.

"You come all the way out here at midnight, you must be up to something," I tell him. And then I know I said too much. I look at Wallace's face there in the moonlight and see him putting two and two together.

"I might could say the same thing about you," he says and, turning on his heel, he walks back to the truck.

I stand there, chest so tight I can't hardly breathe. Jed—he's slow, hasn't caught on yet—just walks backward after Wallace, never taking his eyes off me. Then he gets in the truck, truck turns around there on the road and heads back the way it come.

I wait till they're out of sight—till even the sound of their meanness has rolled away—angry tears just spilling out of my eyes. Moon shoots out again making day of night, and I go back in the weeds, pick up the laundry bag, and head home, so disgusted with myself I don't know what to do. April Ruth, I say, you aren't nothing but one overgrown child, trying to make things happen same way you did back when you was nine.

The bushes pull at my coat, and I jerk my sleeve free. Branches reach out and scrape me across the face, but I just push on. Seem like I'm punishing myself, taking the woods 'stead of the road. One foot slips off into a gulley, my leg goes with it, and it's all I can do to keep from falling. I feel the baby turn his little self around inside me, and I edge over to a stump and set a moment, one hand on my belly.

And all of a sudden I think, April Ruth, you may be young and stupid, but you ain't evil. I could have come back to Foster just to devil him. I could be fixing to walk out on this child once it's born. I could be sleeping around or drinking myself to death, but I wasn't doing none of those things.

I wait till the moon slips out again, then start off once more. I'm thinking how in the whole year I worked at the City Chicken, I wasn't late once—only sick a couple times with my monthlies. Didn't I prove they could count on me? Didn't I show I could learn? You hold your head up, girl, I tell myself, but just as I break through the trees, I see a light on in the house. Foster steps out barefoot, zipping up his pants.

"April, where the hell did you go?" he says, his eyes still full of sleep. "I swear I heard you yell, and was lookin' this house over!" He stares at my face and then at the laundry bag, and gives his head a shake to clear it of cobwebs.

Took all my strength back there just to buck myself up, but now I got Foster mad at me. Feel the corners of my mouth tug down, and last thing in this world I want to do is bawl. I come in and close the door. Foster faces me there in the kitchen, waiting.

I take off my coat, my sweater, my scarf, my boots, and Foster's old woolly cap, him watching all the while, lips half-open, like he's counting the clothes I lay down.

"F–Foster," I says at last, "the Harley brothers was on their way over here to steal your truck." And then I tell him bit by bit what happened, swallowing after every five words or so.

Foster goes on staring like I am out of my head crazy.

"You ever think how you could injure that child you got inside you?" he asks. "You ever think how you could get pneumonia?"

I swallow some more.

"You're doin' just like you used to, April!" he says. "Get an idea in your head and take off. I told you this is *my* problem; it's got nothing to do with you." He picks up my boots and puts them in the closet.

The tears leak out in spite of myself, but this time they got a different flavor. "It wasn't like I was just riding around with Thomasine," I tell him.

"Shouldn't have been out there at all," Foster says, and goes on picking up my clothes like I'm a child come in from the cold. And suddenly I know what it is between us.

"Foster," I say, "I ever leave you again, it'll be for the City Chicken."

Now I got his attention all right. "What you *talking,* April Ruth?" He come back in the kitchen and stare at me hard. "What are you *saying?* Don't you get enough to eat here? Don't I treat you nice?"

"I'm not talkin' *nice,* Foster, I'm talkin' family. I got to be where when one person makes a mistake, it's everybody pitches in to help out. Someone has something to celebrate, the others is in on it too—everybody's life all mixed up together. Didn't never have that back in the trailer, and I want it now." The tears is coming faster.

Foster pulls out a kitchen chair and sits with one hand on each knee. "You think I don't want that too? You think I don't miss my family?"

"Sure you do," I tell him. "But you got the bridgeworkers like family to each other, everybody lookin' out for the other person. You told me yourself how it is."

"When I asked you to come back, April, I didn't intend to saddle you with my gambling debts," he says.

This time I look him square in the eye. "Now you listen to me, Foster Williams. We both of us brought something into this marriage we didn't intend, and if you're going to help raise this child of Gus Freeman's, you got to let me help pay your debt." By the time I get the last word out, my voice is trembly again.

"Don't you *worry* about them Harley brothers," he says. "I'll work it out."

"We're you and me going to do it *together!*' I tell him, and now I'm shouting down the walls. Shouting and crying both at the same time. "I ain't just some dollbaby you can wind up to play with when you come home at night!"

"April, what's got into you? Of course you aren't just a doll-baby. Never thought you were."

"Oh, no?" I says. "You cook the dinner, I set the plates; you wash the windows, I wipe the sills; you drive the truck, I play the radio. Whenever there's somethin' important to be done, Foster, I'm the one not doing it."

"Well, I can think of a few times I've let you try it, and a bigger mess I never saw."

"Maybe the time wasn't right," I tell him. "But when *I'm* ready to try something new, Foster, *you* got to be ready for *me!* Can't just keep me locked up in a drawer, play with me when you git home." The tears is coming again.

Foster stares like maybe he's hearing me for the very first time. "I never meant for you to be locked up," he says quiet-like. Then I see the way his lips is twitching. "But there was times I wished to God you were."

"*What* times?" I wipe my eyes on my sleeve.

"Time you cut off your hair, for one."

"Foster, I've *growed* some," I tell him.

He reaches out for me then, smiling just a little, but I pull my arm away.

"Okay," he says. "If you want to take a little money from your account each week to help pay that debt, I don't mind."

But I'm not taking no chances. I reach around to the counter and grab the grocery list.

"*Write* it!" I say, and hand him a pencil.

"What?"

"Write it down. Say how I'm your wife and this is a family."

Foster studies me some more, his lips hanging open. Then he takes the pencil and writes just below where it says "mustard and eggs."

"Say how I got as much right to share your problems as I got to share your bed," I say.

Foster writes that too.

"Now *sign* it," I tell him.

Foster rolls up his sleeve, twirls his hand around once or twice, and then, in big scrawly letters, writes, *Foster Preston Williams.*

"That you?" I ask, pointing to the "Preston." Don't want him tricking me.

Foster puts one arm around my waist. "That's me," he says. "Now you think we could get some sleep?"

Here I married a man, didn't even know his full name.

***

We're snuggled up together like spoons in bed, Foster behind me, hand on my belly.

"What if the Harleys come back?" I ask.

"Won't be tonight," says Foster. "That scream'll be ringin' in their ears for another day or two." Foster can fall asleep quicker than a cat in the sun, and two, three minutes later, I can tell by his breathing he's gone.

I'm not one bit tired. Maybe feel better than I have in my whole life. I liked the way we was lying, both facing out in the same direction; strange how you can take pleasure in things you'd never once expect. I smile at the window. Smile at the wall. Foster makes little bubble noises with his lips, and I reach down and pat his leg.